"'*Why are all your characters freaks?*'
he burst out during a phone call.
At first I thought he was joking.
My position was that all characters are
freaks because, essentially, everyone in
real life is a freak, in their own particular
way. This had been a constant in my
thinking and my fiction from the start.
It was precisely what I wrote about:
everyone is as fascinating and as fucked
up as everyone else. If you look hard
enough and sympathetically enough
at anyone, you will see that they are
freakish and unique and wonderful."

FANCY MAN

PAUL MAGRS

Lethe Press

Published by Lethe Press
lethepressbooks.com

'Glittering Fag' first published in *Raise #2*
'Baubels' first published in *Fable (Queer Life Issue)*

ISBN: 978-1-59021-654-5

Author photo by
Clair Macnamee

Cover and interior design
by Inkspiral Design

INTRODUCTION

I MOVED TO A NEW PUBLISHER IN 1998. AFTER THREE NOVELS AND A collection of stories I was moving on and writing a new book. I wanted to write something grand, set over a larger span of time – maybe twenty years or more. The novel was to be the story of a young orphaned girl who falls into the hands of her slightly unscrupulous aunty and who makes good and bad choices and good and bad friends as she moves into her twenties, discovering new places and relationships as she goes.

In many ways (I now see) it was the story of myself in my twenties in the 1990s. But it was also the story of Isabel Archer in Henry James' *The Portrait of a Lady*, a novel I'd read with great attention and enjoyment during my last summer in Edinburgh.

In essays I read about Henry James there was talk of architecture and the structure of his novels: these faultless erections of his. I thought: I'll have a bit of that, then. So I decided that my Wendy would follow a similar path to James' Isabel. In a kind of cover version of the old book she would begin in one city and move to others, resisting temptation and the lure of wicked people wanting to exploit her. It would be all about money and finding love and trying to find a place to live and who to trust and what to feel. It would be about sex and self-delusion...

And I wrote all of this in the gaps I could find in my life during my first year lecturing at UEA in Norwich. I was teaching the MA course in Novel-writing, long-established as the oldest, most successful course of its kind in the UK. Most of my students were older than me and some looked askance at someone they clearly felt was callow and not famous enough to be teaching them. Here was this self-effacing northerner with a daft sense of humour telling them all what to do and sharing teaching duties with the Poet Laureate. I often had quite a fight on my hands when it came to showing people at UEA I knew exactly what I was talking about.

In the midst of this I was struggling with my *Fancy Man*. At some point along the line my new editor – who had apparently loved my earlier books, even sent me fan mail about the first – decided he hated this new one. He couldn't stand what I was doing with it.

'Why are all your characters freaks?' he burst out during a phone call. At first I thought he was joking. My position was that all characters are freaks because, essentially, everyone in real life is a freak, in their own particular way. This had been a constant in my thinking and my fiction from the start. It was precisely what I wrote about: everyone is as fascinating and as fucked up as everyone else. If you look hard enough and sympathetically enough at anyone, you will see that they are freakish and unique and wonderful. If I had a constant theme, this might be it.

Anyway, the editor wasn't happy about that.

'Everyone you write about is a transvestite or grossly overweight or they have no legs or something else horribly wrong with them, or they believe in aliens...'

Yes, all of this was fair comment.

Then he said, 'Don't you know any normal people in real life? What's the matter with you?'

Up till then he had seemed such a kindly soul. Really, a gentleman, with interesting stories of his own to tell. But he had seemingly gone off my writing overnight. I remember a parcel of manuscript coming back in the post and when I unwrapped it I found that he had crossed through almost every single page with thick, greasy pencil. (It reminded me of the pencil with which my grandfather the butcher used to work out sums on bloody parcels of meat.)

He'd left hardly any words at all still standing on those four hundred pages of *Fancy Man*. It was the weirdest thing. I was in a panic. What was I to do with a book where all the words had been crossed out and were somehow wrong?

He told me that I kept going off and getting too interested in secondary characters. He thought I must keep my main character the focus in every single scene. I didn't agree with that idea at all. Surely one of the great pleasures of novels is all the detours you can take? A novel is a forest we are invited to lose ourselves in.

My then-agent didn't help much.

My work was developing, as it should, changing from book to book and yes... perhaps this one was even wilder than its predecessors. But why would anyone set out to write a book tamer and less demanding than their last one?

This one had a suicide cult, alien replicants, nasty old witches and a cameo by Marlene Dietrich. All these things were delightful to me. If I made them delightful on the page, I was sure my audience would follow me.

My then-agent said: 'You should develop and mature more sensibly. You should mature by writing less about northern working class people. Write about more middle class people. Write about the south.'

For some reason it wasn't until 2003 that I sacked her.

As it happened, *Fancy Man* was all about moving away from home and finding a whole range of different kinds of people coming into your life. But I guess the message from that daft agent and that daft editor was: only write novels just like other people do. If you want us to sell them and other people to buy them, you've got to make it all a bit more... conventional.

I just couldn't. I couldn't see what they were talking about when they said make it more normal. Looking back, I can catch a glimpse of the kind of thing they might have wanted me to do. Make the romance more orthodox. If it had to be gay, keep it light and vanilla. Put in fewer unicorns and alien replicants. Keep the sex fluffy rather than quite so in your face. Less melodrama, fewer cocks, fewer flights of ludicrous fancy. And maybe don't make every single character a writer..? (In 'Fancy Man' almost every single character is busy writing novels, memoirs or letters, or they are bursting into some kind of ragged verse to express their feelings. But this was just a joke of mine. In any other literary novel (Iris Murdoch, say) no one would turn a hair if all the characters were writers, philosophers or critics. Why shouldn't that also be true in novels written by me? In novels about hairdressers, shop girls, lottery winners..?

Because it isn't very realistic or true to life, comes the answer...

But I never started off writing novels in order to be true to life. I wanted to be true to my characters and a fully-imagined world of my own. I wanted to interrogate the myths and lies of realism and break it apart from within. When you come from a working class background the literary world expects you to write gritty realism, so you can look back on squalor and make everyone shudder. Well, fuck that for a game of soldiers, I thought.

The other route you can escape into as a non-posho literary author is horror, sf or fantasy. But they were kind of a boys' gang then, and mostly still are. What I really wanted to do was to take the outrageous tropes of those bastard genres and put them into literary novels. I wanted to create a wonderfully spicy stew of fictive elements...

Anyhow, somewhere between teaching all those courses that year, fighting to convince people I knew what I was on about, and editorial difficulties and ultimately the cancellation of my fourth novel (did I fall or was I pushed? The book was cancelled either way...) I lost my confidence. Somewhere between the devil and the deep blue sea. I found myself alone with my manuscript and all my confidence suddenly gone. My great new editor had said my book was nonsense and my agent couldn't help.

The book, as far as I could tell, was ruined.

This felt just like being a tightrope walker, jolted out of his delicate spell of concentration. He looks down, sees the ground, and wobbles. He needs to get his balance back right away or he's going to plummet to his doom.

So I put *Fancy Man* away. Up in the attic in the house I'd bought in Norwich. Every copy of the manuscript. The one where I chopped it down to half its length. The one where I excised all the Magical Realist elements. The one where I chopped out all the aliens and cocks. The version where

I edited out the long section set in the brothel above the gay sauna on Leith Walk, run by the woman with no legs. The version where I'd hacked each scene into exquisitely arty, poetic fragments... Every single copy I put away out of my sight.

Then I went and did my best to forget all about it. My year with Wendy and Timon, Aunty Anne, Colin, Belinda, Captain Simon, Uncle Pat. I abandoned the freakish lot of them, people who'd been as real to me as anyone I knew in 1998.

I got on with life. I started a whole new novel in 1999 – *Modern Love*, which was a very dark domestic thriller with no fantasy at all and lots of murders. It came out with a different publisher – my third – in the year 2000, when I was thirty.

Time moved on. Eventually we moved cities and jobs and houses. I chucked out boxes, folders, files, papers, letters and manuscripts. I chucked out, I thought, every remaining version of the doomed 'Fancy Man.' My partner Jeremy despairs at me throwing stuff out. I prefer to clear the decks, but he won't hear of it.

Anyhow – fast forward to 2016.

There's the marvelous news that Lethe want to republish my first three novels, with new covers, introductions, added extras and contemporaneous short stories. I'm cockahoop. Writing these introductions for them, I still can't resist grinning at the very thought of these books being made available again.

Then, when I'm racketing about in old boxes in the Beach House at the bottom of our garden (we live in Manchester now, in a leafy enclave down by the railway lines) I find something interesting amongst my old files. Amid the letters and old stories and notes and ideas I find 'Fancy Man' again.

I assume at first it's the tidied-up version. The truncated version. The bowdlerized or bastardized version. But it's none of these. It turns out to be the four hundred page version. It turns out I hadn't binned it after all. Not even in a fit of pre-millennial self-loathing and pique.

Here it is. It spent six years in the Norwich attic, then ten years in the Manchester cellar and then a year or two mouldering in the Beach House. It's damp and blotchy and warped.

I read it all again, very slowly.

And I love it, all over again.

It seems very me. Me as I was at twenty-nine. Not as hampered and crushed down and worried and care-worn as I became a little later on.

It's like finding a little clone of yourself, or a recording of your voice with your friends, or a set of photographs of a happy time you didn't even know had been printed.

So.

I feel confident all over again about the *Fancy Man* phase of my writing career. The novel reads like a missing link in my books and it should rightly slot into 1999 – right between *Could it be Magic?* and *Modern Love.* Now the whole story can be told. It's been restored and polished up and put with the others.

I hope you enjoy it. Even though it's full of freaks, oddities, aliens and cocks. Welcome back to the end of the twentieth century.

Paul Magrs
Manchester
April 2016.

FANCY MAN

ONE

My sisters were fearless and I could never understand that. I was the youngest, so was I the protected one? They bred and fed me on the titbits of the world they saw. I thought the world was something that would gobble you up, soon as look at you. Some days I became too scared to leave the house, and certainly night saw me indoors.

My sisters were out on the streets. "Like cats on heat," our mother would say. It was a harsh way of putting it, but I could see she was scared for them. My mother was scared of the whole world. Mandy, my eldest sister, said it was our mother who unsettled me.

I was the third child. The dregs. I was the last scrapings from our mother's womb, the last spitter spatter of use from our father's balls. Half-heartedly they whipped me up, my eldest sister said, and I was the best they could muster.

Was I offended?

I pictured this conception. I saw it in the fluffing up of pink candy floss, when they jab a naked stick into the vibrating metal tub and you watch, standing at the candy floss caravan window. How the strands and strands of spun pink toffee whirl and attach themselves in a claggy, gorgeous beehive. I loved the way it looked like genetic material coming together in a hasty massing of life.

So I wasn't offended.

My eldest sister also said my mother breast-fed me and she was so short on milk I got curdled, watery stuff like the water you have left after poaching eggs. Our mother had hit a fearful, confused middle age by then and her milk no longer came with brio.

My sisters watched her feed me in the evenings and they looked at each other. They were amazed by her loss of nerve. By then we were in the poorest place we had ever lived. It was the hardest of times we had fallen on: all of us in one room, sharing a balcony and walkway with hundreds of other families. Under layers and layers of balconies. It was the first home I remember. My sisters lost no time in telling me that we had come down in the world, and that I was their Jonah.

My two sisters looked at our mother and were embarrassed by the squelch and slap of my feeding noises. They stared at her tits and the fatness of the orange settee.

They said that was when they started to feel scorn for her. She had let us all down, they said.

We lived off the Golden Mile. A breath (a smoky, lipsticky, fish and chippy breath) away from the promenade, where all was glitter and tack and nostalgia.

The Golden Mile makes me think of...

Fat ladies on toilets

Skinny men at keyholes

Magicians pulling rabbits

Strongmen flexing and testing their muscles

Blue comics...

I love the word blue (don't you?) for everything risque. It puts me in mind of...

Colour of oil and rare sea birds

dredged onto beaches

nuns' knickers
tadpoles
bush of pubic hair in the dark
Bluebeard himself.

Between the gold-painted Tower and the hoops and skirts of the rides at the fair, the sea sucked... pushing up the rubbled belly of the beach... drawing back a long slow suck of sand...

At night you'd get the illuminations on the water... an underwater jamboree competing with the shore... showing up green and gold and red, the letters on signs and logos and hoardings reversed and a-quiver... the lights leeched out like blood flowing over your teeth—gingivitis—when you suck your teeth too hard... and your gums, soft, swollen, bleed.

This was my town.

MY MOTHER WOULD SING AND SING AS SHE WORKED IN THE KITCHEN. She cleaned things till they shone, even formica. Home smelled of bleach to me. Bleach still reminds me of home. My mother would wash and hang the dishcloths on the shiny, silver taps to dry. Nothing smelled worse than a foisty dishcloth, she said.

She would sing a song about her golden chances passing her by. It's the only line of that song that I remember. What was that song? When I asked her she would say, 'Was I singing?'

For years I spent more time with my mother than the others did. They were at the age of going out and not coming in again until they had to. Crawling home with the dawn, with their money all spent and yesterday's knickers back on.

"Those sisters of yours," my mother would say. "They're running wild. Now, you'll be a good girl, won't you? For your poor old Mam?"

WE LIVED IN THAT TOWN UP AGAINST THE SEA... AND WE WERE barricaded from the sea by the Prom (diddley-om-pom-pom)...up and down, all weathers, folk would go up and down the Prom...in the long stormy winters...we were scared of floods, even though we lived in a tower block...but the water could still get in, up the shafts of lifts...rising level by level...and then the concrete pebble-dashed chipboard towers would tumble and topple...I could see the whole of north-west England crumbling into the brown grey sea...bad as that perilous crust of California.

They sent out sandbags in preparation—like in war-time—to lie at our doorways, to hold back the tide...like Midas, or Ming the Mighty, or Moses...or, who was it? Canute! Oh, my head for names...watch out for my memory. I might be what the expert—the bloody expert—Mandy calls an unreliable narrator. Ay, that'll be right. But I'm one who's been surrounded by unreliable narrators, all my life... buggers! ...everyone I've ever known... they've all been up to it...telling their own sides.

And watch out for when I jump ahead of myself...and tell some of the story in advance. Don't worry. I live in the end. In case you were worrying. I already know the surprises to come.

I hate surprises. Life springs too much shit on you as it is. Astrid, the woman in the Leith Walk launderette, would have something to say on the subject. "Jesus God! What are you trying to murder me, with shock?" She was a German Sikh.

And yet...I don't like softening blows. I hate prolepsis. Like nibbling as you're cooking. Means you're not hungry afterwards.

And watch out when I go third person! It's still me, still all me! To me it's just like looking in a mirror and trying my hair a new way...doing something different with my hair my eyes my face...But believe it or not...I'm fairly consistent. I am! I am!

SOON IT BECAME A GAME TO TAKE WENDY OUT. THE TWO OLDEST SISTERS did it for a laugh. The town about them was so familiar by now that it held no terrors. They could fettle anything. They could jab a single, slender finger and tell anyone to go and swivel. They were sluttish and shrewd and their tights were sheer on the long, long legs they'd taken from their mother. Their mother had blue, pulpy veins coming up at the backs of her legs, especially at the backs of her knees. But the legs of her two eldest daughters, Mandy and Linda, were practically flawless. Up and down the promenade they clicked in unison, in stilletos, drawing the glances of lads and women outside the arcades, the pubs, the late night cafes. Up the promenade following the shabby illuminations and the music that went with them was Motown, all different songs, coming jumbled up from pub doorways.

Mandy and Linda brought Wendy out. Sixteen. She's of an age to get out and have some fun, they told their mother.

"I don't know," their mother said. "She's very young for her age."

Mandy, the eldest, tossed her headful of marmalade curls. "You've kept her soft. You've kept her too babyish."

"Well, I still don't know."

All this as Wendy sat with them at the tea table, fiddling with crumbs on the gingham cloth. She walked her fingers on the blue and white centimetre squares. She closed her eyes and walked her fingers. If both fingers rested on blue, then she'd go out with her sisters. If both landed on white, she'd be staying in. If she had one on white and the other on blue, then she'd go out and walk right into her True Love. She'd never have to go out again. Life would come easy after that.

SO THIS IS HOW IT WAS TO BE PART OF THE CROWD. SHE THOUGHT THEY would be more aggressive. It came as a surprise to her, that people stepped aside to let her past. She thought you'd have to fight to find your way. But Wendy knew she had it easier because her sisters went first, cutting a swathe.

They stopped outside of the waxworks. Here there was a glass box the size of a phone booth. Inside it rested a puppet clown, life-sized, his bald white head pressed against the glass.

Mandy told Linda to put ten pee in the rusty metal slot. 'Watch this,' she told Wendy.

The clown shook himself alive and they drew back.

He waggled those white hands like landed fish. He threw back his head and roared with horrible laughter. He belly-laughed fit to burst and it echoed inside the glass cabinet, crackly like something on the telly. The clown's face was rigid, with his scarlet lips shiny like boiled sweets, drawn back and his teeth poking out. His plastic tongue waggled as he guffawed, thrashing about, stotting himself deliberately off the glass.

A crowd gathered to see the hilarious clown.

"It's awful," Wendy tried to tell her sisters. The laughing went on forever. The tape in his head must be on a loop, she thought. You could hear the thing hiccup when it started again.

Wooo—whoooo—woooo

A woman beside Mandy went funny when she saw the clown. Throwing back her own head she screamed and screamed and grabbed Mandy's forearms. She laughed and gabbled in her face, right up close. Mandy jumped back and shook her off. The old woman kept ranting like the gift of tongues: It's funny, isn't it? Tell me it's funny as well. Others around were joining in. It was infectious and jolly, wasn't it? It was meant for fun. It was meant for joining in.

Mandy was cross now, and led her sisters away. It was dark and time to go for supper. She wanted to sit on a high stool at a chrome-plated bar and eat fish and chips, swinging her legs and watching out the window at who went past.

"What did you think of that clown?" asked Linda, the plumper, middle sister. She was in a skinny rib top which did nothing for her. It had horizontal bands of orange and purple.

"I hated that clown," was all Wendy could say. "It was like something out of a bad dream."

"You," Mandy sniffed. "You never think anything's funny."

"That's not true!" Wendy cried. "I like a good laugh!"

If there was one thing their mother had taught them, it was that laughter was the best medicine. Their mother had forgotten her own best lesson. These days she hardly even cracked a smile. She was in tonight, ironing. She had a pile hip-deep, she said, and what would they all be wearing next week, if she didn't do it? Wendy said they'd all do their own, but their mother wouldn't hear of it. She knew her two eldest wouldn't dream of helping out. She'd brought them up spoilt. They wouldn't do a thing around the flat. No, tonight their mother was indoors with an Ali Baba basket full of laundry and the telly on. Tonight was the final of 'Opportunity Knocks.'

She wondered about her girls, out on the town. These were busy nights on the promenade. All sorts of people were abroad. But her girls had to learn to get out. She'd never wanted her daughters to be the type to hold themselves back. And she was sure she could trust Mandy and Linda to look after the little one. They loved each other really, her girls.

But couldn't girls sound vicious sometimes?

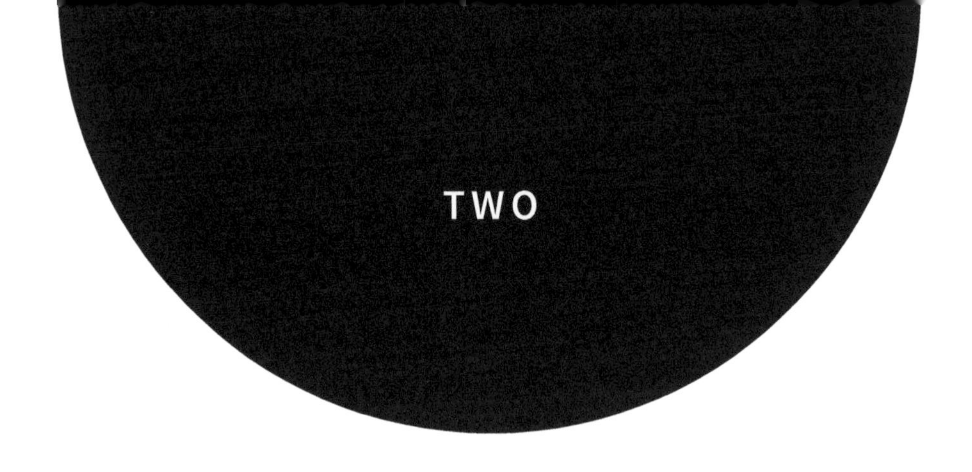

TWO

Sometimes it was like I was the favourite sister and Mandy felt she could say things to me she wouldn't tell Linda. I loved these times, my face scalding over.

We made Linda stand outside the place where we had our fish and chips. Poor Linda, kicking her heels on the pavement and watching through plate glass as Mandy and me took our seats at the gleaming counter. "Only two stools," Mandy had trilled. "You'll have to do without, our Linda." And to Linda's stunned face she added, "We can't make our Wendy do without, can we? Not the baby. What would our mam say?"

So me and Mandy watched Linda lean against the glass as we had our supper. I stared at the flattened part of our Linda, the orange and purple stripes of her.

"Sometimes she's got no sense," Mandy told me. "She's like a big lump."

Feeling horrible and thrilled, I agreed with her, sucking up a hot strip of golden batter.

Mandy went on. "Remember when we had that big scene, when Linda said she couldn't sleep on patterned sheets and pillowcases?"

I nodded. Mam had been upset because she couldn't afford new, plainer bedclothes. So Linda was stomping her feet and yelling, Fine! She'd strip her bed down and sleep on the bare mattress. Mam was shouting back that no daughter of hers would sleep on a bare mattress.

It turned out that Linda would wake in the middle of the night and look down at her pillows and sheets. In the dark the giant pink and blue petals of the print scared her. She mistook them for blotches of blood, come some way out of her body. Often she thought her ears bled in the night.

"There was a reason for it," I said to Mandy. But she had taken up staring at the man serving behind the counter. A black man, with the darkest skin you've ever seen. He was in a pinny striped red and white as toothpaste and he wore a white cardboard hat, folded to the right shape. I thought he must fold a new one at the start of every shift. It looked just like one of the white card trays he was shovelling chips into. He worked silently, under illuminated boards of prices and faded pictures of different dinners. Besides the mushy peas, I realised, everything they cooked was beige.

"I really want to have a black man," said Mandy suddenly, in a different voice. She was fixated on this one. She watched his hands work, binding someone's parcel in reams of newspaper. "Just to see," she added. I thought, this must be the kind of thing she can tell me and not our Linda.

"Isn't that a bit...I don't know...a bit racist?" I said.

She looked sharply. "What?"

"Wouldn't he think you were just after him because he was black? For the novelty?"

"Nah." She was always sure of herself. "He'd be pleased. And it's not just because he's black anyway." She tossed that hair. "They're meant to have right big dongers. Haven't you heard? I'd just like to see, for once."

"Just for once," I repeated and I must have turned scarlet. I went back to watching Linda, watching us from outside.

LINDA:
Mandy thought that our sister was an experiment.

We stood her in front of things, to get her reaction.

When she was very young we stood her in front of the radiator, to see if she would melt.

Later, we tried to dye her hair. We used: tomato soup, gravy browning, lemon juice, olive oil.

When you're a middle sister (like me) you have no power. Not unless you are distinctive, and I was never distinctive. Mandy was special and big and Wendy was special because she was small.

I could only ever watch and marvel. My sisters seemed so original. Where could I begin...to even make a mark?

I was a lump. I'm not pitying myself. I was a lump, I don't care. I'm stubborn, unchangeable. But I'm also steadfast, reliable.

When I grew up and went out to work they put me on the make-up counter in Boots and I stayed there. I tell women how to make the best of themselves. I like it.

Mandy was jealous of my job, when I first got it. 'You! How can you get women to make the best of themselves?'

And it is true that I was never glamorous like our Mandy is glamorous. She seethed for a week or so and boycotted Boots. Then I started bringing stuff home—free samples and whatnot—and we were friends again.

I tried explaining to Mandy. She would be too lovely for my job. She would be too intimidating behind my glass counter. Behind the racks and rows of mascara brushes and the gorgeous coloured tips of lipsticks. She'd be too lovely.

I on the other hand put the punters at their ease. I was every woman. I looked the same as everyone else. I stood as good a chance as they did of looking nice, given the right make-over. They'd look at me and think... well, I look better than her, and she's stood on display.

So there I was again, pacifying Mandy. Volatile Mandy who could flare up for fun. You had to watch your step with her.

I felt like warning the men she went out with. I saw them step out onto a minefield. I waited for them to snag trip-wires, to find their feet caught under the flat, deadly weight of mines.

Mine mine mine. Mandy could blow us all to smithereens with her selfishness.

She walked into any room expecting all eyes on her. Soon that made her wearily expectant. She hated the way she made eyes light up. But woe betide any that stayed dull for her.

Oh, she could treat people disgracefully.

Just when Mam was getting her life back together, getting herself a new beau, a dapper little man from the old-time dancing, Mandy shoved her oar in and ruined things.

The dapper man came calling on Mam. He came in gleaming dancing shoes. Mam was readying herself in her room. I'd never seen her so breathless, so enjoyably anxious, since dad had left us, years before. She fussed on in her room and we looked at the little, proud-looking man.

He came floating into the kitchen and Mandy punctured his sails. She looked at his shiny dancing shoes and said, 'You only wear them so you can look down when you're doing the waltz and see our mam's knickers.

How mortified he was. How mortified we all were.

Then Mam came in, looking all dolled up, and she saw how we were. Mandy looked smug. Then we saw how she had written in the steam on the glass kitchen door that our mam was in love with the dapper man. Words to that effect. It made them even more nervous of each other.

Other times he came Mandy would lay out our father's photos on the mantlepiece, and leave out things that had belonged to him, all about the place. His old slippers by his chair. As if we were expecting him to wander back in. We weren't, but the dapper man took fright and never came back to call on Mam.

Poor Mandy.

People who are cross all their lives worry me. I'm waiting for them to go off with a bang. Mandy would shriek and veins would bulge out on her temples.

Once she got me down on the floor and kicked me, in the stomach, in the face, wearing her good new shoes. We weren't kids then. I was sixteen. There's a nasty streak in her. Even I—her closest relative—would say that about her.

Mam once said: "You know, don't you, that you'll never be as closely related to anyone as you are to each other. Not even to me." She looked along the line of us, proudly. "You virtually are each other. There's all the same stuff in you."

She wanted us to look after each other and do well.

She tried to instill that in us, as if she knew she wouldn't be around to see how we'd turn out. She could see it all coming.

Mandy used to laugh at our mother for her fear, but some people can feel a cool shadow on their heart. They know how things will end up. They know they haven't got long. She was like this, I think.

She tried not to fret, but she let it out just enough to make Mandy rebel against her cautions and scruples.

Mandy brought danger home.

But secretly I think our mother enjoyed the marvellous creature her eldest daughter had become.

"When I was your age, I'd never have dared..." And our mother would laugh. She'd learned to laugh again at our exploits. Not just Mandy's, mine as well. Because sometimes - now and then - I had my moments, too.

I wish our mother could see how we've all turned out.

That seems the most important thing now.

That's all I wanted to say.

Back to Wendy.

They told me it wasn't really going on the fair if you didn't go on something that scared you. Me, I liked the animal house and the hall of distorting mirrors.

In the hall of distorting mirrors we came out as each other. Mandy laughed to see herself looking dumpy and short. She could afford to laugh, it was so far from the truth. Linda went tall and straight as Cher. She was the only one of us to improve herself. My head went down to a pinhead, my boobs swelled up and my hips were a mile wide. That was the funniest thing all night.

We came out and queued for my favourite...pink candyfloss! And that was when my sisters decided it was time to test out my bravery. Or to teach me bravery, I suppose was the idea. Anyway, they dragged me across the other side of the Pleasure Beach, to a roller coaster that was built of iron and sun-bleached wood. Its expanse rolled for pointless miles, sheer into the night. The ground about it shook with pressure, and all I could smell as we waited in line was tar.

They took me on the roller coaster because they said it was

easy. When you went on it, it wasn't like you had to do anything. You sat down, made yourself comfortable. You pulled the chipped metal bar down in front of you and that would hold you in. It felt slack and heavy and I had no faith in it. I sat in front of my sisters, and they sat side by side. We climbed aboard on a flat stretch where you could make believe this was a toy train, a normal train. You could pretend you weren't about to climb and climb and climb...

I hated most the going up. Slow grinding to the top of the world...
Closing my hands on the rail and closing my eyes
On the first dropping away.
On the first one I could see the beach, the full sweep of it,
and bugger me if the Golden Mile isn't curved after all,
and not a straight line at all.

A mile away, the pointy tower tried to plunge itself into my heart,
On the drops and slow ascents there was all the time in the world
for the beetliness of cars
the antiness of pleasure-seekers below
and what shocked me most
was how I jumped out of my seat

the whole way I hardly sat down.
Climbing on, Mandy and Linda had told me
the worst thing you can do is
raise both hands above your head...

You'd be sucked out,
protective bar or no
protective bar.

By gravity, by air pressure, by magic,
and you'd plummet,
spectacularly...

You'd be in smithereens,
Linda said.
You'd meet the train again as it grimly looped the loop
You'd drop on your pals, and kill them as well

And I knew
I just knew
In the seat behind
my sisters were waving both their arms in the air
they didn't care
They sang at the tops of their voices for as long as they could,
and then they started screaming for joy.

Almost straight away afterwards they wanted to go on the Mad Mouse. But first they laughed at my face.

"Wendy love, you've gone green!"

"She can't even open her mouth!"

I wanted to sit upstairs in the Wild West cafe opposite the Mad Mouse while they had their go on it. It was a smaller ride than the roller coaster, but it was even more hair-raising. From what I could see, anyway. Its drops were harder and its corners joltier. They got into a carriage the size of a mini and knocked themselves blissfully sick on something that looked as solid as a bag of four-ply wool. Their car had mouse ears and a tail that flapped behind, shedding sparks.

I went to the cigarette machine. I was clumsy getting the cellophane off a pack of Embassy Milds. I didn't really smoke usually. They tasted harsh.

Mandy and Linda came to collect me.

"She doesn't look well."

"She shouldn't have come on with us, if she knew she was going to take bad." This was Mandy, who would only indulge you so far, and then she would turn.

"I haven't taken bad," I said, tossing away my fag ends and standing. My left leg felt a bit numb down one side, on the hip and ankle. I thought it would fade as I followed my sisters back through the Pleasure Beach. I thought it was from the way I'd been sitting on the ride.

Awkward. I was awkward. I ached, and I could still hear the rumble and shriek of the rails.

THREE

How do I account for laughter? Where do I begin? It's the hardest thing to write about, after love.

I knew a man—and don't let this go any further—who would laugh like a drain whenever he came. He didn't think it funny, the wrench and splash as he let go his load. It was just his natural response. Like a tickle. Like something had caught his fancy just right. I loved to hear him howl like that, and rock his whole body and curl up like a clam, and go so vulnerable, the very instant after stretching his furthest, pushing it hardest.

Such a relief. Such a release.

If I wanted to write about laughter, well then I'd be stuck.

You can tell a funny story in written words. But written words can be hi-jacked by just about anyone. Anyone can read them in a new tone of voice and kill them stone dead.

Just because something is funny now, doesn't mean it always will be. In Victorian times death was the funniest thing around. It had them rolling in the aisles. Now we laugh about sex, about sauce, and death is taboo. How shocking they would find us, how shocking we find them.

See? I'm back to sex. Why do I link laughter with sex?

When our mother and father were together and still making love, it was my mother's laughter we heard through the wall. Even above the jouncing of bedsprings, the plaintive grunts of our labouring dad. Of course we all three had our ears pressed up to the wallpaper. Above the radio dramatics of their humdrum copulation we'd get our mother's raucous laughter. Sometimes derisory, other times complicitous, always full throttle. With her laughter she would egg his fucking on.

TIMON, THE BOY WHO WORKED IN THE FISH SHOP ON THE GOLDEN MILE, he told me that he wanted to write the funniest stories in the world.

"But what's funny?" I shrugged, slumped at his bar, sounding jaded as only the daughter of a great laugher can sound.

"Anything's funny," he smiled, shyly almost, prodding the fish in the hot yellow fat. "'Almost anything's funny." Then he told me the story of the rival fish shops, one of whom had taken revenge by tossing a dead cat into the other's deep fat fryer. The dead cat contaminated everything and put them out of business. I gave a hollow laugh and saw that Timon's humour was the type that relished others' misfortunes.

Then I pictured the dead, battered cat chasing dead, battered fish under gallons of oil.

"Tell me about your mother," Timon would say again, because I had him intrigued. I shrugged.

It was about this time our mother was taken ill. I wandered out of a night to escape the density of air at home. Everyone sat round waiting. I was the youngest: I had to pretend I didn't know what we were waiting for. Mostly I slipped out into the world my sisters had been preparing me for. I went to see Timon in the fish shop on the Golden Mile. He was a writer. His head was full of all the funny stories he would tell, given half a chance.

"You see all the world come by this place," he'd say. "I could tell you a thing or two." When I asked him to tell me, he'd shake his head. "You'll have to get a bit older, honey."

I never told my sisters I had a new friend. I had a new friend black as the sea when the illuminations come on. I had a new friend who knew funny, dirty stories and wanted a chance to write them down.

I told him about my family. About my eldest sister and her interest in him. He snorted. "Girls like that always want to know."

"And do you...have a big one?"

"This from a child!" he exclaimed in mock horror. Then he smiled. "Like a horse," and he gave the counter a brisk wipe down. "But don't go telling your sister." He glinted mischievously. "She's a bit brassy, isn't she?"

And I gasped, never having heard anyone criticize the way our Mandy looked, or the way she went on.

"The one I really want to know about," said Timon in a slack moment near midnight, leaning across the counter and ruffling up the pile of ready newspaper. "Who I really want to know about, is your mother... one of the greatest laughers in the world." He said it like she was famous, appreciating that, to me at sixteen, that's exactly what she was.

Once she said, laughter is my gift to you. I can't give you much in life besides what you already have. But laughter costs nothing. This was when we were very young.

She came to our school Christmas concert. We were at the same junior school she once went to and she arrived, peering round, full of nostalgia. The school hall smelled excitingly of cigarettes and cologne as we waited behind scenery to come out in cardboard masks and sheets and tinsel. We could see our mother, sitting near the front with our quiet father. They were listening to the headmaster's speech, which he always gave and which, she said, he used to give when she was a girl. He was aiming jokes over the kids' heads and trying to appeal to the parents. My mother realised only then that the jokes he told were quite blue.

The head called out raffle prizes. Everyone had donated tins from the back of their cupboards and the school secretary had done them up like hampers in red cellophane with bows. Mam said, when she was at school there, she always wanted to win a hamper, but they never did. And then, when she was a grown up, her number suddenly came up. Two little ducks, twenty-two. Starting to laugh, she stood up and said, "But I never win anything!" What we won was quite a small hamper. Just a box with tins of butter beans and custard, nothing very Christmassy in it.

She went up to the front to fetch it off the headmaster and he was still trying to make the parents laugh. Mam was wearing a tight old dress with no arms and she kissed him smack on the forehead. Afterwards she wished that she hadn't bothered...his forehead was shiny with sweat. But his eyes nearly came out of his head and everyone laughed, so it was all right.

In those days my mother was huge. She was never really fat...just solid through and through. When she started to lose that size she started to lose her humour. When she grasped the headmaster on the school stage it looked as if she could just squeeze him up. She hated losing that strength.

Her laugh. It came out of her like a force of nature. Me and my sisters used to love to start her off. It was like a reward to hear her go on and on, to start as a rumble somewhere deep inside, then to hear it catch fire and send her helpless, send her shrieking. She laughed until the tears rolled down and for us at least it was the most infectious laugh in the world. We aided and abetted that laugh. We coaxed it out and fanned its progress with laughter of our own. We'd sit her in cafes and wait for someone across the room to give a chuckle or a sudden guffaw and our mother would start. She couldn't help herself.

"You're like witches," our father would say, hounded out of his own house. "This is what it must be like to be with a coven of witches."

Our mother thought he should get out more, have more fun. She made him take her out, down the Big Club, as they called it, one Friday night. They had a blue comic on. Dad blushed the whole time. Our mother would laugh at anything that had to do with bodily functions, as she called them. The blue comic that night knew he was onto a good thing, with our mother at one of the front tables. She shamed our dad.

The comic got her up on the stage and she kept on laughing, clutching her knees. He locked her in a shiny black cabinet and the idea was that he'd shove swords through, like a magician. You could still hear our mother, muffled inside, and this the audience loved. And then she went too far and lost control. The blue comic drew attention to the pee spreading out from under the black box. She'd warned him before she'd stepped inside, "I'll lose control of myself," she'd said, as if putting her on the stage made her capable of anything. The blue comic dodged her pool of pee and shouted, only half-joking, that she'd electrocute him if it touched his mike cable.

Our mother came back that night and woke my sisters and me and told us all what had gone on. How she peed herself laughing on the stage. Dad was in the bedroom doorway. He'd had a few and bravely said, "Have you no shame?"

Mam stood and towered over him. "You want to get yourself a sense of fun. What do you fellas do, anyway? You go to the gents and widdle all over the floor. I've seen it. It's only pee."

He grunted. "When have you seen the inside of the gents?"

She ignored him.

Nothing more was said that night, and all the laughing stopped. At breakfast time the next day Mam was down in the mouth, and it was up to us to bring her round. It always was. But it wasn't difficult to start her going again. People will laugh at anything if they really want to. You just have to let go.

I USED TO TALK TO TIMON UNTIL HIS SHIFT ENDED AND THEN WE WOULD walk each other home. He lived alone, not that far from our flat. That year the illuminations down our stretch of the shore were all about toys. From the streetlamps we passed were hung teddy bears, ringletted dolls, aliens, giant ray guns.

Timon told me what he envied most about me was my family. "There you are, going back to your full flat, all your sisters about you. And I'm going back to my lonely, cold place."

And if that wasn't a hint to be asked back to our kitchen for a mug of tea and a plate of sausage sandwiches, I don't know what was. I'd already told him this was the way we would all meet up at the end of the night. Whoever was in first got the frying pan on. Usually it was Linda and I'd come in to find her snipping off sausage links with her pinking shears. I asked Timon back for some supper. He agreed in a rush and I thought, you bugger.... you only want to see my sisters. I was convinced he wanted a more mature me.

"I'm an orphan," he told me and I realised then that he was younger than I thought. There was a spring in his step on the last bit of our journey. He was heartened by the thought of going home to our real family.

"You have to understand, though," I said, "about our mam being ill. She'll be in bed, or she'll be under a duvet on the settee and she probably won't be bothered with visitors."

"I'll creep in like a mouse and be very polite," he said. "I'm quite respectable, you know." He plucked at his T shirt, sniffing. "But I smell of fish and chips."

SOON AS WE GOT IN I KNEW SOMETHING WAS DIFFERENT. THE TELLY WAS on, but there were no voices to complement it. Our mother had recently got herself a video and she would sit up into the early hours of most mornings and watch old monster movies. Whenever she was watching you'd hear her own ribald commentary. She was working her way through the lifework of Godzilla and, as I came down the passageway with Timon, I could hear Tokyo being once more ripped apart and stomped on. But I couldn't hear Mam's derisory cackles. At once I felt scared, thinking she'd been taken bad. There was a strange black coat on the rack in the hall and I thought it might be the doctor's.

We pushed into the living room and it was full of silent faces. They were bathed blue from the Godzilla movie and, for want of anything better to do, they had fixed their gazes on the screen.

My mother was sitting up on the orange settee, with the blue patterned duvet pulled over her legs. She sat stiffly and painfully and she was flanked either side by Mandy and Linda. How normal they looked, each with a best cup and saucer on their knees, staring at the visitors. The best tea service was laid out on the coffee table, even the elaborate, fragile pot. "These are the oldest and best possessions I have," Mam had said, time and again, fingering their gold trim, their crimson flowers. "Break a single piece and you'll never be forgiven."

Timon looked at me. This wasn't the free and easy, chatty, raucous, smokily aromatic suppertime he'd been led to expect from us. I was too busy staring at Mam's visitors to help Timon out. He stood beside me as I stared and stared at the neatly-dressed couple on the dining room chairs, which had been pulled out especially for them.

It was dad, in a dark suit and tie, with a young wife who had her hair cut in a black bob. You could tell she was a severe-looking person, but here she wasn't so sure of herself. They had two very small babies in yellow hanging around their feet. Dad's new family.

Then I realised that everyone was staring at Timon and me. I burst out to Dad, "Well, we don't want you back now."

"Wendy!" Mam said, and the strange woman and Dad—how much like newly-weds they looked, all dolled up—squirmed on their wooden chairs.

"I've not really come back, Wendy love," he said, hardly looking at me properly. "Look how you've grown up!" he said, with a feckless sigh.

Timon spoke up then, telling me he'd just go on home if it would be easier. "No," I said. "Everyone, this is my best friend. He's called Timon."

In that full, still living room, he really did smell of fish and chips.

I asked Dad, "Why did you never want to see us? Why didn't you want anything to do with us?"

"Wendy, I did..." he said, and then he stopped himself.

"Are these your new babies?" I asked. They were roaming around the carpet like little creatures. He nodded.

That was when Mandy's patience went and she stormed out of the room and into the kitchen.

I followed her in.

She decided to fry sausages. Clang went the pan on the gas ring. Poor Timon, I left him in the living room. Later he said it was all right, because they all fell quiet again. They went back to watching *Destroy All Monsters* and first one, then the other yellow-suited baby climbed into his lap. Kids loved Timon.

"I don't want Dad here," Mandy growled. She couldn't find Linda's pinking shears and she tried to pull the sausages apart instead. I fetched her a knife. "What makes him think he can swan back in, years later, with his lovely new wife and kids?"

"Did you think his wife was lovely?" I asked.

"She's stuck-up looking," Mandy snapped, furiously lighting the glass with the unreliable clicky thing. The small kitchen filled up with pungent, unlit gas. Then it lit. "Dad would think stuck-up was lovely. He always wanted to better himself. Mam and us weren't good enough for him."

"Don't say that!"

"It's true. Weasly little bastard." She sniffed as the pan began to hiss.

"He's only come back because somehow he's found out that she's dying."

I froze. Someone had said it at last. I might have known it would be Mandy. Mandy with no respect for silences, convention, other people's hesitances. I took in a sigh of, I suppose, relief. "He knows she's going to die," I repeated, to get the taste of his knowledge and her death in my mouth. The taste of burning sausage was there too as Mandy angrily swished them about in the pan, unsticking their undersides. "Cheap meat," she cursed.

"It's cancer-cancer-cancer," she sang. "That's what we've all not been saying."

I knew my face was white. I asked her and kept my voice straight, "How did he find out?"

"This whole country's smaller than you think, Wendy. Word travels. There are so many connections. If you want to know anything, all you have to do is put your head down in the right place."

"What's he come back for?"

"It can't be her money."

"Then what?"

"I think he's come for you, Wendy. You're the youngest. You're the one who still needs seeing to." She looked at the burnt pan, swore, and emptied it into the pedal bin. The pedal was broken and she was faffing on with the bag inside while I digested the thought of being taken off somewhere by my dad and his new family.

"Mandy, I'd rather die."

"That's hardly very fucking tasteful," she said, straightening up. "And who's that black fella you've dragged home?"

I shrugged. "Works in the fish shop. You've seen him before."

Her eyes bugged out. "That's him? What are you doing with him?"

"He's my best friend."

I sat at the kitchen table. Mam's Cats calendar she'd bought off the Salvation Army was lying open. Whole weeks had been ticked, crossed and circled in a variety of felt tip colours. Someone's cryptic system of marking off time. "Mandy," I said. "I can't leave here. They can't take me, can they?"

Mandy sat opposite me and, taking both my hands, said the best thing she ever said to me. "Nobody can make you do what you don't want to."

MANDY WOULD COME HERE AND PLAY THESE MACHINES, THOUGH SHE never knew the rules. Some of the others who came to play knew you had to—well, look at the words on the lit-up buttons—hold, stick, nudge, all that. Even the pensioners, the old girls coming out with a handbag full of pennies and hope in their hearts knew the rules for gambling on the machines. Mandy would come down here and she just wouldn't know. What was more, she didn't care. If I'm going to win, I'm going to win, and no amount of holding-sticking-nudging will help me anyhow. When she came down after midnight, full of hell, full of temper, going hell-for-leather on the one-armed bandits, those at the machines either side of her would look worried. She'd be slamming in the coins and yanking on the bandit's arm and making the cherries, bells and stars thunder so violently round and round. And if she won she wouldn't stop even to count up her winnings.

AT HOME THE MIDDLE SISTER LINDA WOULD BE STUCK FOR THINGS TO DO. She sat beside her mother and watched whatever was on. *House of Dracula* in black and white and not very scary. She felt a daring leap of disgust in herself. Her mother was so feeble, the scary films she watched weren't scary. And then disgust at herself: her mother's helpless face and how she lapped those tame horrors up. Past midnight they watched Dracula chase Frankenstein chase the Wolfman.

"I always loved the Wolfman," her mother sighed at last. "He could never help himself." She looked at her plumpest daughter and said, "Why did I always fall for fellas who couldn't help themselves?"

Linda saw then how much flesh had dropped off her mother. How haggard she looked, even though she was made up with all the free samples Linda's new job could fetch home.

"Why are you looking at me like that?" her mother asked.

MANDY WENT ON PUSHING COINS INTO MACHINES. USED ALL HER TWOS and moved onto fives. These were the coins she had saved over years, saved them in biscuit tins and hidden them under bunk beds. Not even touched them when things got tight. Carried them when they moved from home to home. Tonight she'd brought them to the arcades on the prom and she'd brought them in a suitcase, heaving it along behind her, scuffing the leather.

She swore she wouldn't leave till all the coins were gone. Her rainy day money pissed away in the dark before dawn. Besides the money, all she had at home were her clothes, which she could cram down into two bin liners. Without the weight of all her capital she'd be free and easy to go, cleared for take-off.

Still she kept winning on the bandits, buying her more shining time in the gambling hall. A boy stood at the next machine, working through his own hoard of five pences. She could see him watch her working on hers. He pulled his bandit's arm with more deliberate concentration, as if that could have any effect and he actually did all the holding and nudging and winking you were meant to do. He was filling up his own silver tray with jackpot after jackpot. Mandy was glancing across to him as much as he glanced at her. She took in his belted raincoat, real leather, and his jeans, tight and faded that way, along the proper contours of his crotch. A sexy relief map in shades of blue.

Cherries Cherries Cherries.

"That's you won again," the sexy boy told her.

"I always fucking win," she snapped.

AND WENDY WANTED TO GET OUT OF THE FLAT AS WELL. IT HAD MADE her claustrophobic before, but her father's visit actually tainted the place. It wasn't even a nice place to go at the end of the night.

She had looked at her father and thought, everything could have been so different, if only you'd wanted it. Their lives could have been any way—better, worse, just different—if his influence had been there. Their mother had influence, but she was inevitable, unquestionable, she was their one constant. He was useless, but he was theirs, and the potential he had for disrupting them made Wendy feel sick. Of course there was no question of her going with him, his new wife and their brats when whatever happened to Mam happened. And that could be years away, anyway.

She had looked at those two babies asleep on her friend Timon's lap and thought: that's a brother and a sister I had and never knew. She didn't feel related. She felt nothing. A twinge of softness at the sight of babies, the sight of babies nestling onto that man who had moved her of late, but that was all. And that was a proper lesson, too. Someone can have your blood and same heart, their nerves can spring from the same source as yours and you need never know. Alarm bells needn't ring. She thought, relations of every sort are chance.

In the kitchen Mandy took me aside. "You're too young to have a boyfriend."

"That's not what he is."

"Maybe that's not what you're calling it, but don't kid yourself. You just be careful."

"Mandy, I'm not daft. And he is just my friend."

Mandy looked tired. "If Mam was herself, she'd be telling you things. Have you got all your facts straight?"

"I'm already on the pill for my period. So even if I was..."

"He could get himself locked up if anyone heard he was touching you."

"No he couldn't and anyway...he's not!"

"Our kid. Look at you."

I was embarrassed now.

I went into the living room, where *Valley of the Gwangi* was playing. My mother hooted with laughter, raucous as she could manage. She wanted her daughters to see she was keeping her spirits up. "All right, love?"

I nodded, sitting down with her, pulling a corner of the blue duvet over my own knees. I stared at cowboys flinging lassos at a twitchy, animated Tyrannosaurus Rex.

Mam said, "Your Aunty Anne's coming."

Se lay on the beach with Timon. It was dark, so hopefully no one would see when they walked into town with damp sand caked all down their backs. And she'd thrown herself down without a thought for dog dirt.

Timon said, "I didn't know you had any family in Edinburgh."

"Aunty Anne's my mam's sister," Wendy said. "I haven't seen her since I was a baby. She came to my christening and gave Mandy and Linda a budgie in a cardboard box with holes poked in. She didn't want them to feel left out on my big day. Man said it was a daft present because it cost her a fortune to buy a cage to put it in and then the bird karked it anyway."

Timon sighed, watching the clouds slide off the moon. Soon Wendy had exhausted the subject of Aunty Anne's coming visit. Neither of them could see the sense in it at all. The woman was a stranger to all of them.

Wendy said, "Mandy asked if I was being sensible...with you."

Timon turned to look at her. He had sand in his hair and it looked like soft brown sugar for coffee. "Like how?"

"She said you could get locked up if you touched me."

He smiled. "Just as well I don't want to touch you, then."

"You don't?"

"God, no. Well. Yes, I do, I just...oh, you know, Wendy. You're just a young lass and all."

"Sixteen."

"Legal, anyway."

"You're not much older."

"It's all the difference."

She turned away. They listened to the slow noise of the sea. "I wish I hadn't said anything now."

"It's best not said." He waited a bit. "Look, Wendy. Give yourself time."

"I think things are going to change. I think it's all going to be different."

"Don't be in a hurry to grow up."

"I don't see why I shouldn't want to grow up fast," she said. "At least then you have a bit of power over your life. You don't have to be scared of the future not being your own."

"You can feel like that at any time, hon."

"If I was grown up now, I could do things right."

Timon laughed at her and she thought how it took skill to laugh at someone and still make them feel all right.

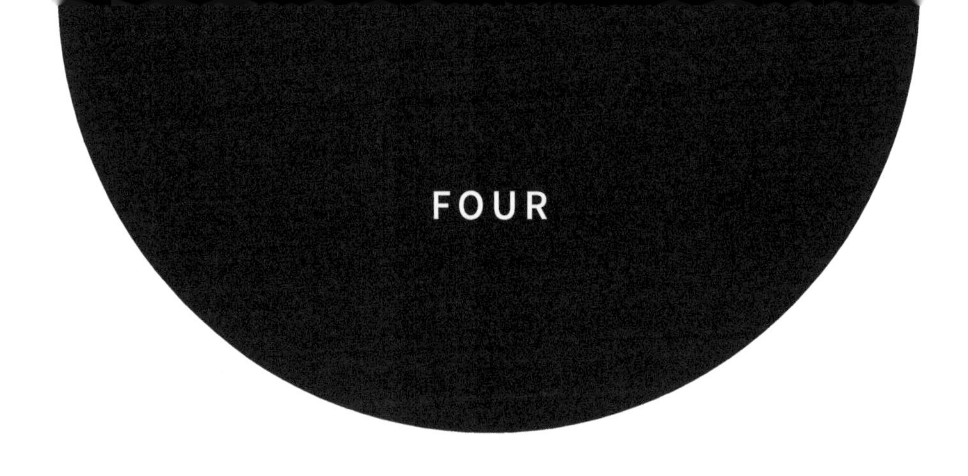

FOUR

ALL THE SISTERS WERE SENT TO WELCOME AUNTY ANNE OFF THE COACH. It was due to arrive on the seafront late in the afternoon. A dull, warm, May afternoon and the sky was bleeding into the sea. The rocks on the shore looked to Wendy like the expensive, irregular cubes of brown sugar they put out on tables in the better sort of cafes. She watched Mandy resting against the metal rails, stretching her long, brown arms in the sun. She looked unimpressed with the whole idea of their aunt's visit. Linda, on the other hand, was excited.

"It's here, she's here," Linda cried, when the coach came round the corner. It eased itself onto the Golden Mile, a full half hour late. "They'll be getting cooked on board that. It's got tinted windows." Linda made herself ready to help their aunt down.

The coach had brought her across the Pennines and the moors. It had chugged and twisted through endless country lanes all the way from the North Sea. For the third time Linda said that their aunt would have looked at two different seas that very same day.

Then the doors flew open and they caught their first proper glimpse of

Aunty Anne. First they saw a wild headful of white hair, standing almost on end, as she allowed herself to be helped down the steps by the driver. Gregor, his badge said, in his brown nylon suit and his carefully brushed toupee.

She was fatter and older than their mother. But, when they caught their first full look at her, all three of them thought that Aunty Anne had been made up to look like a comedy version of the woman their mother had been. A gabbling giant of a woman, clutching the sides of her expansive, too-hot coat and laughing at herself as she almost slipped on the coach steps, and seeing her nieces for the first time in ten years. "'Oh, let's see my lovely girls. These are my beautiful nieces!"

Wendy could hear Mandy squirm with embarrassment, hoping no one she knew would come past, or at all, while Aunty Anne was with them.

SHE TREATED HER LEGS LIKE THE MOST PRECIOUS THINGS SHE OWNED. "I may never have been much to look at," she would say, and then hoist up her skirts a little to show off her tan tights. "But look at these! I've been blessed with legs!" She went to the old-time dancing and it was this that had kept her in trim.

They found that Aunty Anne would repeat this line about her legs as a kind of nervous tic. Whenever a gap in the conversation needed filling, she'd slide up her skirt and do a modest high kick. "Look at this!" And, "If I really tried, I bet I could kick as high as my head!" And then she would have a go, right there in the living room, with their mother lying down on the settee, watching on.

That first afternoon of the visit, Aunty Anne looked solemnly at her younger sister. "I've still got the legs of a girl!" said Anne, surprising them all. They couldn't see their mother's legs because of the duvet. *Fifteen to One* was on the telly, a ruthless, hectic quiz. Their mother asked them to turn the sound down.

"She always had incredible legs, your Aunty Anne. Mine were two sticks next to hers. You ask her nicely, she'll do the splits for you."

None of them rushed to ask.

"I couldn't anymore," laughed Aunty Anne. She tried to get them all laughing, and their mother tried, but they couldn't.

They were worn down by the heat of the afternoon. It was cooling now, but the heat seemed to stand in the room. Briskly, Aunty Anne said, "And what are we going to eat tonight?"

Their mother shouted after her, as she went to take over in the kitchen: "It's a bit of a mess in there. We haven't got any of the right things in..."

On their way up to the flat, Aunty Anne had lagged behind as the girls went up with her cases. She stared at the flaky paint of the stairwell, the broken lights. "This is where our Lindsey's ended up," she said, then looked shamed because the words carried up the stairwell, so they all heard her. Someone had dropped shampoo down the stone stairs, and it oozed and spread in the heat, making the stairs smell of pine needles and soap. "It must have spilled out of someone's shopping bags," said Linda cheerily. "Usually it smells of piddle down here."

THAT FIRST NIGHT THEIR AUNT DID THEM A FRY-UP, ONE OF HER specialties, she told Mandy, who pulled a face. Linda trooped out to the corner shop for the things they needed and their aunt acted shocked by the prices.

"That's what you get when you live in a holiday resort!" She turned away from the cooker, to smile at Wendy, who found that she'd been staring. "Do you feel like you're always on holiday?" asked her aunt.

"No," said Wendy, who'd never until that moment thought of living anywhere other than Blackpool.

SHE BOUGHT ME A SILVER CARDBOARD BOX FILLED WITH CHOCOLATE serpents. The box was tied with green ribbon, springing open at the slightest touch as it sat on the cool white table top. Aunty Anne rapped her knuckles on the cafe table. "Real marble. That's quality that, Wendy."

She had brought me out alone for afternoon tea. I went expecting it to be something of a ceremony, but I wasn't sure why I'd been singled out. She sat me down and presented this box of minty chocolate serpents. We peeled them free of foil and crunched them up, laughing, as we waited for the waitress. Aunty Anne had smudges of milk chocolate round her mouth and I didn't feel I knew her well enough to tell her. This was three days into her visit and she was still new.

Already, though, she had dyed her hair a stark, matte black. Same wild style, now a solid black. Our mother shook her head. "She never could make up her mind about things like hair." Mam had a lot of patience with her sister, maybe because she hadn't seen much of her over the years.

One night I heard them talking late. My sisters and I were eating in the kitchen and Timon was my guest. I sat proudly beside him as he wolfed down hot sausage sandwiches. We ate them with a lot of pepper and his eyes moistened when he realised, and Mandy watched him like a hawk for signs of weakness. But he swallowed peppery sausage down without exclaiming or sneezing. Mandy and Linda were drinking him in, all the while.

Mam and Aunty Anne were supposed to be watching Peter Cushing in *The Beast Must Die,* but they were talking in quiet, earnest voices. I could hear them through the serving hatch, which we never closed.

"I found it hard enough bringing just one up," Aunty Anne was saying. "Though Colin was a worry. I can't imagine what it must have been like, seeing to three bairns, all by yourself."

Mam didn't seem to want to talk about it. "You just get on with it, don't you?"

"I wish I'd come through more to see you, to help out."

Mam wasn't a great one for accepting help though. She was pleased to see her sister on this visit, but every time Aunty Anne did something—swooshing around the living room with the hoover, clattering dishes in the sink, or ironing in front of the telly—our mother's eyes would burn into her back with envy and resentment.

Aunty Anne said, "We haven't talked about this properly, but afterwards...I'll sort everything out."

Mam waved her hand, putting this conversation off.

Aunty Anne protested, "But we never talk about important things, not until it's too late. Our family's always been the same."

"I'm tired, Anne."

"I'm just saying..."

"Leave it for now. Not much needs sorting, anyway. I've not got much to pick over."

"There's the girls."

A pause. I was glad my sisters were busy talking with Timon. I was glad I was the only one listening to this.

Our mother said, "Only Wendy needs seeing to. Only she needs your help, Anne. The others are old enough now."

"She's just a baby," said our Aunt.

AND AFTER THE SILVER, CHOCOLATE SERPENTS, EATEN IN DEFIANCE OF THE signs that told us we should not consume our own foods on the premises, we had cinnamon toast, which came in long, ginger fingers, sparkling with crusted, caramelised sugar. Aunty Anne bit into a finger and wrinkled up her eyes with pleasure.

"We used to come here every Saturday morning, me and your mother," she said. "When we were girls we thought cinnamon toast was the best thing in the world. We thought it was very continental."

I tried to see our mother and aunt in this worn, still luxurious cafe. I imagined them as two giggling girls, already big for their ages, swooning over their Saturday elevenses. I thought she must have been romanticizing: putting the girls they had been into a more genteel era. They seemed a million miles from Mandy, Linda and I, trolling up and down the Golden Mile and nipping in for chips with Timon.

"You're very like your mam at that age," Aunty Anne told me, and I nodded and smiled, knowing very well that I was nothing like her.

I was in my best going-out frock for that afternoon. It was Mandy's. I'd wriggled into it, knowing this was an occasion of sorts and, true enough, Aunty Anne had just finished pouring the tea with an elaborate flourish of the dainty, impractical strainer when she started to tell me All About Herself.

With the glorious indiscretion I was to get used to, she launched directly into the tale of how she and her husband, my Uncle Pat, had stopped loving each other.

I was agog.

AUNTY ANNE:
That's how simple it was. I stopped loving him.

One day I was making him breakfast,
his and our son's,
and all of a sudden, that was it.
Bang and Pow, like Batman, or the Annunciation.
I didn't have to stay.
The truth was as clear as the toaster before me.
The toaster you had to whizz bread through
twice, because it never got hot enough.

I stopped loving him and it had gone overnight, like germs
sometimes do.

Our son was grown up by then, and there was no reason to stay for his sake. I spread the toast with I Can't Believe It's Not Butter, and I laid out jars of marmalade, plum jam, lime jam, blackcurrant. The sun came through them bright and stickily and I started to dare myself:

Leave, leave, leave,
You don't love him anymore,
You could go this afternoon,
After the gasman's been this morning and had a look at your meter.
My heart set up a mad tattoo.
I could go.

Colin, our son, was ill, of course, and nothing would change that.
Did I tell you he was ill, Wendy? We don't
really talk about it.
It was my biggest staying-or-leaving factor, but
he would never get better.
What I did would make no odds.

Colin came into the kitchen, looking so skinny,
so helpful. No longer a child
so did he need me?
Ask him outright:

If I walked out this afternoon,
What would you think of me?

I day-dreamed him
saying back, Mother,
get yourself away,
If you don't love him...
Well, then.

I had a tingling up and down these legs of mine.
There was a dance going on somewhere,
somewhere I didn't know about yet.
Someone was picking out a tune
for me, and I
had a dancing partner
I had yet to find.

I just knew Colin would understand his mother.
I've brought him up a clever,
sensitive boy, a credit
to me.

So this is me. I left my family and Scotland
behind. I moved to the north of England
where I snared myself
a lover—yes!—me!
Well, look at these legs!
They're bound to hook new admirers.

Here's a picture of me with my new lover.
Not much to look at, perhaps.
Not to a young girl like you.

I go back, every six months, to see my son,
They live in the centre of old Edinburgh.

I'm like Mary Queen of whatsit
Going back.

I left and first I told my husband I'd fallen
out of love,
He took it on the chin.

"You were a young girl when I took you on,
and I was already knocking on."
He looked me up and down
still handsome, proud, my hair
at that stage,
a fabulous tangerine.
"I should have seen this coming one day.
Some young fella whisking you off."

I laughed. "Nobody's whisking me off!"
But off I went.

I followed the A1 through the Borders,
across wild Northumberland
endless Roman Roads, perilous with sharp
crests and sudden
dips
I settled in Newton Aycliffe
A place called Phoenix Court

And word came that the old man I'd left behind
had become a millionaire.
The Saturday after I left
his six balls,
and
            his bonus ball
popped out
in perfect sequence.

And bugger me if I hadn't
burnt all my boats.

WENDY'S FRIENDSHIPS.
I said I wouldn't do this...nip ahead of the bookmark, as it were...I wouldn't show off my foreknowledge, but...it has struck me that there are things in common through all the stages of my life. Namely, these extraordinary women I have known. I've surrounded myself with these personalities the whole time. Early-learning with my two big sisters, I suppose...so I've always needed these big women around me. I pass from friendship to friendship...not that I exactly leave friends behind...but new friendships have a habit of becoming more pertinent, of seeming that way...and there are tHose friends you must let go of for a while. Doing their own, peculiar things. I have found that you can't keep hold of everyone at once.

If friendships are worth anything, you'll find some way to keep it all carrying on, under the surface, or away to the side. Then one day... but there will always be lulls. It's worth being aware of that. At first I found it upsetting, that one day someone is your best mate...you'll share anything with them...like now, with Aunty Anne divulging the truth of her cankered love and her lost millionaire...at that moment it seemed a promise that we'd always be this intimate. Intimacy always ends up making you think it's forever. But you have to get wise. Intimacy is a great flatterer. It's very easy to put on...you simply draw closer, lower those lids, that voice...There would be times to come when Aunty Anne simply wouldn't dream of telling me what was going on. When she would clam up tight and I could only roughly surmise and rely upon my other friends. Yet it's bollocks depending on just one person, that's worth knowing. Anything can happen to them. Limit your damage potential.

So...I've spread my affections wide. Concentrated bursts here, here, here, in a largish semi-integrated group. Loosely-held formation. Like sympathetic bombs, setting each other off, should anything happen to me.

You've got your friends because, to you, they are extraordinary. But the stuff that makes them like that also makes them sometimes weird, clammed-up, shell-fishy like that. Sometimes hard to get on with.

FIVE

IF I WAS TIMON, I'D FEEL CROSS ABOUT OUR MANDY. ESPECIALLY THESE days. Especially after all her success. I don't know if he remembers how she grilled him all through that summer. I don't know if he even knew then that's what she was doing. I could see what was going on. He knew things she wanted to know and she got them out of him.

"Timon," she would say, "how do you know what to put in a story?"

"That depends on if that's a story-story you're talking about, like a story you tell, or a short story, or a novel."

She considered. "Say I mean a novel."

"Well then, a novel. Now you can put anything in a novel." He looked out across the road. We were sitting with pints on a bench outside a rough pub. I was having shandy. "I suppose you could put anything in a story for telling, and a short story too." He shrugged. I saw that he was looking at the way the flower baskets hanging from the eaves of the ladies' toilets were swaying. I liked the way Timon noticed things. I tried to notice things through his eyes.

"So there's no difference then?" Mandy persisted.

"All the difference in the world."

She asked, "Is it length?"

I looked at her sharply. She was back on Timon's dick again. Sometimes she couldn't leave it out although, as far as I knew, she'd never seen it.

Timon smirked. "Length has something to do with it."

"How long should one be? A novel?"

"The best novels in my opinion," he said, "have very particular lengths. My favourites are 187 pages and 328 pages."

Mandy blinked. "How could anyone write so much?"

"But they do," said Timon. "Sometimes, once you get started, it's like, when will you stop? Where will it all end?"

"Is that what it's really like?" She fluffed up her auburn curls. I hated her when she did the coquettish thing. I was getting too hefty, already, to copy that.

"Sometimes I'm writing and I think it's a good job I've got friends and the fish shop job, just to get me away from the page."

"It's your life," said Mandy. "It's your vocation."

This last word hung in the air for a bit. When Mandy sloped off, a little later, I mulled it over. "Where did Mandy learn a word like vocation?" I asked Timon.

He looked at me like he didn't know what I was on about. He was back to noticing things. The old women waiting for each other outside the ladies', checking in their bags for their purses.

After that, I started noticing Mandy doing things that were unusual for her. She was reading like a mad thing and I would see her in places I'd never noticed her before, as if she'd sat down and started to read without even knowing where she was. In the shopping arcade she perched on the pensioners' seats by the rubber plants and the fountains, *Sense and Sensibility* in her hand. In McDonalds' front window I saw her as I breezed past and she was sucking a milkshake, coming to the end of *Mill on the Floss. Bleak House* lay drying out on our bathroom radiator because she'd dropped it in the bath when she'd tried to light a bathtime ciggy. I saw her in the park and she was flipping breathlessly to her place in *Madame Bovary* and at last I felt courageous enough to go over and ask her what was going on.

She tilted that perfect, sunburned face and shielded her eyes. Maybe it was coming out of the book and into the sunshine, but at first she didn't seem to recognise me. "I don't know," she said in reply to my peeved question. "I suppose these are the books I always wanted to read. I promised myself that when I finished my exams, I'd read the books I always wanted to read."

I'd forgotten she'd even been doing exams. There had been such a fuss in the family, two years ago, with everyone persuading Mandy to stay on at school to get her A levels. We begged her. She gave in at last as if she was doing us a favour. Now that time had been and gone and her exams were finished with, without their hardly being mentioned.

AT THAT TIME IT WAS MOSTLY JUST ME, MANDY AND TIMON. WE walked along the beach in the daytime, sat in the cafes along the front, we went round the Pleasure Beach, though I didn't go on the wilder rides. The person who was missing was Linda. She was working in Boots all the time. She said she was saving up for her bottom drawer. We would go in to see her, but there's only so much you can say to someone when they're working behind a counter. Best to save it till they come home. But we'd go in and try out make-up samples on each other. I saw that Linda actually knew what she was talking about and, when she explained something, about your skin's ph value or your moisture or whatever, she put on this special, breathy, posh voice.

Linda wasn't coming out with us at night either. Now she had a bloke. "It's inevitable," said Aunty Anne. "They start working and they meet people. They meet up with fellas. That's how it all starts up. Then you don't see them for ages."

Our mother listened to this and I wanted to kick our aunt's shapely ankles for being so tactless. Mam wanted all of us around her, and here was Linda running about the place with a man.

He was an insurance clerk. He wasn't well-paid but he wore a dark-striped suit to work and she said he was bound to rise. He told our Linda that, if he married her, he'd insure every part of her body for a separate, astronomical amount. She meant that much to him. And, if they went in for babies, he'd insure her every time against twins. Linda glowed when she told us this.

Mandy sneered. "He sounds like a wanker."

Daniel the insurance clerk looked out of his depth, the night he came to see Linda at home. He came straight from work in his dark suit, and he had his sleeves rolled and this smell of office sweat and cologne that I quite liked. He had dark curly hair you could see he'd be happier just shaving off, and his shoes were very shiny, which reminded me of what Mandy had shouted at Mam's one-time fancy man. I wanted to tell our Linda: don't let him waltz with you.

I suppose we tried to squeeze him out. Not maliciously, not concertedly, but we didn't put on any airs for this insurance clerk. We acted naturally and, if he couldn't deal with that: hard lines.

That night the flat was full. As soon as he came in I saw through his eyes how ramshackle and neglected we had let the place become. With Mam being ill the housework had slowed to a standstill and things were no longer immaculate. We dusted the rooms that our mother spent her time in. She hated dust lying on surfaces and ornaments. She thought it would choke her. Little bits of human bodies, she said, going up her nose and into her lungs. She must have watched a movie about a dust monster.

She was watching *The Mummy* when Daniel was introduced to her. She was very white and you could see she couldn't be bothered with guests. She made a brief, gallant effort and asked Aunty Anne to turn the telly sound down. It was an exciting moment, with Christopher Lee swaying bandaged-wrapped, emerging from a swamp. But our mother listened carefully to what Daniel had to say for himself. "I liked the way he was very sure of himself," she said afterwards. "He's the type you could take anywhere and he'd make himself at home. But he looks the type to always want his own way."

By then Aunty Anne had well and truly settled in. She was sitting in her peach-coloured slip with her bra straps dangling down when Daniel was shown in. She'd forgotten he was due. "Help!" she mugged, and slipped past him to find a housecoat. She had a polythene shower cap on, waiting for her henna to take. You could see the henna under the cap, like the seamy clods of mud all over Christopher Lee.

Timon and Mandy and me were in the kitchen, and we were next on the list for Daniel to meet. Our kitchen was more cheerful since Timon had helped up to paint every sill, fitting and cupboard door in alternating patches of blue and yellow. We were talking in our bright kitchen and smoking. Smoking was allowed at home again. Our mother had started and she swore blind it had bucked her strength up. Cigarette burns had started to appear in her duvet, like tiny bullet holes.

Daniel came into the kitchen and tried to join in with us. We were just chatting and flipping through magazines. Mandy had *Tess of d'Urbervilles* open and her legs hooked over the edge of the table. Daniel told her he had read *Jude the Obscure* for his O levels, but he had thought it was very old-fashioned. People found it much easier, these days, to get themselves educated and rise through the ranks and make a success of themselves, didn't they? He didn't think Thomas Hardy was very relevant to their world anymore.

"Personally," said Mandy, "I hate things being relevant."

Timon looked up. "Is relevant the same as pertinent?"

Mandy slapped the Hardy face down on the table and rummaged for her ciggies. "Relevant comes with more strings. Relevant means that you have to feel like you're learning something."

"I hate to split hairs," said Daniel, "but..."

"Don't split hairs then," said Mandy. "I like your curly hair, by the way."

"You do?"

"Come on, Daniel," said Linda, and led him back to the living room, where the volume on *The Mummy* was back up.

LATER DANIEL TOLD LINDA THAT HE WANTED TO RESCUE HER FROM ALL that. From where she'd come from. Linda gasped. Then she slapped him, then she kissed him. So that was Linda.

Mandy said, "She's selling herself short to that little creep. Just because she's a big girl, doesn't mean she'll get no more offers."

"She's a sexy lady," said Timon.

We both looked at him.

"Who said you had any say?" asked Mandy.

He spread his palms and gave one of his gawky laughs.

"Don't ever compare one of us to the others," said Mandy. "Sisters don't like it."

"I wasn't!" he protested, laughing, refusing to take her seriously, which is why, I think, they never seriously fell out.

We were walking along the prom and Mandy changed the subject and starting asking how many characters a novel should have, and how many chapters. Timon was telling us that the arabic word bab meant both chapter and door. He said, don't put too many doors in your house or the roof will fall in. And too many people can't run around. And Mandy was asking, should the shape of a chapter be a dramatic W or a dramatic V and should a whole novel be shaped like a cathedral? She wanted to know all about structure.

"Mandy," said Timon. "Are you thinking of writing a book?"

"Me?" she said. "Where would I begin?"

I WAS IN BOOTS WITH LINDA AND SHE WAS GETTING ALL OF HER PERFUME samples out. I loved the tiny, coloured bottles and was wondering if I would like to work in that environment, where you got to handle nice things all day. But I was very different to Linda. She loved the shop itself. She loved handling the money, getting her fingers dirty with the smell of money, then dousing them with perfume and rubbing moisturizer and lipsticks onto the backs of ladies' hands. She loved the crush and push of the shop's shiny aisles. I would hate all that. To see a crowd go by and not be in it.

Whenever we tried out the perfume samples I'd get splashes of all kinds of smells up both my arms and round my neck. I'd come out of the shop smelling ridiculous and too flowery or musky. Once when I came home Aunty Anne said I'd have all the cats on the block coming after me. But I tried these things out to kill the time and not look like I was there just to talk to Linda, which I was.

I tried out one of those fragrances that can be used by both sexes and it smelled like watermelons. I held the bottle wrong and, peering at the nozzle over my sunglasses, squirted myself in the eye. I shouted out and Linda shushed me.

Then Mandy was there. She'd dropped her usual cool and was all excited. I was still shouting about my eye. "What's your problem?" asked Mandy.

"She squirted herself," said Linda. "What's that you've got?"

Even with both eyes full of tears and my face squinched up, I could see Mandy was waving a green slip of paper.

"Honestly," she said, "you can hear you two right across the shop."

"Oh, you can't, can you?" moaned Linda. She started to straighten up her clinical uniform and to put her testers away.

"You'll be getting the sack," said Mandy, mixing it.

"Don't say that!" said Linda, who was very superstitious. Daniel the insurance clerk was trying to cure her of that.

"I could put a complaint in about you two carrying on," said Mandy.

"Yeah, yeah," said Linda. "Tell us your news, anyway."

Mandy grasped my wrist. "Don't rub your eyes. You'll make them worse."

"Tell us your news!" said Linda, through gritted teeth.

Mandy threw down her green slip of paper. "It's the day of my exam results!"

We were shocked, and ashamed of ourselves for forgetting.

"A, B, and fucking C!" she crowed.

Linda was hopping up and down and I was hugging our Mandy. "You got them! You got them! Have you told Mam yet?"

"Not yet," Mandy laughed. "I'll tell her tonight, when we're all there."

"A, B, C," said Linda, leaving out the 'fucking', because Daniel was trying to train her out of swearing too. "You make it sound so simple!"

MANDY:
What do you call that moment? The moment you realise what you want to be?

This was one of those questions I asked Timon. The many questions I asked Timon that summer. He was a mine of information. He had opinions on everything and I liked to tiptoe through them. He was like beach-combing.

He thought and his eyes lit up. He said, "That's your epiphany, that. Your moment of realisation, Mandy." He laughed. "Something new, coming true."

Wendy was walking along with us. She tutted and repeated it.

"Something new, coming true." She was never very literary.

In the middle of the shopping arcade Timon turned to me. "And what is this epiphany you're having, hon? Is it gunna change your life?"

"Timon," I said. "I fucking hope so."

Then he said we should all go to the top of Blackpool Tower, and I could have my epiphany up there.

He had a sense of occasion, that boy.

The elevator took us up, up, up.

Under the Tower they have ballrooms for the waltzing and tangoing and foxtrotting that Aunty Anne went in for. They had an indoor circus with chimps dressed up for a clarty tea party.

The higher we went up the Tower, the more things crammed into our sight. The waxworks, the piers at either end, the death-defying womanly curves of the rollercoasters. Too much to take in. The higher up you get, the more you end up having to concentrate on just yourself. Else you get dizzy.

"'So what's your big surprise?" Wendy asked, and there was that answering-back quality to her voice. She was at that age.

I imagined that in the cramped, perilous space at the pinnacle of the Tower, I was wearing the hooped skirts of a Victorian lady. They ballooned in the breeze above the Tower's iron gantries. I listened out for the heavy rustle of the silk. I supposed that you'd never get up here in those skirts.

I said, "I want to go off and do nineteenth century literature."

"I thought so," Wendy nodded.

"In all those books," I said, "all I can see is me."

They both looked at me funny.

No matter who wrote those books—young or old, male or female—they all wrote about me. A woman of eighteen, stepping into the world, waiting to see what it will bring her.

"A beautiful woman of eighteen," I added. "It's all my story."

"Well," said Timon. "That's what you'd call an epiphany."

Wendy looked suspicious. "So what are you going to do?"

"Literature at Manchester Poly," I said, "And I start in the autumn."

SIX

THAT SUMMER THEIR MOTHER DIED. SHE WAS AT HOME ON THE SOFA, which was just as well. She would have hated to die in hospital. "And you know what us lot are like," said Aunty Anne. "Something would happen, a whole series of horrible somethings, and none of us would get to her bedside in time. She would pass away all by herself, because we were still waiting for buses."

As it was, their mother died with her family standing around her.

"All my eggs," she whispered, and they looked at each other.

Her hair was just growing back, into a tufted, punky style that suited her. But she looked drawn and tired out. They had known for some weeks that this was the last round of her fight.

"You've been in and out of this hospital," said Aunty Anne. "They'll be sick of the sight of you."

Their mother smiled. "I had more false alarms when I had our Wendy." She looked at Wendy. "You were doing the hokey-cokey for a fortnight."

Wendy nodded. She stood and watched, shocked by how calm everyone was. Their mother was dying and so they were all on their best behaviour. Their mother was dying and they watched it like they might watch from the Golden Mile as the rides on the Pleasure Beach burned down.

SHE HAD MANAGED ONE LAST TRIP INTO THE WORLD. SHE WAS IN A wheelchair, which Aunty Anne soon caught the knack of pushing. Aunty Anne was laughing the whole of this period, but if anyone elbowed in to help push their mother's chair, she would turn ferocious. Cheerfully setting her own weight behind her sister was the one practical thing Aunty Anne could do. She could lend her sister those marvellous legs, for a week or two at least.

Sunday best, walking abreast, the whole family went to visit the waxworks on the Golden Mile. Their mother had a hankering to see the Chamber of Horrors. Timon came with them, and he was the most shaken by the grisly spectacles they took in that afternoon, following the wheelchair's slow, squeaking progress from tableau to tableau.

"Isn't it scary!" whispered their mother, and the girls had to agree. Threads hung from the dark ceilings, brushing their faces like cobwebs.

They passed through the Vestibule of Murderers, the Grotto of Stranglers, and the Annexe of Slashers. They watched jerky, animatronic bodysnatchers pulling parts of waxy bodies out of holes in the waxy ground. The parts looked mushy and useless, but the snatchers looked pleased with themselves. Dry ice curled everywhere, sea green and blue. A mad husband was dunking his wife in a frothing and steaming bath of acid. Then came the best part: the Hall of Monsters. Vampires squatting in clock towers, feeding the bats and frightening the hunchback. Those same vampires issuing suavely from behind bedposts and wardrobes. Frankenstein and the Wolfman were in a woodland setting, both cursing their heritage as, behind them, the creature from the black lagoon came dripping up the shore. In a golden tomb the mummy was clutching its bandaged head as it came back to migrainey life. How pleased their mother was to see them in the flesh.

Finally there was the Anatomy Exhibit, which was only for adults. It was full of life-sized dummies, mock-up, simulacra of bits of bodies. Cross sections and amputations, remains and souvenirs. It showed all the things that could go wrong with you.

"It'll be like a freak show," tutted Aunty Anne. "I'm not going there. Let's go and see Fred Astaire and Ginger Rogers. Now, she had a pair of legs, didn't she?"

Their mother didn't want to see the Anatomy Exhibit anyway. "Too much like real life," she said.

THE MOST SOMBRE ROOM WAS THAT FULL OF FAMOUS RULERS. IT WAS AT the end of their trip out. The displays were roped off, as if these really were eminent and important persons that commoners weren't allowed to touch. It was the least popular room, especially on a hot afternoon.

"Look at all the jewels!" said Aunty Anne. "Imagine they were real!"

Wendy thought her aunty sometimes sounded like someone who had always been poor. And yet there was her husband, apparently a millionaire. They all watched the spotlights glimmer on theatrical jewels.

Their mother took a large orange out of her handbag. She waved it at Mandy. "Here, love. Nip over there. Shove it inside her dress."

Mandy's face lit up. She took the orange.

Aunty Anne started to laugh. Linda said, "You can't..."

But Mandy was over the rail in a flash. No alarms went off. No one noticed. She put the orange where her mother had told her, and gave Maggie Thatcher a third tit.

Their mother had brought a whole carrier bag, full of sick room fruit. "I'm sick of the sight of fruit!" she laughed. "Fruit makes me think I'm ill!"

They progressed into yet another chamber of famous people. These were the real stars. The daughters took their instructions, and the pieces of just-past-their-best fruit that she handed them. Ceremonially, they jumped the braids and trip-wires and put:

A banana down the skin-tight dancing pants of Michael Jackson.

A pear down the back of Arnie Schwarzenegger's bathing trunks.

A whole pound of clementines down the front of Barbara Cartland.

Grapes in the hands of a supine Liz Taylor, and

an apple, like Magritte, like Wilhelm Tell, on the head of Superman.

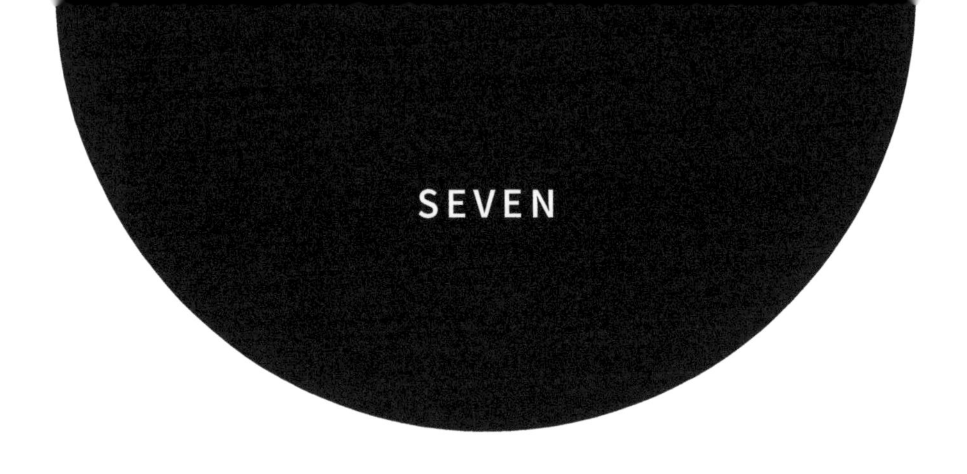

SEVEN

THEY THOUGHT OUR MOTHER WAS RECKLESS. THEY THOUGHT SHE WAS brassy and loud and that made her reckless.

Then, when she became scared of everything, they lost patience with her. Why couldn't she be brave any more? Why wasn't she laughing in people's faces, or hurling herself into the wind? People need other people to be brave.

They thought her life had made her timid. Her husband had walked out and started another family. She became increasingly poor. She brought up three girls alone, and then she became ill. She took a whole load of hard knocks. This eroded her courage, they thought.

But I knew our mother better than anyone. She was always a worrier. She was never as defiant as people thought. I saw her close that front door and cry hard tears. When there had been a stand-up slanging match outside on the walkways, or down in the street, and our mother was involved, she'd give as good as she got, or better. But when she was back in private, those defences would fall away. She'd look shattered.

She had spirit, but not entirely the sort they thought she had. She was quieter than anyone would believe, especially in the years when she was laughing her head off. Even when it seemed she did everything she could to draw attention.

ALL THESE THINGS TO DEAL WITH. HER BITS AND PIECES. WHO'D HAVE thought she owned so much? Would anyone want any of this?

Looking at her living room (and it was hers now, not ours, as if her going had pushed us out and the things there were already in the past) I realised that there was a horse motif throughout our mother's choice of ornaments. I couldn't say I ever noticed it before. Horse brasses hung dully on their black leather straps. Horse shoes were nailed above doorways for luck. Pictures of horses pulling ploughs or carriages were in the hallway. Her china shire horses lined up along the bar's frosted glass. Even the soda syphon had a horse's head.

Only now she was gone was I seeing things.

She had three shelves of novelty tea pots, all for show and never use. They were in the shape of cottages, castles, Blackpool Tower, Dusty Bin, the Rover's Return, a red phone box. I lifted up all their lids and peered inside, finding buttons, toggles, two stamps and some old earrings, not very nice.

THEY ARE SOME KIND OF FAKE GOLD AND ONE OF THEM IS CRUSTED IN black and brown, with a wizened bit of what looks like scab. I drop it back into the teapot when I realise that what I'm holding is the earring that Mam ripped out of Mandy's head. I'm looking right at a chunk of Mandy's earlobe. These earrings have been hidden inside this house-shaped teapot, ever since the night Mandy came back late and announced that she had given her virginity gladly to a boy called Martin.

The earring—once yanked out of her ear—got thrust into this pot, bloods and shreds of flesh and all, and forgotten about, as Mandy howled and bubbled. Linda called an ambulance and when it came we all raced off to watch Mandy get stitched up at three o'clock in the morning.

Mandy was fourteen and I was eleven and she told me, to reassure me, that it was just a grown-up row they'd had. She and Linda never skimped on the details they hoped would educated me, and that included those of her deflowering. They wanted me to know what I had coming to me. They wished someone had explained things properly to them. Our mother was never a very skilful explainer.

Mandy had wanted to lose her cherry in the open air. After the Pleasure Beach that night she had taken Martin, who was in her composition class, to the park, and they rolled under the trees. She let him push a finger into her and then, nervously, both afraid they would buckle and snap it, his tight cock. He pressed on for two or three strokes and then he got scared he would come inside her. She said to push in a couple of times more, just so they'd be able to say they'd actually done it. He fucked her like he was washing up the very best dishes, gritting his teeth. Martin, relieved, pulled himself out and tossed himself off in the long grass. Mandy watched interestedly. Then he tucked himself away and helped her up. She came home, and that's when Mam hit her, for the first and only time in both their lives.

AUNTY ANNE SAID SHE WAS NEVER A ONE FOR LOOKING A GIFT HORSE IN the mouth. She said this and she wasn't trying to be funny, but the things she was referring to were all horse-shaped. Our mother's ornaments, horses of different sizes, textures and colours. Bequeathed to our Aunty Anne by my mother's slim will. They presented themselves to her as a quandary. What do you do with a load of horse-shaped household objects? And, as Aunty Anne pointed out, it wasn't as if she was settled in her own place. If she had her own house—fine—maybe she could consider filling it with horse memorabilia. But she doubted her lover in Phoenix Court would be thrilled if she brought these things to him.

They made quite a collection. We laid them out in rows on the living room carpet. Horse-shaped everythings, even teaspoons. Our mother's will had stipulated that if anything with a horse on it was to be found in her flat after her death, it was Anne's. Our Aunt was surprised as any of us. On the day of dishing out the bequeaths and leftovers, Aunty Anne found herself looking at hundreds of gift-horses.

We brought them out from under the bed. They were on shelves, in cupboards, on top of wardrobes.

"I could open a restaurant and the theme could be horses. I could display these to the public, for a charge." Aunty Anne was full of schemes like this.

"But do you like them?" Linda asked pointedly. She didn't, that was plain. She was looking at a stuffed donkey from Spain. It was wearing a sombrero.

"I don't really like them, no," said Aunty Anne.

It seemed a terrible thing, to criticize a dead woman's taste.

"Then you'll have to get rid," said Mandy. "We can't leave them here." Bit by bit we were cleaning out the whole flat. No one quite said that we were leaving forever, but it was obviously in the air, with every neglected corner that got swept, every cubbyhole that got emptied.

Aunty Anne decided she would sell of her horses at a car boot sale on a Sunday afternoon. None of us had a car, so that was something to work round. She thought about borrowing one, but then a very nice man in charge told her she could lay her wares out on a wallpapering table instead. So she set about flogging her horses.

She found that she was a very successful saleswoman. She haggled and hectored and hooted with laughter. There was such a commotion around her stall that no one could go by without looking. All of Saturday night she'd been up making toffee and cakes and scones, using up the bags of flour, icing sugar and spice that were left in our mother's kitchen cabinets. Aunty Anne was selling cakes for thirty pence each.

Gradually she let fly our mother's herd...

She made forty-seven pounds and announced that she would take us all out to dinner.

TIMON WOULD GET HER USED TO BEING NORMAL AGAIN. MANDY TOLD him, "You're the only one who can bring her out of herself."

There was little Wendy wanted to do except sit in the mostly-emptied living room and watch videos. Her mother's horror videos were almost unbearable to her, because each time the monster crept up on the heroine, Wendy could hear her mother shouting out: "He's behind you!" She could hear her mother cackle and groan each time a dodgy special effect burst or splashed or lurched onto the screen. She could hear the mocking shrieks of her mother in the gratuitously bloody bits. But Wendy went on, through hot, still afternoons, watching every one of the tapes.

When Mandy asked him, Timon readily agreed.

Wendy only shrugged when he said, Come out. Face the world again.

He took her into pubs and they would sit whole afternoons and evenings away. They drank themselves drunk and sober again.

THAT MAN OVER THERE, LOOK HOW LONG HIS SWALLOWS OF BEER ARE. He's really drinking it down. Gollop gollop. His eyes are wide and his eyebrows go up like he's being forced, but no one's forcing him. I can see right up through the end of his glass and his mouth opens and shuts in close-up.

What's Timon saying to me?

THEY SAY A CHILD CAN'T IMAGINE THE WORLD GOING ON BEYOND THEIR own death. That the point of maturity is marked by the realisation that life goes on without you. My own horrid epiphany was that the world went on longer than my mother. I couldn't believe it.

Ping ping ping.

Snapping the apron strings.

AT THAT TIME I COULDN'T CONCENTRATE ON ANYTHING. I COULDN'T listen to a word Timon tried to tell me. I'm sure he was telling me sensible, supportive stuff. He had lost both his parents. He knew the territory. And I, who by then had spent a year hanging onto every word uttered by this big, beautiful man...ignored him.

In the pubs where we sat smoking the afternoons away I would look at the carpets and think about how they were stiff with bitter. For some reason I found the long, sunny afternoons hardest to get through. I became fascinated with the scarred varnish on the bar and tables, and thought about how, for generations, they had been scoured by spirits. The place was sodden with booze. Its medicinal tang hung in the gloom.

IF THEY ASKED ME, HOW DID I RESPOND TO MY MOTHER'S DEATH, WHAT would I say? There wasn't much I could say.

Did I, like Linda, throw myself into my work?

I had no work.

Linda won herself awards for her immaculate service. Got herself promoted. Now she was allowed to do in-store make-overs. Lovely. Shoals of nervous women brought their unmade faces to her counter, and fidgeted there on stools, submitting themselves to her expert fingers.

Her insurance clerk Daniel wanted her to go higher and higher.

Take your beautician's exams, Linda!

She wanted to be a Doctor of Glamour. A Professor of Beauty.

Because he was good at getting things insured, Daniel was promoted, too. He bought a house on a new estate, out of town, where all the houses were in cul-de-sacs and made of gingerbread. They stood with discreet distances between them. Neither saw any reason why Linda shouldn't move in straight away. Our mother had died. The family was already broken up.

Mandy, Timon and I helped them to move. Daniel covered their new, barely-dried walls with brown hessian wallpaper. They had Swedish-type furniture, all bought to match. Minimalism, Daniel informed us, was his watch-word. Linda didn't look so sure. She liked things that would draw the eye. In their new house they didn't even have a three piece suite. They had bean bags in different colours, and scatter cushions. Aunty Anne wasn't impressed.

"You show all your drawers, sitting in these," she said, smoothing her skirt as we all sat in bean bags. It was the evening of their moving in, and we were eating fish and chips, starving after all the lugging around. Linda had fetched them in as a treat for the workers. You could tell by the look on Daniel's face that he wasn't keen on us eating in his new front room.

Aunty Anne had come to inspect the place once the work was over. "Am I showing my drawers, Daniel?" she cawed. She loved to find new ways of distressing him. "But look at my lovely legs!" She lifted them in the air, slumping sideways in the orange bean bag.

MANDY'S RESPONSE TO OUR MOTHER'S DEATH WAS TO PLUNGE HERSELF further into the nineteenth century. Even the way she talked started to change. She talked in whole sentences and would put on all these silly voices, like someone in a book. She was making plans for moving to

Manchester, and met a man on one rainy, flat-hunting trip. They had frothy coffee in Meng and Ecker's after a matinee of *Saint Joan* at the Royal Exchange. He was in a sky blue plasticky coat and she knew almost immediately that he was the one. His half moon glasses had yellow-tinted lenses and he talked knowledgeably about cubism and modernism and Virginia Woolf and, by degrees, Mandy said, she could feel herself being seduced. "The moment he got onto stream of consciousness...I was lost..."

MEANWHILE I WAS PRETENDING TO BE OF DRINKING AGE, AND TRYING out every drink ever invented. Settling on which would be my tipple. My downfall and demon. Campari and lemon. Egg nog. Lemon vodka. Peach Schnapps. Southern Comfort and lemonade. The sicklier and stickier the better. It was as if I was determined to make myself ill. And I was still but a child, with the same sweet tooth. I discovered After Eight flavoured vodka. But I never threw up, not even drinking these ever-sweeter confections. I kept them all in. I made my own self as sweet as could be and, through a dreadful summer of mourning, steadily fermented.

Timon, watchful, matched me drink for drink. Even took the same drinks as me. And he, poor lamb, was violently sick every time. Sick as a dog.

I ADDICTED MYSELF TO THE JUKE BOX. I PUT ON THE SAME OLD SONGS. There were to be found in juke boxes in pubs all over Blackpool, their labels coloured yellow, their numbers rubbed away with use. These are the songs I can't listen to now:

Land of Make Believe—Buck's Fizz
Does Anybody Miss Me—Brenda Soobie
Ever Fallen in Love—Buzzcocks
Anyone who had a Heart—Cilla Black
Runaway—Del Shannon
Story of the Blues—The Mighty Wah
A Little Loving—Dusty Springfield.

This last one was playing when Aunty Anne came in to, as she saw it, rescue me from myself. In she burst. And I was holding down ouzo. My head full of fennel fumes and Timon turning green at my shoulder. Aunty Anne's face was set. She had been planning this showdown for days. She had carefully planned what she would wear for coming into bars alone, hunting for me. She looked eccentric and determined, in a yellow sheepskin coat and a wide-brimmed green fedora. She looked almost artistic.

THIS IS WHAT AUNTY ANNE SAID.

"You're not doing yourself any favours. You're spoiling yourself. Isn't she, Timon? He's a man, he knows. No man will look at a woman who's spoiled herself."

"I know you're upset about your mam. We all are. But you can take upset too far. You can wallow in it. Look at your sisters. They aren't sinking into...sinking into..."

"Despondency," said Timon.

"Thanks," I snapped.

"They aren't, though. They're getting on with it. You just have to get on."

I asked her, "What am I meant to get on with?"

I asked her again, "Where do I begin?"

AT THAT POINT I THOUGHT I WAS GOING TO BE HOMELESS. EVERYONE would tootle off to their own, new homes, and they would all forget that I didn't have one.

Aunty Anne had decided that she was coming to my recue, and taking the situation in hand, she made Timon collude with her.

"You, young lady, are coming with me."

OUR MOTHER'S DEATH MADE US THINK ABOUT THE FUTURE AND WHAT WE should all be doing. As if she had just been a prompt: now it's your turn. Prove to me. Do something of your own.

The others jumped to it.

But they knew where they were jumping.

How could I plot out the shape of my new life?

I didn't have any idea of shapes.

Now, of course, I know shapes. I've had years and years of shapes.

They're easy. Live any sort of life and you throw out a shape.

Even if you think you don't form anything, and that what you've lived is insignificant: a shape is still there. Even an inconsistent, collapsible shape. Even a rubbish one.

Y= mx + c. That's what I found out later.

I wish someone had told me that at the start.

I took O level maths only recently, in these my later, idle, workless years. I learned all this stuff about graphs, about making and plotting one shape into another. Transformations. So maybe if I'd listened in school, early on, geometry would have seen me through.

Fact was, I had no talent, or ambition.

I couldn't beam and flatter and smear on lip-gloss and make other ladies spend spend spend.

I couldn't force my eyes to follow print through the thousands of pages of tersely formal, decorous prose that Mandy loved. I could never keep track of the names. Charlotte Elizabeth Jane Sarah Agnes Fanny.

And why would I want to do what my sisters did?

So both a career and a further education were out.

What was I to do?

"First," said Aunty Anne, "we go to Edinburgh, to your uncle."

So we travelled north.

EIGHT

DUBIOUS AT FIRST, BUT THAT DOESN'T HURT, DOES IT? A LITTLE circumspection never hurt anyone. In his long life Captain Simon had learned a thing or two about not getting his fingers burned. So when he was making new acquaintances, when he went into a fresh situation, he kept his soldierly wits about him.

But which army had he served with? What kind of soldier was he? You and whose army, Captain Simon? Nobody knew.

He wore a yellow coat with shining buttons, braid and epaulettes. His medals were impressive and buffed up, and he had a stainless white moustache, curling up at both ends. He was a bit of a mystery, and he claimed always to have a knife slid down inside one of his boots. He was an expert in jungle warfare, he said.

So Captain Simon was careful. He didn't go into anything without checking it out first. After some months though, he found that he actually enjoyed going upstairs to visit the top flat. Seeing what the old man and that young lad of his were getting up to. Always something different. Pottery or war games, papier mâché or poker. They became Captain

Simon's main diversion.

Mostly the old man and the young lad sat in their flagstoned attic kitchen, drenched in lovely, clear daylight and, to all appearances, didn't do much of anything these days. But they talked, and that's really what the Captain loved to go up there for. The craic, the Irish called it. Blether, the Scots said, and that was more appropriate here, though the old man wasn't Scottish.

Captain Simon would ascend the staircase with the custard yellow walls and scarlet trim at ten thirty in the morning, knowing that the old man and the young chap would already be sitting at their table. On the scarred table between them would be the ransacked newspapers and the day's post. They seemed to get more of their fair share of both. The old man's stringy plants and saplings would be out on the table, under the window, getting their share of the daylight. A pot of the strongest coffee the Captain had ever tasted would sit among dozens of cups. If you listened very carefully, you might hear the cafetière whine. That was something scientific, to do with the pressure of hot, wet air. The young chap had explained it.

Some morning the old man might even have a bottle of red wine open. He drank it from a tumbler, like fruit juice. He sat back on a cosy swivel chair in his scarlet dressing gown that he would wear all day around the house. He went around in bare feet, even though there was no proper carpet in the hallways and the floor was covered with spelks. These late-in-life-millionaires, Captain Simon would marvel. How they made him smile. Taking a flat in the Royal Circus, filling it with not-very-luxurious nor outlandish belongings. Living quite simply and not filling the place with yachts and sports cars and dolly birds. Thinking they could just move into the Captain's life like this.

At first the soldier had guessed that the old man and the boy were lovers. They boy bustled about, chivvying round the rather donnish gentleman. The Captain assumed that their contented flirtatiousness with each other meant they were partners. But they weren't. The son, Colin, put him right on that count. Colin had laughed fit to burst. "Hear that, dad! He's got us down as an old married couple!"

The father glanced over his 'Scotsman' and said something to the effect that it was often the way, when the child was stuck at home with the remaining parent. Captain Simon thought about this. It made it seem as if Colin was there seeing to his ailing father. If anything, though, it was the other way around. The boy was thin and white, wore a little goatee beard, and he was so obviously ill with that horrible disease.

Their bleary, brilliant camaraderie pleased Captain Simon and day after day he kept coming back to smoke with them. He found that he could roll a joint better than either of his neighbours, and he hoped his skills might bring him into their little gang. It had been a long time since Captain Simon was part of a gang.

ONE MORNING THEY SAT DRINKING WINE IN THE KITCHEN, PLACIDLY listening to the sounds in the hallway as the men laid the cable for fifty new TV channels. The old man was flipping through the satellite TV magazine, marking in red felt tip the things he couldn't miss. Juggling the fifty channels.

"You've got a new toy," said his son, trying to read the listings upside down.

"You should be glad," his father said gruffly. "So many new multi-millionaires go completely off the rails."

"They get their heads turned," smirked Colin, who loved clichés of every sort, and collected them.

"It's true!" said the old man, whose own reason for loving clichés was that they were true. "You should be relieved I can still get pleasure out of simple things. Like having fifty TV channels to choose from."

His son looked at the shows he had ticked in red. "And getting all hot and bothered over *Charlie's Angels*."

'I'll do no such thing!' His mobile phone gave a trill. Captain Simon really liked that noise and often thought of asking how you went about getting yourself one of those phones. He knew it was something to do with subscribing to, belonging to, a web of some sort. He'd have liked to carry his phone in his inside pocket, to have that noise going close to his heart. Captain Simon enjoyed only the very nicest things.

The old man was impatient with whoever had called him. "You're breaking up. This is useless. You sound demented, woman." He sighed.

'Your signal is nothing like strong enough.' He switched her off and tossed the phone back onto the table. "Anne's still on the train. And I couldn't hear a word she was saying."

Colin looked up sharply. 'But she's still on the way?'

"More's the pity," the old man said. He prodded the very last little bit of the joint at Captain Simon. "You haven't met my darling ex-wife, have you?"

The Captain gulped. In the year he had come visiting he had never heard such a person mentioned.

"She's a harridan," said the old man. "A gorgon, a siren, a terrible monkfish of a woman. But, as she'll no doubt tell you, she has the legs of an angel. What does she dance like, Colin?"

Colin said dutifully, "Like nothing on earth."

"She's coming here?" asked Captain Simon.

The old man harrumphed. "If she bets you that she can still do the splits, don't take her up on her bet." He went to fetch a fresh bottle from the cupboard under the eaves. 'She'll do herself an injury, showing off one day." He straightened up suddenly. "Colin, could you fetch that for me?" The boy tutted and did as he was told. "The other thing, of course, is that she's bringing your cousin with her."

"Which one?" asked Colin.

"Oh, I don't know. They're all the same to me."

Instinctively Captain Simon had taken out his handkerchief, flapped it once briskly in the air, and set about polishing up the brass of his buttons and epaulettes.

YOU CAN'T GO ANYWHERE WITHOUT BUMPING SOMEONE YOU KNOW. Mandy warned me once that the world was smaller than you ever thought.

When I was small my mother took me to department stores and we'd go up and down in escalators and all the lifts and the departments looked the same. She drilled me on what to do if we were split up. Especially in the Sales, which were ferocious. Sometimes Mam was easily distracted. She said, stand right still. Don't go haring round and round and shouting after me. If you stay in one place, I'll do the moving round. I'll go to every floor every corner every nook every cranny. Soon I'll be there. Soon I will find you.

So I'm not to worry about meeting new people. About going to new and bigger towns. Committing myself to brand new stuff doesn't mean I'll never get the old again. Everything but everything comes back.

ON THE TRAIN WITH AUNTY ANNE. PAST CARLISLE, I'M FURTHER NORTH than I've ever been before. What am I expecting? To drop off the frozen crust of the world? The countryside looks the same. Brownish cows or horses grazing.

I feel jumpy jumpy. Not like me at all. You can take the girl out of Blackpool...You can take the girl out of Blackpool.

Aunty Anne picks up my small world theme.

"One of the reasons I had to get out of Scotland was that it's smaller than you think, the bits that people live in. You see the same old Scottish faces everywhere you go. Now don't get me wrong, I liked living there and I won't hear a word against it, but it got ridiculous. I went on a walking holiday to the Western Isles and left, right and centre I was bumping into faces I knew. In lonesome spot hotels they'd seek me out to play dominoes or make up a foursome for tennis. You can get enough of friendly faces gathering round." She fiddled with the aluminium strip of the teabag in her plastic cup.

I'd already pointed out to her the young man just up the gangway from us. A sexy skinhead, well filled out. He had been in our Linda's class at school. Used to hang out with our Mandy and Linda for a while last summer. David. We hadn't seen him since them. Now here he was, on our train to Edinburgh.

The sun slanted in, lighting him up quite prettily, and I kept looking over. It's my new habit, this looking at men. Before, I'd only ever bother looking at Timon. Now, I was staring at anything that went drifting by. Or sitting there, swinging his boots up onto the empty seat beside him, wadding up his jacket for a pillow. Staring at a magazine with a nude picture on the cover—that woman from the series about aliens living on our planet and she's the one who finds them out. She's never nude in the series. Now he's falling asleep, looking less and less hard.

Aunty Anne went shunting up the aisle, looking for a payphone. When she was gone I deliberately caught that David's eye.

"You've grown up!" he burst out, as if he couldn't stop himself. Then he blushed. I was watching Aunty Anne, still pushing up the train, saying her excuse me's, and I was thinking what a big behind she had. I had never thought of the size of her bum before, she always drew attention to her special, delectable legs.

I thought about freezing this David out, now I had his attention. I didn't know how. I said, "I've left school, an' all."

"You're Wendy, aren't you?"

I nodded and we grinned at each other.

"I used to knock about with your sisters. I'm David."

"I remember."

For a while—I was just a kid then—he'd come in and watch telly with the family. Even our mother thought he was sexy, but she would never have said that. She called him a skinny little article and he could make her laugh and she would pat the settee cushion next to her, inviting him to sit. "*Creature From the Black Lagoon*?" she'd announce, and it was like she was offering him a posh drink.

"Our mam died," I told him.

He looked shocked.

"It was cancer," I said. "It wasn't, like, a vampire or a creature from a lagoon or anything."

He gaped at me like I was weird.

I said, "Remember how she used to watch all them films?"

He nodded. "Look... I'm sorry."

I shouldn't have said anything to him. Aunty Anne was right. She said people don't like it when you bring death in.

Aunty Anne tells me, 'Stay close by, lovey,' at the station with everyone milling and knowing where they're going and of course I don't. I'm flung the mercies of people I don't know from Adam. I stick to Aunty Anne as she goes to commandeer a porter... she wants a wheely pushy thing, she can't think of the right word for them.

"A trolley, madam?" and with a flourish the cheeky monkey pulls one from behind a pillar. Just what she wants. She seizes the handle, tutting. She can't be doing with cleverness and bright sparks making a monkey out of her. She tells me to load all our bags on the trolley.

I love the way everyone gets off the train and hits the platform, knowing where they want to be and hardly breaking their stride, parading over the white, speckled, shiny ground.

There's that woman in the smart cut orange woollen suit that Aunty Anne so admired. The woman sounded very posh to me. She had a table and two toddlers, had them cutting coloured papers up and keeping their attention all the way from London, 'where we live,' to Edinburgh, 'where we have a little flat in the New Town.' A kind of Arabian fella was at their table in his robes and he got roped in, all jolly, to help the kiddies draw and cut up princesses and animals with long, peculiar legs. Ahmed helped the kiddies stick the cut-outs on the carriage window, so the sun shone through and lit up their different colours. "He's a nice man, Ahmed, isn't he, mummy?"

"I'm sure he's a very nice man, darling."

They were going now and Ahmed was off in his other direction. I found I was staring, just like I'd earwigged all the way up, even though the chat was getting on my nerves.

Then, when Aunty Anne's back is turned, here's that David—the skinny skin skinhead—pushing a folded, raggy slip of paper into my palm and I know by touch, by osmosis of some sexy, flirty, successful sort, that it's got his phone number scrawled on it. He wants me to call him up some time now that we're both in Edinburgh. And I have nights to fill, nights and nights to fill.

I see him flash by—a streak of sharp, grinning sunlit boy—hoisting an army bag over one shoulder and he's away. I tuck his note into my pocket. Aunty Anne is flapping her arms at a taxi. It grumbles up and sits ticking at our kerb.

NINE

WHEN THEY ARRIVED THERE WAS THE USUAL FLURRY AND FUSS OVER NEW guests. Wendy hung back, tired from the six flights of stairs, and watched them behave. Reunions: mother and son (fond, wary), husband and wife (very formal, very wary). Wendy took it all but knew, as the real stranger in their midst, that she was the actual object of scrutiny.

They were urged to set down their bags in the hallway—the carpetless, messy hallway—and leave off putting things in their rightful places until they had a cup of tea and settled themselves. "We don't care if the place is a state!" cried Uncle Pat. He flapped the sleeves of a voluminous scarlet dressing gown. "Come into the kitchen!"

Wendy followed them down the passage. It certainly was a state, as if it had been half done-up and then abandoned during redecorations. Bits of old carpet and newspaper partly covered the old boards. The phone and the Yellow Pages had been slung in the corner. "Don't you feel," the old man called out to Wendy, "when you get off the train that you're still vibrating and shunting along? I feel like that for a whole day afterwards."

"I've not been on a train before," said Wendy, and realised it was true.

The flat seemed to smell of veggie burgers, coffee and cigarettes. It seemed to Wendy a funny place for a couple of millionaires to live.

The cousin, Colin, hadn't said a word yet. He was so skinny and not what she'd expected at all. Aunty Anne hadn't said much to prepare her, but somehow Wendy had pictured a strapping lad in a polo shirt, hairs sprouting out on his chest.

They were ushered into the kitchen, a bright, stone-flagged room with an old-fashioned range, potted plants resting everywhere and a sloping ceiling. The old man dashed over to the cooker and was busily turning over veggie burgers on the grill. It was like walking into an indoor barbecue: there were already guests at the kitchen table that Wendy didn't recognise. Aunty Anne was looking daggers at the interlopers.

"Ah," said Uncle Pat. "These are our downstairs neighbours. Captain Simon, and his captivating sister, Belinda."

They nodded hellos at the curious couple. Colin was finding them chairs to go round the cluttered table. Belinda was a very fat woman in a candy-striped mini-dress. She had white hair kept back with slides, and very broad, white knees. She shook out a bag of sugar mice onto the table. 'I've been saving these until you came,' she said, in a very broad, posh-Edinburgh accent, the first that Wendy had heard.

Her brother next to her was in some kind of uniform. "Are you back for long, Anne?" he asked, Aunty Anne, thought, very forwardly.

"We don't know as yet," she told him.

Wendy saw her uncle and cousin Colin exchange a look.

HER ROOM WAS BESIDE THE KITCHEN AND SO SHE COULD HEAR THEM talking when she went to bed, or first thing in the morning. Sometimes she lay awake with excitement, full of the idea of herself in a new place.

The girl she'd been would never let herself get het up about a change in circumstances. The girl she used to be would have been sickened. She wasn't used to excessive enthusiasm. But the moment Uncle Pat had shown her the green spiral staircase up to her own room, she knew this would be different. She had her own space, with walls freshly painted an eggy yellow, and a skylight wider than she could spread her arms. This was directly above her bed and, when she lay staring up, she seemed to be lifted up to the sky. Smashing.

That first morning, when Uncle Pat had showed her to the spiral staircase, just beside the kitchen, he had said: "For as long as you stay with us, this will be yours." His battered face flushed with pleasure as she tested her feet on the iron rungs. She was starting to warm to him. The skin of his face was shiny like the bottoms of her mother's old, worn moccasin slippers.

This was the first uncle-y thing that he did for her: showing her this room and saying that it was hers, letting her try it out for herself alone.

She poked her head into the gorgeous yellow of the new room and gasped. She looked down at him again, this foreshortened old man in the crimson silk of his overlarge dressing gown. He gave her a small wave and walked away. He didn't seem Aunty Anne's type at all.

MOSTLY COLIN WAS IN CHARGE OF WENDY. HE KNEW ALL ABOUT nothing, he admitted, but he liked lovely days out and Uncle Pat had decided that Wendy would have to learn all about the city on a series of lovely days out. When Colin and Wendy went out alone, they generally ignored the history and legends and the buildings, all the things they ought to pay attention to, and sought out the shops that were so swish they displayed only two or three items in their windows, or the cafes that offered the sickliest looking cakes.

When Uncle Pat came out with them he thought that Wendy would like to hear all his memories of the city. How much it had all changed. How, nowadays, everything was geared to pleasure and he was sure that was a marvellous thing, a positive thing. He talked to Wendy as if she was considering Edinburgh as the place to spend the rest of her life.

One day that first week they had a late, lazy lunch in the Scarlet Empress, Colin's favourite cafe. They took the window table at the back and looked out at the cramped, green garden.

"Mark you," said Uncle Pat, "I talk about pleasure, but all the jazz clubs and the cinemas down this end of town appear to have vanished. They've whistled off to those multiplex places, haven't they? People find they like different things, I suppose. They've gone off old picture houses, full of honest vulgarity. There was one with long steps, like a draw-bridge down to a hut where you bought your tickets. It was like going up into a castle, the castle where all your dreams played out. They had wooden Corinthian columns that were rotting away inside..." He looked up to see Wendy smiling. "Oh, I feel about a hundred and six explaining this to you. Yet I still feel six years old inside. I do, you know. That's never left me."

Colin was playing with a salad. "I wish I did."

"I like hearing about what it was like before," said Wendy. "You must have lived here for years."

"Years," agreed Uncle Pat. "But now that you're here..." he paused. "I'm sure you'll find plenty to keep yourself busy now that you're here."

THEY WERE FINDING OUT THE KINDS OF THINGS SHE LIKED TO DO, AND trying their best to please her. She didn't know herself what she liked anymore. She was happy to let them lead her around. Colin took her to the galleries: on the long, leafy walk along the Waters of Leith to the Museum of Modern Art. He was silent much of the way as they crossed and re-crossed the river and dams and ducked the overhanging trees. In the cafes they visited Colin liked to read or simply watch the people at other tables. Wendy took this time to write letters to her sisters or Timon. She found that she wanted to read, too, which was a novelty for her. She begged Timon to send her some stories he had finished, and wished that he would hurry and get on with that novel of his. But he was so precious with the things he wrote. He said it made him feel too vulnerable, showing even someone he trusted his unfinished work. And all his work was unfinished. He could tinker on with stories forever. There was always something to correct. To a perfectionist like him, Timon wrote, the words he wrote never quite chimed in with real life. They slid off the surface and spilled away. He preferred just telling her the stories he thought up or heard. In fact, he thought, he would never publish anything in his lifetime. Let them find it when he was dead in a gutter. And anyway, he told her, she should be immersing herself in new things, not his old stuff. Wendy considered what he said. "Something new, coming true," she reminded herself.

When Uncle Pat took her out it was so he could talk to her. She got the feeling he didn't get much of a chance usually, and he was a right old gas-bag. Colin was by nature quiet, it seemed, and Captain Simon was chatty, but not very forthcoming or, actually, that interested in what anyone else had to say. Wendy could tell her Uncle was pleased that she listened to him going on. He took her peculiar places, too, that she would never think of. With him she went to dingy but cosy cafetierias down the rougher end of Leith Walk, where they watched the racing on a portable TV. He took her to the launderette to meet some of his cronies, who greeted him and her with a certain dry-lipped jocularity. She realised that he was showing her off. "See this? This is my long-lost niece."

She even started going out places with Belinda, the big woman from downstairs. Belinda must have been fifty, but she dressed much younger and liked to think of herself as closer to Wendy's generation. She wanted to know whether Wendy would be a pal of hers, and come out clubbing and dancing in the evening. Why not, Wendy shrugged.

The only person not to make an effort going out with her and showing her round was Aunty Anne. Now that they were here and settling into the flat in the Royal Circus, Anne seemed to have lost a certain amount of interest in her niece. She spent her time at the car boot sales held in multi-storey car parks around the city, picking up bits of old tat—pictures and ornaments mostly—for a few bob at a time. These she would sell in the auctions held down the Thistle Street warehouses on weekday mornings. She was making a bit of extra pocket money, she said. Colin raised an eyebrow. "Actually, I think she's making a fortune. She says she discovered this latent talent for flogging things. When did she find that out?"

"Ah," said Wendy. "That was when our mother died." She explained the situation with the collection of horses.

"That's awful!" said Colin. "Fancy just getting rid like that." He sighed. "My mother hasn't got a sentimental bone in her body." They were having coffee in the sculpture park at the Musuem of Modern Art. It was one of Wendy's favourite things so far, sitting amongst the distended, silvery bodies sporting on the lawn. She wasn't sure she agreed with Colin about her Aunty. She must have something sentimental in her, or sympathetic at least, to have brought Wendy here in the first place.

SHE NOTICED HOW GREEN IT WAS. THEY LIKED TO HAVE LOTS OF TREES in this city. It made the place seem fresh to her. You could be in the thick of the busiest street, diesel fumes lining your throat as you squeezed past the queue at the bus stop, and all you'd have to do is turn the next corner. Bound to be a bit of green there. Trees lush with leaves held in clusters, in long, fat fingers. Bunches of bright greenish bananas in their thousands. She knew from the little biology she'd studied that what trees breathe out, she breathed in. The whole city seemed to breathe. At least, it seemed that way to Wendy, who lived in a yellow room at the top of a tall house and she could leave the skylight open. Let the breeze into her room, let it pick up and whirl her few belongings about: the lightest of them anyway, her letters. She loved to let the wind push its careless paws into her room through the gap in the ceiling.

AFTER A FORTNIGHT OR SO WENDY WAS SENT A LETTER, PRINTED GREEN on green notepaper, asking if she would like to join something called Job Party. It was a club that met three times a week in an airless office behind the DHSS. If she attended three times a week, they would pay her benefits no bother, the letter said. She read this out at the kitchen table.

"Benefits?" asked Uncle Pat, peering over a piece of his own morning post. "Are you on benefits?"

"I sent her down the day after we got here," said Aunty Anne. It was true, it had been the very next day. "She's left school. She needs to see what her entitlements are."

"Benefits," sighed her Uncle, going back to what, by the look of it, was an involved letter of his own. "There's no need of benefits while the girl's staying here. There's plenty of money around the place." He harrumphed and Aunty Anne slid her hazel eyes into a sidelong glance. Wendy wished she would stop doing this at her, every time money was mentioned.

This was the quiet—or relatively quiet—part of the morning, just before the sun rose directly over their roof and made the whole flat too hot. The post had arrived with its usual crash on the bare hall floor, and they were absorbed in it, half-heartedly feeding themselves breakfast as they went. As usual Aunty Anne was the only one without letters. She commented once more that Wendy seemed to share her Uncle and cousin's talent and habit of getting lots of mail. They paid her no attention. Glumly Aunty Anne wached the three of them read as she spread marmalade an inch thick on wholemeal toast. She was waiting for the arrival of Captain Simon in his yellow jacket. Just lately she had started to think of him as a very dashing older man and found herself keeping up her side of a gentle flirtation. She bit into satisfyingly hard strips of orange peel, squashing the rind between her teeth. Funny that she should start to fancy an old man under her ex's nose. However, she thought, such are the mysteries of sex. That's all there was to it.

Wendy, meanwhile, was starting to dread the idea of Job Party. She remembered Timon once telling her how they'd forced him to go on one of these things. That was before he found the job in the fish shop. He was put in a group with seven others and the teacher-type person had talked to them about things like re-training for The World of Work. Timon had hated the enforced silliness of the whole thing. Sitting round with strangers and discussing what would fulfil them all. Mind, Wendy had thought at the time that Timon was too fussy. He probably thought he was too good for all of them. He said it was very like his experience of Creative Writing workshops—and he'd stopped going to those, too, for the same reasons. At least at Job Party nobody expected you to 'get' their poems. And Job Party gave you free stamps and stationary, and they had come in handy for sending SAEs with stories to literary magazines.

All in all Wendy didn't want to go to Job Party. She imagined being the youngest there, and the one with the least idea about anything. An older man, someone quite repellent that she'd be kind to on the first day, would become fixated on her and maybe he would stalk her, finding out where she stayed and following her home, hanging about in the darker, leafier corners of the Royal Circus...

To get it out of her mind she went for a walk.

She was still exploring Edinburgh, finding new things all the time and coming to the realisation that this now (or for now, at any rate) was the city where she lived. Where some people did nothing but rollerblade across the pavements and squares, where black taxis went darting everywhere, all the time, and every patch of wall was plastered with flyers for night clubs and shows. And what pleased her was that she didn't know exactly how long she would be here. Up till now she had been tied to school and family—to Blackpool, in fact. Which, while not being boring exactly, was still home. This was the first city of her choice. Well, Aunty Anne's choice, really. Although Wendy needn't have come if she hadn't wanted. She might have stayed in Blackpool alone, or with Linda—or even gone to Manchester with Mandy. She still could. But all this, everything here, felt like her own choice.

She had noticed how, in their time here, how subdued Aunty Anne had become. She was no longer the overbearing figure she had been in Blackpool. Her ex-husband worked on her like an antidote. His placid erudition took the fizz and the sting out of her brashness. Wendy was astonished to see Aunty Anne submit to Uncle Pat, especially when he told her outright to shut up. Aunty Anne was a different person when she was with Uncle Pat and, Wendy thought, that was probably what had made her leave him. Wendy liked to see how people changed, depending on who they were with. Only a very few stayed the same and Colin was one of them. It didn't matter who he was talking to.

So Wendy was getting to know them all. And she was pleased she wasn't at all over-attached to Anne. Since arriving, the two women had really gone their separate ways. Her aunt had become self-absorbed and quiet. She had promptly dyed her hair black, then white again, and then a glorious pink. Colin told Wendy: there's the danger sign. And it struck Wendy for the first time how much Aunty Anne must be missing Wendy's mother, too. She'd be thinking of the wasted years, when she'd never gone to visit her sister. She'd be wondering how many years she herself had left.

"You'd feel like living it up, wouldn't you?" Wendy asked Colin. "'You'd throw caution to the winds."

He nodded. "Hence the pink." He did a kind of facial shrug. "She looks like a cockatoo. Isn't 'throw caution to the winds' a very old-fashioned phrase?"

Wendy nodded. "I just like it."

Colin smiled. "Me too."

Throw caution to the winds. And here Wendy was, getting butterflies over starting Job Party.

She crossed Princes Street, which was furiously busy at this time in the morning, and she resisted visiting any of the shops. She passed the galleries—the National with its sphinxes lying sentinel on every corner and dossers propped against pillars, petting their scrawny dogs. Up the several dozen steps of the Mound, and into the Old Town. She was getting to know her way about.

What would be the worst thing they could do to her at Job Party? Ask what she intended to do with her life? She could make something up. She wasn't daft. She could tell them a downright lie—or pretend to be her sisters or Timon. Borrow someone else's intentions for a while. Or they could make her take a rubbish job for a while. They had that power.

She went to the museum. In the vast and airy entrance hall they had a proper totem pole, several storeys high. Vases and teapots and earrings. She imagined how expensive everything must be. In the stuffed animal department she sat down to stare at a glass case the size of their old kitchen. It was crammed with specimens of almost every kind of bear on the planet. Some standing, some rearing, some curled supine. All of them were growling out of the corner of their mouths.

"A scene like this," she said, gazing at them, "would never happen in nature."

So she looked at this display for an hour or more.

It was the way they looked so companionable she liked.

All snarling.

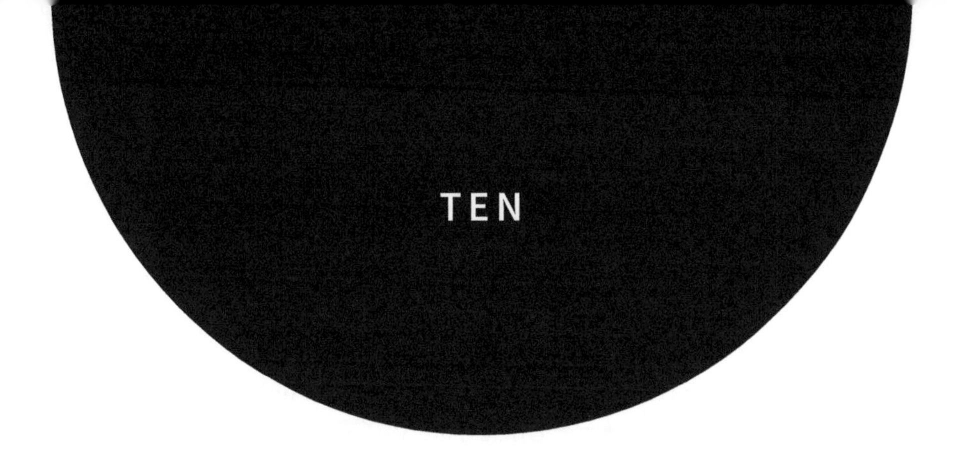

TEN

AUNTY ANNE DECIDED THAT WE WERE GOING OUT SHOPPING TOGETHER. We were going to do Princes Street: all of the department stores I hadn't seen yet. Princes Street reminded me of the Golden Mile, only with no sea and no illuminations.

I couldn't go until I'd read that morning's post.

> You haven't told us anything yet about what's going on. You know you've still got a home here. With us. We've got a spare bedroom. Daniel has booked us up to go to Tunisia, which is the desert. Two weeks in July we could do with the rest. We'll have to remember and take lots of sun block and all the right stuff for our pale skins. I'll look silly on my counter if my skin burns, won't I? Anyway you take care of yourself Wendy. We have a lawn now, Daniel laid it last Sunday.
>
> Lots of love,
>
> Linda.

Dear Wendy,

We've buggered it all up. Wasn't it me who was supposed to be going off to the big city? You were the little'un. You were sitting put, while I found adventure. Yet there you are.

I want to know all about it.

Are they treating you nicely? Are you settling in? I don't remember much about Uncle Pat. We never saw much of them, really. All I remember is me being tiny and Uncle Pat telling me—it was at somebody's christening—that chickens are so stupid that they commit suicide every time it rains. The rain taps them on the head, they look up and it falls down the holes in their beaks and then they drown. Rubbish. So I think of him as a daft old man telling bairns rubbish. Is Aunty Anne behaving herself? Is she spending all his money? Are you living in the lap of luxury?

Look at my new address. I know—it's not a Manchester address. I've moved. You're going to say I'm stupid, I know. And you've no right to! You're still four years younger than me. Just because you're swanning about in Edinburgh doesn't mean you can—oh, anyway, sod it, yes—I've left Manchester-city-of-my-dreams behind already and come to a small dingy town instead and all for some fella.

Reader—I married him.

No, not quite. But I chucked in my university place for him, even before term began. Am I mad or what? I'd even bought my set texts. I'd read them and everything.

We're in Lancaster. A bit more north. Well, you know where it is. And if you don't, you can look on a map. The smallest place I've ever been. A little castle with prisoners still inside, a canal with red and green chuggy boats going up and down and lots of mill workers' houses. There's a university on a campus out of town. It looks like a whole load of cereal packets and washing up liquid bottles. Looks like they made it on Blue Peter. Maybe I'll transfer my course to there. We're still talking it over and seeing what we can afford, and living in a rented house by the canal. From the kitchen window I can watch the swans go by.

Nigel had to come here, that's the reason for all of this. He's started a PhD. He's going to be a doctor. He's found this old out-of-print woman (I mean, a novelist) who nobody knows about and whose books he loves. I haven't read any. This was the only place they'd have him to research her books.

Write and tell me I'm daft. Or write and bully me into getting back to my degree. Write and tell me to get something done. What am I doing? I'm tending houseplants. Putting up curtains. I'm fixing up the little house by the canal—lovely!—and having a fine old time. Nigel has a car and we run about the place. Lake District. Last weekend we went to see our Linda and that posh bloke of hers. A happy foursome. How we made me puke. Maybe I'll get fed up with all this soon and do something mad like run away. I could hitch up to Scotland in an afternoon and come to see you. Land on your doorstep, Wendy. What would you think of that?

Tell me about it all, anyway.

Nigel's up in the bedroom, reading. Doing his research. He thinks his old, out-of-print woman might still be alive. Wouldn't that be something, he said—taking his head out of one of her musty old books—to find her alive and well after all these years! He said this to me when I took him up a cup of tea and a sandwich, an afternoon snack for him. He still wears those yellow glasses...and his blue coat.

I'm not even reading these days. You know all those doorstep-sized Victorian novels I used to get through? Ravenously? I look at them now...on my new mantlepiece, all their spines happily broken, thin white lines scored on them to show how well-read I am...and now I can't be bothered. I picked up *The Woman in White* today and couldn't get into it. One of my favourites. I cleaned the cooker instead. Even the grisly bits under the rings.

They're too big, those books. And, in them, no one goes

on normal. Or not very. And there's no sex. I don't know why I never saw that before.

lots of love...

Mandy.

AUNTY ANNE TOOK HER TO JENNERS. AS THEY PASSED THROUGH THE TALL double doors and shushed into the dark, perfumed, cavernous interior of the store's ground floor, her Aunty pushed two fifty pound notes into her hand.

"What's this?"

"Your Uncle Pat wants you to buy something nice to wear."

"What?"

"He wants to take us all out for dinner, and..."

Wendy jumped to her own defence. "What's wrong with my own clothes?"

"Nothing," hissed Aunty Anne. "But..." She shook her head. "Look, are you going to argue about being given a hundred quid?"

"Yes."

"Why?"

"Because he shouldn't spend his money on me. He's already putting me up, and..."

"Just take it. He's got stacks, remember. And I'm not getting any of it, after all." Aunty Anne hurried over to the Elizabeth Arden nook.

"Wait a minute," Wendy went after her. "Did you ask him for this?"

Aunty Anne ignored her. Wendy asked again.

"I just said that perhaps you could do with some new..."

Wendy could have slapped her. "You'd no right to ask him for money for me! And there's nothing wrong with what I wear!" She looked down at herself, at her denim shirt and jeans, her scuffed trainers. Then she was aware of the other women swishing past the cosmetics counters. Glamorous women with sunglasses pushed up and perched on top of their heads, their hair slick, all dressed up in satin trouser suits.

"You're a child," Aunty Anne snapped. "Someone has to take you in hand, tell you what to do. Your mother can't anymore."

Wendy turned red. "My mother never tried to, anyway. Even when she was here."

"Hm," said Aunty Anne. "She let you all go your own way, didn't she?"

Wendy nodded. "What's wrong with that?"

"It doesn't always work. Sometimes people...have to be guided more."

"Rubbish."

"Nobody's ever told you how to dress, Wendy."

"I don't need telling! I'm happy how I am."

"But everything you wear looks so...cheap."

"You mean tarty?"

"No—cheap! Like you're wearing things out of a cheap shop."

"Most of my things come from charity shops."

Aunty Anne gave a look as if to say this proved her point. She ran a hand over the display of lipstick tips. Wendy thought of dog's willies.

"It's got nothing to do with you," Wendy snapped. "It's not up to you to see I get brought up like a proper little lady."

Aunty Anne looked sceptical.

"Don't look at me like Mary Poppins."

"Ha! Don't you have a temper, eh?"

Wendy stomped off.

AUNTY ANNE FOUND HER IN THE LADIES' DEPARTMENT. THERE WAS A whole display of tartan slacks with elasticated waists. "It's all clothes for old women up here," said Wendy.

"Not all," her Aunt said coaxingly, and nodded to a section where they had flouncy, silky, ribboned gowns. Wendy rolled her eyes.

"That's what they wear to...like, university balls and stuff. Horrible."

"What would you like to wear?"

Wendy shrugged. Aunty Anne offered her the hundred pounds again and this time, with a sigh, Wendy took it.

"You touched a nerve," Wendy told her. "Ever since I've been in this town, I've felt like I'm not dressed right. I was comfy at home, the way I was. I never thought about it."

Aunty Anne was nodding sagely. Wendy went on. "Here, I've felt like I ought to look different, be different...change myself somehow. Is that because it's a big city and everyone's so smart?"

Aunty Anne was fingering the collar on a nice suit. "Partly that. It's also your age. You're bound to want to change."

"I don't want to. I just think maybe I should."

"Try things out," said Aunty Anne. "You can afford to."

Wendy looked at the ladieswear. "Not here, anyway." She stashed her Uncle's money away.

Aunty Anne was looking at her strangely.

"What?" Wendy prompted.

"You're doing very well."

"Thanks. What at?"

"Settling in here. It can't be easy. Getting used to the flat, living with new people. Your Uncle Pat isn't the easiest person to live with. I should know."

Wendy felt like laughing. Next to Aunty Anne, she thought, Uncle Pat was a doddle.

Aunty Anne said, "He's very fond of you. I can tell."

They were heading for the escalator. Wendy smiled. "It's hard to tell with him. He's so skitty."

"He likes you a lot," said Aunty Anne. "He said last night, what a tonic you were to have about. Because you're not old or ill."

Wendy, smiling, shook her head. "I'm not old or ill."

"So you're doing really well."

"Well, thanks!" They were back in the hall of perfumes, where the counters gave of a pale, chill light. Aunty Anne headed straight to the samples. Wendy said, "You sound like a school report."

Aunty Anne squirted herself with a small green bottle, sniffed her wrist a grimaced. "You've made a good start. He'll not forget you." Then she gave Wendy one of her significant looks. "Do you want to try this?"

It was the most awful flowery scent. "No, thanks." Wendy was suspicious. "What do you mean, not forget me?"

Aunty Anne tutted. "You know...in his thingy, his will. When he passes away, eventually."

"How can you think that!"

Aunty Anne smiled kindly. "Of course I can! I can think it on your behalf, you silly thing. I can't think it on my own behalf. I won't be getting anything. Not his poor ex-wife. And I don't expect to." Anne put down the last of the samples and rubbed both wrists together, crushing all of her scents in one. "Shall we go?"

Wendy's voice was calm. "I'm not here to beg for that old man's money."

"Oh, lovey, come on. None of us can afford to be that noble."

"I feel sick."

Aunty Anne gave her a gentle push, and nudged her elbow. "Would you really turn up your nose at all his millions?"

"You've brought me here to beg...to..."

Aunty Anne became flustered and cross. "Not 'to' anything. What was I meant to do? Of course I brought you here." Her voice had gone too loud. "Now, look...don't spoil it. Come on, let's find a shop for trendy young ladies...and let's blow that money."

Wendy crinkled the notes in her pocket. "I wish you'd left me at home."

Aunty Anne drew herself up to her full height. Even with a scarf wrapped into a turban to cover her hair, pink bits were poking out from under and she looked ridiculous. It was like candy floss under her turban, Wendy thought. "I think you're kidding yourself, Wendy. It was your choice. You thought as well as I did that you deserved a crack at ending up in that old devil's will. You're not as innocent as all that."

Wendy kept quiet. She couldn't look her aunt in the eye.

Anne said, "Let's get you dressed up. Come on. He's serious about going out to dinner. He doesn't want you looking scraggy-arsed, does he?"

THE NEXT TIME I WENT TO THE MUSEUM I HEADED STRAIGHT TO MY GLASS cabinet full of all the kinds of bears in the world. They hadn't budged an inch. I liked this about them...but, I realised, what I also liked about them (a lot) was that, on the other side of that outside wall behind them...was a Balti restaurant. Did the Balti people know? It was probably their toilets, at the back of that place. I imagined fellas peeing up against urinals. And I was pleased, because I imagined them suddenly getting X-ray specs and seeing all these splendid bears.

The extinct room made me think, too. In one corner they had the tallest bird that had ever walked the earth. It was shaggy like horsehair. Ten foot tall. And I knew for a fact it backed up against a green grocer's.

I waited to see it come to life and peck a hole in the wall. Give someone a fright. I would sit here for an hour or more, looking at stuffed beasts. It calmed me down.

ELEVEN

HER NEW TOWN—THE NEW TOWN, AS THEY CALLED IT—WAS IN A GRID. Streets like a crossword. Three across. Two down. Starts with a V, six letters, second last letter R. Wendy zig-zagged everywhere she needed to go. It was Georgian architecture, Captain Simon said. Obviously the product of a tidy mind. Of a whole host of tidy minds. They all had tidy minds in the eighteenth century.

"A tidy mind!" said Aunty Anne, as if she had never heard of such a thing. It was breakfast time and, while the others were reading their post, she was flipping through last night's Evening Post. There had been a collision in space between an unmanned supply ship and a Russian space station. It was the worst space accident in years. Aunty Anne had found herself talking about these things quite a lot recently, with Captain Simon, whose hobby, he said, was outer space. Anne scanned through the small piece on the accident, genning up.

Wendy, meanwhile, was thinking about spending the day zig-zagging around town on her bike. Aunty Anne had given her an old bike, which had been left in the outhouse in the shared garden. It was as good as new.

Uncle Pat had bought her a blue riding helmet and, although Wendy wasn't convinced that she looked right on a bike, the new blue helmet settled the matter: she would have to make an effort.

But the traffic on the streets of Edinburgh was very fierce.

For the moment, she put it out of her mind and read Timon's letter.

> I'm flakey. I'm flighty. You know I am, hon. So I'm rubbish at writing to absent friends—but I've been missing you, even though I'm hanging out with other people. You know how it is.
>
> I don't want to go making you jealous with talk of all my new lady friends. I've been seeing a bit of your sisters, of Mandy and Linda. I even went up to Lancaster to see your Mandy in her new house. Did you know she'd pulled out of her course? Silly girl. I told her: you'll live to regret this. You'll look back one day at all your golden chances—Oh, fuck off, Timon, she snapped, you horrible black bugger. So that shut me up, and we went out for a drink. We didn't take that silly stuffy boyfriend of hers. He hardly said a word to me the whole time I was there. I think he was jealous. I can't see why Mandy sticks it with him. She reckons he's the dog's bollocks in bed, and I couldn't work out if that meant he was bad or good.
>
> You know, Wendy, you never told me about that trick your Mandy does—with those metal bangles she wears. When we sat in the bay window of the City Bar, she pushed both bangles inside her mouth, to stretch her lips as wide as they'd go. She looked frigging awful, bless her. She says, Timon, why do the men never look at me now? And I laugh, because when she does that, she looks like a monster. Your Mandy's been doing that trick too much. She went to the doctor, he told her to stop. She's stretched her lips and the bottom one is bending curling over and it won't go back. The Doctor said, my dear, you are losing your elasticity. That's what he said. You must stop this nonsense at once. So there

she is, hon. That's the shape your loopy sister is in. I'm ok. I'm writing still. My droll little stories. (Very little). I'm on the verge of selling something (I think).

love to you....

Timon.

Timon's letters would always come like this. No real information in them. Nothing like the ordinary stuff people put in letters.

Usually it would just be a postcard's worth of stuff like the above. And...he'd probably made it up anyway. Had Mandy really started to lose the elasticity in her lips because of a trick she did with bangles? Mandy had always pulled faces... She loved to turn her beauty grotesque. But was she actually hanging and flapping open? In Lancaster? And had she really gone to the doctor? Timon, I wish you would write me sensible stuff.

Whatever Timon wrote, it was never the product of a tidy mind. Wendy sighed and went off with her helmet on, to ride around the city.

Aunty Anne and Captain Simon Sing a Sexy Duet About
Collisions in Space.

Or...Aunty Anne wishes this was a duet.
She bursts into spontaneous:

Singing songs at our age,
Old man, we must be fools...
Ah, you rotten devil, Captain Simon
did you do something valorous once?
or maybe repetitively some times?
These days...
I'm bumping into you on the stairs
the echoing stairwell between these flats
where I stay with my ex-fella
and your best friend,
and the pigsty where you live
with your funny

fat-kneed sister: how can you bear her?
hanging around all the time...
Strange old thing, as obsessed with
space as you are, I've heard.

We bump each day nose to nose on the steps
I hold in my breath as we pass...
hold my hand in your skinny old hand
like holding a handful of spam
you need someone warming you up...
ships squashing by in the night
or fuel ships, fuel ships that go
colliding with Russian space stations
(I thought you'd appreciate
a racy, spacey turn of phrase)

Oh, Captain, I'm thinking of us in no gravity
of us in no clothes
in no gravity
turning and turning
head over heels, tit over bum
cock over clit over
coiffure...
do I shock you my silly old darling
old man?
I feel I can take this liberty,
say, I want to be the first to
fuck
an old man
in outer space
(how kind no gravity will be on
brittle old bones! And nothing will
sag!)
I want to shunt our station out of its
worldly orbit by

shagging
What a word!
A word I've not used before...
but one that makes me think
of...rumbunctious, woolly-arsed humping
in zero atmosphere
our faces all flushed up...
old goat, have you really
got a hairy bottom?
In my mind I can see it
And it's like the full moon

And all that comes from our bodies
all that will float free...
will slide weightless and loose in
the absence of air...
globules of me and specially
of you, rubbed off
and like slow confetti
revolving
all about us.

"I have to talk to you," Captain Simon said, stopping Aunty Anne on the stairwell that morning.

She drew in a breath. "Right," she said.

"It's about...affairs of the heart," he told her.

And they made a date and a time, a place.

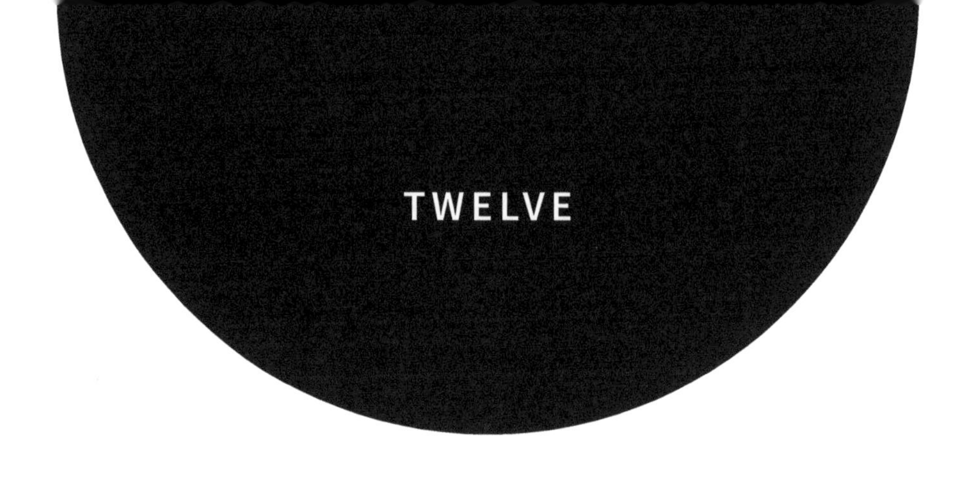

TWELVE

WENDY GOT ON WITH COLIN IN THE FIRST INSTANCE BECAUSE THEY discovered that, sometimes, there was nothing that both of them liked more than to go out of a night and talk about nothing. About bums and tits and to have a giggle. It was a relief to find this out. All the conversations Wendy had been having (for ages, it seemed like) were about the future, and death, and what to do now. Oh, give me some space. Give me a drink and a fag...and a pal to go on daft with.

She was off the sickly sweet liqueurs. That turned out to be a passing phase. "Liqueurs!" Colin laughed. "Lick your own!" Her coached her in drinking bitters, lagers, stouts. Something with some body and gall. Drinks that were fizzy and dark, which had volume and daring, that were heady and fulsome. And that were never, never sweet. "Face it," he told Wendy. "When you're young and pretty like we are, you can't afford to order anything sweet. We have to temper our native sweetness with..." He shrugged. "Bitter, mostly. And gall."

Lately, even when there wasn't a disaster, or things to sort out, it had seemed to Wendy that some people just adored raking up trouble. They stirred around for it in the mire. They itched away at it, like they would at a scabby wound. They can't be content. Neither Wendy nor Colin wanted to be made to think or dwell particularly heavily on anything just then. They wanted time to enjoy each other's company.

It was the next act of a gentle comedy. The settling down period. Everyone starts to enjoy each other. Wendy was getting to know her gay boy cousin: a lovely boy. He's a lovely boy, my Colin, said a tipsy Aunty Anne one night. Not been out much, not seen much of the world. Just this town. He flung himself on the mercy of this town. Its...nightlife. Aunty Anne couldn't bring herself to say the phrase 'gay scene', or even say in so many words that Colin was gay. She said that he wasn't the marrying kind.

Colin had found his own niche, his own coterie, in a very cosmopolitan and—you'd think—a very permissive, sophisticated city. Come midnight, Colin would be out on the scene, somewhere in town, up the East End. His father and now his mother, turning a blind eye to his absence at the late night kitchen table, where the grown-ups (the grown-ups! The pensioners, really!)—Uncle Pat, Aunty Anne, Captain Simon and Belinda, all sat about, stewed to the gills, on a variety of wines and spirits.

What time did Colin slink home in the morning? Well, that depended. But when Wendy was about and she was his companion on his jaunts (and they weren't only weekends—oh no! Tuesday, he claimed, was the best night of the week. So bang went the old working class Friday-on-my-mind crap. Tuesday was king!) When Wendy went with Colin, he came back earlier. Dragging in over the threshold at two, maybe, to see the dregs of the party in the kitchen. With his young cousin to watch over, Colin got up to less mischief. Which was a good thing, they all decided.

And Wendy...

It had just hit her that she was in the loveliest city she had ever visited. It was late summer: a summer that seemed to be lasting forever. The wide streets were full of standing heat, of air that barely moved and quivered to the touch. And crowds, crowds dashing to plays and bars and places to pleasure themselves in the afternoons.

It has just hit Wendy that she has nothing in particular to accomplish. Wendy the chronic under-achiever has nowt to do! Somehow it isn't fair, she thinks...but dispels that thought. If I just stand my ground, and refuse to decide anything (about my future—oh boy) then I can just about enjoy this trip.

She was already skiving off from Job Party.

Wendy knew that at the back of her mind Aunty Anne would be worrying. (Oh, but what new preoccuptations must Aunty Anne have now? Her hair was yellow—triumphant, near-gold, like stalks of corn, or rape in a field in May.) Despite what went on in Aunty Anne's life, with the back of her mind she'd be fretting that Wendy was footling and tootling her time away. And actually, in the end, was going out to bars and cafes with Colin—queer bars at that!—any different to the desultory pubbing and clubbing she'd got up to with Timon immediately after her mother's death? Was she just going back to drinking her afternoons away? She was, wasn't she? Was Colin any better an influence than Timon?

Wendy hated comparing her friends, one to another.

All my life, she thinks, my friends have been the most important thing.

Of course Aunty Anne would think that Colin was a better influence than Timon. She was bound to. Colin was her son, and perfect, and all...

(But a bum bandit! A delicious bugger! And diseased and all ..!)

And yet...and yet...this isn't the same as spending all her time in dingy, seedy Blackpool pubs. It isn't the same at all. Wendy knew this was because Anne had grown up in Blackpool too. Everything there was backward for her.

Wendy's efforts here in Edinburgh were towards a goal. Getting that money. Getting that money.

No, says Wendy weakly, sadly. I never thought that.

Oh, pish, laughs her aunt.

Wendy tried to ignore her. She concentrated on her friends. Friends are what help you pass difficult time. She lavished her time upon beautiful, frail Colin.

IT WAS COLIN WHO HELPED HIS MOTHER TO DYE HER HAIR GOLD. WHEN he suggested it she was pleased that someone was taking notice of her hair. The sun had begun to fade the pink out of her and she needed something new to perk her up. She knelt on the bathroom mat with her head over the bath and let Colin pour jugfuls of warm water over her head.

"You've got long, gentle fingers, Colin. You could have been a hairdresser. Did you ever think of that?"

"Hm," he said. Over the years his mother had kept urging three different careers on him. For her he cut the very model of a hairdresser, a priest, and a doctor in a hospital. And he hadn't grown up to be any of those things.

The packet said twenty minutes for the bleachy dye stuff to take. They both knew from experience that the longer you left it, the better the chance of achieving that burnished gold effect you were after. "Nothing more disheartening," Anne sniffed, "than taking off your shower cap, rinsing it all out, and discovering that nothing has changed at all." She proposed to sit in her shower cap and let her hair ferment for a good hour. They went into the living room to watch something, anything, on cable. A TV movie—something tragic and/or uplifting—that would be perfect. Anne draped a towel around her shoulders, in case a trickle of bleach should escape and get onto the regency-striped settee. She knew that by leaving her hair cooking so long she was dicing with the possibility of it all dropping out...but these were the chances you took. She desired golden hair.

They settled down to the film, which was confusing. It was about domestic violence, as far as Anne could make out.

"Where's Wendy today?" she asked her son during the adverts.

He shrugged. "Out and about somewhere. Making friends."

"Don't you feel left out?"

He didn't rise to the bait. His mother was a great one for teasing. "Not at all. I'm glad of the rest. She's exhausting to be with. Always asking questions."

"Is she?" Anne frowned. "She doesn't ask me many questions. In fact, she gives the impression of being a proper miss-know-it-all."

"Not at all," Colin shook his head.

"Oh well," said his mother airily. "So long as she's learning something... from someone."

"What does that mean?"

Now it was her turn to shrug.

He asked, "What's the point, mum? How come you brought her

here?" This was very direct for Colin. He took his mother off her guard.

"You know," she said. "I explained. She's a poor orphan now, is Wendy. Her mother dying only a matter of weeks ago, and all...and her two sisters are selfish, really: one pursuing her career, the other her education...and both of them are more interested in the fellas they've managed to hook for themselves..."

"It seems to me," said Colin, fixing his gaze on the creamy ointment inside his mother's plastic hairnet, "that you're trying to mould Wendy into something. To educate her and bring her on."

"Mould her!" laughed Anne. "Into what? My own image, I suppose."

"Yes!" he said. "That's what I think you'd like."

She looked irritated suddenly. "As if I could! She's got a strong will on her. Oh no, Colin. You talk like she's...I don't know, a bit of old cloth I was going to run up and make into something new. But Wendy will do exactly what she wants to do with herself. She's already let me in on that little secret."

He laughed, turning back to the film. He'd lost track now, of what was going on, who was who. "Has our Wendy given you a telling off, Mum?"

"Not exactly," she said. "But I know full well that the girl has got a mind of her own."

"She's very frank, and you're very frank," he said. "So you know just what to expect of each other."

"I suppose so," said Aunty Anne. "Little minx."

"You're both very natural," Colin smirked. "Shall we see if that gold has worked out?"

She felt her covered scalp with one careful hand, as if she could tell the new colour that way.

He took Wendy to a bar where everyone looked up when you walked in. It used to be an ordinary pub, but they'd festooned fairy lights here and there and put Bacardi on special offer and tried to make it gay. Upstairs a transvestite in a scarlet frock was in charge of the records and kept putting on songs from the shows. *Oliver!* of all things. Colin and Wendy were the only ones upstairs. They sat and the DJ pulled down a giant TV screen, apparently from the ceiling. She zapped it with a futuristic remote.

A weather woman twice life-sized filled that end of the dance floor.

Wendy was saying, "I suppose I like your mum, because...because..."

"Ah, we never know why."

"I always know why," Wendy said. She stared at the transvestite, who was staring balefully in turn at the giant weather woman. "It's because Aunty Anne doesn't expect you to like her. She doesn't care. Everything she says is like high-kicks, like doing the splits. In your face."

Colin was sceptical. "Do you really think so?"

"All that business about her legs," said Wendy. "All that 'Look at me! I'm fantastic!' It's all so defiant. It's all not-giving-a-fuck."

"Maybe."

THEY WALKED BACK HOME ACROSS THE NEW TOWN. WENDY WAS JUST getting used to how the nights here went on later. It seemed ordinary now to start the evening off just before midnight.

"The town's full of ghosts, you know," Colin said. They were passing the trees at the bottom of Calton Hill. "If you come by here in the early hours, sometimes you can hear them rustling about..."

"It seems a very haunted place," said Wendy, still feeling like a tourist. "All the history."

"Of course," said Colin, "You have to have suffered in your life to see a ghost. To really see a ghost."

"I didn't know that," said Wendy, "What are you...like an expert?"

"In ghosts or in suffering?" He looked at her. "I'm only teasing. I don't believe in ghosts, do you?"

"I don't believe in suffering," she said.

"No?"

"I don't believe in showing it," she said. "Best thing you can do is grit your teeth and keep your gob shut."

"Sometimes it's not as easy as that."

"If you can, though, it's worth doing. Mind," she said thoughtfully, "if it looks like you've never suffered, then no one bothers with you. You look as if you're too hard."

"Is that what you think you look like?"

"I don't know. Do I?"

"No, you don't look too hard."

They walked on and decided to stop for chips. "The main thing," said Colin, "Is to try and be as happy as possible."

Wendy looked at the whole lit up front of the chip shop. Its papier mache octopi and mermaids. "That's what I came here for," she said.

THIRTEEN

I DON'T THINK I CAN BE A VERY NICE PERSON...BECAUSE I CAN'T ALWAYS see the best in people. I look at them sometimes and they just seem awful. Their bodies seem awful.

I watch Aunty Anne on the phone in the hallway, gassing away to one of her cronies. Or maybe someone she's doing business with. Wheeling and dealing Aunty Anne, ducking and diving. She's breaking off nubs of crusty bread and feeding herself as she talks, mumbling and swallowing as she rabbits on...num num num...and I can't bear the thought of her warm spit mushing the bread down.

I look at people and think what a bad design they are. Aunty Anne here has to eat and talk and breathe out of the same bit...the same hole in her head (she's a mouth-breather, of course, and a very noisy eater) and how easy, I think, it would be for her to choke. And I look and I can't help thinking I'd like to write to a glossy magazine and ask if my...antipathy is natural.

Am I alone in imagining the people I know sitting on the toilet? Doesn't everyone do this? I picture my uncle, my aunt...when they shuffle off down the hall to the loo (and wasn't it the French who called it loo not because of l'eau, but rather le oo, for the two holes of oo being eyeholes in the wc door for cheeky peekers?) They lock themselves in and you can hear the thunk of the seat going down, then the rattle of them farting down the pan...It's become like a mania: I can see them in my head. I do it with the people I see on the street. See flabby pale thighs and skirts hawked up, knickers and trousers dropped round ankles, turned inside out, exposing all their innermost secrets.

Sometimes you can see too much.

MAYBE PART OF WENDY'S GENERAL DISGUST WAS HER FINDING THAT SHE attracted people to her. She was coming of age (what an old-fashioned phrase!) and what people saw in her was nothing less than a fine pair of listening ears. People latch onto me! she moaned, tossing in her white feathery bed.

I get people telling me all sorts of things, bizarre things...and they all think I'm interested. And, of course, usually I am. Sometimes it wears you out. All these new friends.

And I still get letters from my sisters and Timon, and they just make me sad. These people who know what I'm really like aren't here to corroborate me and the new things I'm doing. Cycling, for Christ's sake. A new place gives you freedom to become unsettled and turn into what you want. But how do you really know what's happening to you? Can your identity outride your circumstances? Can I mould myself? Or will others impinge on me?

Aunty Anne's had a stab. Uncle Pat has taken to me and treats me like a frilly little girl. That meal we had out, he made such a fuss. When I'm with him, I horrify myself, turning all frilly. Colin has made me into his best pal—his fag hag, as he says—and I wonder if I like that name. He's expecting me to fully-fledge into a grown-up drinking pal and he expects innocence and sophistication all at the same time. He expects me to amuse and console him.

In a way I need to depend on Aunty Anne and her knowledge of what it was like in Blackpool. But Aunty Anne has lost interest in me, I think. She has got her own plans.

So I concentrate on new people. Colin...and now Belinda, Captain

Simon's dappy sister from downstairs, who has decided to be my friend.

It seemed to Wendy that no one had ever been able to tell Belinda that she could be dressing nicer to suit her shape. Maybe she had never had anyone close enough or brave enough to tell her. She was fat and in her fifties and forever squashed into tight polyester mini-dresses. The day she decided to befriend Wendy and came up the spiral staircase to Wendy's room, she was huffling and all asweat. She clanged up the iron rungs and poked her head into the yellow room. That day she was in swirled green nylon. Wendy felt instantly sorry for her, as she always did for people who didn't make the best of themselves.

Wendy had been taking a nap. It was too tempting not to: the long afternoons in all that yellow, with the sunlight cramming in. How scarlet and tousled the woman from downstairs looked, coming in to spoil Wendy's peace.

"They said that you'd done this place up nice," said Belinda. As she spoke she never quite met Wendy's eye. Wendy had noticed this before. She thought the woman must be profoundly shy. Whenever she came to visit she brought presents and offerings, almost like paying a toll. Most often she brought pink sugar mice, which she would empty from a paper bag onto the table. This place was used to stroppier visitors than that, who saw no need to make excuses for their presences: Aunty Anne, who treated her ex-husband's flat curiously as her own, and Captain Simon, who seemed a regular, if dull-ish fixture. Especially in these cable TV days. Recent afternoons had seen Aunty Anne watching with Captain Simon. Wendy had seen them in the windowless living room and their afternoon raptures put Wendy in mind of her mother and all those gaudy horror movies. (But, Wendy nagged herself, Aunty Anne and Captain Simon... were they really just watching the telly? Was all that sitting about just them having an excuse to sit for hours, tight together? Uncle Pat kept out of their way. To Wendy's eye something seemed to be brewing there. Maybe that's what Belinda was here for: 'Tell your Aunty to get her hands off my lovely brother!').

"The others said you'd got your room nice," Belinda said again, gazing with approval at the nick-nacks along Wendy's original mantlepiece.

Bits she'd picked up in the junk shops of the Old Town: Seventies kitsch, mostly, and a few ethnic artefacts. A beaten tin toucan from a Mexican shop. Wendy sat up, pleased with her new things. Belinda plonked herself down on the end of the bed. Now here it comes, thought Wendy. The woman's come to talk All About Herself.

Belinda, however, talked mostly about her brother, the gallant, the valorous, the magnificent Captain Simon. She had cared for him and loved him all her life. Only she had known him back before he'd grown those white, twiddly mustachios, before he'd turned bald as a coot, before he'd started to wear a yellow uniform jacket. She adored him: he was her Don Quixote. She had seen to him and protected him, and naturally, their brotherly-sisterly bond was barnacle-strong. He was like the moon in eclipse to her and she could see nothing of the sunlit world around him.

"I know my brother like nobody knows him," she told Wendy.

"That's good," said Wendy. She kept her voice neutral. She was pleased they had each other.

"Yes, it's good," said Belinda impatiently. "It's always been good. It's always been fine." She stopped and chewed the inside of her mouth. Holding something back.

Ah, thought Wendy. Here comes the real coming-clean. The woman is jealous. Jealous as all hell. She knows someone's been yanking her brother off her.

And it's you, Aunty Anne, isn't it?
You've got your purple steel-tipped talons
into this poor woman's brother...
Oh, Aunty Anne
why can't you be honest about things?
why not do things out in the open?

The sun was at its hottest now. Wendy wanted to stop talking with Belinda and hang her head out of the skylight, stand on her mussed-up bed and look out over the streets. Pant with her tongue out like a dog on a long car journey. She fought down a yawn.

"He's not the same person," said Belinda at last.

"Do you think he's spending too much time up here in this flat?" asked Wendy. "Too much time with my uncle? Does that bother you?"

The woman looked stung. "I couldn't begrudge the lad his afternoons out with his pals," she said. Wendy shivered at the way she called a man in her sixties a lad. It made Belinda seem suddenly huge and schoolgirlish.

"But you do mind really, don't you?"

Belinda sagged down. "He's not the same man."

"You mean he's changed. He's changed a little bit."

Fiercely Belinda shook her head. "He's not the same man at all. You've got to listen to me, doll. What I'm saying is very simple, but no one would believe me...and I'm going out of my head. Now, I live with the man and I know him better than everyone, right? And what I'm saying is, these past few months, he's not been the same man. He looks the same and does most of the same things. But...but but but." For the first time since coming up into that room, Belinda looked Wendy straight in the eye. "My brother has been *replaced*."

ONLY THAT MORNING WENDY HAD RECEIVED ANOTHER POSTCARD from Timon. He was all enthusiastic about his new philosophy. Oh boy, she thought. A new philosophy: all he needs. Something new, coming true. In his post card Timon declared that he was learning to listen to people properly. He was learning to keep his own mouth shut and to really listen. He had sent Wendy a picture of the Golden Mile at night and written on the back that he was taking up the very thing that she wished she could give up. He wanted, he said, to be a naive receptor. He'd read something some old novelist had said—the very woman that Mandy's boyfriend was obsessed with: Timon had read of book of her essays while staying there. And this old bird said that a writer had to be ignorant. Purposefully he/she had to unloosen all the great stacks of knowledge in their heads and let it float away downstream. Determinedly, you had to know nothing. Then you had to be a listener. Then you had to be a naive receptor...of sense impressions, of general chit chat. You had to stop being clever-clever.

Wendy rather resented this coming through the post from Timon.

He ended his card with:

> 'So I'm not the clever fella I was!
> Oh no!
> I'm not the clever fella I was!'

Wendy put the letter away with the others. He's a naive receptor now, she thought. She wondered what that made him before.

WENDY BLINKED. "REPLACED?"

Belinda sighed. "You don't really want to hear this, do you?"

"No, go on." Might as well now.

"In this fallen world," said Belinda. "The survivors fall into two distinct camps. There are holograms and there are replacements. The hologram people have stopped being flesh. They're what's-the-word... insubstantial. You could poke our finger right through them if you tried. That's the hologram people. Your cousin Colin is one of those, poor lad."

Wendy stared at her.

"And then," Belinda went on, "there are the replacements. They are fleshly and are built to last longer than mere holograms. And a replacement is what I've been given, rather than a brother. Do you understand?"

She looked into Wendy's eyes as if she was trying to hypnotise her.

"I don't understand you," Wendy said. She felt that the grooves in her mind had sealed over and the words that Belinda was talking were gliding right over her, and could find nowhere to lodge and make sense to her.

Belinda groaned. "You think I'm bananas." She stood up and slapped her knees, as if to get the blood flowing. She brushed her skirt straight. "I'll leave you to it."

Then she was gone, back down the spiral staircase.

FOURTEEN

DO YOU KNOW WHAT THAT COLIN SAID TO ME? FIRST OF ALL I THOUGHT he was dead cheeky, saying this. I get touchy when people try and say things about my mam. They might mean the best but I get protective. She isn't here to defend herself, so I'm watchful.

Colin said: "You and I should make the best of ourselves. There's no way we should waste our lives, you know."

We were crossing the busy street. Two sets of lights, top of Leith Walk. Spot of breathless jaywalking. "I wasn't planning on wasting my life," I said.

"I was just thinking," he went on, when we got to the pavement. "They were unique, your mum and mine. I mean, women in their position, of their generation, their class. You know, they were unique in human history."

He stopped to look in windows. Colin was interested in everything. The mauve and pale yellow gerbera in the florist's window, the six foot cacti, the knobbly bread studded with olives in the front of the deli. Colin walked round with his eyes on stalks. It was the smells I liked.

I thought he was having me on, the way he was talking. I felt alert to satire, and asked him what he meant exactly. And I thought about Aunty Anne and my mam, watching *The Blood Beast Terror* right at the end, on our old telly. Aunty Anne holding a tassled cushion up to her face to block out the terror. My mam laughing out loud at it. Women unique in human history: Colin was saying it again.

"I mean the Pill," he said. "They were invented by the Pill, those women, and the time they lived in. They never had to have kids. Me and you, Wendy, we needn't have existed. They had that whole necessity and obligation removed. And they chose to have us anyway. Your mam had three of you." He looked at me. We were right outside a second hand record shop. Vinyl Villains. "We got born anyway, against the odds. Our mothers flying in the face of cultural and biological fashion."

"I suppose so," I said lamely.

"I feel obliged to make things up to them sometimes," he said with a sigh. "And not footle and tootle it all away." Footle-and-tootle was one of Aunty Anne's phrases. I liked the way Colin used it without thinking.

In the record shop window he saw 'The Best of Cilla Black' for two pounds. Cilla in the Sixties, dressed as a cowboy in orange slacks, cravat and black stetson. Big cheesy grin. In went Colin to ask the assistant to fetch the LP off the window display and play him some tracks. Check for scratches.

I stayed out on Leith Walk, thinking. Soon 'Anyone Who Had a Heart' cane drifting out the open door. I knew Colin would buy the record and play it obsessively for a week or more, as he always did. Until he'd driven us all crazy with the same set of songs. It's what he always did. He loved women singing old-fashioned songs. Poor Colin. He liked things that sounded dated. Everything that once thought itself state-of-the-art and got left behind. Colin said he got a very particular frisson from things that had dated. It was the way those things kept hopefully in view, wanting to come back.

Colin wished he could slow down all of time. If time was slow enough for me, he said, I might do something with my life. I might slow down the changing colours in my blood cells.

When he said that I would picture his arteries and veins and cells like the moving blobs in a lava lamp.

On Leith Walk I listened to Cilla Black—'Step Inside, Love'—and watched Colin, rapt, indoors.

COLIN TOLD ME HE WAS ASHAMED OF HIMSELF, OF HIS YOUNGER, treacherous self, who had wanted to belong to a different family. He lay in the sun on Gayfield Square and explained how, at eleven, he'd developed a crush on the whole Familie Schaudi from his Longmann's basic German book at school. It was a purple paperback, all floppy with use. Each lesson came in the form of a comic strip about the Familie Schaudi, each week getting up to something new (never anything very exciting), each time involving new items of vocabulary that the class would be tested on after the weekend. Ten words a week. It sounded like a doddle to me. That was the old O level, Colin said. I myself am a product of he National Curriculum, of GCSE's. How much broader is my knowledge base! I told Colin how much harder we'd had it compared with his lot. They made it all so much more difficult. I left school without a single qualification. That, mind you, was meant to be well-nigh impossible.

Lying there in the patches of shadow from the trees that ringed the park, Colin gave me a funny look. He'd pulled off his top and he had shorts on. He'd brought an old duvet cover from the airing cupboard to lie on. How grey he looked amongst the still-livid reds and blues of Spiderman. My cousin lay spreadeagled on Spiderman, who seemed unperturbed, still shooting out his webs. Colin's skin didn't look very healthy at all.

He went on about his crush some more. How he wanted to belong to that family and not his own. To run about the town with lanky, blonde, clean-living Hans and the pig-tailed Lieselotte and Lumpi the daschund. Calling out Gruss Gott! to the shopkeeper (and learning, one by one, the German names for the shops they kept). When one week's story was about Hans' English penfriend coming to stay, Colin said he'd been bitterly jealous.

"Did you have any crushes when you were at school?" he asked me.

"Can't really remember..." I said. But I do. Cool, aristocratic Lalla Ward. The willowy Time Lady Romana, swishing about on Doctor Who.

"I was an awful, precious, queeny child," he said. "Most of my teachers loved me, except one, Mrs Thompson, who decided she was my deadliest enemy. Once when I was about eight we had this row, this heated row, in front of the whole class. I'd written about my weekend and she tore a strip off me—she denied there was any such thing as chilli con carne."

Colin drifted off then, thinking.

He remembered that same teacher telling him off in gym class, when they were all sat round cross-legged. He was stroking the tiny fair hairs on the legs of the boy sitting next to him. Mrs Thompson called out angrily: "I don't think you want to be doing that, Colin."

But why not? he wanted to know, but didn't say anything at the time. The boy with the legs wasn't complaining.

Wendy looked at the titchy, tickly hairs of his goatee beard, lit up in the sun. Golden and red filaments. The red ones were, if you peered right close, pink. "Get away!" he said, opening his eyes to see her looming over. "Don't look in my face!" She was blocking out his light. He liked the inside of his eyelids to stay bright red. He imagined it was healthy, all good for him. Vitamin D or something, flooding straight into his head through his eyes.

She asked him how long he'd had his little beard.

"Why, don't you like it?"

"They've all got little beards," she said. "All the gay men here."

He shrugged, still lying down. "They think it makes their faces longer."

"You've already got a long face."

NOW SHE'D SET HIM OFF WONDERING IF HE REALLY WANTED TO HAVE A beard. All through growing up he'd never imagined having one. He never thought of beards as having anything to do with him. The metal work teachers at school, all three of them, had beards. So did Obi Wan Kenobi. Now here he was. This was the person he'd turned out to be. He said, "It doesn't take much to set me off thinking about the different ways I might have turned out."

Wendy was taking off her shirt, bunching it into a pillow and lying down. Showing off her little bra top from Flip to the whole of Gayfield square. From one shirt pocket fluttered a sliver of paper. A phone number on it. That David, the skinhead on the train. It was only barely legible after the wash. She hadn't phoned him yet. Maybe now was the time.

Colin hadn't noticed her staring at the number.

"This is how I'll be now," he was saying. "This has got to be my prime. Twenty-three. As prime as I'll ever get. This is my ultimate incarnation."

"Incarnation," she muttered.

WHEN THEY WERE OUT AND ABOUT TOGETHER THESE WERE THE THINGS that Wendy was apt to forget. Those three things would come back with a little jolt sometimes. Not a major shock, just an odd reminder, like getting her change back in John Lewis' and staring at the exotic Scottish pound notes.

She would remember that Colin was queer, that he was going to die, and that he was a millionaire. These separate facts would push themselves into her view, where she would quietly marvel at them.

The queer part of it wasn't that unusual any more. The disease wasn't either, after the year she'd been having. It seemed that everyone she knew was busy making the best of their time, even the ones without a time limit. The hardest, strangest, unswallowable fact of her cousin's life was his money. She didn't believe in it. True, if they were in town and miles away from home when it rained or he came over tired, he didn't think twice about flagging down a taxi. But he never exactly threw money around. And he never carried more than twenty pounds on him. "Just like the queen," Wendy said.

"Someone's going to get their shins kicked," he muttered.

"Oh, I'm sorry if..." Wendy didn't know yet how far she could push the jokes about queens.

"I'm having you on, doll," he said. "You can call me what you want."

She liked the way they called each other doll here. The gay boys and girls used the term a lot. In the Scarlet Empress they had flyers and posters for nightclubs with pictures of Barbies and Action Men in drag. She wondering if the doll-calling had anything to do with that, or vice versa.

Call me what you want, Colin said, and looked like he meant it. He felt like her best friend these days and that made her feel guilty for squeezing along some of the others. Wendy was always having to ask the objects of her affection to breathe in and squeeze along. There always had to be room for one more and she was always falling in love, these days.

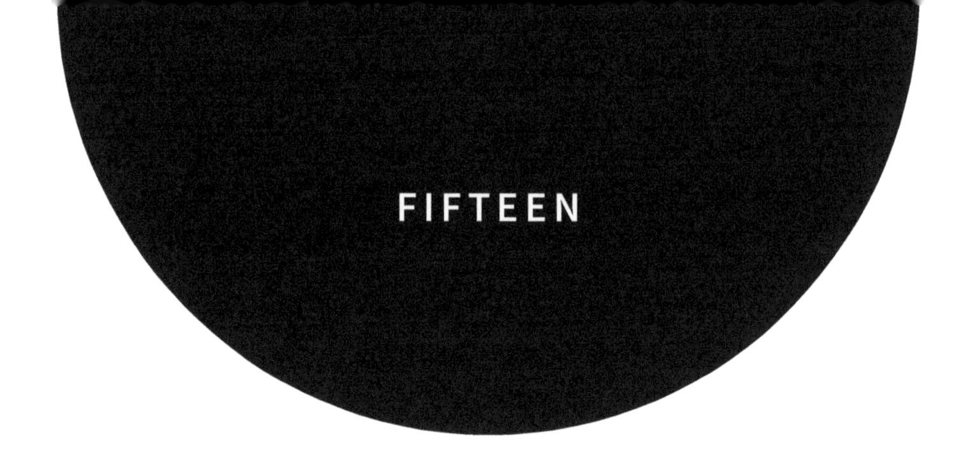

FIFTEEN

ON LEITH WALK SHE FOUND SOME OF HER FAVOURITE PLACES...

With Uncle Pat she went to the bookies, the cafeterias and the charity shops. She loved to look in the windows of the boutiques that sold material for saris. Gold and green fabric dotted with millions of sequins. Swatches of multi-coloured cloth wrapped on headless dummies. The glitziest of fabrics drapped on those dummies in the dowdiest fashion.

Soon Uncle Pat stopped coming out with her. He spent the days indoors. With each day it was getting hotter and it was too much for him. He was ailing. Wendy asked Aunty Anne about his health, but her aunt brushed aside the suggestion that Pat was getting worse.

Four storeys of flats lay on top of the shops down Leith Walk, so that there was a great concentration of life. There was a lot going on and this made Wendy feel at home. You could see the windows of flat upon flat, with paper lanterns, cheese plants and Chinese wall-hangings on display. When you walked down the street in the morning, there were always bin bags stacked at each lamp post for the bin lorry, and there would always be at least one exhausted three piece suite waiting with its cushions burst apart. It was as if the people here were forever chucking out their old tat and buying new.

She started going with Belinda to the launderette where Belinda always took the Captain's dirty things in a vast pink wash bag. Belinda propped it in an old pushchair and they walked gently across town. Outside the launderette was a life-sized orange Sooty bear, with a slot in his head, collecting money for the blind. He was chained to the front door and the links were as thick as Wendy's wrists. Wendy would stare at Sooty as she chatted to Astrid, the German woman who ran the launderette. Belinda got on with her washing. She wouldn't say a word until her washing was underway.

Until then Wendy was left with Astrid, who fascinated her because she looked like a film star, all dusky skin and bright eyes, and she had no legs. Astrid would be sitting on the bench between two full Ali Baba baskets, shaking out and folding other people's newly-dried washing. You could smell the static cling on the various clean bits and pieces. Astrid wouldn't be sitting really, of course, nor kneeling, or squatting. She was propped on the bench: folds of rich, glittering cloth gathered under her, protecting her stumps. To Wendy she looked sufficient to herself, busily folding and it didn't seem incongruous that there weren't two legs coming down off the bench from the truck of her body, that her golden sari just tapered away, nothing coming out of it, not even a mermaid's tail.

Astrid had one of those red dots on her forehead. Like a religious red dot on her forehead. Oh, I'm ignorant, thought Wendy. I should know all about these things. Other cultures. I know nothing. I don't even know about my own.

She stopped staring at the chained up Sooty and gazed at Astrid once more, who hummed unidentifiable songs as she dealt with skirts, babies' romper suits, men's workshirts. Her hair fell in two black plaits that hung down lower than her stumps.

"What has Belinda been telling you this week?" asked Astrid. She looked amused. "She's always telling someone something."

Wendy looked from Astrid to Belinda, who was wedging her silver coins into the machines. Maybe everything Belinda said, she said for a joke, or a dare. Maybe she and Astrid were having everyone on.

"She's been telling me all sorts," said Wendy, feeling out of her depth. "All of her stories."

"All her stories," laughed Astrid, deep in her throat. "Jesus God, not all her stories. The woman is a menace." She raised her smoky voice. "Have you been corrupting the ears and youthful innocence of this child with your tales? Belinda?"

Belinda barked with laughter. "Of course I haven't!"

Wendy said, "She told me that the world can be boiled down to two types of people: holograms and replacements. That's what she said."

Astrid turned to Wendy. "Did she tell you she thinks her brother is a replacement brother?"

"Oh yes." Wendy had thought it was a secret.

"You will scare the girl," said Astrid.

"It wouldn't harm people to know what's going on," said Belinda, gazing at her washing.

"So now you're in the know," said Astrid.

They all settled back then to watch Captain Simon's things go round. Slap slap slap.

Astrid said, "What Belinda hates...can I speak for you on this, Belinda?"

"Go ahead."

"What Belinda hates is the trivialisation of the situation...of these holograms and replacements. You know, like in that TV series that everyone was going mad about. All of them cash in, they rush to cash in on the situation. And it's a serious situation! Jesus God, is it serious! To have a brother replaced like that!" Astrid stopped her folding and glanced at Belinda. "How am I doing so far?"

"Very good," said Belinda.

"So all this replacing and these holograms...where are they coming from? Who's doing this?"

Belinda said, "Do you want to know what happened to me?"

Wendy gulped. "I think so."

The shadows in the narrow launderette seemed to squash in, drawing the three of them closer. They knew it was only the sun going in over dowdy Leith Walk, but the effect was remarkable. "Jesus God," whispered

Astrid, over the shunt and squelch of the washer.

"It was 1964. Edinburgh Airport. Picture the scene."

Astrid and Wendy concentrated. They put their imaginations to work. Wendy pictured a generic airport. She could see Belinda there, decades younger, not an ounce slimmer, in a mini dress of course, and dashing about, excited about her first trip abroad. It was quite a trek, down to Spain.

It was chilly in the waiting lounge, her thick arms and thighs were mottled red. Still she wore sunglasses, a wide-brimmed hat, and already she had blown up her beach ball.

"And we were delayed and delayed all of an afternoon...and all for a private jet, buggering up the schedules. So we knew it was someone famous coming in."

"Who was it?" asked Wendy.

"Yes, who?" chimed Astrid, though she already knew.

"It was Marlene Dietrich," said Belinda, smacking her lips on the name. "And I met her on the runway, when the press went out to greet her and she came down off the little staircase from her jet, holding onto the arm of her swanky beau, and clutching her hat onto her head and her bag to her side. I had been dragged along with the press because my boyfriend at the time—Alastair, a pimply boy who was taking me to Spain—worked at *The Scotsman*, and he threw caution to the winds, wanting a few words from Ms Dietrich."

"You met her!" said Wendy.

"More than that," said Astrid, pursing her lips, knowing what was coming.

Belinda took a deep breath. "Marlene and I were *kidnapped*. The two of us, together, taken against our not inconsiderable wills. I was in my holiday clothes...and Marlene was in baby pink Chanel. And she had on a wig of the brightest, tackiest yellow nylon. Which came as a surprise. She had on shades so dark you couldn't see those famous eyes. She howled and yammered like nothing on earth when...when *they* insisted that she removed them."

"When *who* insisted?" said Wendy.

"Just wait," said Belinda.

"Jesus," said Astrid.

"The men from space," said Belinda.

Astrid gave a small cry. She pointed at Belinda's washer. The door hadn't been properly closed and glistening soap was spilling out onto the floor. Wendy dashed over to jam it shut.

"Well done!" called Astrid.

Belinda looked piqued that her story had been stalled.

Wendy wasn't sure that she wanted to hear any more. She couldn't believe her ears. The calm, easy way Belinda was telling them this. She herself felt responsible, as if she'd pushed Belinda into a corner and demanded the full story. She'd only done it to call Belinda's bluff. Now here was Belinda apparently believing herself. It was a shame.

"Shall I go on?" Belinda asked. It was dark again in the launderette. Rain had started up on the Walk. "There was, of course, a ban and a hush-up in the Edinburgh press and then the world-wide press. It was, potentially, a very big story. Imagine telling the whole world in 1964 that a nice Edinburgh lady and the world-famous movie star Ms Dietrich had been taken off together in a terrible flash of unearthly..."

"'I believe," said Astrid, "that the word they use in the world of today is 'abducted'."

"This wasn't the world of today," said Belinda ominously. "This was back even before man walked on the moon."

"You're saying you were kidnapped, with Marlene, by aliens?" asked Wendy.

"I was amongst the gentlemen of the Scottish press and the people who worked at the airport and who were looking after Ms Dietrich. We clustered round her. One minute she is saying, in her ever-so famous tones: 'I am here to make a movie! I am to be Mary Queen of Scots! I love Scotland! I have always loved Scotland!' Next thing we all know a great big black shadow rolls over all of us, obscuring the brilliant sunshine. We all look up. Everyone gasps. Big space craft overhead. Shouts. Yells. Then a big flash of light. Like the space men are taking a gigantic Polaroid of us. But they weren't. They were kidnapping—abducting—Marlene and me. The only ladies present. When the glaring light died down and everyone could see straight again...we were well and truly gone. And so was the space craft."

"I don't believe this," said Wendy.

"Every word she says," said Astrid, "is gospel."

"How do you know?"

"Because Astrid came with me to Paris," said Belinda.

"What's Paris got to do with it?"

"In 1990 I went to Paris," said Belinda. "To catch Marlene before she died. I had to see her one last time. Astrid came with me."

"You went with her?"

"It was marvellous. Jesus God, it was a life's ambition realised. She had fallen on...what you call it...hard times, old Marlene...but she was a remarkable woman still and nevertheless."

"And you believe all this story?" asked Wendy.

"All of it is true!" cried Belinda. "True true true!"

> Dear Timon,
>
> I've passed your address on to someone I've met here. Today she told me a real humdinger of a story. I said, write and tell it to my friend Timon, because he's a famous writer, or he will be one day, and he can tell the story to the whole world. So now she's very keen. She's called Belinda and now she lives downstairs, but she says that in 1964 she was held captive at the North Pole by...well, I'll let you hear from the lady herself. She wants you to ghost-write her autobiography.
>
> Colin said that you only see ghosts—by the way—if you have suffered. I thought anyone could see them. You won't have suffered enough, not with your easy life.
>
> Get in touch and write me a sensible letter. No more of this nonsense about Mandy's lips and how she's stretched them. I didn't believe a word of that.
>
> One more thing—do you think you're a replacement or a hologram? Holograms are people you can walk through. So insincere they hardly exist. Replacements, on the other hand, are real: I mean, you can touch them, but they aren't the people they think they are. They mean well, but they're still replacements. Which are you, Timon? All of the above

is TM copyright Belinda-from-downstairs. All her ideas are about how the world has been infiltrated by replacement people and none of us is real anymore. The invasion has already happened and we aren't who we should be. That's what she reckons, anyway. Maybe she'll explain it all to you on a postcard. Belinda, her theories and her stories (which she believes...!) are my present to you, Timon.

Don't say I never give you owt.

PS Don't lose your elasticity! Whatever you do.

love,
Wendy.

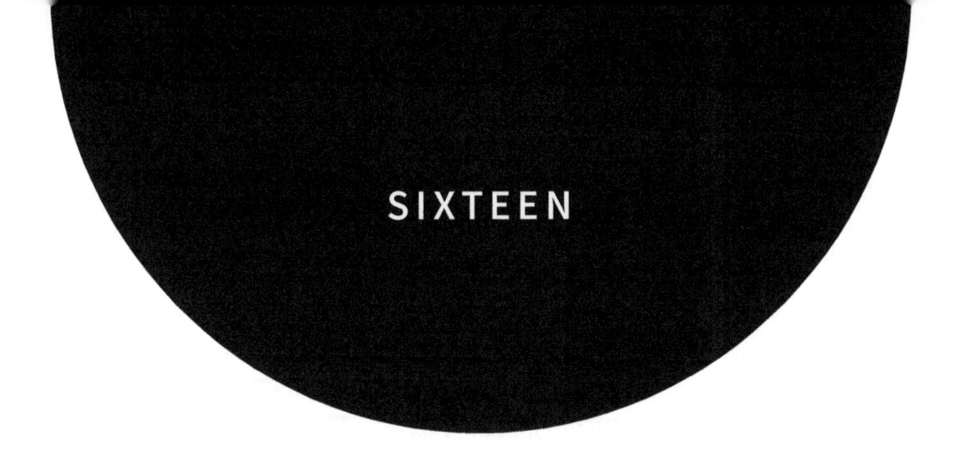

SIXTEEN

He wasn't a skinhead anymore. Wendy didn't know it yet, but she wouldn't be getting him as a skinhead. In the few weeks since she'd seen him on the train and he'd slipped his number to her on the platform at Waverley, David had been letting his hair grow out. Now he looked (or so he'd been told) tufty and sweet and, at first, Wendy would miss him when he walked into the club where they were supposed to meet. She was still looking for her skinny skin skinhead.

David had been working in a record store in the West End. He was one of twenty who took turns behind the tills, easing the neverending stream of customers with their clingfilm-wrapped CDs. CDs slapped on counters made such a brittle, satisfying sound. He loved the noises of this summer's work. The crashing of the tills and all the electronic white noise. He knew all the music. Surrounded by music, he would remember what was in the charts this summer for the rest of his life. Edinburgh had been his chance to make himself trendy and he had taken to the city happily, growing in his thick, dark sideburns, buying tartan Doc Martens and a range of trendy tops in different colours. He saw bands in pubs and bigger bands on tour, drank lager, ate nachos most nights, dabbed crunchy granules of speed on one finger and brushed his teeth with them, so he could dance and still get up to work on the till next morning, his hair sticking up funny where it was growing back.

He socialised with the people from work. Early on there had been a few nights with Heather, who was part of the extra staff they took on for the sales season, but that had stopped. "I used to have a vampire fixation," Heather had told him, "but that fizzled out." She was one of those people to whom everything in their life was just another fad. David decided he wasn't prepared to be that.

He moved into a flat with a bloke from work, in Thistle Street, an alley of warehouse flats above the auction rooms. He was just two streets down from the shop on Princes Street. Now he was living in the centre of town, four storeys up a fire escape. He moved all his things into the flat in only five trips up the clanging fire escape. His flat mate Rab had much more stuff. Thousands of dog-eared records and rather startling books in cardboard boxes. David only hoped they didn't choose to move out on the same day. Or that Rab didn't move out first. He'd hate to have to offer to help Rab move his stuff.

In late August Wendy gave David a call and he blinked three times before realising who she meant she was.

"I didn't think you were going to bother!"

"Oh," said Wendy. "You shouldn't lose faith so easily. I'm around."

THEY MADE A PLAN TO GO OUT LATER THAT WEEK. WENDY PUT THE phone down. The phone was still on the bare boards in the hall. You'd think Uncle Pat would buy a phone table or something. Then she thought, maybe this is what I'm missing—talking to and seeing someone closer to my own age. Everyone I know here is older. Even Colin is. He's nearly thirty. David sounded so young.

THE SUN WAS BACK OUT. THIS WEEK WAS THE HOTTEST SO FAR. TODAY Aunty Anne made and effort and said, "Let's get some sun-bathing in—up at the Botanical Gardens." She had been slightly friendlier the last few days and these trips to the park had become the thing that aunt and niece did together, upon which no one else—and certainly no male person—impinged. Wendy had duly gone with her aunt and lay on the grass, on a prickly tartan blanket.

Anne lay back, fleshy and unashamed in skimpy shorts, baring her marvellous pins to the numinous sky, and anybody else who went passing by. Spreadeagled beside Aunty Anne, Wendy felt overshadowed and wanted to slink off to the cover of the trees. The new Chinese Garden lay over the brow of the next rise and she longed to go and sit in the simple wooden pagoda in the shade. Not waiting for Aunty Anne to fix her with a look, as she could at any moment, and ask: "Have you met a nice boy yet?" or, "Aren't you wondering why my eyes are twinkling?" (She really asked this and yes, indeed, her eyes were twinkling merrily. To her shame Wendy pretended not to hear her aunt's question. Though, of course, she was dying to know what had put that twinkle there.)

Oh, to be like her sister Mandy and her Aunty Anne and not give a tuppence ha'penny for anyone's opinion. Wendy would try to make herself brave and work herself up to a certain pitch of brassy nonchalance, but then her nerve would snap at its tautest and she'd be left dangling and all self-conscious. Today she was amazed at herself, how coolly she had talked to David on the phone. "Yeah, I'll come out dancing. Only somewhere where there's actual songs to dance to, with gaps between them...and so long as they're songs that I recognise." David had been only too pleased to let her have her own way. Maybe she'd blown her summer's worth of cool on that one phone call.

For some reason she was reacting badly to the sun. When she was little she'd been able to run around the beach and about the streets all day in the brightest sun. These days, each time she came home from bearing her arms, legs, stomach and the top of her head in the Botanical Gardens, she would end the day feeling sick with a splitting headache.

"I've never been cursed with sun-stroke," said Aunty Anne, advancing with a cold compress and asprins. "You're like your mother. You'll be peely-wally all your life."

Wendy flushed, hearing her mother called like this.

Aunty Anne was turning a fine, glossy mahogany. Those legs of hers were lacquered and finely turned like something off one of the precious antiques she saw being sold each morning in the auctions she was still attending. She was still patiently picking up bargains and tips about the selling game. "I'm an exquisite antique!" Aunty Anne would call out, strutting about the flat, showing off her tan. "And just look at these gorgeous legs! Couldn't you eat them?"

"For God's sake," said her ex-husband. "Put all that flesh away. You'll shame us all. Next to you, we look like we're wasting away." It was true. The more gloriously robust Anne became that summer, the worse her son and his father looked. Anne would emerge each morning from her purple satin-lined room in ever-skimpier and garish and daring outfits and the two men would still be shuffling about in their dressing gowns. Only Colin sometimes flung himself down on the grass in Gayfield Square, onto his old Spiderman duvet cover. Father and son were declining together and Anne's ebullient health was a rebuke to them: get out there and enjoy it!

Her advice—about anything—was always the same, thought Wendy. You've got to go for it! Seize the day! You've got to go and get out there!

But they wouldn't. The old man had taken a turn for the worse. And mostly Colin didn't leave the flat till after eleven at night, when the sun had safely slunk away past the conservatory on Calton Hill, which looked to him like a baleful nipple on a single tit.

This afternoon Wendy lay next to her dozing, basting aunt and wondered once again if she was footling and tootling her time away. Colin might well have been more help and support to her in her quest for something meaningful to do. (Meaningful? When did that come about? The word had never occurred to her before. All she needed was something to take her mind off loss and displacement, to give her a propping up and a structure for the things she got up to. Jesus God! (How infectious Astrid was) she was seventeen and meaning wasn't really that high on her list of priorities.)

COLIN WAS NO HELP? NO, I WOULDN'T SAY THAT EXACTLY. HE WAS GOOD to me. A very maternal boy, I think he was at that age, with the mothering instinct thwarted in him and coming out and splurging over his few friends when he and they would let it. He could be crowding and oppressive with his care and his wheedling the truth of the matter out of you...Right from my first days in their luxury rooftop pad, he wanted all the truth out of me.

Maybe, I thought, he's a naive receptor, like Timon.

Belinda said he was a hologram, and therefore not to be trusted. But Belinda's world-view was just bizarre and although I liked her idea of splitting everyone in the world into two categories (how convenient!) I wasn't convinced. And, as yet, I certainly wasn't convinced that she and Marlene had been experimented upon at the North Pole.

Colin's problem, I would say now, and perhaps it was my problem too, was that he couldn't think of anything more delightful than being a seventeen year old girl. And he told me this, he told me this himself. This good old reductionist version of a gay man's sensibility came straight from the horse's mouth—so don't write in! If I'm being reductionist about queers, about Colin himself, then so was he and, in that unguarded moment, he was happy to be. He actually said, 'To be you and pretty and seventeen and have it so easy and not be queer and have fellas chasing you! Lovely! You're so lucky! So ordinary!'

It was my...situation he adored, more than me myself. I imagined that he was sneaking up on me, ready to pounce...not to seduce me, of course, but to oust me. He wanted to know why I wasn't having a better time than I appeared to be having. And he lost no time in suggesting that if he was me, why then he'd...have a humdinger of a time. Humdinger was his word. I'd started using it too, I'd noticed, along with doll, along with Jesus God! Along with telling people not to lose their elasticity. I always picked up things like this. Verbal tics cling to me.

"Time to get back," said Aunty Anne, peeling herself off the grass. Shreds of green were sticking to her darkened underside.

"How come so early?"

"Your Uncle Pat gets back from the consultant soon."

I must have looked blank.

"Don't you remember? He was at the hospital today."

I'd forgotten.

"About his...problems." With a downward glance Aunty Anne alluded to his general area of discomfort. She shook out her blankets.

I couldn't believe it had slipped my mind. And, a month ago, when the appointment had been given him, I'd solemnly promised to go with him and hold his hand. He hated hospitals. He hated anything that smelled of an institution. "Institutions smell," he told me, "of gravy, flowers and fresh excrement."

"Who's gone with him?" I asked.

"Colin did," said Aunty Anne, leading the way back to the path. "Even though he hates those places too. They depress him, and I'm not surprised." She sighed.

"Why didn't you tell me?"

"I thought you knew!"

"Why didn't you go?"

"I hardly think that's proper. I'm his ex-wife. They're poking on with all his insides."

Sometimes I just didn't understand Aunty Anne.

WHEN WE GOT BACK TO THE FLAT IT WAS EMPTY.

There was a postcard on the met from Timon. It showed a picture of an egg-headed alien, glowing yellow.

> Wendy, who are these people you're knocking about with? What are you doing, telling them they can write to me? I've never met any of them in my life. Are you giving out my address to just anyone? This Belinda woman is obviously bananas. And lonely. I got a card from her the same day I got your note. A kind of preface to telling me what she calls, 'the whole shazam shebang and kit kaboodle.' She thinks I'll write a story about her. I dreamed last night that it was me being abducted. You know I hate that shit.
>
> love (even so)
> Timon.

SEVENTEEN

THEY DIDN'T KNOW WHAT WAS WRONG WITH UNCLE PAT. HE CAME BACK late that afternoon and how we fussed around him.

"I can sit my own self down!" he grumbled, heading for his favourite swivel chair, in the brightest patch of light. It was strange seeing him in clothes. He was wearing a tweedy suit with a beautiful silk tie, loosely knotted, a peacock green and blue. He tilted his head back, sighed and closed his eyes. "Serious things don't seem so serious once you get home," he said. "Once you step through that door, it's like they all fall away."

Aunty Anne said, "Hush now and get some rest. Do you want something to eat? There's some bacon I could fry." I could see her big hands twitching, keen to do something practical, which for her usually meant one of her slapdash fry-ups.

For a moment Uncle Pat looked vexed. Then the strength drained out of him. "No, I'm all right. Colin fetched a...muffin, I think the word was, from the stall outside the hospital. I ate it in the waiting room. Do you know, the whole business of being looked at has tired me out."

We all sat down and watched him. I don't know why. If I'd come back from something serious—the acute surgical out-patients' consultancy, no less—I wouldn't want faces peering at me afterwards. But we were waiting for him to tell us that everything was all right. It made you realise how thin he'd become, seeing him in his best suit like this. We were too used to him swishing about like Prospero in his voluminous scarlet gown.

Colin said, "They were very nice to us. They let me go in with him."

Uncle Pat opened his eyes. "In case I forgot to tell them anything, or didn't listen properly to what they told me."

"I didn't have to do anything. He was great," said Colin. Then he turned and gave me a distinctly funny look. I blushed.

"What did they say?" asked Aunty Anne. She went to put the kettle on, her feet shuffling impatiently on the flags, wanting to dance.

"They felt all over my abdomen," said Uncle Pat. "All my skinny old stomach. It was a very nice, very young Canadian girl with cool fingers and a very lucid way of talking. She said there's very definitely a mass down there."

"A mass?" said Aunty Anne.

"Something inflamed, she thought," said Colin. "They don't know. They want to do emergency scans."

The phone rang in the hall. There was no answer phone. Or rather there was, but it was faulty and only recorded actual phone conversations and played them back to the next person who called. Not very useful. I dashed into the hall, straining to hear about Uncle Pat's scans.

"Wendy? It's David."

"It's a really bad time," I said.

"What?" He was at work and the shop noise was fierce behind him.

"It's a really bad time to talk," I shouted. Behind me I could hear Colin counting things off on his fingers.

"He's got to go back for an X ray, a barium drink..."

"A barium meal," his father corrected him.

"Whatever. It's where they light you up inside and video everything swishing about. And an ultrasound, too."

"That's what they give pregnant women!" cried Aunty Anne.

"Maybe it's twins," said Uncle Pat gloomily.

"Wendy, listen," David was saying. I could tell he was serving someone at the till at the same time. "Right. If I could just ask you to sign where it says 'signature'..."

"What? David..."

"*Going Places* on Friday night, Wendy. It's a club."

"I can't do this now, David."

"You can't come out?"

"Yes I can come out, but..."

"I can't stay on long...Seven o'clock at the Assembly Rooms on George Street. Friday at seven! Dress up retro! See you then!" The shop phone went dead.

"They say that the barium meal tastes disgusting," I heard Uncle Pat say. "For some reason I picture sitting down to this funny, lumpy plate of chemicals, forcing it down with a knife and fork. Or the foaming jug of poison that Dr Jeckyll swigs down."

"Oh god," said Aunty Anne, sitting herself down as I came back into the kitchen. "This is just awful."

I looked at the three of them. For the first time they properly felt like my new family. At the back of my mind I could hear that voice of Mandy's singing, as she had of our mother: 'It's cancer-cancer-cancer.' Mandy demystifying everything as usual. Mandy saying the unsayable, singing the unsingable. I was gripped by the need to say the word myself. Say aloud to the luxury kitchen: It's cancer-cancer-cancer. Just to get the word out. Sure that it would make it easier.

Yet the word was already there. It might as well have been written on each of our foreheads, as we all looked at each other, stuck for the next thing to say. Like in the Rizla game, where everyone writes a famous person's name on a thin cigarette paper, licks and sticks it on their neighbour's forehead. You can't read how you've been labelled and, by asking questions, you have to guess.

"I'll come with you next time, Uncle Pat. Your next scan. What is it, this barium meal? I'll eat it for you, if you like."

He smiled.

I LET THE SMELLS OF THE LAUNDERETTE WAFT ABOUT ME AND I HEARD Belinda's drowsy voice go on, today describing in fine, wonderfully recalled detail, about the surgical instruments—specialized, gleaming—that had been used on her thirty something years ago. Beside me Astrid gasped and oohed, though she must have heard the story countless times before. I closed my eyes and concentrated on the clean smell of detergent, and of fabric conditioner, rich and pink, sloshed into the tubs by the handy capful. You could smell old fish and chips too, in the rumpled balls of old newspaper under the benches. Astrid had some difficulty picking up after her messier customers.

"A lovely, funny woman." Belinda was, on request, mistily recalling Marlene. "Rather harsh, of course, and odd. She never looked anything less than immaculate." She sniffed, rubbing her knees. "Even in her late, bed-ridden years."

Astrid pitched in. "Even then. That was the only time I ever saw her, in that down-heel Paris apartment and I thought Jesus, that woman is still every inch the superstar."

I said, "Tell me about the Paris trip."

"1990," said Belinda. "Picture the scene. Astrid and I went for a long weekend."

"We had planned for months," said Astrid. "Scrimping our pennies together."

"I was going for a Chanel frock..."

"But that's a whole other story," said Astrid.

"The real purpose," said Belinda, "was to see Marlene again, all those years after we were kidnapped. Five days we were in that strange craft together, high above the icy wastes of the North Pole. She must remember me, I thought, even though were hadn't been in touch for over twenty-five years. In the five days we shared each other's company we poured out our hearts to each other. Now, the memory had faded a little at the edges. It seemed to me, by then, like a curious dream."

Astrid said, "So we presented ourselves at the buzzer downstairs from Ms Dietrich's apartment. A shabby green door. It wasn't hard to find. I was like you, Wendy. I thought that Belinda's story was all film-fan flim-flam and fabrications. So we buzzed...and..."

"We buzzed the intercom," said Belinda, "and Marlene could hardly say go away, bugger off, don't disturb me. Not to the woman she'd been held captive with all those years ago. Who'd suffered the same weird indignities."

What indignities? I was dying to know. Belinda was going to tell me that she'd made love with a man from outer space. I was waiting for it.

Astrid's marvellous eyes lit up. "The intercom crackled. 'Oh, it's you!' went the voice and, Jesus God! Even on something as mundane as an intercom that voice was suffused with...what is the phrase?"

"Jaded tristesse," said Belinda.

"And Marlene, I swear, she said: 'Hullo Belinda...come on up, old girl.'"

BECAUSE ASTRID WAS IN HER CHAIR, THEY COULDN'T TAKE THE UMPTEEN, winding, creaking steps. They had to wait instead for the antiquated lift. In the lift Belinda trod on a mouse. The place was a horrible mausoleum, and as they were winched to the top Belinda felt sadness panging in her ample breast. In the hallway at the top, the carpet had lost its pattern and colour.

"Oh, I wish we hadn't come."

But Astrid was excited. "Why on earth?"

"Poor Marlene, putting up with us in her twilight years."

And Belinda thought of her own, lovely spacious flat in the New Town, in Edinburgh: of its perfection, even if it was cluttered by that brother of hers. At that moment she didn't feel well disposed towards Captain Simon. Wasn't he, after all, the real reason for this peculiar, peremptory reunion? For Marlene, out of everyone on the planet, would surely believe Belinda when she said that her brother, Captain Simon had been replaced...

Marlene was sitting up in her bed, under a dowdy duvet. An uneaten lunch of clear soup was on a tray to one side, a vase of pink carnations turning brown at the edges stood by it. A Baby Belling was plugged into the wall beside her. She wore an expensive headscarf and dark glasses.

"Belinda! Sit yourself down, girl! Pull up a pew..." Then she glared at Astrid. "Jesus God, that woman has no legs."

Astrid looked stung and didn't say anything.

Marlene scrabbled at her bedside table for her ciggies. Lit one. Oh, thought Belinda mournfully. Where were the Black Sobranies of your glory years? And the gold tipped holder and Zippo Noel gave you? She remembered the two of them smoking like schoolgirls in their cell on the weird craft, using up the last few delicious cigarettes (and the oxygen). Watching the lilac smoke unfurl as they wondered what would become of them. "Fame does not matter here," Marlene had told Belinda. "Up here in the stratosphere we are equals."

And Belinda's heart glowed with pride.

THE STORY WAS INTERRUPTED BY THE MAN FROM THE PLACE NEXT DOOR. Tom, in his tracksuit bottoms, was one of Astrid's other regulars. Wendy had already heard about him. At the back of the launderette you could smell the chlorine from the footbaths next door. Wendy had asked Astrid: is there a swimming baths next door? Or in the basement? And she had imagined a subterranean pool, leaf-fronded and tiled in blue and gold and steamed mirrors, the ceilings dappled and crazed with watery reflections. Astrid smiled and explained that next door it was a gentleman's club and it extended underneath the launderette. A special gentleman's club where the gentlemen paid their money to take off all their clothes to sit in the underground pools together, or in small wooden cabinets, partly dressed in old towels as the temperature rose...

All this underneath the launderette! And Poundstretcher!

Wendy was enchanted by the thought of all this beneath her feet. Gloomy dripping caverns full of naked men, beneath the black and white tiled lino. They weren't specific nude men she saw, just an undifferentiated mass of male flesh. Nobody she would have to talk to.

She stared out at Leith Walk: the push chairs getting shunted past, the dogs, the granddames, the pensioners and pissheads. She wondered if they knew what was going on beneath their feet: the underground men.

Belinda had gone back to talking about the surgical implements with which she had been examined. "They were spotless, mind."

The man from next door was pulling up to Astrid's bench a hamper full of—he flung open to lid to reveal—soiled and dampened towels. Astrid winked at Wendy. "Tom and I do a roaring trade from the gentlemen who wish to take off their clothes and sit in the heat of our shared basement." The man in the vest top and tracksuit bottoms smiled at Wendy.

"It must be nice," said Wendy. "Lolling about down there."

Tom grinned. "Spending languorous summer afternoons in the hot timeless dark of someone else's cellar. Forget your cares!"

Astrid said, "Doesn't he talk funny!"

"It would be like being a mushroom," said Wendy, and made Tom laugh.

ON FRIDAY NIGHT I DECIDED I WOULD TAKE COLIN ALONG WITH ME FOR support. He didn't have any other plans. I wasn't about to go and meet a man I hardly knew without back-up. I wanted to know what Colin thought of him.

Colin didn't know what to wear. He tried on a few outfits and they all looked much the same. Different T shirts to hang off his skinny frame. Three pairs of immaculate, probably new jeans, in navy, white and black, to be winched in tight around his waist. I sat on the end of his bed and watched him try things on and I was amazed by his waist. He made me feel colossal. I could fit his waist between the span of my two hands. He jumped out of one outfit, into the next, into another, like jumping through hoops, revealing between each one his pale boy's body, his white Calvin Klein's.

In the end he settled on a green T shirt and, in the pub round the corner, he tipped the first drink of the night over his white jeans. That night we spilled more alcohol down the pair of us than either of us drank. It was the night of wasted booze. We were nervous.

We walked up from the Royal Circus. I was in a T shirt and jeans, too. It was too hot a night to go dressing up and clarting on and I wasn't sure, anyway, if I was that serious about making an impression on David. Dress retro, he'd said. Whatever that meant. The club he'd suggested was a monthly one, that moved venue each time and played old-fashioned music: tunes from twenty year old adverts and TV shows. The whole point of this, Colin warned me, was that it was an...ironic disco. You danced between inverted commas to easy-listening music.

"And I'm not sure if it's really on at the Assembly Rooms," he said. "I think your boyfriend's got it wrong." Colin was peeved because of the gin stained down his crotch.

We had cocktails in a piano bar on Frederick Street. A horrible pianist sang Stevie Wonder songs at us. This was a street full of restaurants and we struggled through a well-fed crowd and smells of garlic, ginger and spices. I hadn't eaten anything since breakfast time, when all the talk of bowel problems had put me off.

Colin was right. The Assembly Rooms on George Street were silent. The windows at the front of that imposing building were dark. No David.

We saw a poster that said the club had been moved at the last minute to a marquee on Princes Street.

"We're already an hour late," I said. "Let's just go home."

"No way!" said Colin. "I want to get a look at your fella."

"He's probably seen this is empty and gone home," I said feebly.

"He can read the signs as well as we can. Come on!"

DAVID WAS PHONING AUNTY ANNE. HE'D BEEN IN THE MARQUEE TENT on Princes Street since the start of the evening. Aunty Anne said that it sounded hellish at his end of the phone.

"Wendy's gone to the Assembly Rooms," Anne shouted to this voice who said he was David. She was dubious about giving out information like this.

"I got the venue wrong," said David. He was crushed into a corner of the bar. The club was far too full. He doubted that Wendy would get in now, even if she'd found the place.

"Well," said Aunty Anne. "It looks as if you've spoiled her evening."

The phone went dead. David put the receiver back.

Everyone around him seemed to be in gaggles, all of them wearing ludicrous, outmoded outfits. They must have raided Oxfam: the men had groomed and smarmed themselves into lounge lizards from Martini adverts. Many of the women had come in evening gowns and gloves up to their elbows with fingers so tight they could barely bend at the knuckles. There was a great many feather boas.

David drank alone at the bar, unsure if he should stay. He could feel the slightly dizzying effect of the speed starting up, but that might have been the noise level, crackling against his eardrums. He imagined granules of speed tootling through his veins...off to who knows where. His brain, maybe, dissolving and busying along.

Being here wasn't the same experience when you were alone. It wasn't the sort of place where you came to cruise around. He had come dressed in a plum velvet smoking jacket, and a frilled blue shirt. They hadn't come from Oxfam: he'd paid a fair bit of money to get the retro right. He felt the comforting nap of his velvet sleeve as a few songs went by...

Call Me

The In-Crowd

The Windmills of Your Mind

You're the Devil in Disguise

Where Do I Begin?

This last, sassy number performed by the great, still-living Scots-Caribbean songstress, Brenda Soobie. As the song shimmered and slunk to its climax David happened to glance at the marquee's entrance, where each newcomer was having their wrist stamped with an ultra violet stamper. And there was Wendy, looking around and smiling hopefully, in a Wombles T shirt.

EIGHTEEN

We went back to a flat in the centre of town, one of the back streets I hadn't explored, which was dark and cobbled, with warehouse doors locked and bolted down for the night, and fire escapes stretching up to the flats which, I realised, must fill the upper levels of all the buildings here. Colin came with us. It was after four, and we had danced through the whole night, finishing in the shopping centre beneath the marquee, where the music was pumped down onto the galleries, fountains and pools of the mall. We were exhausted and Colin came along with us. None of us thought about it. It wasn't as if I was going *back* with David. It hadn't come to that. We'd had a laugh and he hadn't made any moves. It seemed that one minute we were dancing to the final few songs and then we were halfway up this perilous fire escape, and Colin was saying, "This is where my mum is making her fortune. Give it a couple of hours, just after dawn, and she'll be here. Driving a hard bargain." As David unlocked his door at the top of all the steps, Colin said, "Mum's making her fortune as if it was a competition. But Dad got his in a fluke. If she succeeds in making it, it will still be his. She doesn't see that. If it's a competition, it's like giving it straight to him."

Then we were in David's flat, which he shared with his friend Rab, who lay tripping on the green velvet settee, his daschund stretched out on his chest. He was feeding the dog cold sausages and listening to some kind of hard core dance music, with one of the Beat Poets intoning over the top. Even though it was a warm night Rab wore a colourful tea cosy hat as though he'd just come in and flung himself down. He said he'd been in all night. David turned down the music and made us strong, sugary tea. He flung open the tall windows and explained that they were so high up here that they need never worry about burglars slinking in. He cursed Rab and his habit of pulling all the windows shut.

"It's the noise from outside I can't manage," said Rab, putting his hands over his ears. "It's too much stimulus. You can have too much stimulus."

David snorted with laughter at this.

It was then we realised that the Christmas decorations were still up. Ratty tinsel hung from the pictures on the walls, the window frames and the many parched yukka plants.

Colin settled himself down to look through Rab's records, and started playing a few, picking up the needle and replaying particular tracks. Rab lay back and let him play what he wanted. The daschund raised its head to stare at Colin.

David and I drank our tea in the kitchen alcove. It was better organised than you'd imagine for a kitchen belonging to two careless straight men: they were vegetarians. Plastic tubs were labelled bulgar wheat, green lentils, mung beans. David was telling me how cheaply you can live off pulses and beans and sprouts. He ransacked their homemade spice rack, opening jars and getting me to identify spices by smell, my eyes closed. Paprika, cumin, garam masala. He showed me Rab's favourite cookery book, one with silly cartoons of a very badly-drawn 'lady vegan' as they called her. "You don't have to worry about eating cheaply, though," David smirked. "Isn't your uncle a multi-millionaire?"

"Not quite." The subject of his money embarrassed me. It was true, I'd become used to eating very well since I'd been in Edinburgh. I wouldn't touch instant coffee now, or soup out of a tin. How strange the boys' jars of dried, earthy foodstuffs looked to me. All their food was stockpiled here: just add water and see.

The strip lighting was harsh and made the rag rugs glow with colour. As I stared David caught me up in his arms and started to nuzzle at my neck. This was his move and, after all, I was rather relieved. His stubble had started to grow in: it was almost dawn. Here you could see across the high rooftops of the city to the docks, and the pink dawn smudging into the vague tangerine of the streetlights. I was too sensitive, or my skin was. When he kissed me I felt too raw, like he was peeling me away. He told me I tasted nice and all I could imagine tasting of was lager and cigarettes.

Across the room Rab had fallen into a stupor and Colin seemed to be asleep, curled awkwardly on rucked-up mats.

"We should have gone home earlier," I said.

"I'll be buzzing all night," David said. "I won't sleep till lunch time."

"You'll miss the best part of the day."

"Yeah?" He kissed me again and then he licked my eyebrows.

"What was that for?"

But he didn't explain. His frilly blue shirt was sweat-dampened still. When I leaned against the kitchen counter, he came with me, and I could feel the tight, mysterious knot of flesh in the front of his trousers. He asked me if I wanted to come to bed for the few hours until morning.

I let his question hang in the air for a moment.

"Have you ever slept with anyone before?" he asked.

I told him that not really, no. But that a friend of mine, Timon, had shown me a thing or two on the beach at Blackpool, late one night.

I didn't tell you about that, did I? It wasn't much. We never made love. I badgered him, friend to friend, to show me the kind of thing I might have to expect. I did it for a laugh, frankly, but I had Timon on that I was ignorant. I made Timon show me his glorious hard-on as we sat on the mucky sands down from the Pleasure Beach. In the moonlight it was like some weird crustacean that had wandered out of the sea. He breathed in little gasps as I took it in both hands like a microphone. Bless Timon. He could hardly get it back inside his pants when I decided I'd seen enough.

So when I went into David's small room, sat on the bed, and watched him strip himself bare, I could look at him like an expert. I took his sticky, excitable cock and the soft bag of his balls in both hands and drew him down onto the unmade bed.

At six in the morning I led the sill-drowsy, dopey-sounding Colin on the walk back to the Royal Circus. He was terribly hung-over.

"You never fucked him," he said, aghast.

I shook my head.

"I mean," said Colin. "He's a sweet, rough-looking boy, if that's what you're into...but..."

"We never fucked," I said, through gritted teeth. "It all happened naturally. He licked my fanny for a while and came in his own hand. Then he fell asleep."

"Marvellous," said Colin scathingly.

When she lay on her bed it was nearly seven and too light to sleep. There was no blocking out the light in her room. She listened to Colin down in the kitchen, having a final, thoughtful cup of tea by himself, then pad off down the corridor and into his room.

Minutes later another bedroom door clicked pen. Someone was up early. Wendy closed her eyes. She heard two pairs of feet shushing into the kitchen. Then two voices, talking carefully to each other.

"It's bad enough here," said a man's voice. "But it would be even worse downstairs." It was Captain Simon, sounding grumpier than I'd ever heard him.

Aunty Anne was with him. I could just see her in that fake fur trimmed robe of hers, pulled to cover her bosom. "It's like a French farce," she yawned.

There was a peaceful lull.

Captain Simon said suddenly, "All the same, I think it would be better...for all concerned, kind of thing...if we didn't get up to anything like this...ehm...anymore."

Aunty Anne's voice came out harsh. "What's your problem?"

"No problem. I think what we're doing is unwise."

"Of course it's unwise, you old fool. That's the point, isn't it?"

"It isn't my point, Anne."

"Love like this isn't sensible," she said. "It isn't tameable or well-mannered. Of course it causes problems."

"I'm not in love with you," he said, affronted.

"Not love then," she said. "Desire. Destructive passions."

"Well, I can't be doing with them anymore."

"I see."

"Pat is my friend. I sit with him, I drink his drink, enjoy his company. This is betraying him. And he's ill, too. This is wicked."

Aunty Anne didn't reply for some time. "So I'm wicked, am I?"

"I think you're a very...impressive woman, Anne. You're glamorous and sexy..."

She made a bitter, dismissive noise. "You're no special friend to Pat. He's told me what he thinks."

"About what?"

"He said, only the other day. About you. About you being a greedy old devil, hanging around, seeing what you can scrounge. He thinks you're waiting for him to die, seeing what you can get. Don't you think he gets enough begging letters?"

"That's not what I'm here for."

"You're not here for me, either, are you?"

"No, Anne, I'm not. I'm afraid you've rather compromised me."

"I've compromised you?"

"You've ambushed me. You've made things impossible for me."

"That's right. Blame the woman. The vile, ungovernable appetites of the woman."

His chair legs scraped on stone as he stood up. "If that's how you want to put it."

"You misogynistic old bastard."

"I love honest women. Good women."

"Like your bonkers sister."

"Don't call Belinda. She's twice the woman you are. Your niece is a good girl, too. No, it's you, Anne. You're a greedy woman. You don't have a shred of fellow-feeling or compassion in your..."

There was a loud crack then, as she hit him. He received the blow silently. There was a second crack, as she hit him again. Then the doors banged and he was gone. He went downstairs to his own flat.

I lay, still unable to sleep, listening to Aunty Anne sob out her heart at the kitchen table.

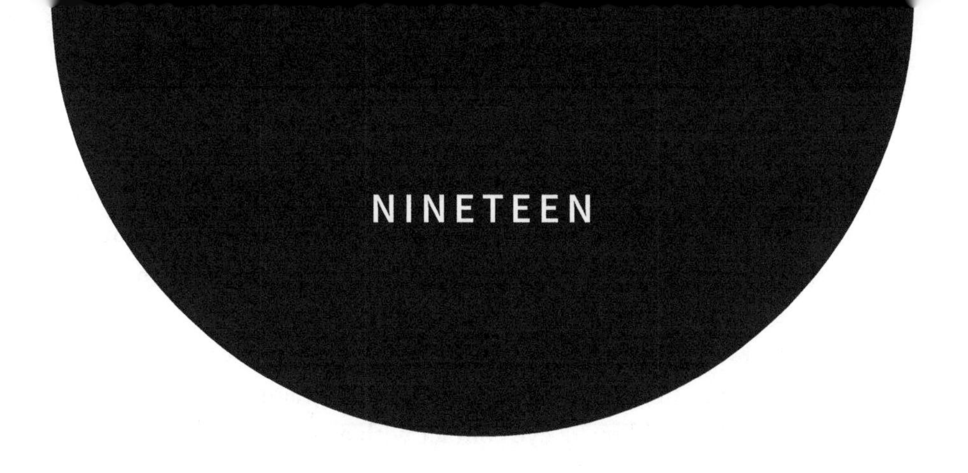

NINETEEN

THE NEXT DAY—AND MAYBE IT WAS GUILT—I WENT TO JOB PARTY FOR the first time. I was setting out, remarkably untired after the night I'd had, and Aunty Anne caught hold of me.

"You came in much too late last night."

By now I knew it was best not to go on the offensive. "I know. We lost track." I looked at her red-lined eyes. "I'm sorry."

"You have to learn how to do the right things, Wendy. What's right and what's wrong. I'm sure your Uncle Pat doesn't mind you getting out and enjoying yourself, but he's in no fit state to worry about you."

I nodded.

"There's a right way and a wrong way," she said. "And you can only push it so far." She stared at me appraisingly. "You want to push it, don't you? You want to find out how far you can go."

I shrugged.

"All right," she said. "You're a good girl, I know."

She let me go then. Colin hadn't emerged from his room yet, but I felt sure he'd get a talking to as well.

Job Party consisted of six others who all looked up, surprised, when I arrived still wearing the blue cycling helmet Uncle Pat had bought me. I was the mysterious Wendy, who was meant to be languishing with glandular fever, or so my explanatory notes had told them.

They were an unpromising bunch. Most of them were men over thirty. The woman in charge talked brightly and pragmatically, twisting in her chair so she could make eye contact with everyone in turn, making her heavy earrings tinkle. She talked about opportunity and re-training, but seemed to know a little about everyone there. She asked me to explain to the group what my ambitions were. It was something they had done for each other at their first meeting.

I made something up. "I want to write a novel, just one novel in my lifetime, that everyone will read and that will change lives."

They looked at me. Luckily, I'd heard enough from Timon and our Mandy to substantiate this wild claim as my own ambition. They encouraged me. But they also said what a precarious ambition that must be, being a paperback writer. I was told to expect lots of rejection letters. That I must be prepared to fund my ambitions by taking all kinds of ordinary day-jobs, but that would be what would teach me about life, about people, about the World of Work.

"I once thought about writing a book," said Janice, the woman with the earrings.

One of the older men perked up. "They say everyone's got a book in them."

"That's right, Derek," she said. "And I've got good life experience. That's what it's all about. Experience."

The group looked at me then, and I felt about six years old.

One of the other older men, Douggie, started telling us about the novel he'd written at weekends ten years ago. He had two photostatted copies in his desk at home. "It was about my experience of the Sixties. Paralleled with my father's being tortured by the Japanese in the Second World War. He wouldn't talk about it usually, but I interviewed him for hours. I tried to get a publisher. I said it was about father-son conflict. When I was made redundant I thought, this is my chance to make a success of myself. I read the thing again. And it was hopeless. I realised I couldn't even string a sentence together. It looked like a bairn had written it."

The only other woman, Sandra, said she'd written off to Mills and Boon once, to get the tape of instructions they sent out to prospective writers of romance. "It was so complicated, though. You're not allowed to get inside the man's head, which was all right by me, because how do I know how a man thinks?" She looked at the glum faces around her. "And they said you have to know all about your characters. You have to know them inside out. I thought it would have been a bit of pin money for me. I never got started. I wanted an exotic location, so I got a batch of brochures from Thomas Cook and pored over them for hours. I still have the tape somewhere, would you like it?"

They looked at me and I smiled. Janice, the woman in charge, said she hoped they'd been some help to me. And maybe I should look for jobs—perhaps in publishing—in the back pages of the Times Literary Supplement.

WALKING HOME I WONDERED IF I COULD GET A JOB IN A RECORD SHOP. But David had said that in the interview they ask you about current bands and records and really, I knew nothing. I only knew the things I liked, and they were all old things, or things that weren't popular.

I stood outside his Megastore and wondered if I should go in. I could pretend I was after a form for casual staff. It would be something to write on my slip for the DSS, to prove that I was making an effort. David might think I was chasing after him. Let him phone me instead.

I went next door to the Body Shop, where they had a vacancy for part-time work. It was like stepping into our Linda's world, considering a job in a shop like that. I walked home, thinking dreamily about facial scrubs and eye gels.

ALL THAT WEEK THERE WAS NO PHONE CALL FROM DAVID. HE LED A BUSY life, Wendy told herself. And so did she, she added.

In the Scarlet Empress one day she saw his friend Rab, sitting opposite his daschund, who got a chair to himself. Rab was writing in a notebook, barely stopping to tap out his cigarette ash. Wendy said hullo and broke his spell.

"I've had this sentence going on for almost twelve hours non-stop," he said crossly. "Now I've lost its thread."

Rab was, he explained, a master of convoluted sub-clauses. He wanted to write a book-length something, maybe a novel, that was all one sentence. Wendy rolled her eyes. Everyone was at it.

"You're the girl from that night," he said, staring at her. His eyes were still jerking left to right, she noticed. Wendy tried to see what he had written, but it looked like scrawl. "Dave's wanted to phone you," he said smugly. The daschund yapped at this, as if Rab was giving away secrets. "But he thought you had gone off him. You and your mate, the little queer fella, upped and left at the crack of dawn. Dave didn't get out of bed till tea time."

"I left him a nice note."

Rab shrugged.

Wendy sighed. "Tell him I don't hate him. Tell him to phone me."

"You phone him." Rab was still wearing that tea cosy hat. She wondered if he was bald. "Listen," said Rab. "He's a nice fella. I'm only saying this because I know him and I don't know you. He's too nice for you to go messing him about."

Wendy drew back. "I'll phone him, all right?"

Rab nodded and went back to figuring out where his sentence was going.

It must be a city of words, thought Wendy, ordering herself some more coffee. A city where everybody wanted to be writing. The streets of the New Town seemed clear-cut and easily cryptic as a crossword, but the intrigues and the endlessly elastic sentences of the people who lived here ran any which way they wanted.

"YOU'RE A LOVELY GIRL," SAID CAPTAIN SIMON TO HER ONE NIGHT WHEN she walked into the kitchen to fetch a glass of water. "A really lovely girl. Isn't she, Pat?"

Uncle Pat twinkled. "Apple of my eye."

"You shouldn't be drinking booze, Uncle Pat. Not on top of your pills."

"Listen to how she thinks about me!" cried Uncle Pat, as if she had said something startling. "See, Simon! That's the kind of woman you want.

A thoughtful woman like that."

"I've done with the female of the species," said Captain Simon.

"Pish," said Uncle Pat. "It's never too late to enjoy a pretty face around the place. Your sister's a fine woman. Where's she tonight?"

Captain Simon chuckled. "She's gotten the hang of my telescope. She's sworn on pain of death to treat it kind. I left her star-gazing. She'll be happy for hours."

BELINDA SAW SOMETHING IN THE NIGHT SKY OVER CALTON HILL. SHE was certain of it. That very night she got the knack of mastering the telescope, its beautiful, brassy complexity: she looked up into the orange-tinged sky and saw exactly what she had been looking for.

All in the eye of the beholder, Wendy might have told her. You were looking at the world with strange-tinted glasses.

Nevertheless, excitably, Belinda stole into the flat above. Everything came right for her that night. The door melted before her. She was a ghost, slipping inside, and up the spiral staircase, to shake Wendy, her accomplice, awake.

Belinda could still see the impression, the blaze of light across her eyes as she watched Wendy stir herself.

"This is your chance," she told the girl. "To see the proof that they exist. The visitors! And to prove I'm not bananas after all."

What she really meant, thought Wendy, dressing hurriedly in the curious dark-before-dawn, was that this was her chance, Belinda's chance, to find the proof in the pudding.

Up Calton Hill in the middle of the night.

They staggered into the creeping dark of the Royal Circus, and found themselves a cab with its yellow light on. The gods are on my side, thought Belinda gleefully.

To the base of the hill. They hopped out at the Scottish Parliament buildings and they set off, up the slow, spiraling path. Belinda led Wendy, sure that the next bend in the rocky, gravelly path would give her evidence. Something had come here tonight. Belinda's shoes were white with rock dust in the gathering light. All they could hear was the slither of gravel under Wendy's boots. The light was turning blue.

They could see the observatory, unmanned, staring out over the town, and the docks to the north. A thousand trees bristled round the base of the hill.

Belinda, in hushed tones, started to explain one of her theories.

"It is the reason that the space men were attracted to Marlene. They already knew of her and her luminous beauty. Celebrity travels further, you see. Sound waves, light waves, space waves from our planet, from the television and radio, travel forever, until they encounter the other people, far away. The space people know about our celebrities first, well before they know about ordinary old us. They know nothing about our struggles. But I got gathered up by accident, in a female job-lot with Marlene. I was their only clue to what everyone else in the world is like! And they're coming back for me."

They paused for a rest on the terraced path leading down to London Road. Wendy wondered how long she could leave it before telling Belinda that there was absolutely nothing here.

"There are people," said Belinda suddenly. "Standing against that wall. A line of them, look, with spaces inbetween. Men."

They both stared and, instinctively clutching each other, started to walk towards the gathering.

"They saw it, too!" said Belinda happily. "See!"

As they drew closer they saw that the men were standing singly. They made for one burly man standing by a lamp. He looked perplexed by them as they approached. Belinda wasn't shy.

"Are you here for the UFOs too?" she called, saying it all in one word—yoofo's—like Americans do. The man gave her a sickly smile. He looked straight past the pair of them.

Wendy looked sideways, at the next man along the wall. She saw another join him. And she realised.

"Let's leave them to it, Belinda," and started to walk away.

"But...but if they're having one of them Close Encounters..."

"I don't think you want to be part of it."

Wendy led her friend gently but firmly down the hill, and onto London road, through a knot of more men, drifting about in the dawn. She flagged them down another cab.

On the terraced pathway, with his back against the rough wall, an astonished Colin watched his cousin and their neighbour leave the hill behind. Colin was having the erect and oddly tapering cock end of a shy boy called Gary pushed into the hole he'd worn in the crotch of his favourite jeans. The hole hadn't been worn on purpose, and nor had the jeans: this was an ad hoc al fresco adventure.

Colin, against the wall, hadn't taken a single breath since he had seen Belinda and Wendy straggling over the grassy brow of the hill, coming towards him. As he realised who they were, he thought, how light and blue the light is becoming, just as Gary's thin hard cock jammed its whole way into his jeans. And suddenly it was very squashed in there.

Colin imagined that Belinda would come straight over. The boy would yelp, filch himself out of Colin's jeans, and hare off, down the crunchy gravel decline. Belinda and Wendy would barrel up to him. "Fancy seeing you here! Did we scare your friend off?" Belinda would be huffing and puffing in the dark, disconcerting the other men around them, and causing them to drift off.

But Wendy and Belinda had gone. They had taken one look and hurried away again. They hadn't even seen me, thought Colin, as Gary suddenly made him spunk up into the dark grass. His come hung amongst the dew like cuckoo spit.

TWENTY

I want a dirty old man
who'll cover me with his dirty kisses
and his floppy old skin
I'll soothe his wrinkled brow
and cheeks and arms and legs
I'll let him shuffle about me
indulge me
let him Lolita me

CAPTAIN SIMON WAS HANGING ABOUT WENDY THESE DAYS. EVEN THOUGH his pal, the oldest man in the building, was in hospital, the Captain kept coming upstairs for his coffee.

Winter months now and they drank milky coffee laced with whiskey, with Glemorangie from Jenners. They drank it with the stove crackling away in the kitchen and it was acrid and smoky. They watched the snow patter against their window above the dark trees of the Royal Circus.

Captain Simon was paying court to her in a charming, chatty old way.

He and Aunty Anne ignored each other and nothing more was said about it. When she stumped into the kitchen in her winter-thickness woolly gown, it was tied tighter and secure and she brushed straight past the Captain. Poured her tea, fried her bacon, lit her first cigarette saying, "Good morning cigarettes, good morning Wendy." Captain Simon would lower his head until she was gone, singing, down the still bare-boarded hallway into the bathroom. The tiles in there were new. Colin had ordered them and seen them cemented into place, all around their bath. Golden and every one mirrored. Aunty Anne sat herself in a scented, herbal, foamy tub each morning and wiped condensation from each small mirror in turn. She glared into them and told herself she was a handsome and voluptuous woman and never more so than now. Her hair was back in its basic, Liz Taylor black. Challenged, aloofy, queenly: Liz Taylor is who she settled on being.

"Your Aunty despises me," Captain Simon said.

"You were a bit unfair with her," Wendy told him.

He looked sheepish. "You know about that then?"

"Aunty Anne tells me everything," Wendy lied.

Sometimes she would look at the Captain and wonder if anything Belinda said about him was true. If he was indeed a replacement of some sort, and not the genuine article, not the original old man, then perhaps he was something else underneath. But he was a hard nut to crack. He came for coffee, made polite conversation, and looked at her.

All had gone quiet downstairs in the Belinda camp. She hadn't seen any more lights in the sky. She had even given up looking. Captain Simon said that she'd done something to his prized telescope, had altered its delicate mechanisms, and he wouldn't let her use it again. Belinda had become somewhat cool towards Wendy, though Wendy couldn't think what she'd done to offend her.

Then one day Wendy was heading up to the top flat and Belinda poked her head out of her front door. Her face was red, cheeks crazed with broken veins and her white hair stood on end so Wendy knew she'd been running her hands through it, as she did when she was perturbed and thinking furiously. The half can of hairspray she emptied into it each morning would make her hair stick like that, ravelled into a thoughtful knot.

Belinda had very finely-tuned ears and she could tell who was coming up the stone steps by their individual treads.

"I've got something you ought to read," she told Wendy and led her inside the flat she shared with her brother. Please, Wendy thought, don't let it be another magazine about UFO sightings. In the past few months Wendy had had newsletters of many dubious sorts pushed under her nose.

Wendy sat herself on the faded chintz, while Belinda rushed off to the kitchen, calling out that she'd prepared some lunch, and would Wendy like some?

The flat was decorated with the kind of ornaments you had to order from the back pages of Sunday colour supplements. Belinda would be paying this lot off in monthly instalments for years to come. Crinolined ladies twirling their brollies and clutching pink roses, plates on special hangers printed with Highland scenes, with Royalty, with the cast of *Star Trek*. On the dresser there were three china babies, life-sized, slumping in a huddle, eyelids squeezed shut, all three dressed in knitted outfits.

Belinda emerged with a tray of chicken kebabs and urged Wendy to dab them into a peanutty sauce she herself had 'blended from scratch'. The sauce fizzed with heat. Wendy wasn't hungry (she never was after a session at Job Party) but she ate them anyway, prising off the sticky meat with her fingers first and making a great show of enjoying it all. When Belinda jumped up and suggested they wash it down with a Martini, Wendy had to say no nicely. She knew to be careful around Belinda. Like many pale people, her thin-skinnedness meant that her feelings rose up easily to the surface. You could see in terrible close up sometimes what was going on inside Belinda and so it wasn't worth hurting her feelings.

Eventually, finished her own drink, she straightened up and Wendy heard her fat knees give an almighty crack. "Now, read this," Belinda said, and made her friend put down a half-eaten kebab and gave her a few sheets of paper. A letter.

> My dear Belinda,
>
> Our friend Wendy has done us a great service—she's brought us together by accident—bless her heart. I'll confess now that I thought she was having me on when her first

letters arrived and she told me she was getting you to write to me. And when I got your letters I thought it was a big piss-take. I thought you were a fruit loop and Wendy had set me up. But now I know it was clever young Wendy bringing us together. She must have seen the many points of contact we have! When I read you I can hear your speaking voice. I can hear you in my head. I feel I know everything about you.

So... blessings on Wendy's head. She's made an amazing difference to my life. I believe in new things in my life and love the people who bring them to me. I believe in something new coming true.

Today I read all twenty-seven of your letters again and you were as large as life once more. I have your whole life story. When I read you it pans out once more.

Now I have just re-read this letter so far and it's very urgent, isn't it? I've never written in this tone to you before. I have to let it all out, though. Last night I sat on bench on Blackpool Promenade, read you and thought it through. I sat till late on, till the crowds thinned out and I realised I was falling in love with you.

I never believed in the people who fell in love through letters. I used to laugh at the people who fell for prisoners on Death Row. The granny who made her ten year old granddaughter write to a serial killer and how all three found themselves besotted. I thought those people were deluded. They'd drummed their better sense into submission with their banal, secretive, confessional notes. And yet I believe in writing, don't I? I always felt you could seduce with writing and that you could be seduced. Why only when it's folded up between printed covers? Why not when the pages come hand-written, hand-posted and smelling faintly of the sweat of the writer's brow, fingers, palms? Their saliva *swalk*ing the envelope's gum. I never thought that someone would seduce me like that.

You've got me over a barrel. I can't work. In the fish shop

I turn all butter fingers, dropping things and the floor is filthy. I can't write anything apart from letters to you. I draft them laboriously, waiting to jam-pack them with images of different colours, to send you flashy prose that will ring bells when you slit open my envelopes. What material you send me, what an inner life you have. I copy out your letters and try to insert myself between your lines. I read and wait for your face to come up from beneath the surface of your writing. You must be in there somewhere: the real, bodily you.

When I try to pin you down, you're gone.

Something in here makes me want to read more and more of you. Devour every scrap of you. Send me your shopping lists, your jottings, your memoranda! I would breakfast on your ephemera, your idle thoughts and sighs. For lunch I would break open your diaries, your considered day-to-dayness. All afternoon I would snack on your poems, keeping a dish of stanzas by my side as I worked. In the evening, however, I would feast myself on your body of prose. Your life's work would be my rich pickings till dawn: supper and dessert lying heavy on me all night.

Can you believe all this, Belinda?
Girl,
you've gone and turned my head.
Tell me the rest now
Tell me what you look like
All my love,
Timon.

Wendy stared at Belinda. "What have you been sending him?"

"Nothing special. He asked about my life, my history. You know, all about the events leading up to my... abduction, and then afterwards. My life now."

"You've made him fall in love with you." Wendy rattled the paper. "He loves you!"

Belinda shook her head, sighing. "He certainly comes over as keen."

"Keen!" said Wendy. "He's gone crackers."

Belinda took the letter back. "All of that about me. It arrived this morning." She folded it back up.

Wendy's mind was racing. "What are you going to do about it?"

"But that's just it," said Belinda. "I'm sure he means well. I feel awful." She sat down carefully. "It's as if I've laid him a trap and the poor boy's walked into it. And I haven't laid him a trap! I haven't."

"He's half your age," said Wendy.

"And look at me. He hasn't got a clue."

"He wants to know what you look like. You'll have to tell him."

"I can't. Who can love me when I look like this? All the weight I've been putting on. I'm a massive woman now." Through the winter months Belinda had been eating steadily, as if building herself up to face winter. Wendy felt ashamed of herself, seeing how upset Belinda was. Yet she still wanted to goad the woman into proving the discrepancy between Belinda-here and Belinda-in-the-letters. She couldn't think what had got into Timon. She had never heard him go on like that before and she couldn't help feeling suspicious. In the past Timon always claimed he was immune to love. He was the watcher, the sideliner, the self-determined wallflower watching the dancers. Love left him cold, he said: he thought it was a sickness. He claimed never to have entertained a romantic thought. Nothing turned him on. His body was an assemblage of parts that would respond readily to the usual stimuli, but he was rarely inside it. Wendy remembered his detached look. The way that night on the sands at Blackpool he had looked down at himself, at his smooth tight belly and his cock like it was someone else's as he let Wendy look him over and take him in her hands. She felt jealous, plainly and simply, now that Timon was letting himself out of control.

"He thinks he isn't deluded," said Belinda. "And maybe he's not. But one sight of me would cure him."

"Don't make yourself miserable about it."

"I've got to nip it in the bud."

"Doesn't he know how old you are? Haven't you said anything about what you're like?"

"Of course I have. The letters are all about me."

"Then maybe he knows what you're like."

"I missed things out, of course. There are gaps."

Wendy realised then that it was these gaps Timon had fallen for. The holes in Belinda's story and her account of herself had lured him.

"Do I put a stop to this?"

Wendy felt like saying yes, of course she should. But that would be out of her own selfishness. That would mean she herself would be fighting over Timon. She didn't want that so she said, "No, write to him again. Tell him the full story. Put him in the picture."

Belinda's face crumpled. "That's a good as saying, tell him to take a hike."

PUT HIM IN THE PICTURE.

When Wendy left Belinda had an idea. She opened the dark wood dresser and hunted through boxes of letters from other people, magazines, scrapbooks of clippings (about Marlene, about the Visitors) until she unearthed a particular photograph album. Lime green, ring bound, picture of the Mona Lisa looking smug on the front. Old family and friends, mostly Polaroids, which were faded now, given an extra sheen of poignancy by the fact they hadn't lasted any longer than fifteen years. Half these faces she hardly recognised. A family gathering for the Royal Wedding in 1981. Here she was. Somewhat younger, somewhat slimmer, in a patriotic frock she had stitched from cut-up flags. A painted Union Jack bowler hat on her head. I look deranged on this, she thought. I can't send him one of me looking like Britannia, pissed and deplorable.

The thought nudged at her, that maybe she oughtn't feel so bad. Not to be too hard on herself. Timon was a sensitive soul: a careful, beautiful man. Surely, to fall so helplessly in love, he already knew all about her. Her outwardness was just a covering for everything he adored and he would love that too, because that was part of her.

She flipped the thick album pages. Here was cousin Christine at twenty-six. With raven hair about her shoulders and those flashy blue eyes. She was holding an exotic drink up in toast to the photographer. Belinda unpeeled the sticky film, and out came cousin Christine. She hurried to her writing table before she lost her nerve.

ON THE BUS TO THE INFIRMARY THAT AFTERNOON WENDY MULLED over the letter she would send to Timon. She would be interfering. Too right she would. She'd be sticking her nose in where it wasn't wanted.

The more she thought about it the clearer it seemed. Now she was sure that what Timon saw in Belinda was raw material. She was a slab of pink flesh that had him drooling. Not for your usual reasons, mind you. He saw her as a repository of stories. Of hare-brained, crackpot tales that were all the more delicious for the ardent way Belinda believed every word of them. Wendy remembered how she had felt compelled to listen to Belinda those afternoons in the launderette, with Astrid urging the story on. We're all in this together, thought Wendy sadly, goading Belinda to make a fool of herself.

As the bus pulled up by the infirmary, the black Victorian, turreted castle in which her uncle was whiling his sickness away, Wendy was thinking that what she really wanted to do was read the twenty-seven letters Belinda had sent Timon. What had she been telling him? All of that flying saucer stuff? Since when was Timon in love with alien stories?

Then she put the whole lot out of her mind as she went off to buy carnations to take to her uncle. She wondered if he'd find Belinda's doings amusing. It was hard work, filling the two hours with chat every day.

WHEN WE TOOK THE OLD MAN TO HOSPITAL HE WAS IN TERRIBLE PAIN. For weeks he had been covering it up, with his bluff smiles and his mockery at our concern. Eventually we persuaded him we should call him a taxi and get him to Casualty. It was a Saturday morning. Aunty Anne, Colin and I waited in a green waiting room with the chairs bolted into the cement floor. We watched a drama going on for an American family of four. They were only here for a few days and the eldest daughter had clonked her head on a pavement in Teviot Square, rollerblading with the shirtless show-off boys. As they waited to heAr how concussed she was the mother sobbed and their youngest played a bleepy, percussive computer game. Meanwhile the nurses were undressing Uncle Pat, lying him under blankets he said reminded him of baby blankets, they were so blue. They pushed and prodded at his stomach again and he told them he was due to see the consultant next Thursday. He'd been good: he was waiting out his turn. He was only here today because his family had forced him to come. They fret, he said apologetically. The nurses went off to find him a bed on a relevant ward. They told him—and then they told us—that they were keeping him in.

AUNTY ANNE WAS THINKING, WE SHOULD HAVE BROUGHT HIM EARLIER. She was expected to get a good telling off from the doctors when they came to see her. They should know what it's like, though. Aunty Anne knew: she'd had her own health problems, and she'd put going to the hospital off and off indefinitely. Eventually she'd end up thinking, I'm in too much pain for this to be normal. Do I qualify as an emergency yet? Even when Pat's pain got that bad—and she could still read him plainly, as if there was still a link between them—he didn't want to bother the nice people at Accidents and Emergencies. The previous weekend he had queued for his GP, who tutted and hmmed and sympathised like anything. Weeks had been going by. Weeks between tests and more tests. The pain would abate for a while, then return redoubled in the middle of the night. But time flies, doesn't it? Especially when you're older. We'll have you seeing the consultant again in no time. The GP patted the old man's knee.

How you got used to pain. And you won't go on about it, because it gets boring. Who wants to hear the gripes and moans of an old man? They're expected to be like that, and Pat didn't want to live that out. He kept mum as much as he could about the pain his folded-in, ruinous insides gave him. And I let him do that, thought Aunty Anne, shocked by herself. I let him go about like that, getting worse and worse. We all did.

IN WARD TEN, WHERE ALL THE PATIENTS WERE WAITING FOR ACUTE Surgery, the bed sheets were pink like blancmange and the curtains were a streaky green, the same green as the pyjamas given to the man who was meant to be in the bed next to Uncle Pat. He was rarely where the nurses put him. He told Pat that it was when they got you into bed that they had you where they wanted you. This pot-bellied neighbour hobbled around his bed all day, ignoring the nurses and the three old women who came to visit, bringing books about the war. Uncle Pat couldn't tell which woman was his wife. Still standing, his neighbour listened to the woman gassing and he pointed to the picture of the ship on which he had served. "It's famous then!" said one of the old women. He went back to looking for things in his bedside locker, and checking the level on his bottle of dilute orange. A tube led out of his pyjama fronts and hooked into a bag of custardy pee, which swayed on a small wheeled rack at his feet. This he tugged along after him carelessly. "Watch your... little bag," one of the old women warned.

"It's all right," he said. "It's firmly attached." To prove the point he gave his bag a sharp kick.

It depressed Uncle Pat looking around the ward too much. The floor had black and white tiles and the room smelled—as he had once gloomily anticipated—of flowers, gravy and shit. "It's all bums this week," the sister had informed him happily. "You're all in for your bowels down this end." Uncle Pat lay and stared at the ceiling and eavesdropped on the next bed.

Until Wendy arrived with her carnations. She kissed him on his white hair, which looked almost yellow on the pillow.

"You should get me put down. I reckon they should put all old people down when they get to be a burden on the State."

Wendy thought of the last time she came visiting with Aunty Anne. Her aunt, aghast, standing on the NHS lino, going: "And you a millionaire! A millionaire in a room with twenty other bodies! As far as I can see, a millionaire is obliged to go private!"

Uncle Pat was looking up and down the ward. He hated chuntering on like he was doing now, especially when Wendy was here, giving up her time. Yet he couldn't help it. She arrived and he started to speak and it all came rushing out. "Look at these old buggers in here. I get this cruel streak, you know, all over me, when I looked at them. That old woman over there, opposite, getting propped up by the male nurse. She can't even sit up to get her pills. They have to hold her till they go all the way down. I think it's cruel, keeping her alive. What's she got to look forward to?"

Wendy wanted to rally him and make him feel more optimistic. Then he blocked her by shifting the subject. He started talking about old people's Homes. The places you got shoved into when there wasn't much hope. Wendy tried to say that needn't worry him now. His money put him out of reach of anyone else. It could save him.

"You could be one of those wily, rich old men. Who own islands and wear silk cravats and sailor caps. The ones who marry bimbos eighty years younger than themselves and get into the papers. With your money you could end up a father again at a hundred and three!"

"That's just grotesque," he smiled weakly.

Her uncle was a winner late in life. His millions had come too late to make him comfortable. Getting put away with everyone else was still a fresh fear.

"I've got a scheme, you know," he said with sudden relish. "For a much cheaper old people's Home. Do you want to hear it?"

She wasn't sure that she did.

"I reckon that they could save money by cutting their heads off. They could transplant three heads onto one old body. What do they do now? Bicker and do jigsaws. It would save space. I can see the day when they'll do that. At first the idea appals you, but they'd sell it as a good, modern concept and pretty soon we'd all be saying, ooh, yes, it's sensible really. Three heads are wiser than one, and all. Three sharing one old body's pain. And we'll have old people with three heads. Or maybe three brains in one huge, old skull. Like the Mekon, in a dressing gown."

"Who's the Mekon?" Wendy asked.

"Don't you know who the Mekon is?"

She shook her head.

"Eeh, lass," he smiled. "What about Dan Dare? Whatever happened to Dan Dare?"

Wendy didn't know what to say.

"I know, I know. He's my age, and pulling his pee around after him, in a plastic carton on wheels."

TWENTY-ONE

Dear Wendy,

I'm having a kiddie. That's given you a turn, hasn't it? I've just fiddled on with the litmus test that I bought from Boots, dabbing it in my wee. You're the first person I've told—Aunty Wendy. I want you to be a crazy, maddening Aunty like our Aunty Anne. I've decided that's what you'll be. By the time you get this I'll have told Daniel too, so technically, you won't be the first.

A sprog. A fucking sprog. That'll put the tin lid on my degree as well.

And I was getting it sorted, too. Maybe next year, starting here, in Women's Studies. I've been getting to know people on campus. I've talked to them in the white plastic, smoky luxury of the Nelson Mandela coffee bar. I look at them and think, I can do what you do. I can think the things you think.

I've bought this shaggy black coat from Oxfam. I look

like a bear in it. I sit on the mini bus and ride through town to campus and hug my secret to me. Really I've known for weeks I was going to have this sprog. I feel quite cool about it. I can see me, sitting on that bus in my furry, ratty old coat with a pushchair, a snotty kid on my lap.

There's a Professor here. I'm making a bit of extra money proofreading his opus. A book on the eighteenth century Gothic. Daniel got me the gig. He knows how finickety I am. I take a chapter at a time from the Professor's office and at home I go line by line through his patient descriptions of ghosts and ghouls, his tender accounts of eviscerations and beheadings. I pick open his typos and his inconsistencies and mark them all down. A doddle, as you'd say. He's a shaggy old professor, dark and messy as my new coat.

He's going to look at my first short story and give me his expert opinion. He promised to. Did I tell you I'd written a story? I've caught the bug. It's very short. Maybe not very good. Don't tell Timon. He'd rip me to pieces.

My baby is the size of a comma. An errant piece of punctuation, holding my life up. But I reckon I'll keep it. Let that sentence develop. Give birth to something, at any rate.

Lots of love to you, Aunty Wendy!

For your soon-to-be-fat, fecund and best sister,

Mandy.

WHILE I HADN'T HEARD A THING FROM THISTLE STREET, FROM MY trendy Megastore boy, David, it turned out that behind my back Colin had been going round there. He and David and the bloke in the funny hat were now firm friends. "I need some straight friends my own age," Colin told me later. "Life is separatist enough." I tutted. He blamed me for his seeking friendship elsewhere. While I was talking with Belinda, visiting his father, racking my brains as to Timon's motives, Colin was clambering up the fire escape in Thistle Street, playing records and eating pasta and pulses with the vegetarian boys. He was telling them, "It's the fire escape that makes this place. It makes it something special coming here." On their fourth storey platform they were cultivating herbs and potted flowers. "Normal steps leading up here would make it just like anywhere. The fire escape makes it all into a film."

Rab looked up from his latest unending sentence and agreed with him, even though he could never catch his breath when he got to the top.

"I'm thinking of moving out to my own place," Colin told me. "Maybe up a fire escape." Yet I knew he wouldn't. He tried to look as if he didn't care about his father's illnesss. On the day the old man was due to be opened up and looked at, Colin was waiting there with us for results.

Colin said to me, "David wants to see you. He thinks you hate him for being a lousy shag."

"He wasn't!" I said, but I didn't phone him up. I thought I was going off men. Colin was welcome to them. Maybe he was working on seducing David or Rab. By all accounts they were generally too stoned to notice anything.

And all this while my sister was pregnant. I wanted to go and see her. There was no word yet from her about how Daniel had taken the news. Something told me he wouldn't be best pleased. He was the selfish sort.

I wanted to go down to Lancaster, to help her buy things in Mothercare. But they were taking Uncle Pat into theatre, drugging him and making him say the alphabet backwards. They said he'd be a right mess inside, all his various scans had disclosed that much. They wanted to see what was in there, what was nestling dark and busily against his bowels. When I imagined him going gently off to sleep, dreaming that they could cut the badness out of him, it was that trustingness that held me in Edinburgh. I had to be there for him. Beneath his bluster and mordant humour, he had far more trust in doctors that I did.

It was cancer-cancer-cancer and I'd already seen that once this year.

I WANTED TO GIVE TIMON THE BENEFIT OF THE DOUBT. I THOUGHT OF HIM as the friend of my youth. That pushed him a long way back in time and to hear that he had turned wicked, had been exploitative all along, really pained me. I decided to believe that he had fallen in love with Belinda. I always wanted to believe the best of my friends.

Belinda certainly believed in him. In those chillier days, when we set about wearing heavier and greater layers of clothes, when the windows each morning were mapped with careful lines of frost, she had apparently lost her anxiety. A new confidence overcame her. Her face shone: winter was her element, I realised. Summer slowed her and in the heat she had to drag herself around the place. November saw her nimble and sure-footed. Her correspondence with my friend went on. And meanwhile, I heard very little from Timon. He wrote me a card for Hallowe'en.

> Since when was I in love with alien stories?
>
> Oh, it isn't that. It isn't what I love Belinda for. What do you take me for, Wendy?
>
> She writes to me full of trust. She writes as if I don't even exist. I'm a patient ear listening to her telling me things she's never told anyone. It isn't material. I would never consider it that. It's a gift to me. Given with her whole heart. No one's ever given me anything like that before. I love Belinda because she's honest without knowing that's what she's doing.

Wendy wondered then if it was Timon who was being taken in. He was being reeled in by Belinda's easy tale-telling. Wendy didn't swallow his view of Belinda as honest and trusting. Who knew the woman better? Belinda had the measure of Timon. She was seducing him with an effortless, flattering attention. Thirty-four letters now, he told Wendy. He was in love with Belinda's imagination, her world-view, her determination to divide the world into replacements and holograms.

AND WHICH AM I, BELINDA? HE ASKED HER ONCE.

Her reply came back: 'Don't be either, Timon. I don't want you to be either real-fake or fake-real. Both types spend their energy on seeming genuine. I want you to give me all your energy instead.'

WENDY WROTE TO HIM: "BUT DO YOU BELIEVE IN HER VISITORS? HOW can you love a woman you think is mad?"

He said he would believe in whatever her picture of the world was like. He wrote:

'I always understood that these visitors weren't absolutely real, in the everyday, measurable, empirical sense. (Sorry, they may yet be real, for all I know, and eventually we could have to get used to the everyday sight of visitors walking up and down the high street. But not yet.) I always understood, I think, that these visitors were the stuff of metaphor, and realised as such by the people who longed for them to come. They were sticky, cobwebby stuff, vaguely associative and from the same source as our collective feelings about things beyond what we can touch. It used to be stars, stars of Hollywood musicals, that we dreamed about, and before that, saints.

'I don't know what the difference is between visitors and stars. We use the idea of them to the same ends. At least, I think, Belinda does. It's why I love her story of being kidnapped with Marlene Dietrich. The visitors taking out Dietrich's womb and Belinda's womb and hoarding them in their spacecraft's freezers. It's an image that appals and delights me. Belinda has made me see herself and Marlene swishing in white furs up and down the impersonal Escherlike corridors of that visitor craft. I can see them pausing to peer out of a portal, at the permanent twilight of the Polar Cap. Belinda has made it all natural to me.

'She has this view of the sublime—of everything that exists beyond herself—and written herself into it. That woman's got guts.'

I HAD NEVER HEARD BEFORE THE DETAIL OF BELINDA'S AND MARLENE'S twin hysterectomies. With each telling the story became more lurid.

I decided to try common sense. To Timon I scribbled a note:

'I don't care if you believe in space men or not. Just lay off Belinda. She's vulnerable and could do without falling for the likes of you.'

NEXT MORNING BELINDA CAME TO ME LOOKING EXCITED, FRIGHTENED, and as if she had been crying. She had another of those postcards showing a yellow, almond-eyed alien.

"He's coming here!" she chattered. "He's coming to see us all. Writing can only go so far, he says. He wants to see me!"

Timon was about to become Belinda's visitor.

TWENTY-TWO

IF SHE SAT BACK AND ENJOYED THE LATER AFTERNOON HERE, THE JAZZ they were playing over the café speakers, the sun slanting in and lighting up the pink chalices of the lilies on her table, Aunty Anne could almost imagine she was here out of choice. But this was the hundred minutes or so between visiting hours at the Royal Infirmary. She was attending both hours today and so, when the first was up, she had found herself blinking outside the stark black frontage of the hospital, and decided to while her time in the smart café across the road.

She ordered quickly, and was given fat poached eggs on toast soaked through with salty butter. Flecks of parsley had been thrown over the whole lot, over the crisped bacon, too. Looking round at what others were being served, it seemed that this was the habit of the kitchen here: they shook a handful of green bits over everything. She ate hungrily, digging into the soft yellow bulge of her egg. Under the heavy knife is felt like an eye. She mashed a spiky, decorative tomato into the toast, enjoying the spoiling of the dish, reducing it to yellow smears and black crumbs.

Pat had said he might try for a little nap during her absence. The sister of his side ward said that, if she really wanted, Anne could stay all afternoon with her husband. But they decided it was best if she went away and came back a little later, refreshed and full of new topics of conversation. What they didn't want, after all, was to be sat staring at each other while they were on the ward.

At about this time they'd be bringing food round on a trolley. They would give him his two usual cardboard cartons: one of a clear brown soup, the other, a runny, raspberry jelly. Pat said it was a very strange thing, not to feel at all hungry. He was letting the drips in his arms, the snaking tubes that punctured his wrists in tiny bites, do all his feeding for him. Anne watched him take a mouthful of the purple jelly and its tartness surprised and repulsed him. After only a week he was out of the habit of tasting things.

Anne had asked his named-nurse Sandra, a big girl who wore her apron tied too high on her waist, what time opening hours would be finishing tonight. Sandra laughed at her. "Opening hours! Like a shop!" Anne coloured and tried to smile. She was only asking because she would have to catch the store later one. There was nothing to eat in the flat. With the old man gone it had become like a poor person's flat, with nothing in the fridge and no one willing to phone up delivery services or takeaways to bring them mobile banquets in cardboard packages on the back of motorcycles. "Banquet for six, sir!" These last few weeks Pat had developed a passion for home-delivered Chinese food. He said he liked it because it never took much chewing or digesting. He wouldn't be getting anything like that in the Infirmary, not sticky spicy ribs or duck in plum sauce. He seemed to be lapping up the attention, though, now that he was on the post-operative ward. The nurse who had seen to him on the previous ward kept on dropping by to see how he was keeping.

They had opened him up and looked around inside for over an hour. His skin was tent-pegged open. Afterwards the surgeon had told Pat and Anne that they had stapled him back together—thirteen aluminium staples—without touching a thing inside. He was sent back to the world like a wrong delivery. They were going to try other methods, the surgeon said.

Anne hated seeing him treated the same as everyone else. When the elderly woman volunteer with the too-even teeth came cackling round with her bread trolley, Anne thought that Pat would be getting steaming, soft rolls from a local bakery. Instead the woman took a slice of brown from a plastic bag and wrapped it in a paper napkin for him. He's a millionaire! Anne wanted to shout. He doesn't want your rotten bread.

What had Anne brought him? Flowers once or twice, then the horrible mistake, the first time she visited, of unloading a bagful of sweets on his bed: *Rolos, Polos, Curly-Wurlies.* They'd been stashed away in a drawer because he couldn't eat them and he pulled them out for his other, hungry visitors. She'd even brought him an early Christmas Selection Box.

Maybe, she thought, I can pop by Tesco Metro tonight, if I get out early enough. Get a few essentials. She thought of buying Chinese cook-in sauces and spring rolls, giving the kids a treat, so they could eat like they did when Pat was home.

After a while she felt out of place in the café. Her tatty yellow coat was attracting attention from the staff, as was the bag of sharp green cuttings the named-nurse had pruned expertly from the flowers Anne had brought, insisting that they be taken home and planted, to come up good as new next year.

Everyone else in the café was young, good-looking, affluent. Anne felt like an old sheep sat there in her good winter coat. She went back to the Infirmary, determined to ask someone in charge how long before he could come home to wait for their so-called other methods.

"He's had a mishap," the nurse, Sandra, told Anne when she returned to the ward. There was no sign of Pat, but she could see the tell-tale snail-trail that went from the side ward to the patient toilet. She had dodged it on the way in and she came hoping that it wasn't Pat's. The shit was runny and dark and it smelled like old people's shit, like something held too long in the body. Years ago Anne had worked in an old people's Home, just menial business, and this brought it all flooding back.

Very clearly the thought came to her, as she watched the nurse set to work cleaning up the mess, that she was going to lose Pat all over again.

Because she kept thinking this, and because he, scrubbed and wearing crisp new pyjamas, felt abashed after his accident, they took a while finding things to say to each other in this session.

At last she said, "Colin seems to have found some new friends. We don't see a lot of him in the flat."

"Good," said Pat. "He'll need new friends."

"Wendy hasn't seen that boy again. She's moping about a lot. That Belinda woman depressed her. She depresses me. But Wendy won't tell her to keep away."

"Belinda's heart is in the right place."

"Did you hear that she thinks the aliens are after her?"

Pat said tiredly, "I heard something like that. It's good she's got an interest."

Aunty Anne rolled her eyes. "That brother of hers is always on about outer space as well. They're both cracked."

Pat smiled. "Simon told me that his sister is convinced that he isn't himself. She's accused him a couple of times of being a replacement for the old Captain Simon."

"See? I wouldn't want to live alone with her."

"She's harmless," Pat grimaced, wanting to slide a little further down the bed. His wife flapped around him as he eased himself painfully into place. "God, that hurts when I move. I asked Simon if Belinda could be right. Do you know what he said?"

Anne shook her head.

"He said, 'Pat, bugger knows if I've been replaced. You'd think I'd be the first to know, wouldn't you? But Belinda reckons she's right. She thinks I'm trying so hard to be the real me that I've convinced even myself.' That's what he said."

Anne shuddered. "That kind of talk gives me the creeps, I must say."

"It fits, though, doesn't it? Do you feel like the same person you've always been? I'm not sure I do. I think I've got a memory of always being the same, but it takes very little thinking to put doubts into my head."

"That's just change. That's growing old." She was impatient suddenly. "And anyway, there's more changes happen to a woman in a woman's life than happen in a man's. Captain Simon should shut his trap. He knows nothing."

Pat said thoughtfully, "Changes go on inside all of us."

When their time was up she found that it was raining, at first softly, soothingly, then with increasing violence. The plastic bag full of cuttings rattled at her side all the way to Tesco Metro. In an impulse she threw it in the bin outside the shop, neatly turning on her heel and ignoring the Big Issue man by the automatic doors.

SHE HAD WORKED NIGHTS, MOSTLY, IN THAT OLD PEOPLE'S HOME. IT MADE her feel much more vital than she usually was, bustling around the old dears, fetching round the trolley, doling out their greens and their gravy. The night Pat had spent on the High Dependency Ward, following his operation, she had sat with him for hours, and the air of urgent efficiency, the sudden bursts of activity amongst the nurses, the smells and the groans, brought it all back to her. You saw everything, were spared nothing. You saw what people came down to. Their brute, basic functions.

An odd memory: one that made her chuckle, but wasn't funny really. Of taking an old woman to the toilet. A blind old woman who wore six pairs of knickers. Somehow she'd smuggled extra layers on and Anne had knelt before her, tugging down pair after pair. The last pair refused to budge and Anne tugged and tugged until she realised that she was yanking at the poor thing's rough old skin.

And Sam, the porter, who'd loved her and taken her out a few times after their shifts ended. Her first and only infidelity. He was Irish and red-headed and she loved his creamy skin. She could picture being back in his Ford Capri in the woods somewhere out of town. He told her the story, in his slow, lugubrious voice, of his grandfather that worked in the steelworks, who'd fallen into the vat of molten steel. He'd been messing on with his mates and next minute he was gone, sucked down inside the vat. All they found afterwards was his wedding ring. The rest had been boiled away, adulterating the steel. Sam the porter used this story to tell Anne to go back to her husband and her little boy. She needn't be spending her time in the woods with the likes of him.

She had almost put that whole episode out of her mind. Wheeling her trolley round Tesco's through the late night rush, it all came back. Pat was of an age and condition to be in that old folk's home now. Did that mean she was too? When had that happened to her? She went to look at the hair dyes. Maybe blonde again. She didn't have to age gracefully. She'd be getting no grandkids. That was a blessing. Our Lindsey never had to worry about getting that old. She was out like a light in a couple of months. Anne found herself crying in the haircare aisle.

Then Belinda was there, pushing a trolley and her friend Astrid in her wheelchair.

"Jesus God, what's the matter?" said Astrid, though Anne barely knew the woman.

"Come with us, doll," Belinda said. "We're getting a taxi down to the Royal Circus. We know your man's sick. You needn't be out shopping when..."

Anne shrugged her off. "He isn't my man anymore."

They drew back from her.

"I'm sorry," Anne heard herself say. "I will share that taxi, if you don't mind. Today's just taken it right out of me."

By the time they led her through the checkouts Belinda had brightened up. "You've no need of buying groceries, Anne. I'm cooking in your kitchen this evening."

Anne eyed her blearily. "Pardon?"

"I'm laying on a special banquet. You've got a new visitor today. My young man is coming to stay."

Astrid, loading groceries, raised her eyebrows. "Jesus God," she said.

TWENTY-THREE

AM I READY FOR NEW PEOPLE, NEW THINGS? TIMON WONDERED. PERHAPS he had been too rash, deciding to come to Edinburgh. But he was sick of imagining things, dreaming up what Wendy would be like by now. He was sick of the vagueness with which he pictured Colin and Uncle Pat. And Belinda, of course, though her photo had gone part of the way to solving that mystery.

She was gorgeous. Or had been. The photo seemed to be an old one, a sun-faded Polaroid. He took it out of his book, where it was marking his page. He should be prepared to find a Belinda a little older than this. The face in the photo was flawless, framed by two dark wings of hair. She smiled and held out a brimming cocktail, the umbrella teetering at the glass's edge.

He watched the slow hills of the borders slide past and tried to let the train's urgent noise drum his apprehension down.

Of course I'm ready to come up against the new, he thought. There's nothing left for me in Blackpool. Shit job, no friends. Even Mandy, far away in Lancaster, apparently madly gestating her foetus, had fallen out of touch.

I like new things. I never get nervous.

His butterflies, then, were all from love.

I'm a naïve receptor, he chanted to himself. I soak it all up.

Since Newcastle he had been sitting opposite a couple from the States. The man was almost inactive, staring ahead through shades, wearing a baseball cap, feeding himself yoghurt. He kept wanting to eat things and his wife had a handbag full of chocolates. She confided in Timon that the chocolates in America were bigger. In America, everything was bigger. "When I first left Scotland," she said, "when I first left my birthplace and went to the States, I craved Cadbury's. And yet now I'm back it's the other way round." She pronounced the names of exotic-sounding American sweets and Timon smiled. Her accent was hybridized. She didn't know where she wanted to be. She gasped out excitedly at every new view, and pulled on her husband's arm, calling him 'Ho-nee'.

Everything excited her: finding the missing teaspoon in her bag, the kind woman across the aisle offering to fetch coffee for them, seeing landmarks on the north coast that she recognised. "Is this Berwick-upon-Tweed? Ho-nee, this is a lovely place where I visited with my grandma, by the ocean. That is the ocean, isn't it?" She waved her hands, scattering sweet papers. "No, it's the sea! The German sea!"

The old man asked if it wasn't the Pacific Ocean. Then he fretted that the kind girl bringing them coffee wouldn't manage, and would trip up on the way back. His wife said, "She'll have some kind of tray to bring them on. You'll see, ho-nee."

Timon wanted to talk to them some more, but he felt sick with nerves. They were old people and he thought he should get some practice in, talking with old people, since that seemed to be who Wendy was hanging round with these days.

He stared at the woman's turquoise knitted top and his heart went out to her. Beside her the old man looked affluent and better-dressed. An exercise book came out of the woman's bag and she slid it under the old man's nose. "This is our joint journal," she told Timon. "It's your turn to write something, ho-nee."

He waved her away. She persisted, showing him a page of notes. "Did you like what I wrote, ho-nee?"

"I didn't have time to read it in depth," he said stiffly. "But it made sense. It was all right."

"I want to get it down. So we can entertain ourselves later, ho-nee, with all the things we'd usually forget. Like a souvenir. I wanted to write down about that place we visited. About those girls we saw, ho-nee. About the unusualness of the way they were dressed."

The old man sighed.

They were quiet until the train reached Waverley Station. When the crowd surged up to the window and everyone on board started making for the exits, she flew into a panic again, getting all their things together. Timon helped them, said goodbye, and hoisted his backpack down off the rack. He hated leaving them behind. He wanted to hear what the old American said to his wife when they were alone together.

Then he was on the pale platform, under the dirty, translucent ceiling of the station.

John Menzies, Wendy had told him. We'll meet you outside the paper stand. Timon breezed along in the crowd, as strangers greeted each other, sought out porters, lit cigarettes. He felt buoyant and wanted to explore.

Wendy's hair was different, much shorter, and stiff with wax. She was in a purple t-shirt of some velvety material. She was even wearing a dark lipstick. She ran up and almost knocked him over. They clutched each other and it was some moments before Timon saw Colin standing there awkwardly, grinning. He was dressed almost the same as Wendy, both of them too lightly for winter. And yet the air here seemed quite mild.

"Look at you!" Wendy gabbled. "You look gorgeous!"

Timon shrugged, embarrassed.

"Colin, take his bag..."

"I can take it," Timon protested. Colin looked far too skinny to pick it up. "Where are we going?"

Wendy looked shifty. "We can't go straight to the flat. They're cooking and getting ready for you."

"For me?"

"Belinda's cooking something special."

"Is she?"

Wendy took his arm. "So we have to keep out of the way for a couple of hours. Come on. Let's get a cab to the Scarlet Empress. Get a few pints down us first."

Timon laughed. "You mean you won't make me drink martini and liqueurs and god-knows-what flavour vodka anymore?"

"Oh no," she grinned. "Those days are gone."

Then, with practiced ease, she got them a cab.

ON THE WAY INTO TOWN COLIN HAD ASKED HIS COUSIN, "WILL I FALL IN love with him?"

"I hope not," she said. "There's far too much of that going on."

"I'm always falling for straight blokes."

She wondered if he had his sights on David from the record shop. "Timon doesn't really pay attention to what people think of him. He thinks he's invisible."

"He's interested in what Belinda thinks."

"That's what worries me about this."

"And Belinda's got herself all worked up. She's frazzled about getting the roast potatoes done. And doing the Yorkshire puddings right. She thinks he'll like them. Belinda seems to think Blackpool is in Yorkshire."

Wendy thought Colin was being cruel. He was going to enjoy this.

"He'll write about us, won't he?" said Colin as they crossed Princess Street, by the great black tower of the Scott memorial. He was making Wendy jittery with his questions.

"Not if I ask him not to."

"He'll try, then?"

"Timon writes about everything. He's obsessed."

"And you're still his best mate?"

"He never lets me see what he's written. I'm not sure I'd want to read what he's put about me."

"If he ever mentions me, I'll want to see it."

Wendy looked at him. "You'd love someone to write about you, wouldn't you?"

"I'd find it very flattering, whatever it was. It's a great compliment."

"You'll have to get yourself noticed then," said Wendy.

Then they were caught up in the flurry of the arriving train. To her

Timon looked the same as ever. Blithe bordering on cocky, as if he knew exactly where he was going. Once she'd asked him how he managed to look so composed. He said he hummed little tune to himself, inside his head. A constant soundtrack to everything he observed. That sounded mad to her. But it explained the way he was distant sometimes.

The cab they took got stuck in the traffic round George Street.

"You look immaculate," Wendy told her visitor. "How is it that when I travel on a train, I come off at the other end looking like a bag of shite?"

He laughed and shrugged. He seemed shy with her. She wondered if that had anything to do with his recent effusions of apparent love. He was trying to talk to Colin.

"You're not Scottish though, are you?"

"I've lived here most of my life, but no. I still identify as English, at a push. I'm not as closed-in as the Scottish tend to be."

"Is that what they're like? Belinda's born Scottish, isn't she?"

Wendy nodded. "One of the few real Scots living in central Edinburgh. And she's not know for being closed-in. Colin's give to these sweeping generalisations."

"You know what I mean, though," Colin said. "Scots have a great capacity for ignoring what's going on right in front of them. Like when Princess Diana died. Off went the Royals to church at Balmoral, the very same morning. And in the service, the death of Saint Diana wasn't mentioned once. That's exactly it. Put a lid on it. Ignore it. That's the Scots."

"But that was more to do with the Queen," she said. "I think you're being unfair."

"Well," said Colin. "I've been involved with more Scottish people than you have."

For the rest of the trip to the Scarlet Empress on the slow decline of Broughton Street, Wendy thought about the Sunday Diana died. Coin had wept throughout the day, for the death of a princess, an icon, someone he saw as bringing common sense and the common touch. Aunty Anne had taunted him with her hasty theories of conspiracies, cover-ups, secret service shenanigans. Colin retreated to his room and played 'Candle in the Wind' repeatedly. "I'll never get to meet her now," he said, later that night.

In the café they managed to secure Colin's favourite table by the window, and spread out the large yellow menus. The proprietor, chuckling, bald, in vest top and PVC trousers, greeted them and Wendy asked for three pints and a snack of bruschetta, tomatoes and Mozarella.

"But we mustn't eat too much, or Belinda will be cross."

"I can't believe I'm going to meet her, after all," said Timon.

Colin rolled his eyes. "Do you see yourself as a Lancastrian, then?" he asked Timon. "Do you think of people like that? As belonging in places?"

"I'm a free spirit," said Timon frankly, as their fizzy lagers arrived in wet glasses. "I was born in London. I don't like it there much. But I can live anywhere. With people, more than places."

"Might you stay in Edinburgh, then?" From Colin it sounded like a challenge.

Timon was soaking up the atmosphere. Brenda Soobie on the café speakers, singing 'What now, my love?' "I might just," he said easily. "We'll just have to see how it goes." He turned to Wendy. "Is this a café just for faggots, then?"

"Faggots and their friends," she said.

"How nice," he said, tartly. And Wendy thought: that's one in the eye for Colin. Serve him right.

"It's very cramped in here," Colin complained, once their bread and tomatoes had arrived.

"I've felt cramped all day," said Timon. "That train was murder. I was sitting with this very old American couple and you know what I'm like, Wendy. I heard all the ins and outs of their lives. All their marriage stories. She was a war bride, coming back to bonny Scotland for the first time. She couldn't remember hardly anything. It was sad, really. She couldn't remember which was furthest north—Aberdeen or Inverness."

"People never know anything about Scotland," said Colin. "They don't know what it's like north of Edinburgh. Just a funny little appendix to England. A few mountains."

"Surely it's not still like that," said Timon. "Not now."

Colin shrugged.

"So you felt cramped and claustrophobic all the way up," Wendy prompted. "Forced into hearing the confessions of those Americans. Oh, you love it really, don't you?"

"It's hard not to feel pressed in by it after a while. The woman wouldn't shut up. She was so on edge. I thought her hubby was going to punch her. I just did what I always do. Breathe easy, create your own atmosphere around you. Make your own head-space."

"Head-space," repeated Colin absently, collecting up one of his clichés. Timon eyed him warily.

"That's how I get by," he went on. "Then I can breathe." He looked around again. Out of the window the tiered garden looked autumnal. The rooftops were prettily bleak. "It's a picturesque place."

"And a very picturesque group you're joining!" laughed Colin. "We're a picturesque bunch. Just you wait and see."

WHEN COLIN WENT OFF TO THE TOILETS, WENDY SAID TO TIMON, "What are you writing?"

"The usual stuff. Bits and pieces. I sent a whole load off to some publishers and it all came back saying it was nice, but I had to write something coherent and substantial." He took a long slurp of lager. "Can you think of anything?"

"You won't write about here, will you?"

"Nothing's happened here yet," he laughed.

"But it will. And they wouldn't like it."

"I'll be good, Wendy."

"You turn everything into your funny stories."

"I can't help it."

"Is that what you're going to turn Belinda into?"

He looked serious. "You're really suspicious about me and Belinda, aren't you? But you shouldn't be. I've never felt as connected to another person as I am to her. Can you imagine what it feels like, being in the same city? It's like I'm aware of her, nearby. Her mind, everything. Waiting for me."

"She bought the biggest chicken you've ever seen," Wendy said. "For dinner tonight. Everything's been given over to your arrival."

"Good."

"So don't mind Colin if he's a bit sharp."

"He's all right." Timon drained his glass. "Are we having another?

That booze is really hitting the mark." Wendy waved at the waiter. "What does he do anyway, your cousin?"

Colin slid back into his seat. "Are you talking about me?"

"Timon was just asking what you do."

"What I do..." said Colin. "People always ask me that. You get defined by your function. Like a bloody tool kit."

"That means he does nowt," said Wendy.

"A gentleman of private means, of private income."

"Thanks to the National Lottery," Wendy smirked. "And, of course, Astrology Annie."

"The day we won the Roll-over she forecast it would be a father with a son who was a very pretty young man with time on his hands. And it was me."

Wendy explained. "Astrology Annie is a saint in Colin's pantheon. Second only to Princess Diana, and a little way in front of Madonna."

"Who's never been the same since she was cast as Evita."

"Right," said Timon. "Don't you get bored, though?"

Colin flushed. Their new drinks arrived. "I've got things I like to do. I fill up my long, empty hours. Nothing as elevated as writing, though." He was about to add, "or working in a chip shop," but he bit his tongue.

"Writing has never felt like a job," said Timon. "I've made bugger all money out of it."

"You will one day," said Colin generously.

"Maybe I'll write a novel about Wendy," said Timon suddenly. "One day, when we can all see what she's made of her life."

"You dare," she said.

"And I'll do a bit of it in third person, like a biography, and some of it in first and get it as close to the tone of your eventual, grown-up self as I can. And then I'll claim it's all your own work. So you'll have to get on and do lots of scandalous things for me."

Colin laughed. "I'll drink to that. To Wendy—and everything she'll get up to."

Wendy blushed furiously.

TWENTY-FOUR

"HELLO AGAIN, TIMON," SAID AUNTY ANNE GRACIOUSLY AT THE DOOR. She took his hand and didn't know what to do with it. "Show him his room, Colin. Belinda's changing downstairs. Dinner's almost done, apparently."

"I can smell," Timon grinned. The hallway was scented like every family Sunday he had ever been invited to. Belinda had topped everything with rosemary—carrots, peas, potatoes, and on the chicken's humped and basted back. It was a trick she'd learned recently. Aunty Anne whirled away with a smile. She'd worn a new M&S print frock for the occasion. "Wendy, could I have a little word?"

Once Timon had been safely led away, Wendy was grabbed by her aunt. "I've had the most awful thought. Have you warned Belinda?"

Wendy stared at her. "What about?"

"Sweetheart," said Aunty Anne pointedly. "You and I know and love Timon a great deal, but a stranger cannot help but notice how black he is."

"Black?"

"Does Belinda know he pen-friend is black?"

"I suppose so. I don't know what they tell each other."

Aunty Anne narrowed her eyes. "Wendy, if this is all a bit of mischief-making, then I take a very dim view. And so will your Uncle Pat. You want to see how she'll react to a black man, don't you?"

"What?"

"You're testing her." Aunty Anne looked piqued. "And the rest of them. Thinking you're oh-so-right-on and politically whatsisname. Now, have you made it plain to Belinda what colour he is?"

"Does it matter?"

"Of course it does! She's in love with him. Well, with the idea of him." Aunty Anne tried to compose herself. "For all her mini dresses and knocking about with young people, you may have noticed that your friend Belinda is actually a quite naïve and old-fashioned person. I'd have thought you'd have had more sensitivity than to land her in a predicament like this."

"I think you're being..." Wendy took a deep breath. It was hard work having one of these hissing arguments with her aunt. "I think you're being ridiculously over-protective. And insulting to both of them. Has Belinda ever acted like a racist in front of you? What makes you think she's like that?"

"I'm giving her the benefit of the doubt. I see that you don't think that's important."

"This is all just you. You're putting your own racism onto Belinda."

"Me, racist! He can be bright blue for all I care! And I never invited him in the first place. That young man means nothing to me. It's Belinda I'm thinking about."

"Yeah, right."

"I hate that tone of yours, young lady. You've lost all respect."

"You've got to respect my friends."

"Wendy, don't you see? To some people, the colour you are is very important..."

"This is the woman who dyes her hair every other day."

"Don't be stupid. I mean colour as in race. It's to do with who you come from, and where."

"Bullshit," said Wendy. She wanted to finish this conversation. "And anyway, Timon's an orphan. He doesn't know where it is he comes from. Can't you just accept him for what he is?"

"I can," said Aunty Anne frostily. "I'm very good at accepting people for what they are. I've had to be an expert, haven't I? I just hope Belinda's like that too."

"Aunty Anne... Belinda claims to have been to space and had sex with her visitors. Is interracial marriage going to be such a shocking thing to her?"

"Now you're being ludicrous. And who said anything about them getting married?"

TIMON HAD UNZIPPED HIS RUCKSACK IN THE NEWLY-DECORATED GUEST room. It was painted forest green in here, with blue skirting boards and floor. Colin had supervised the furnishing in his father's absence and he lapped up Timon's enthusiasm. He watched Timon shake out his luggage onto the new duvet and found himself staring as the newcomer yanked off his shirt and shoes, at his nipples which looked almost purple and bruised. Timon shucked off the rest of his clothes, changing hurriedly for dinner, and saying how starving he was. From his pile of belongings he plucked out a fresh yellow shirt.

Colin—although he could have kicked himself because of it—was already half in love. "I'll show you where the kitchen is." He added, as Timon followed on, "I'm not getting changed."

"You look pretty smart as you are."

Colin head swam with lager and praise.

In the warm, rosemary-scented kitchen, the long table was laid with the best silverware. Aunty Anne had set out the places and glasses herself, refusing to let the jumpy Belinda touch any of the precious pieces. "We were given this tableware on our wedding day," she explained mistily.

Already installed at the table in her wheelchair was Astrid, who looked up when Colin and Timon walked in. "Jesus God, he's a fine-looking man," she gasped, dropping the spoons she'd been rubbing. "Is this him?"

"This is him," said Colin.

Timon stared at Astrid. "You're in a wheelchair."

Astrid nodded.

"And you're... Asian."

Astrid looked perturbed. Then she realised. "I am not Belinda."

Colin hurried to smooth things over. "This is Belinda's pal, Astrid. She works in the launderette."

"I have my own business," said Astrid, and let Timon kiss her hand. Wendy came in.

"Astrid, you're here too! It's proper gathering of the clans."

"Jesus God," said Astrid. "That Belinda has got her knickers twisted and no mistaking it."

"Are you German?" asked Timon.

"Somewhat," said Astrid, deadpan. "He is very curious about me, everyone, no? Belinda will be quite jealous. But tell me about Wendy's sister and her unborn child. You have seen her most recently, I hear...?"

While Timon talked with Astrid, Colin set about corking wine. Wendy sidled up to him. "I've had a right ding-dong with your mother."

"Surprise."

"I think she feels usurped."

"Usurped! She doesn't even belong here!" He grunted as the cork came free.

"That's harsh, Colin."

"She's been getting on my nerves recently. Fussing around Dad and all. As if she thinks she'd better make up to him before he pops his clogs."

"Don't say that He'll be all right."

Colin changed the subject. "Hey, I like your mate Timon."

"Really? I thought, the way you were going on, you disapproved of him."

"That's just my secret weapon. He'll be begging to be friends with me. And he dropped his drawers without a by-your-leave or anything." He smacked his lips and poured out glass after glass of Chardonnay. "What a beauty!"

"Oh, fuck," said Wendy.

Aunty Anne appeared in the doorway. "Belinda's on her way up, everyone."

They went very still.

"Have a drink," Colin told Wendy.

Timon was sitting beside Astrid now and the both stared at Aunty Anne in the doorway. Now they could all hear Belinda's heavy tread on the stairs beyond the front door. She was walking very carefully, trying not to drop something. The door clashed behind her and she was coming up the hallway. No haste, almost ceremonially.

Timon looked at the others' apprehensive faces. Then at the doorway. Aunty Anne stood aside, and there was Belinda.

The same Belinda as ever, in her best pink frock, her massive arms held out before her, carrying a home-baked, home-decorated cake. It was overrun with pink sugar mice and she had piped on the top: "Welcome, Timon!" A number of indoor fireworks hissed and burned merrily all around his name. Above them her face was radiant, expectant. She'd put on a new colour of lipstick. Fuchsia, fresh, sticky, and her hair was tied up in ribbons.

Timon was standing slowly, out of his chair.

"Welcome, Timon!" cried Belinda, stepping in the room, as if she was reading the cake aloud.

"Belinda!" he laughed, and ran to her.

CAPTAIN SIMON WAS NOT A HAPPY MAN. WHEN UNCLE PAT CAME HOME and gently installed himself in the kitchen, the door was flung open and the Captain came crashing in, brimming with complaints about his sister's behaviour. "They've taken over," he moaned. "They're at it day and night. Humping and pumping like animals. Whenever my back's turned. Belinda is becoming a floozy and it's an embarrassment. She told me yesterday—while I was eating my tea, mark you—that she'd been ravished by her black boyfriend on the very same table that very morning."

Pat chuckled. "It's their honeymoon period, Simon. It'll all fizzle out soon."

"Big black bastard," glowered the Captain. "I've asked her, what does she want, taking up with the likes of him?"

"Oh, hey, now," Pat said, wincing. "I don't hold with that kind of thing. Timon's a nice enough chap. And he thinks a lot of your sister. There's not a lot you can do about that."

Captain Simon felt reprimanded. "Ay, well. I get possessive, you see. No-ones come between me and Belinda. A fella is likely to be protective of his little sister, isn't he?"

"She's doing all right, Simon. She's having the time of her life, by all reports."

It was from Wendy, on her last few visits to the hospital, that Uncle Pat had learned of the most recent events at the Royal Circus. He was glad of anything going on, any distraction from his coming home. He didn't want a lot of fuss around him. As far as he was concerned, the doctors had given up. They'd looked right inside him and seen how far the disease had progressed. Far too far. A man who'd hardly been ill all his life, who'd never actually spent much time in a hospital before, had become too ill for surgery. Now he was home, supposedly waiting for them to decide what to do with him next. More queues, more botch-jobs. He was waiting, he knew, to die. He was pleased things were going on around him when he returned. He didn't want a whole load of weeping and wailing. Everyone round here acted like a bunch of old women already as it was.

Aunty Anne appeared, lugging his things from the hospital, all of them wrapped in new, shiny NHS bags. She looked overly bright and cheery. "Shall I put these away?"

"Sit still for a while, Anne. Come and talk with us."

"I'll just..."

"Come and sit down, woman."

She obeyed him then, which was surprising. It was like having a whole new range of faculties, he thought, this business of dying. People actually started to listen to you. He'd have to try that out some more.

"We've just been talking about Belinda's new young man," said Pat.

"It's her first real boyfriend," said Captain Simon.

"She's running about like a young girl," said Aunty Anne. "There were out dancing last night. He's certainly very taken with her. He says it was instantaneous: as soon as he clapped eyes on her. He would have known her anywhere, he said."

"They've gone mad," the Captain tutted.

"It's nice to see people in love," snapped Anne. "I believe in true love, don't you?"

The Captain glared at her.

"It's very odd being out of the ward," said Pat suddenly, gazing out of the window. "I was thinking all the way here in the taxi. Whenever do you spend two whole weeks indoors without even stepping over the door? Never. It was like the rest of the world had stopped existing."

"Well, it hadn't," said Anne brusquely. "Quite a lot has been going on."

"Good," he said. "Now I think I could do with a little siesta, before Colin and Wendy come in. I'll need some strength for talking with the young'uns and catching up with their gossip."

Anne helped him down the hall to his room.

IT WASN'T THE SAME. WHENEVER WENDY MANAGED TO GET TIMON TO herself and Belinda wasn't tagging along, they still never talked the way they used to. He was holding something back and she wanted to tackle him about this. He admitted that when he was with people, all he was thinking about was Belinda. About her grand, brave, soft white body. "She envelops me! She covers me! She takes me in and won't let go."

"That's more than I need to know," said Wendy.

"You've never had this," said Timon. "You can't appreciate it."

She scowled. "And you used to be so cynical about all that." She couldn't believe that Timon was hankering after someone other than himself. That he no longer felt free to roam about and take things in, lose track of the time in his explorations. She'd been looking forward to showing him what she had discovered in Edinburgh: all the things she knew he'd love, the places where people talked and carried on, the colours. She had discovered the paintings of rooms and flowers by Anne Redpath, an artist who had once lived in the Royal Circle. Now Wendy was seeing the town through the smeary brilliance of Redpath's colours: midnight blues, salmon pinks, crimsons and buttery yellows. She had searched her new city and realised it was for sights and places she could show off to Timon. Now he was here the impulse to drag him off to see the chained Sooty outside the launderette, the slabs of granite across the brown Waters of Leith, where you could sit in the sun between the overhanging mesh of branches. She wanted to buy him the cakes in the French patisserie that she imagined were flown fresh overnight from the continent: the chill of night-flight still on the cream and dusty icing sugar, in the raspberries crammed between pale layers of pastry. She had the textures and smells of the place to offer him. The Timon of old would have relished them, would have followed her anywhere, but now he looked as if he was humouring her. She could see by his face that he was just eager to get back to Belinda, who seemed to leave her bed only rarely now that winter was settling in. Wendy had hardly seen her, just heard the odd, disquieting detail from Timon. It was hard to picture Belinda as quite the sexpot Timon described. He made her over into a chuckling odalisque, an ample, wombless Olympia, welcoming home her Nubian slave. Whatever Nubian meant, added Timon. All Wendy could see was Belinda wrapped up under her duvet, hugging her polar bear girth in a colossal hug, congratulating herself on a wonderful catch.

When Timon actually found the time to go out into town with Wendy, they found it easiest to talk on neutral subjects and on those they still might agree about. Both hated the idea of anything coming in the way of their friendship. Yet Wendy couldn't find Timon anything but changed.

They were walking up Queen Street, past the iron railings which hemmed the trees in the private park. All the black wood and metal was rimed with frost and the pavement was perilous with dirty ice.

"Did Mandy tell you what her Daniel said about the baby?"

Wendy shook her head. She hadn't heard a thing from Mandy since she'd sent her a congratulations card.

"The first thing he said was, of course they had to get rid of it. They couldn't afford it. It was ridiculous. And how could she let it happen."

"I always thought he sounded like an arsehole. She's not listening to him, is she?"

"Last I heard, she'd told him where to get off. They aren't happy bunnies, anyway. He's just thinking about his PhD, and where the next lot of funding's coming from."

"Mandy really wants the kid," said Wendy. "It's funny. I never imagined her being like that. In her letter, though, she sounded really happy. Excited. It's a long time since she's been like that."

"She's got a fight on her hands with Daniel. I met him, you know. Didn't like him much. Not much chat in him. And he said he couldn't see the point in anyone ever thinking they should write fiction. All the great fiction has already been written. We don't need any more, cluttering the place up."

Wendy plunged her hands into her thick coat pockets. "Mandy should come here! Stay with us!"

"You're building up quite a little colony here," he laughed. "What would your uncle think of you inviting all and sundry?"

"She's our Mandy."

"Inviting an unmarried pregnant woman for Christmas! We could have a whole nativity. I could be a Wise Man."

"Why not?" She made to cross the road. She wanted to take back some fresh bread from Hendersons'. Colin was making soup this afternoon, his new passion and pastime this winter. "I like having everyone around me," said Wendy. "And why shouldn't I?"

HANDS OVER MY EYES IN HENDERSONS' DELI. I HATE THAT, EVEN FROM people who think they have the right. I'm a touchy-feely person, I think, I mean, I have no problem with proximity and people showing their affection. I wasn't in the habit of rebuffing my nearest and dearest, no, but I always found being taken by surprise rather difficult. Like I said before, life has too many surprises in store.

So: hands placed coolly over my eyes when I'm looking at the wooden racks of bread and I'm deciding between poppy seeds, nutty malt or a milk loaf. I liked the ones that shed bits and grains and seeds on the table, but that was to do with the pleasure of wiping down the table after the meal. I always liked wiping down surfaces, and shaking out tablecloths. I shook out tablecloths over the Royal Circus, hanging from the kitchen window, and watched the seagulls get aerated.

I'm wondering, anyway, what Colin would want me to bring for his carrot and coriander soup, which he was, at that moment, threshing and pulping in his brand new blender. Hands over my eyes and I whirl around with a shout—drawing glances, because the shop is packed—and it's David standing there, in a navy polo shirt, his work uniform. He looks pale and unshaven, but you can see the strong lines of his bones and I think, despite myself, that he is extremely good-looking. I haven't seen him in months. He's clutching two cartons of semi-skimmed milk to his narrow chest. I loved his chest: the tightness of it, the little collection of hairs that sprang in different directions.

"I'm on a break," he said. "Come and have coffee with me."

I looked across the shop and Timon was staring at the salads, the olives and slivers of feta cheese adrift in oil. He was at the stage of romance in which he was finding everything delightful. Getting on my nerves, actually. I caught his eye. They looked red from lack of sleep.

"Can I bring my friend?" I asked David.

"Is that who you're seeing now?" It sounded so juvenile, as if he wouldn't let Timon come along if he was my lover. David realised what he sounded like. "You're buying expensive bread!" he said. "I can't afford that stuff, even though this is my corner shop." Of course, I thought, the flat up the fire escape was at the back of this alley. That hadn't even clicked with me.

When we sat at the metallic green table in the café next door, Timon was telling David how he'd known me for years. He was giving the whole spiel: how wonderful I was, his best friend, a loyal and true companion. Timon thought he was helping out: throwing salt on the fire of David's affections, making grand sparking flames lap up. But David looked shifty. He wanted to ask why I had never phoned him. As we sat there, I didn't know. Something about his flat, maybe. The narrowness of his bed, the cramped floorspace taken up with laundry, the unwashed sheets. I couldn't imagine he'd been waiting on my call.

"Do you think I should be on the Net?" Timon asked. He looked at the punters at their consoles, all along the café's front window. "Maybe that's my true form. Not a big, cohesive narrative. Snippets, fragments, cryptic bits sent out for free on the web, or whatever they call it..."

"I had a go on that, me and Colin. We looked at nude lesbian Barbie dolls with their rude bits blacked out and censored."

"I thought it might put me in touch with someone, with people," said Timon. "I'd probably do it all wrong."

"I like your letters," I said. "Even the short, crappy ones."

"You can't beat instant connection," said David.

"I don't suppose you can." I looked at him. "You've become very pally with Colin, haven't you?"

"He's a great fella," David smiled. "He knows what it's all about."

"He does?"

"He tells me about you sometimes. He said you were right, though.

We'd never have worked out together."

Colin had been mixing it. Wendy felt that he'd been shoving his oar in and telling David these things if not out of malicious spite, then out of some odd desire to explain. She didn't see why he should bother. She didn't want her doings explained to David. And she never said, to Colin or anyone, that she and David 'weren't right together'. That was a cliché for Colin's collection and she was insulted he'd put it in her mouth.

All these men and the things they said to each other. Like a load of maiden aunts.

She left the café with Timon shortly after this. She finished her frothy coffee in one hot glug and told him they were going.

"So I'll see you, anyway," said David, "on the outing."

There was to be a minibusful of them going to the beach that weekend. Everyone. It was Aunty Anne's plan. Wendy wanted to ask David where he came into this, but he pre-empted the question. "Colin's roped me in. I come with the mini-bus, you see. It belongs to a friend of Rab's. And I've got the special thing on my license. So I'm taking you all to the beach."

"Good," she said. "Come on, Timon."

That night they ate Colin's soup, which hadn't turned out quite right: it was a chunky brown and orange broth. He thought that his father—only a few days out of hospital—should be eating easy things like this, but Pat was craving his takeaways. He wanted to phone his favourite Chinese in Toll Cross to send out one of their motorbike boys. It was his favourite Chinese in town because he found the handwritten notice in their window poignant: 'Carry Outs Are Welcome'.

Gamely they ate their soup. Captain Simon had joined them once more, evading the lovers downstairs and their noisy, ravenous supper. They still made him sick.

"What's all this about a trip to the beach?" Wendy asked.

Aunty Anne dropped her spoon with a clatter. "That's a surprise! Or it was meant to be!" There was still sticky soup on her spoon and lips.

"What?" asked Uncle Pat.

"We might as well tell them now," said Colin, with a sigh. Colin and his mother had been plotting together. It was evidence of a closeness between them that might have pleased Wendy, if she hadn't already been cross with her cousin.

"Well, whatever it is, I can't go anyway," said Pat decisively. "How can I go sitting on a beach in November? It's ridiculous! I'll be a frozen old man on the beach. They'll take me away."

Briskly, Aunty Anne sad, "We're taking advantage of the warm spell. You need some colour in your cheeks."

"Where are we going?" he asked weakly.

"Up to Yellow Craigs. It's only half an hour. Lovely, empty beach."

"You'll love it, Pat," said Captain Simon.

"Are you in on this?"

"First I've heard of it."

For devilment, Aunty Anne said: "We've asked Timon and Belinda, too."

Captain Simon grunted. "I'll have to see how I'm fixed."

"We've even asked Astrid," smiled Colin. "'Jesus God'," he said, pulling his face.

"It'll be a right bloody circus," said Pat. "Us lot turning up."

Yet he looked pleased.

EVENTUALLY TIMON WOULD TELL HER IT WAS TRUE: SHE WAS AFFECTED by everything. She took whatever materials, the substances she found about her, crumbled them and used them like—he shrugged—one of those earthy, gritty skin moisturisers from the Body Shop. Granules got into her pores, replenishing and altering her.

"I went for a job interview in that shop," Wendy told him, smiling. "When I was looking for a job. Did I tell you? They had twelve interviews all at the same time, in the cellar store room. They made us play silly games with each other and that's how they decided who they wanted. They had a big flip chart to tell us what qualities they were looking for. They didn't want me."

"You're not listening to me," Timon said.

"Sorry."

She knew he was going to come up with one of his analogies. She knew this and, really, she didn't want to hear it. Her experiences as a body and facial scrub. What flavour, she wanted to ask.

"The only thing that doesn't affect you are the men who fall in love with you. You sail through their influence."

"What men?"

"The men around you. You're not susceptible to them."

"Good. There haven't been that many, you know."

"That David, for one. You're very aloof with him."

"Maybe I am." She hated the way that, because of the hothouse exclusivity of his time with Belinda, Timon had become the expert. "Anyway, David will always be all right. He can adapt himself easily to where he is. He'll always do the right thing for himself. This is exactly the right place for him. He can blend in with everyone."

It irritated her that Timon was still going on about David. Couldn't he see he was out of bounds, now? As winter came on they all saw more of David, who joined the rest of them most evenings at the kitchen table, but he wasn't coming round to look at Wendy. Couldn't Timon see that? She wanted to tell Timon that he was reading things to suit his own view of the picture. David was coming round to see Colin.

"I wish you weren't so offhand with David," Colin complained to her one night. He'd dragged her away from the kitchen, where Uncle Pat was holding court.

"Am I?"

"He thinks you might be homophobic."

"Oh boy." She looked at Colin. "Why should that bother him?"

They kept up the pretence that Wendy didn't know what was going on between them. That was down to David who, a month after the day on the beach, was still hesitant about telling anyone about his coming out. He disliked the phrase. To David it made it sound like if he came out, there was somewhere he couldn't get back into. He wanted some leeway.

I HAD A FLING AT THIS TIME THAT I DIDN'T TELL ANYONE ABOUT, AND especially not Timon and Colin. A fling. Like it's something you casually toss off.

On one of Uncle Pat's last trips out he took me to the theatre. We both dressed up. We went to the theatre that was built entirely of glass. When we stood on the bridge you could see the whole city reflected in its front, the last gleam of sun on white buildings. The city had been packed up into a box. It was all on purpose, said Uncle Pat, who still liked to find things to point out to me.

We walked very slowly, but he wanted to walk the whole way.

There were Christmas crowds in town. The decorations were up. Argos was heaving with people who were flipping through the laminated pages of catalogues and scribbling down numbers. We had a quick look. He wanted advice about something for Aunty Anne. I was no help with that. It made me feel sad to see Uncle Pat staring at all the pictures of jewellery and not knowing what she'd like. We gave up.

That night were were going to see a comedian. Billy Franks, a veteran who still packed out theatres with his one man show. It was mostly old people who went to see him, remembering a string of records he had out in the Sixties, heart-rending tears-of-a-clown stuff that Uncle Pat played for me before we left that evening. Billy Franks had a reputation for unpredictability, warning the audience that he rambled on for hours and they wouldn't be getting home until the early hours. He hoped they'd booked taxis, he always said: the manager had locked all the exits and no one would be freed until he'd spent himself. They loved it: they let him go on, avid for what he'd do next. The posters in the theatre's foyer showed him leering dirtily, his hair wild and thin, and he was clutching a ukulele up to his chin.

"Not the kind of thing you'd usually come to see," Uncle Pat smiled, while they sat waiting to go in.

She said, "Actually, someone told me once I had to see Billy Franks before he threw it all in. A once-in-a-lifetime chance. He used to come to Blackpool every summer, but we never saw him. Mam did once, I think."

"Remember when you asked what I did in the war?"

Wendy blushed. It sounded trite, but recently she had actually asked him that. He'd been pleased, though. He told her what it was like to parachute down on enemy trees. His description had shocked her. The old mad had coloured and said that parachuting scared into the unknown had felt to him like an orgasm every time. An orgasm in the fast, empty air.

"Anyway, I spent quite some time in the war with him." Her uncle nodded at the leering poster. "He hadn't stared as a comic yet. But he was learning his patter. He could really talk. He chatted on when he was nervous. Making you laugh when you shouldn't. I had to hit him once to shut him up. He was endangering us."

"Laughing behind enemy lines," said Wendy.

"Exactly. I haven't seen him in thirty years. He became so successful, and..."

The bells were ringing for the start of the show. The other old people rushed nimbly up the stairs for their places, putting down drinks and holding tickets aloft. Some of the pensioners were in tracksuits. Not for the first time Wendy wondered at how fit-looking, how energetic modern pensioners were. They zipped about on saga holidays, they looked tanned and lean, they knew how to enjoy themselves. Gales of laughter broke out as they jostled for their places.

THERE WERE LONG GAPS IN HIS RAPID BURSTS OF ACTIVITY AND HIS rattling speech. He had every speech impediment heard of and, during his four hours onstage that night, he stammered terribly. It was part of the act, of course, or had become part, and the audience laughed at his fluffs and tongue-tied pauses as much as they did at his ribald jokes. There was that tension between what he intended to do and the moments when he clearly lost his place, his nerve failed, and he flapped his arms helplessly. The audience, Wendy realised, were thrilled to see him teeter on the edge of disaster. As if waiting to see him crumble, burst into tears, or run off-stage in fright. Yet he always rescued himself with his ukulele, holding it up to his chin and tweaking it into a few lines from one of his ancient hits, crooning along in a surprising, unafflicted baritone. Whenever this happened, the audience clapped and cheered and muffled his snippet of song.

Wendy found her mother's laugh coming out of her. Raucous and unexpected, welling out of her at the hoariest, most obvious dirty jokes. The old comic was quite blue. Every punchline had something to do with arses and cock, tits and what he called 'Aunty Marys'. He winked and goggled as if he was being suggestive, but there was no suggestion in it. It was all up-front. Act One ended in a long, circuitous, almost punchline-less joke about giraffes in Edinburgh Zoo. Then he whirled off stage, limping slightly.

A dumpy woman in a spangling black dress came on to fill the interval. She sat at the piano and did them 'Send in the Clowns' and the sprightly pensioners raced for the bar.

Uncle Pat had some trouble getting out of their row. The seats wouldn't flap up to let him past and he realised he'd left his painkillers at home. He was wincing.

"Do you want to go home?"

He shook his head tersely.

All through the second act sweat ran freely down Billy Franks' face, ruining his mascara, his purple eyeshadow. His fluffed-up, dyed-black hair started to flatten. It was soaked and his face was a ghastly, streaky colour. Beside Wendy, Uncle Pat was sweating too, his laughter punctuated by gasps.

Near midnight Billy Franks gave it up and sent his audience home at the height of their laughter. Wendy was relieved: she could get her uncle home.

"We're going round the back," he said. "To meet him."

THE DRESSING ROOM'S WALLS WERE WHITE PAINTED BREEZEBLOCKS. It was in the cellar, and a whole lot less glamorous than Wendy had expected. A spray of irises were on a table and Billy Franks' comedy suit and shirt were slumped on a chair. The man himself sat flabby and white at his mirror, cold-creaming his face clean. He looked around. "A young lady!" and grasped a golden dressing gown, which he pulled on unhurriedly, staring at the pair of them. "It's you, isn't it, Pat?" he asked with a beam of pleasure, quite different to his onstage smile.

The two old men embraced, full of their own aches and pains. Pat said, "This is my niece."

Billy winked broadly. "Oh, right." As if it was in his act.

Uncle Pat laughed. "It is, really. Wendy."

"A lovely lady," said Billy, and turned back to his mirror. "I was terrible tonight, wasn't I?"

"You were marvellous," Wendy said.

"Thank you, but no. I'm putting one over on the audience. I'm exploiting their good natures. They laugh, thinking my gaps and mistakes are part of the show. They're not, you know."

"Aren't you tired of this?" Uncle Pat said. "Week in, week out?"

"Have to, pal. Tax trouble. I never took myself off to retire in Spain. I made all the wrong choices. In the Eighties I should have got myself a big fat lucrative quiz show like all the others did, or I should have retired gracefully to somewhere hot. But I didn't. And here I am slugging it out still. Same old rotten material."

"A bit dirtier, though," said Uncle Pat.

"I know." Billy looked almost ashamed. "Had to move with the times, eh? It's my alternative phase. Good, eh?"

Wendy was embarrassed. Billy was talking about something that was new fifteen, twenty years ago. And 'Alternative Comedy' was something he thought of as just blue but pretending it wasn't. To him it was a disruption of comic tradition and one that had kept him off the telly and spoiled his career. Later that night, drunk and maudlin, he told them of his bitterness about comedy moving to telly and if you weren't on the telly you were cheap and unfunny. "And telly was full of the right faces. All these young'uns with university degrees, all political and proper. Children. Well," he gave wink. "My face didn't fit, did it, loves?"

They were having dinner in an Italian restaurant across the road from the theatre. It was deserted, but it kept open late for them. Billy seemed to know the ponderous manager, who brought their dishes himself. They ordered everything and while Wendy set to work ravenously, Billy and Pat ate little. Billy talked and twiddled a whole basil leaf in his yellow fingers.

"I had a film part, though. My breakthrough. Did you see it? Blink and you'd see me."

"What was it?" Uncle Pat said.

"*Carry On Down The Pit* in 1984. One of their last Carry On's. Can you imagine? A farce about the miner's strike. I did a cameo—recogniseable only to the cognoscenti of the avant-garde comedy fringe. Singing with my little ukulele, with a yellow helmet on my head."

"I've seen it," said Wendy, hoping she had.

"I did a number with Brenda Soobie. Lovely girl. She must be about sixty now. We were covered in coal dust."

"Colin will have the video, definitely," said Wendy. "He loves Brenda Soobie."

"Everyone loves her," said Billy morosely.

They were the only customers in the place. The manager lifted the lid on the piano and picked out a tune. He looked across at them and Billy smiled. He reached under the table for his dirty-looking ukelele and wandered across.

"Listen," Uncle Pat told Wendy.

Billy sang in Italian. A long, complicated song, accompanying himself softly.

When he finished they clapped loudly and he bowed.

OUTSIDE HE TOLD PAT, "YOU'RE NOT WELL, ARE YOU?"

"Not long for this world, Billy."

Billy didn't say anything.

"I'm waiting to jump."

"I'll get us a cab," Wendy called from the road, but South Clerk Street was empty.

"I've got my car," said Billy. "I'll drive you."

He had a purple Volkswagen Beetle with posters for his own show stuck on the back windows. They stopped first at an all-night bakers for crumpets and cake. Uncle Pat rapped on the red door and they were let into a steamy, noisy room with trays lined with greasy paper left out on every surface. "I've come for crumpet."

"Hey, Billy Franks," said the skinny baker. "I'm coming to see you tomorrow night. I'm bringing ma wife."

"I can't do anything for her," Billy smiled. "Have you tried the vet?"

They drove across town, Wendy holding the warm parcels from the bakery.

"YOU'VE DONE WELL FOR YOURSELF, PAT," SAID BILLY, GAZING ROUND AT the quiet flat. "How did you end up with the big house? I'm the famous one."

"I don't own the whole house, exactly," said Pat. He was pouring them whisky. No sign of the others.

"It's nice, though. I'm still living out of my suitcase."

Pat had wanted to bring him back to the busy kitchen, to meet the others. He supposed he wanted Billy to entertain them some more. Or he wanted Billy to see the folk he had around him now. Maybe this was best. A quiet drink. He washed down his painkillers with Glemorangie.

"How long do those things take to work?" asked Billy.

"It's immediate," said Pat. "Magic pills."

"I had a magic pill to cure my impotence." Billy looked at them expectantly.

"It's a joke, right?" asked Wendy.

"No, not really. I made it up. I do that lately. I start the joke without knowing what the end will be. It scares the pants off me when I do that on stage. Everyone looking at you."

He tried again. "I knew a man who took a magic pill to cure his impotence." Billy looked thoughtful. Then he brightened. "His wife couldn't swallow it."

Uncle Pat laughed.

IN THE VERY EARLY HOURS OF THAT MORNING I MADE WHAT THE OLD, showbizzy gentleman called a 'gift of my splendidness' to him. I took him to bed.

Now look, this is the older Wendy talking to you, and it's many years since Billy Franks died, garnering a few, smutty nostalgic columns in the Sunday papers, dead of pills, booze, neglect and a fat purple heart on a jumbo jet. Floored by the altitude, he choked out his last, a few years past the turn of the century. Floored by the air hostess, he would have chuckled, winking madly.

I made him a gift of my splendidness back in 1997 when Uncle Pat had seen himself groggily off to bed and we watched him from the kitchen table, Billy sitting with hiccups in a director's chair, too slewed, it seemed, even to move. He'd been tight for hours, he said, on sheer adrenalin.

I really was splendid in those days, I suppose. I always had large breasts with very small nipples and the old fellas especially loved them. Nipples pink as Belinda's sugar mice. While still in the kitchen I let the old comic pull my dress off, all the way over my head, untwist my bra and hold my breasts in his crab hands. I remembered then that I'd wanted work-hard, old hands on my body. I wanted to feel that. My clean white skin shook in his hands and he was tender. He listened and waited on that pulse. "It's like holding a very young bird," he said. "New hatched. About to fledge."

Like my mam I always liked a man who could make me laugh. He did so all the way to my room. I made my decision and he asked very nicely. I took him in my hands and led him down the creaky boards before he was tempted to start begging. I could see, I could feel his dauntless old pecker pushing out against his pants. I pushed one of his hands into the front of my knickers, loving the snag of his unclipped nails on my hair while he dabbled at me, with increasing confidence. His hand came out buttery and warm.

I must have been prescient at that tender
age or I knew what was
coming or I jumped on the first
chance I saw but for weeks
I'd been telling myself

I want a dirty old man
who'll cover my whiteness
with dirty old kisses
who'll rove over my slimness
with floppy old skin
I'll turn him on:
Soothe his wrinkled brow
straighten out his arms and legs
cool his cheeks
inflame his weakened lungs
let him shuffle about me
indulge me
let him Lolita me

Too old to be Lolita, even then.

His body was crazed with lines, and endless mapwork. Only his thin penis wasn't like an old man's.

"A comic's vital tool," he whispered, fitting it into me, talking more to himself. "The butt of all his jokes." I'd had to pump it delicately to keep him hard. Till the end was wet and pink like a kitten's nose.

We slept in a hug that almost crushed the life out of me. I marvelled at the different textures of our skins. The variousness of his: emery board, elephant hide, richest vellum. I, meanwhile, was tight and replete.

He was the man I once told you about. The man who giggled when he came. He climaxed and roared with laughter, shaking the bed, the pictures on the wall.

In the morning he was gone, leaving a smell of whisky, cigarettes, of basil, crushed into the sheets and my skin.

In Colin's room that night, he and David held still, listening.

"That noise," said David.

"Someone else in this flat is fucking," Colin smirked.

David lay to cover him. He buried them in covers. "December tomorrow."

David stared at Colin. He'd come so far. At first he would close his eyes when Colin kissed him, as if taking medicine. He'd relaxed since then. Things to get used to: beard burn, stubble burn, the double volume of sperm in the bed. The towels kept handy for afterwards. Looks from the others, at first, in the hallway. Loving the noise of Colin. Hearing another man's voice in the dark. The strange, hairy legs beside him when they went to sleep.

When they first spent the night together at David's flat, Rab hadn't been surprised. He watched them, that first time, slink off to David's tiny room. Rab sat on the settee, where he planned to stay all night, speeding and writing his endless sentence.

David said, "I wish you could have an endless fuck like you can a sentence."

"I like endings," said Colin. "I like starting again, fresh. I like putting things in brackets for later, I like feeding them through semi-colons, propping them in parentheses. I like the endless sexy tussle of sub-clause on sub-clause. Those tickly commas. Do you want me to carry on with this punctuation-as-fucking conceit?"

"No," said David. "Just...dot dot dot."

In the dawn Billy Franks drove his Volkswagen back to his digs. Telling himself jokes, singing a loud, tuneless song.

I knew a girl who made me
a gift of her marvellous
youth and her
thighs
and
by my eyes!
Her thighs were a size...!

It isn't true. When I was young, my thighs were delectably slim. I was slim as stair rods.

TWENTY-SEVEN

ALL THE WAY THERE HE WANTED TO MAKE JOKES ABOUT IT. WHEN THEY walked up the beach in a procession he wanted to laugh at the motley bunch they made, carrying rugs, foldaway chairs, a couple of battered hampers. They walked slowly, letting him take the lead, letting him find their spot on the deserted beach. Anne walked with him, a tartan rug bundled up in her arms. He wanted to laugh and ask her if this was his funeral procession: were they going to push him out to sea as a lost cause, watching him dwindle away on the grey, distant water? But something held Pat back from laughing. He was touched they'd all come out with him today. What a rabble they were, though.

"The good Lord's smiling on us with the weather," Anne said, startling him.

"The who?" he said. "Since when did you..."

"Since you stopped asking," she said wryly, still staring at the clear, November sky. The warmth was quite puzzling. "I've not had a complete conversion. You needn't worry."

"A devout Anne is something worth thinking about," he smiled.

"I've thought about God, this past year," she said. "Even before our Lindsey died. Ralph's very big on God, of course. Pictures on his walls. A Catholic."

The old man's mind had gone blank. "Ralph?"

"You see how little you ask?" she said gently. "Ralph's my man."

"Your man. Of course. You don't talk about him much."

She shrugged.

"You've become part of the family again, Anne."

She looked at him. "What a funny year it's been."

They were heading towards a soft hollow of pale sand, set back from the tide. Tussocks of stiff, sun-faded grass kept it in shelter. "Why not here?" he asked, and flapped his arms briefly to alert the others.

"I'm glad," he said, sitting down carefully, testing the ground. "I'm glad that I won't have to think about next year. The years keep on getting more and more complicated."

"I know," she said.

"I just want Christmas. I want it to be a success. Will you stay here for Christmas, Anne?"

"Yes, of course. Ralph isn't expecting me back in Newton Aycliffe."

"You've been away months..."

"He's always busy. He holds these Crusades, in his house. Saving people."

"One of that sort," said Pat, amused.

"So we'll have a... family Christmas."

"Funny family we've got."

They watched the others settling themselves, ranging at close but separate spaces on the sand. Wendy was with Timon and Belinda and hearing about Belinda's trips here as a youngster, about plunging into the freezing sea. How purging it was. She was laughing, throwing back her head. Her brother, the Captain, still in his immaculate yellow coat, was actually carrying Astrid, who had brought her chair, but who knew it wouldn't run on sand. Gallantly the Captain had lent a hand. Her single long plait bobbed on his shoulder. He set her down on a blanket, which Anne was smoothing out. "Here we are," said Anne. "All settled." It was just past lunchtime, the best part of the day.

Colin was talking with David, who'd brought them the van and driven them here. Anne didn't know much about this David, but she decided she'd go over there and thank him in a moment. When his and Colin's rather animated, quiet conversation was finished with. Last came David's friend, Rab, in his odd woollen hat, throwing sticks for his daschund, making it splash into the tide. Rab was the funny, skinny one that none of tem really knew. He seemed reluctant to sit down, to be part of them. Anne could understand that. Other people's family groups could be off-putting, and yet they were hardly the usual family. There was very little blood here. Still, and all. Anne felt a warmth towards all of them and it surprised her. Even for Captain Simon, talking about Germany with Astrid. Anne decided that maybe she had put the Captain in an impossible situation. Of course they couldn't conduct an... affair under her ex-husband's roof. She could see that it wouldn't do. You couldn't rely on other people to be brave. Best to let it come as a surprise, a bonus. You can't simply demand that they be brave. Anne shook her head at herself.

"Have a nap," said Pat. "You look ever so tired."

"I was making sandwiches at seven this morning. I don't know why so early." She lay back in the sand and, with Pat watching her, she drifted off.

WENDY TOOK A WHILE TO DECIDE SHE WAS IN THE SPOT SHE WANTED. "Perfect." She flopped down. "I like this better than red hot and sunny. It's warm and still."

"You're very affected by your surroundings," Timon observed. "I've watched you. You settle in and then... it's not that you blend in, exactly." He looked around, thinking. "Putting you in a place, that's like dunking a biscuit in a cup of tea, hon."

She sat up, leaning on one elbow. "That's not very flattering."

"Has she changed, then?" asked Belinda.

"Quite a lot," said Timon. He discomfited Wendy by looking straight at her. "In Blackpool you wore your youth very close to the surface. You jangled with it, glittered. Like the place itself."

"Oh, very poetic."

"Trying so hard to be pushy and grown up, you gave it all away. Finding something to frizzle your energy away on."

"Oh, energy," said Belinda.

"Here, though... I suppose you're still dashing about. You listen to people better, you know. You give them more time."

Wendy flicked at an insect crawling on her arm. "When Mam died I realised there were so many things I hadn't asked her about. I felt stupid. In the end we'd spent hundreds, thousands of hours together. She told me things about her life, but I can't believe there are so many gaps. There's just a few funny stories left. That's all I remember."

"It's true," said Timon. "That's it. Funny stories and accidents."

"Like when she weed herself in the magician's cabinet, and when she kissed the headmaster. When she got us shoving fruit on the waxwork dummies." Wendy smiled. "But we sat together saying nothing sometimes. Watching silly old films, monster movies. Talking about nothing in the kitchen, eating sausage sandwiches with too much pepper. I think of all the things I could ask her now."

"It sounds like you had a great time," said Belinda, staring up at the sky. She was in a sundress, Wendy realised, of the same yellow as the Captain's coat. Cut from the same cloth.

"So that's maybe why I listen now. Hoping to hear stuff. I miss too much."

"Everything effects you," Timon told her. "You hear enough."

They lay quietly for some time.

"Timon's changing, too," Belinda said. "Since he's been here, aren't you, hon?"

"Oh, yes. I'm enjoying my writing, suddenly. Before I didn't. I made myself cross when I wasn't writing. Now..."

"We have lovely day," said Belinda. "He works at the kitchen table and I make him do regular hours. Like a proper job of work. He's going to be a great success."

"Belinda's teaching me to cook. No more fish and chips. Or, only when we want. She's taught me to wash my colours separate, instead of jamming everything in the machine together." He grinned.

Across the way, Captain Simon and Astrid were playing travel scrabble. The two of them were hunched over the tiny board. "Jesus God!" burst Astrid. "Zygote! What is 'zygote'?"

"Is that the beginning of a beautiful relationship?" asked Timon softly.

Belinda looked weary. "My brother doesn't have beautiful relationships. More's the pity." For the first time she sounded like she wanted him off her hands. Wendy saw that it was she who propped the Captain up, not the other way around. Belinda lowered her voice. "The Captain of old... he never knew difficult words. That's one of the subtle ways in which he gives his game away."

"Oh..." murmured Wendy, not wanting to go into this now. She stared off at the sea, at the island a little offshore and its lighthouse. She imagined growing up on an island with no one around her. Rab was still throwing the stick for the dog. Neither seemed to be getting bored.

"YOU MAKE ME LAUGH," COLIN TOLD DAVID. "COMING OUT ALL THIS WAY, driving us all out. To spend the day with a load of old women, my dad and me."

David shrugged, his chin resting on his knees, which he hugged to his body. He was staring at his new boots. Colin had helped him choose them in the sales—shiny red patent leather. "I haven't seen much outside of Edinburgh. This is nice. A bit of seaside."

"It's true," Colin said. "When you live in the middle of town, everything comes to you. You don't go out much." He wondered why David was looking so glum. "Go and talk to Wendy. You know you want to. Don't let that Timon monopolise her."

"Oh, they're old friends. They have to catch up."

"They've had plenty of time for that," said Colin briskly. "They weren't even together, you know. If that's what you're worried about."

David perked up. "I didn't know that. I assumed they had been."

"There you go. Talk to her. It's the only chance you'll get at... seeing her again. If that's what you want."

"It's not what I want."

This brought Colin up short. "I thought you'd done all this to impress her." He tried to temper his native cynicism. "I thought bringing us all out was your gesture."

"No," mumbled David. "Not in that way, anyway."

"It looks like you've done Dad a power of good."

Pat was taking in slow, careful breaths of the sea air, as if he could drink it in. He looked alert and composed, a rug pulled up over his knees. Although he'd come out under protest, claiming that the whole day was a silly exercise—he'd even used the word farrago—the old man had dressed himself up for the occasion. A newish green tweed suit, a checked waistcoat. His shirt loose on his wattled neck. He gave the impression of paying no heed whatsoever to the various people and conversations around him.

David looked at Colin. "You don't see, do you?"

"Hmm?"

"How many straight male friends have you got, Colin?"

"What? Oh, I don't know." Yet he did know. Since getting to know David and Rab he'd been seeing a whole other world. "What are you going on about, anyway?"

"You've got none, have you? Apart from us?"

Colin shrugged. "It makes no difference to me where my friends are coming from. Or who they're coming with. I go around with you and Rab, I suppose, because we get on. That night I went to yours, with Wendy after the club, the night you and her copped off and slept together, we all got on then, straight away. We've got stuff to talk about. It's easy. We have a laugh. I've probably got more in common with you than all the other queer blokes I've knocked about with."

David was looking uneasy. "And haven't you ever wondered—I mean, has it ever been at the back of your mind—that you might get me, um, into bed?"

Colin laughed. "Why you? What about Rab?"

David said, "Because you talk to me more. You spend the time with me. I thought..."

"Oops," said Colin. "This sounds like the end of something. I didn't think we'd have this problem. Look, David. I thought you knew a little more about me by now. I treat all my friends the same. With a bit of manners, I hope. When I do come across males of the straight persuasion, like yourself, I treat them nicely, but distantly, with full ceremonial honours. I treat them—and no pun intended—like proper ladies." He sighed out his cigarette smoke, disappointed. "So no, I won't assume that just because we've slept together a couple of times you were doing anything other than trying it out. I won't assume we're, like, boyfriends all of a sudden.'

David rubbed his eyes slowly and they both listened thoughtfully as they squeaked in their sockets. Crumbs of sand, inevitably, got in there. "Oww," he cursed, and rubbed harder, complaining.

"Just like a straight man," said Colin, and passed him the water bottle. "Sluice it out. If thine eye offends thee..."

David saw to himself, and eventually sat with very pink eyes and a wet face, looking at Colin. "You still don't see what I'm on about, Colin. I want you to take me home one night soon. I want you to take me home up that fire escape and fuck me on my bed."

Colin snorted. "I don't do requests."

"I'm not having you on."

"Yeah?"

"I've said it all wrong, haven't I?" David rubbed one eye.

"Don't start that again. And yes, you have." Colin thought. "But you like ladies!" he burst.

"Honestly. Is that the extent of your understanding of the..."

"Yes, yes, the complexity of human sexuality. And yes it is.'

David smiled. 'I want you to... do more things to me."

"Do things?"

"I want to try it out some more. All of it. "

"So I'm going to carry on being your little chemistry experiment set?"

"Yes. No. Oh fuck. I like you, Colin. And... I fancy you." He smiled, shy, looking down.

"You do, don't you?"

"Like a bastard."

Only then did Colin let himself realise that he himself had an erection. He said, "I want to go home now."

"Tell them," David laughed.

"I can't..."

"Can we go off in the dunes?"

They looked, and the tussocky dunes receded far into the distance, up to the woods, beyond which their minibus waited. It certainly looked promising. But they saw a whole host of flashing, silver kites lurching and wheeling above them. The dunes were full of kite-fliers.

"Shit. That's because the breeze has picked up," said David.

"Let's stay put, then," said Colin, settling back down. "I can absorb this more slowly, then. At my leisure."

He lay and watched David stare at the empty stretch of beach. It was studded with black and green granite and the occasional waves crashed down as if the North Sea was throwing in its final chips again and again and again.

TWENTY-EIGHT

It was some old portrait painter I read about once who said it. He was asked about his flesh tones. So subtle, so lifelike, so impossible to get. You'd think they were fresh on the canvas, still living, decades after the jewelled worthies and the smug matrons were dead and gone. Asked his secret, the old painted said he mixed his colours with brains.

And when I read that I saw him dabbing his brush in real brains, as if their substance could lend something to the colour, not just grey and white. Other painters had used semen, shit, blood, piss. Their portraits would reek. Untreated, they would smell like the bodies of the unwashed.

I also thought about how it meant putting something of the substance of the person into the picture. It was like voodoo, it seemed to me. Mummifying bits of them against their own image. All I can do with the portraits of everyone I knew is put their brains in with what they said to me.

I look at photos of them all and it's part of my morbid imagination, part of me, that I can picture levering off their skulls and see their brains like yolk inside. The photos aren't very good, of course. Everyone is caught at their worst moments. Most of them have red eyes, flash-blind, cats caught on the prowl. On one set of pictures, Christmas that year in the Royal Circus flat, everyone looks pissed. All except Serena, Aunty Anne's friend, who came to visit on Boxing Day. Serena looks like someone who is used to being photographed. Her head tips forward slightly, so her eyes look larger than they are. Her hands are folded neatly on the lap of her smart dress. It could almost be that she is on her best behaviour for her visit, but I later found that she was almost always as composed as this. Someone had removed her anxiety glands.

Her flesh tones are perfect, even on these rotten, blotchy, precious photos. When whoever created Serena and knocked those pigments together, they were definitely using their brains. She was luminous. Her words were succinct and uttered with perfect, dry diction. It was Boxing Day that Serena arrived, following our two days of haphazard festivities. She came to stay and her style was a rebuke to all of us.

When I look at these pictures of Serena with us at dinner on Boxing Day, 1997, it isn't pissed we look exactly. It's messy. As if we were making an unprofessional job of being ourselves.

MANDY NEVER CAME FOR CHRISTMAS.

Middle of December she sent a card, a letter, and a photo of herself by the canal in Lancaster, holding and showing off her proud bump.

> Dear Wendy,
>
> Daniel is a fart. It's official. Maybe you've already heard from Timon, but Daniel as horrible about the baby. He never wanted it, won't deal with it. It was my choice, he said, I stopped taking the Pill. I took his stuff without even consulting him. I suppose that's true, but he's pretty careless himself. If I wasn't going to have an abortion, than that was it. Nothing's improved since then. I'm getting bigger and bigger. Squeezing him out. I don't go taking him drinks and food anymore when he's working. When we were first together I went on like a fool.
>
> So, soon, I'll be moving out. Taking baby and going.

His yellow glasses piss me off now. Jaundiced view of the world and all. At first I found a little cynicism sexy. I've got to get my act together now.

What other news?

My Professor—remember? The grizzled one who I was proofreading for? Took me to dinner when the book was delivered to his publisher. I got a special thank you in the acknowledgments. He ordered extra bottles of wine. He treated me nice.

He wore a kind of safari suit, wrinkled at the elbows and knees. The best restaurant Lancaster has to offer. Talked to me all night about witch-burnings and magic cults. In another age, he said, he would have been a necromancer. I could have believed him. Paid for it all with his golden card and tried for a fumbling snog in the car park. I put him off.

It was one of those chilly, misty nights we get along the canal. I walked home alone, with only the swans on the black water for company.

I told Daniel his Professor had tried to kiss me. He'd been working all night on his thesis. That bloody old woman of his. I think he's in love with her. Obsessed with finding her, bringing her back out into the open, out of her seclusion. I said, maybe she's happy staying at home knitting, watching telly, doing old lady things. That caused a row. Bigger than the row about his hairy, horny old Professor.

"He tried it on with me, too," said Daniel.

"When?"

"It was a supervision session we had in a pub. He asked me straight out if I swang both ways."

"Swang? Is that word?"

"Yes. His beard tickled when he kissed me."

"You let him?"

"I told him to fuck off. I'm changing supervisors." That was even more pressure on him, he said. Added to what me and the baby are giving him.

Next thing I knew, the Professor was ringing the house daily.

"Are you ok to speak?"

And I kept saying no, and putting the receiver down.

The house kept smelling dusty, cigarettey. I was convinced the floorboards smelled dirty, and were cobwebbed up underneath. In the knotty gaps I could even see the grey webbing. I bleached the boards and they went all patchy.

Then, one day, I let the Professor talk for a little while longer. "It's about the short story you gave me. Success, Mandy!"

"You what?"

"I sent it to an anthology. An annual collection for new writers. I acted as your... uh, agent. And they took it! That's a hundred pounds! The beginning of your career! The letter came this morning."

I met him in the white, fussy Georgian tearooms in town and he showed me the letter on stiff, creamy paper and it was all true. My first story sold and I hadn't even tried.

So there I am, Wendy. The book comes out in March. I'll send you a copy. There's a party in London and the Professor said he'll come with me. I have to write more stories, he said. He tells me I'm a genius and now he hangs on my every word. He wants to write them down, which is, of course, only flattering.

I mean, all I wrote about was Mam, about Blackpool, the Golden Mile, me, you, our Linda. It was a tiny, tiny, short story, about the fair and Mam dying, what she was like at the end. How she used to watch monster movies. At the finish of it I have her down on the beach, on the wet sand, walking out to sea to catch up with Dracula, who's turned into a bat and flying home. It took me ages to get it right. Yet it seems to have worked.

Shall I send you a copy?

If I write a novel that sells millions, becomes a movie, I

could take the baby anywhere.

I have to think about what I should write next.

The Professor has a room in his attic and I'm moving into it this week. I haven't told Daniel yet. Leave him alone for Christmas. The Professor thinks I should write a Gothic novel. He would. A ghost story. I remember what you said once: that to see a ghost you have to have suffered. There's a beginning.

Happy Christmas Wendy—I've no money for presents—but all my love, anyway.

Mandy.

That Christmas Wendy thought: I'm surrounded by bastard writers.

Maybe that's when I decided that one day, I'd get my own back on them all. Eventually I'd learn the skill, the lingo, the patter, and do it myself. With the language and the patience and everything I remember, I could wrest my own life back for myself. Away from the separate me's in pages by Mandy, in the funny, stolen fragments that Timon produced, even in some of Rab's endless sub-clauses. Even he managed to smuggle me in. I want to get it all back, and put it in one book.

My eventual husband, Joshua—we'll get to him soon—he had versions of me. Paintings and drawings of me framed in his exquisite flat. He commissioned people to come and have a look at me. I haven't got any of those pictures. Didn't want them. To me, all of those pictures are saying, "Who does this woman think she is?" The artists were coerced into making me their subject. I came out wrong in those, because I never have to be coerced. I slipped into the things that people wrote and no one had to pay for that. Joshua wasn't happy though, unless he was paying for something. Usually paying over the odds.

Wait for him, anyway. The connections are coming up. Serena visiting was the first palpable link with my eventual husband. The next bit of my life. Aunty Anne was engineering it, without even knowing what she was doing. Aunty Anne always called Joshua my fancy man. In her own way she was proud she led me to him, even at the end.

AUNTY ANNE WAS AS GOOD AS HER WORD, WHICH SHE HAD GIVEN ON the sands at Yellow Craigs, and stayed with us all Christmas. I heard her talking on the phone to her man at home in Phoenix Court, Newton Aycliffe. Ralph the man with a mission, the obese Lamb of God. He held services in the living room of his council house because he was too fat to leave it very often. "He's huge!" Aunty Anne told me gleefully. "He has legs wider than both of mine put together." She seemed to delight in him. "The Lord made me this shape," he told her. "I'm fat for the plan." He was wedged on a Chesterfield settee and often slept there. When Aunty Anne told him she was staying in Edinburgh, he turned out not to be very pleased at all. "I thought you were going out on a mission. I thought it was Scarborough for you this Christmas."

The phone crackled.

"Oh. But I can't leave, Ralph. He's very... near the end. It's our last chance."

More crackles.

Later that night Aunty Anne told me that we might be getting an extra Christmas visitor. I thought, not Ralph! Then she said Ralph had rung her a friend of hers, and asked her to keep an eye on Aunty Anne. Ralph sounded odious to me.

SO WE HAD OUR CHRISTMAS. EVEN THAT GAME WHERE EVERYONE STANDS in line and passes a balloon along, person to person, without using their arms. Uncle Pat sat it out, laughing in the corner.

Astrid sang us German carols on Christmas Eve.

Colin took a bunch of us out to the Oyster bar, where we had tequila slammers at midnight, mixing salt, lemon juice and wasted booze on the rough wooden tables.

Aunty Anne wanted dancing, so the furniture was pulled back and Colin produced his treasured records. We danced.

Belinda cooked for us once more.

Captain Simon knocked the tree over, carrying chairs in the hall. He became flustered, picking up shards of burst glass baubles. "Watch your feet!" he shouted at us, on his hands and knees. "Put some slippers on! Watch your feet!" We laughed.

"Jesus God!" said Astrid, wheeling past crossly.

"Watch your feet," Timon smirked at me.

"Don't lose your elasticity," I told him back.

Mandy wasn't losing her elasticity. It didn't matter that her GP had told her, had given her stern warning that if she persisted in performing that particular trick of hers—with the golden bangles in her mouth—she would go all bandy-lipped, loose-lipped, and not be able to talk. There was no sign of that happening to Mandy's perfect, tensile strength. Her mouth moved with perfect shape: she could hold the shape of any vowel or consonant. She would practise, watching herself. Only, she could open her mouth wider than anybody she knew. She was like one of those tribespeople who put plates in their lips, or rings on their necks and slowly graft themselves into some bizarrely cultured, attenuated form.

Daniel, peering over his yellow-tinted glasses, said her stretchable-but-still-pert mouth was like a snake's. But he would. Odd, for a man who had read, researched and agreed with so much contemporary feminist theory (and whose subject was the great grand-mammy of many of these theorists) that he could be so blithely Freudian, and sexist in his appraisal of Mandy. Carelessly he called her Snake-Woman, Phallic Mother, a loose-lipped swallower of his manly essence. Well.

Our Mandy kept her lips, her vowel-sounds, her talking itself supple by endless practice. Sotto-voce as she sat on the minibus into town, or walked back across the snowy park, or cleaning the cooker, or cooking their tea, she was muttering to herself. She found her syntax was elastic, too: strong and yielding and it could carry a freight of anything she fancied. She started to mutter and come up with her own strings of words the day she stopped reading. She was building up a corpus of work, only very little of it was written down yet. Only this first story, about our mother, our mother dying on the beach at Blackpool at night, watching the strings of lights on the Golden Mile reiterated in the water.

Mandy was roving over old ground, past events, past history. Her muttering took us all in, turned us over, pulled us into her telling. In the snowy park that led from the river to their housing estate, she walked alone in twilight with her Sainsbury's bag and let her mutters grow louder.

Grand loops of improvised words sent out ahead of her. She allowed herself to shout them, call them out like a bat uses its bursting cries to orient itself in the dark. Mandy, testing her voice, liking what she heard.

His attic room was clean and Spartan and he helped her move boxes of her things in during Christmas week. Daniel wasn't home to see her go. He was off on his travels, hunting down the living, non-practising writer he told everyone he revered. He wanted to tell her: I have your clue. I know the key to uncover your texts. I have seen the figure in your carpet. Mandy hoped the old thing—if he found her—would send him away with a flea in his ear.

No mystery, no essence, no secret. Mandy wanted to tell her Professor: don't go making me a mystery. What I am doing is very plain. She began her next story and it was a continuation of her first. But she ravelled it back and began a little earlier. She thought: Where do I begin?

With Timon on the Golden Mile. She thought of Timon, a literate, watching, slant-viewed outsider. In his fish shop, busying himself absent-mindedly, stitching white fish in their hot golden cardigans. Then she thought again and wrote from the viewpoint of a younger sister. Me. She thought about me at sixteen and thinking it was time I saw a little of the world around me. How afraid of that world my imagination made me. My sisters were always fearless, I thought, and I could never understand that. Mandy teased this out of me, making me understand why they seemed so brave and why I didn't feel like that.

That Christmas her room in the Professor's house was cold, of course, with no heating, no rugs and the hard, dry snow bashing against the clean windows. Cruel and scheming, the Professor chilled her and forced her out of the room he had claimed was hers and she was forced downstairs, to warm her bare feet in front of his fire and watch the Professor indulge himself. He opened the best of his wine and made her drink and watch him burning books, book after book, on his real fire. It was his secret vice, he said, one that nobody knew about, that he bought and rebought and annotated afresh new books and then incinerated them, when he felt the urge.

That Christmas Mandy watched his fire and licked the wine off her lips.

I WENT TO SEE MY BEARS AT CHRISTMAS. I HADN'T BEEN IN AGES. THEY were still the same, which I found disappointing, rather than reassuring. Father bear, black bear loomed with his forepaws up in supplication, Grizzly mother shambling beside him, and looking sideways. Various cubs were heaped in colours ranging from burnt umber to ginger: there was even a yellow bear with a curious, simian, old man face. Beside them, in a glass case of his own, the great granddaddy: the recovered skull and chipped skeletal revenants of a cave bear. His jaws were like the front of a Volkswagen Beetle. Timon came with me, eager to see the bears I'd told him about. His Christmas present from Belinda—who was usually so frugal, and timid with her sheaf of credit cards—was a very compact video camera, wit which he'd already been filming us. His batteries weren't very good, and didn't last long and after each hour of filming he had to switch himself on to recharge. He whizzed through batteries because he liked to cut very fast from shot to shot, composing these bewildering collages of views. His own cut and paste technique, he told us, delighted, showing us some of the results on the telly on Christmas night. By then we were used to him looking at us through his machine. When he cut and pasted, swiftly pressing STANDY-BY and RECORD, he gave a shrill bleep-bleep. He cut into sentences, so that when we watched ourselves eating Christmas dinner, it was a jumbled and punctuated version we got, our sentences running abruptly into each other's.

> A cracker with me I want someone to pull a sauce there's more sauce in gravy is too I fetched out the lumps with a strainer that thing isn't on me the state of me you shouldn't you again is it me to say? What do you want to me to for posterity I'll believe that when I see David, he's filming you pull my cracker with me put that thing down did you know your red light's flashing? What does that mean? Anne's in the hall on the phone to that fat Christian charity after all it's the time of the year it is some music on carols and we went four times a day ten candles all lit all weathers I love you Timon get my good side trifle and I put the hundreds and thousands on not very well I'm afraid Uncle Pat is asleep Uncle Pat? At

the table get that bottle down this end of Aye, to you as well
best of the compliments of the season.

Timon filmed the bears for a while. He had decided that he was making a proper film. He put me on my bike, in my blue riding helmet and followed me in the oddly quiet streets of the city when we went to the museum.

It was Boxing Day. Uncle Pat was spending the day in bed. Most of the others were taking it easy, sleeping off the too-much they had eaten the day before. Timon and I were full of energy and we came out to film the bears.

"Your uncle," he said, taking care for it not to come out on the soundtrack. "He didn't look too good yesterday, hon."

"He was exhausted by the end of last night," I said.

These were all the unsayable things, however. We both knew, and so did the others, that Uncle Pat had been waiting for Christmas, he wanted a nice Christmas and then... where would he go from there? Was it over yet? When did Christmas actually end? Epiphany? Our mam always took the decorations down before New Year. They depressed her, she said, once the real day was over.

We walked back to the Royal Circus. I wheeled my bike. Timon said he and Belinda were having dinner together: their own private Christmas tonight. We kissed goodbye on the landing and I still got the urge to ask him outright: was his first reaction to the sight of Belinda the true one? Had this delight been that complete and concealing nothing? I couldn't ask, though and I left him, going up the last flight of stairs.

Inside, home again, I met Serena Bell for the first time.

WENDY KNEW SOMEONE DIFFERENT WAS THERE BECAUSE THEY WERE playing the piano. It was in the living room, which no one used very much. The room was painted blue and faced the dark side of the flat. The piano's lid was always down, and had become rather dusty. Wendy had lifted it once, giving the cool, yellowed keys an experimental tinkle. She couldn't play, of course.

She recalled an instance of Mandy's bravery, her rashness. A school assembly when Mandy was twelve. For some reason the headmistress was asking who could play, who'd like to come out and entertain us? Who'll give us a rousing chorus of something? I will, called Mandy, and the whole school, an embarrassed Wendy included, watched her walk down the waxed floor and get up on the stage, where the teachers sat in rows. I can play, Mandy assured them and sat herself at the stiff-backed piano. She paused and then plunged her hands onto the keys, launching into the rowdiest nerve-jangling noise she could produce. And she wouldn't stop. The headmistress had to pull her away from the stool, and was yelling at her while the notes rushed and rumbled away, subsiding while all the school laughed.

This, however, on Boxing day, was perfect. Schubert.

No one else about, it seemed, except the music. It had that odd timbre on the air, stirring the dust, which meant it was real and not from a record. The records she had most often came home to weren't Schubert. Usually they were Dusty Springfield or Cilla Black.

She went to see who it was and there was a strange woman in a plain black dress. She had come already in mourning, which set Wendy's teeth on edge right away. Her hair was neat and gracefully grey, cut in a bob. The woman tilted her head to acknowledge Wendy and show her intense, alert, grey eyes. But she played to the end of the piece, holding Wendy there. Wendy could only stare at the woman's incredibly long fingers. Wasn't there a story about a boy with long fingers, and the scissor man who came to trim them down?

When the woman was satisfied she was finished, she sank into herself, then stood and gave Wendy an off-putting smile that went up higher on the left side. She held out one large hand for Wendy to shake.

"I'm Serena Bell," she said in an English accent, as if it was a name Wendy should already know. "I'm a friend of your aunt's."

"Oh. She said you were coming, actually. Where is she?"

"With your uncle. He's sleeping."

"She's sitting beside him?"

"They've had the doctor out this morning. Your uncle had a rather tricky time. The doctor tells us there isn't an awful lot they can do." She closed the piano lid. "Your aunt is sitting with him till he wakes," she said again.

Wendy turned to go.

"I don't think they want you to go dashing in, Wendy."

"I'm not dashing anywhere."

"You can see your uncle this evening. It's been discussed. Why don't we take this time to become better acquainted?" She lowered her voice. "If this really is your uncle's final few days, then I gather we may be thrown together rather a lot. So we might as well know each other. Let me make a pot of tea. Your aunt showed me where everything is kept." She started to lead the way into the hall. Wendy overtook her.

"No. I'll do it. Where's Colin?"

"He went out with his friend, before Anne decided to call the doctor. They've gone to something called the Scarlet Empress."

Wendy didn't want be the one to tell Colin what had been going on. Or to explain this new arrival. "Well, why's no one phoned the café? Told him to come back?"

"I think the emergency is now over, Wendy. Neither your uncle nor your aunt want a fuss, you know." She smiled that tight, lopsided grin again. "What lovely pictures they've chosen for their hall. Horses. When you come to visit me in London, you'll see all my pictures. I'm quite a collector, you know. Not that I know anything about them. I'm ignorant, really. I'm not like Joshua, who knows everything about the beautiful things he buys."

Wendy was frowning. She couldn't take it all in. "Let's have that tea," she said.

THAT NIGHT THE KITCHEN TABLE WAS LITTERED AGAIN WITH THE USUAL things: used knives, dirty plates and ash trays, Rizla papers, shreds of tobacco, the tall red glasses that Anne had bought the flat for Christmas. And two sky blue bottles of Bombay Sapphire gin.

Serena Bell didn't drink. While the others topped themselves up and talked, much more placidly than on other nights, she gave the distinct impression of waiting for something. Waiting for everyone to wear themselves out, perhaps, and start behaving properly.

How we must have bored her, Wendy thought later. Serena with her friends in high places, and her lofty thoughts. But she sat with Captain

Simon, who told us about scuba diving of all things, and Astrid, who wondered aloud whether one day they would invent something that would enable her to dive like that and see the glories of the deep.

"One day they will," said Captain Simon. "And a whole new world will open up. You will be the little Sea Maid."

"Jesus God," she said, shaking with laughter.

Aunty Anne looked white and didn't say much.

David drank with us, waiting anxiously on Colin, whose turn it was to sit with his father. I hadn't taken my turn yet. I was dreading it.

When they heard the news—what news? Was anything really going on? It wasn't like waiting for a baby to be born. An old man was slipping in and out of consciousness, limboing gently—but when they heard the news at any rate, Belinda and Timon abandoned their romantic Boxing Day dinner for two to sit with us. We needed more chairs. Outside it snowed on the Royal Circus. Timon lit the stove and I found myself surprised again, at how practical he could be when he needed to be.

Oh, anyway, and Serena Bell's eyes were looking at each of us in turn. You couldn't help but feel judged. She was coolly inspecting us for faults. We all thought that.

"Are you sure now, Serena," said Aunty Anne, pulling herself out of her reverie, "that you've had enough to eat?"

"Quite sure."

"It wasn't very good, I'm afraid. Not really a proper welcome."

"I am glad of a welcome at all in these times," said Serena, and Aunty Anne smiled. Anne's speech was crisper, more exact when she talked to her friend. The way she looked at Serena made you think she was studying her.

"I suppose this is the end of Christmas," Aunty Anne said at midnight. "There's no name for the day after Boxing Day, is there?"

TWENTY-NINE

"THERE IS A SMELL HERE," SAID SERENA BELL SHARPLY, AND STOPPED, taking a keen lungful of night air. "A kind of national aroma of Scotland."

Colin and Wendy waited for her.

"Old smoke and hops and sea, I suppose." Serena sniffed at the wool of her smart black coat. "When I come here, it soaks into me and when I return to London, it's still there."

It was the few quiet days before Hogmanay, and they were taking Serena out to CC Bloom's for a drink after midnight. Wendy was startled that Serena had accepted their offer, and rushed back to her room to change her outfit. She thought Aunty Anne's friend must have been used to much fancier company. Colin, though, was taking careful note of how the woman had latched onto Wendy, going everywhere she went, watching her every move and reaction. She was definitely sizing Wendy up.

"I'd like to see you at my age, Wendy," Serena laughed.

"And how old is that?"

"Just past forty. And then some. I want to see what life makes of you."

A chill crept past Colin then, but he stopped himself. Hadn't he thought similar things about his cousin? Hadn't his father said them?

"It will be busy tonight," said Colin. "You've got a drag karaoke and cheap spirits."

Serena smiled as if he had said something very witty. "Oh, I enjoy rubbing shoulders with all the gay boys. They love me, you know."

"Do they?" said Colin.

"I think my gay friends, my gay London friends, rather identify with me. I've had life's hard knocks. I've reinvented myself. I know about men. About desire. I understand them."

"Edinburgh queens aren't the same as London queens," said Wendy.

"A queen is a queen is a queen," Serena corrected her. "It's in the nature of these things. Despite all appearances, nature is immutable, sweetheart. Whatever they look like, or behave like, what all the queens are doing is simply this: they're feeding off the Dionysian energy of the place. The city."

"You've lost me."

"Look at this street," Serena said. "All these Georgian houses. How pure, neat, straight they are."

"The product of a tidy mind, Captain Simon says," said Wendy.

"Jesus God," said Colin.

"Exactly," nodded Serena. "I believe that cities are the great sites of the age old battle between culture, classicism, purity—the Appollonian project, and that which is repressed, vivacious, diabolic, lascivious—the Dionysian. This walk from the Royal Circus to your little nightclub—CC Bloom's, did you call it?—represents the divide and tension between those two warring worlds."

Colin sniffed. "But I know some rich old queens who live up the posh end."

Serena smiled at him like he hadn't got the point. She said, "I myself love the tension more than anything. That's what people miss out, when they talk about treating queens as ordinary, about regarding them as normal. You see, they aren't 'normal', and nor would they want to be. They're partaking in the eternally queer Dionysian revels..."

"Excuse me," said Colin. "How come you get to categorize everyone?"

"It's my prerogative as a faghag. I've been hagging longer than you've been fagging. So listen and you might learn a thing or two."

That shut Colin up until they crossed shrouded Gayfield Square, London Road, and were safely in CC's. When they turned around, he had vanished.

"Probably he found some friends," Serena smiled, when Wendy started to make excuses for him. "I'm afraid young Colin doesn't like me very much. He never did before."

Wendy said, "I've never heard him sound so argumentative with anyone before."

"He resents me. I've known his mother for years. He should thank me, really. It was me who warned her that he was growing up queer. Saw it a mile off, of course. Gaydar bleeping. And I, after all, was the one who had to talk to and console Anne after his diagnosis. He didn't do anything for his poor mother. He clammed up in himself all that time. I had to explain everything to Anne."

"It must have been very hard for her," said Wendy. They were moving through the crush with their drinks, towards a table. People squeezed up.

Then Serena flung off her black wool coat to reveal a skimpy rubber outfit and black stockings. Wendy stared: you could virtually see the woman's nipples. Serena flicked out her hair, laid her coat on a chair and glanced round to see that she'd been noticed. "My faghag's outfit," she said. "All the queens love a little light bondage. They think I'm hilarious."

The man next to her muttered at her and both she and he guffawed. Serena sat down and Wendy asked, "What did he say?"

"I've no idea. His accent was impenetrable."

DOWNSTAIRS THEY FOUND COLIN IN THE DANCE FLOOR, TALKING WITH an ex. He was glad to be rescued.

"He came running over as if I was his best friend," he said. "And he was the one who was a complete bastard to me. That chef."

"Oh, him," said Wendy.

Serena was looking for a space on the floor to drop her cigarette. "Are we dancing?"

So they danced with Serena, who seemed to jockey everyone around her and fall purposefully into strangers' arms.

"Look at him dancing on that podium!" she shouted. "Looking at his reflection. Whooo!" she whistled. "I love narcissists who can really pull it off!" She shrieked at the boy. "He can't, of course."

Then she was dancing with an older man in a leather harness, and several young women in T shirts that had 'Spice up your Life!' and 'Tits!' printed on them. She came up to Wendy with a bottle of amyl nitrate. Wendy felt immediately sick.

"She," Wendy told Colin, dancing over to him, "makes me feel ancient."

"Yeah?"

"Wouldn't you like to be like that when you're her age?"

He gave her a look.

On the steps of the dance floor they found Astrid, perched in her wheelchair, sucking a cocktail through a straw. "I'm here with Tom," she screeched over the music. "You remember? The nice man from the dirty man's place, where they sit in the nude in the sauna?" Wendy nodded. "He's had a terrible time getting me down the stairs to here. He promises he will dance with me. I tell him, I hope I don't spoil his chances tonight."

"Hey," said Colin. "You've got tinsel tied all around your chair."

"Tom said I had to glam it up. He was right, I think." Then she saw Serena, dancing with the young women. "Jesus God, is that your Aunty's friend?"

Wendy nodded.

"She will be falling out of that dress."

"I think she's pissed out of her head," said Colin. Then he gasped, because Serena was holding one of the women in a close embrace and they were kissing as they danced.

When Serena joined them at the bar, she said, "I kept telling her I was never a dyke. Well, not a very good one. Sometimes these young women just won't listen." She turned to Wendy. "Don't you just love being post-feminist?"

"I'm not sure I do."

"Oh, it was such a relief to me. It was my very own Stonewall riot. I felt free to attack anyone the slightest bit dowdy."

"Ah, Tom," shouted Astrid. "This is Wendy's aunty's best friend, Serena."

"Tom runs a gay sauna," shouted Colin as Tom, grinning, pumped Serena's hand.

"Delightful," said Serena. "You must have a lovely time."

"Wheel me on!" called Astrid. "My request has come on! I bribed the young lady for Tom Jones."

Serena stood to watch with Wendy as the others gave Astrid a hand, and unclipped her brakes. "I rather like it here," she smiled, her mouth going up at the side. "I thought it would be much more earnest than this. And I absolutely love these baby gay boys in their swishing kilts."

THEY HELPED SERENA TO HER BED AT FIVE O'CLOCK. SHE HOWLED AT them to take her shoes off first, or she'd break her ankles in her sleep. "Will you be quiet?" hissed Colin. "My dad's sleeping..."

"Oh, he can't hear anything," mumbled Serena, ashamed.

"He can hear everything," said Colin, and walked out.

"That Tom, the sauna man, is a lovely man," said Serena.

"Hmm," said Wendy, struggling with laces.

"Why aren't there any saunas for women like that? Why don't they think women wouldn't want love like that? Why can't women do their thing? In the dark, in dark cellars?"

"Would you want that?"

"Oh, yes," said Serena. "I want to be in the dark."

The next morning she was immaculate, sitting early at the table in a neat grey suit, sipping coffee from an orange bowl. She was talking to Aunty Anne and they were making plans.

"First stop will be Newton Aycliffe," Anne was saying.

"That ghastly place. There's nothing there. Not for you."

They talked like very old friends, Wendy thought, not thinking they needed to look at each other.

"You must come to London. With me."

"I need to go to Ralph."

Serena scowled.

"Don't you approve of this Ralph?" Wendy asked, and they stared at her. "None of us have met him."

Serena composed her features and would say nothing more on the subject of Ralph. She inclined her head in a suggestion of a bow. "I must thank you for a lovely evening," she told Wendy. "And for removing those ridiculous shoes of mine."

Aunty Anne looked amused. "Wendy doesn't realise that beauty means pain. I imagine she was very scornful of your shoes."

"I don't remember," said Serena.

"Wendy doesn't approve of dressing up and making an effort."

"She looks charming."

"As she gets older, she'll see the effort it takes."

"Hmm," said Serena, gazing at Wendy, who was surprised to find she enjoyed this attention.

"Aunty Anne, you make me sound like a slob."

"In many ways you are. Are you going out like that today?"

"Yes."

"There you are, then."

Serena said, "Your Aunt hasn't kept with the times, Wendy. She doesn't understand. I'm sure, Anne, that Wendy knows very well what clothes and disguises can do. She has a shrewd head on her shoulders."

"Perhaps," said Anne sourly.

THAT MORNING AUNTY ANNE SET TO WORK WITH DUSTPAN AND SHOVEL, mop and scalding water. "These bloody stone floors," she said. "These bare boards! There's hardly anything to hoover. There's nothing like hoovering."

"Why are you cleaning everything?" Colin asked, squeezing between shifted furniture. He hadn't seen his mother do this for years.

"I've got the urge to purge," she said.

CAPTAIN SIMON SAT BY HIS FRIEND THAT MORNING, THINKING IT MIGHT be the last time he'd see him.

Where will I be without you, Pat?
I haven't many friends these days
it isn't like the old days
when we
did we
know each other back then?

Sometimes I think I remember
and I can see you and me and being in
fields and the moving dogs
and leaves stuck-in-grass
it all comes back
You never asked me questions
You thought I was boring, I know
I think I'm boring, too
a boring friend
who always wears the same yellow
coat and I don't remember why
and with you goes whatever
clue I might have had.

Pat slept fitfully through that day and, in the late afternoon, the sky over the Royal Circus already black, Colin was sitting beside him, staring at lit windows when he died.

THIRTY

THE IDEA OF INFLUENCE CAME UP AND IT SEEMED THAT EVERYONE WAS talking about it. Serena Bell spoke again about the two combative spheres in the world, the Appollonian and the Dionysian, and Wendy started to find her persuasive. On the streets of Edinburgh, when life returned to the city, ordinary, ordered life after their rather subdued Hogmanay, she saw men in pinstriped woollen suits bustling round the insurance buildings in St. David's square and they looked browbeaten by Appollonian culture. They swished past the drunks and the down-and-outs, who to her now seemed like the battered survivors of Dionysian rounds.

Whenever Wendy was introduced to someone's view of the world, she found it pervading her own senses and everything started to look that way. She took to Serena's influence as easily as she had taken up Aunty Anne's reducing the world to one divided between women who kept themselves nice and those who let themselves go. Still jogging around in her head was Belinda's point of view over a world of replicants and holograms. Serena Bell's classically composed scheme of things was all the more seductive, however. Serena seemed to give licence to all sorts of behaviour: all was inevitable, everything explicable. At Uncle Pat's funeral service early in the New Year, Serena startled them all by reading Yeats' 'The Second Coming' in a throbbing, passionate contralto. Colin was offended to hear his father called a rough beast—he was sure that's what Serena intended—slouching towards Bethlehem, or anywhere. Wendy thought he should give the woman the benefit of the doubt. Probably she meant nothing by it. She'd just wanted to hear her own voice in the dusky chapel, being melodramatic. At the same service Aunty Anne wanted and got Verdi's Requiem, just like at Princess Diana's do, and she sobbed just the same.

The idea of influence was there all the time. Colin complained that Wendy was getting far too taken in by Aunty Anne's friend. "She's a fascinating woman," said Wendy. "A real survivor."

Meanwhile, Timon was terribly wary of her. "You're mixing in esteemed circles now, hon," he sad. "She's taken you under her wing."

"She gives me the willies," said Belinda. "But isn't she glamorous? She's like one of those paper dollies you used to press out of card, and dress up how you wanted..."

Aunty Anne said, "I think Serena's very taken with you, Wendy." And it was decided that Wendy would accompany Serena to London in the days following the funeral. Aunty Anne was also going south, but only as far as Newton Aycliffe, to see her fat man. She would meet them later in Kilburn, where Serena kept her little house.

The flat in the Royal Circus was breaking up. When Serena had read Yeats aloud in the chapel, Wendy latched onto the words, 'The centre cannot hold', and she suddenly saw that Uncle Pat had been their centre. And now they were going their own ways. Uncertainty was the prevailing mood and when they gathered in the evening, it wasn't with any real purpose. Even sitting at the scarred table, drinking and talking as always, it seemed as if they were waiting for something and they didn't know what.

Serena was down the hall, playing Shubert again, very deliberately and it seemed she was biding her time.

Colin and David were the first to go. They flew to Paris. "I'll see you in London later," Colin told her. "You make sure you look after yourself." He wasn't at all sure he should leave Wendy with the others, but knew for himself he had to get out for a while. He wanted to see David in some completely other context. They were at that stage and needing to spend some time with none of the others about.

Timon and Belinda went to the west coast, taking the camera. There had been a rash of UFO sightings in the press and she wanted to capture them on tape. Her idea was that, this time, they *both* would get themselves abducted. They could be great ambassadors, and she would never be afraid with Timon in tow. They told Wendy this. "Take care, hon," said Timon. "And keep your elasticity." This time it sounded like a warning not to get swayed by anyone else's ideas. That seemed like a joke, coming from Timon.

"You're the naïve receptor," she told him.

He took a laughing gulp of coffee and found it cold. They had sat for hours that morning, saying tentative goodbyes. It was time for them to go.

Belinda wouldn't stop hugging and thanking her for introducing her to this lovely man. "My life has changed," said Belinda, "more than I could ever have imagined."

They left, making Wendy feel like a success.

Serena booked them tickets at Waverley for King's Cross.

"You have the whole of the capital to explore."

Wendy found herself being surly. "This is a capital, too."

"I can't believe you haven't done London before. Do you realise how weird that is? At your age?"

Aunty Anne packed up Uncle Pat's things. She had a variety of charities bring their vans to the front door and made the others carry the boxes down.

"Does Colin know you're throwing out his dad's things?" Wendy asked.

"Oh, yes."

But he didn't. When he returned from Paris, weeks later, he was horrified.

ON THE TRAIN THEY TALKED ABOUT SERENA'S SUFFERING. SHE DID IT lightly and with the utmost irony. Wendy was glad to hear her talk, to take her mind off her adopted town, slipping away.

"Of course I have millions of friends, the world over. And I can put the masks on. I never look lonely or tired. But I am lonely, truly. I despise going back to that house in Kilburn when it's empty and I'm alone. I adore taking visitors with me."

She clasped Wendy's hands across the table. The train was full with people leaving after the New Year and both Wendy and Serena had bags on their knees.

"Most people wouldn't say they were lonely," Wendy thought aloud.

"Most people are without feeling," said Serena. "But they are all damaged and chipped in some way. And I might hide my scratches and knocks under a surface of brilliant irony and, if I say so myself, glamour, but you learn to turn the damage inwards. Like a display of fine china. You have to show them the best side. Pull me out of my cabinet, though, and you'd see. Turn me round in a strong light and then... oh, my dear, I'm a horror!"

She made Wendy laugh.

"One day I'll tell you my story."

Here it comes, thought Wendy. Someone else telling me things. If only it was Mandy with this talent for eliciting confidences. She needs the material. But Mandy tended to make people fall silent. Her beauty and her muttering closed other people off from her.

"But I shan't tell you yet," Serena went on. "You're at a funny age to hear a story like mine. I wouldn't want you to judge me too harshly." Then she bought them a bottle of wine from the refreshments trolley, which they drank from plastic cups, and by York Wendy was fast asleep.

SHE WAS DREAMING OF AUNTY ANNE. THIS HAD BEEN TRIGGERED by Serena saying, as they passed through the low, flat fields outside of Darlington and Wendy's head swam: "Your aunt, of course, has never quite learned the true extent of my wild side. She needs to believe in my civility, my good manners. Anne refuses to recognise any other aspect in me at all. She makes me feel full of contradictions." Serena sighed as they hurtled through Darlington station and Wendy imagined her aunt only a few miles away, already in Newton Aycliffe and already part of her other life.

Wendy was dreaming of Aunty Anne in the small new town where her lover lived and had wedged his apparently glorious bulk in a council house, where he held rapturous services for the local women who came to hear him praise the Lord. Aunty Anne extolled his charisma as a beacon in a place horribly lacking in beacons. It was an odd town, she had explained, full of little box houses like dolls' houses and the people she met there she often found surprising. Wendy's dream brought it to life for her, though she had never been to Newton Aycliffe. Aunty Anne wouldn't let her: "I don't want you to see where I've been living in recent years. It represents the past. You have to go on." She was playing the plucky widow, though Uncle Pat had never been to Newton Aycliffe either.

Wendy pictured a place of yellow brick houses and winding miles of estates, satellite dishes and ice cream vans that patrolled night and day, chiming out 'Lara's Theme', the tune from *Dr. Zhivago.*

"During services in Ralph's house, it was me who had to run out when we heard the *Dr. Zhivago* theme and buy his cigarettes and his umpteen bars of chocolate. Ralph would look up from his prayers to take the change and his Bounty bars."

He was Buddha, stolidly attaining perfection in his council house. Aunty Anne said he lived in a place called Phoenix Court, and she said he had chosen it as the place for his mission just because of the name. Phoenix Court described his purposefully arrested spiritual ascendency with wonderful precision.

Then, even in her dreams, Wendy rushed past the North, and she started to imagine London and everything there.

Serena was still talking when they left King's Cross and took the tube and the overland to Kilburn. Wendy followed without a word, drugged by the train ("Still vibrating the next day!" she heard Uncle Pat say) and did all the things Serena did, asking for a Travelcard, hurrying through the white, dirty hall, feeding her pink slip into the turnstile. Serena kept up her chat all the way down the busy escalator, hardly noticing her surroundings, as if she was walking down her own staircase. Others were doing the same.

Wendy was looking at those rushing heedlessly down the escalators, at the posters for musicals with wads of chewing gum stuck to them. She was overhearing snatches of hundreds of conversations. A man at the bottom of the escalator was busking Jonathan Richman's 'Summer Feeling'. Serena was saying, "I feel drawn to spending my time with those younger than me. Most of my friends are, though you are the youngest now. You must think me ancient. I was born before the Sixties. To you, that must be like being born before the French Revolution."

On the tube Wendy sat beside Serena and tried not to look at people's faces. Her face in the window was distorted horribly in the dark and she was embarrassed, realising that everyone else would see the same reflection of her. When someone at the doorway, clambering past, said "Excuse me," it took her by surprise. She'd heard that Londoners were supposed to be rude.

It was going to be a place where you came home at night and blew black, sooty snot out of your nose. Aunty Anne had told her that. It wasn't like Edinburgh, where when you walked in town and between buildings, the crags came into view. Edinburgh was a city of trompe l'oeil, with sandy-coloured mountains and castles hugger-mugger with Seventies tower blocks. It was a city you could escape after a few minute's walk. London wasn't going to be like that.

"AND HERE," SAID SERENA, LEADING WENDY INTO HER HOME, "IS THE clutter, the clabber, the pitiful ragbag of accoutrements that constitute *me*." She went through the house like someone accustomed to living alone, flicking on all the lights, tossing post aside, making towards the kitchen.

Wendy was taking it all in. The rooms were jam-packed with tasteful objects, hangings and pictures, each placed that bit too close together. Newspapers from before Christmas covered the coffee table. The living room which they passed through, and left untouched, was a homage to William Morris, and the dining room to Robert Mapplethorpe. Serena had her head in the fridge. "Everything has turned sour and stale," she cursed. She plucked out a bag of coffee beans and spilled them into the grinding machine. "Don't you hate the flat, bleak smell of a place when it's been empty?"

Wendy had never live in an empty place. By now, though, she was used to Serena's extra-sensitive nose. She watched her friend go through the rooms, wrinkling it and opening windows. She played her messages.

"Sweetheart, it's Joshua. Christmas Eve. I gather you're away in the frozen north. You're terribly missed here. We'll muddle through without you, I'm sure. Phone me when you return."

"One message," Serena sighed. "What an empty life. No tortured lovers missing me. Not this Christmas. I'm obviously clapped out."

"Was that your friend Joshua?"

"We'll see him soon." Serena brightened. "Shall we rustle up something to eat?" She yanked open the freezer and started peeling plastic films off pasta and sauces, mussels and dips.

"Well now," she said, when they sat to eat at the white table. "Aren't we the lucky ones? Everyone else has to go running around after partners and doing what other people want. Look at us! We can please ourselves." Serena ate ravenously, with much less ceremony than Wendy had watched her eat before. "I'm glad I brought you, Wendy. There's so much more for you here, you know."

Wendy fell asleep in a room decorated by only a few, bright stripes of colour.

"Minimalism, sweetheart," said Serena before she closed the door on her. "Good for our souls, now and then."

Wendy succumbed nevertheless to her usual, overcrowded dreams.

FOR THE FIRST FEW DAYS SERENA WAS MOROSE. SOME OF THE GLIMMER and glamour had gone out of her and she trod through her house in a tracksuit and kept the washing machine going. She cleaned and ironed everything she could lay her hands on. She had no piano here and she spent the evenings staring at expensive contemporary art books with her face twisted in regret. "I wish I could paint... or be conceptual. The truth is, I haven't any talent. When other people have ideas and produce things, well then, I'm brilliant. I can see their ideas, see to the heart of them, in a moment. But I'm blowed if I could ever have an idea myself." She took up another catalogue and laid it on her lap. "Look at this young man. Wonderful. He came from nothing: a backstreet in Blackburn, or somewhere. Now he's putting Anthills in glass cabinets in the Tate and pouring oils into the soil and letting them soak through the colony in wonderful colours. He calls them things like 'Ecostructure I' and 'Ecostructure II'. And this girl, she takes photographs of herself each morning and documents the highs and lows of her life by the way her face looks when she wakes up. My life is my art, too... but why didn't I think of doing this? Although I look shocking when I first wake up. I wouldn't want my morning face hanging in the Tate." She cast the book in its plastic wrapper aside. "I'm sorry, sweetheart. I was meant to be showing you a good time, wasn't I?"

I had spent the first days knocking about Kilburn, looking in the rows of shops in the High Street. I had pastries and cakes in an Irish baker's, sat in the window and wrote Carnaby Street postcards to everyone, until I remember that I had very few addresses for my friends. They were all travelling around. On an impulse I bought a drawing book from a newsagent and drew the view from the café, putting myself in as a stick figure, sitting at the bench with the menu and the tomato sauce bottle in the shape of a tomato. Serena had set me off thinking: why shouldn't I be an artist and draw ludicrous stick figures to record my experiences? I put in a few figures lolloping by, getting about their business. I wished I'd done some drawing in Edinburgh, too, so I would have pictures of everyone. But they wouldn't look like themselves, of course. On my Kilburn drawing, I didn't look like me. The way I'd done my eyes, I looked very cross.

On the way back to Serena's house I passed an old-fashioned launderette called Kleen-as-a-Whistle. What made me go in was the Sooty chained up to the door, in case anyone pinched the money for the blind. Inside I found the woman who ran the place, sitting on the bench and swinging her legs. She had no arms.

"Can I help you?" she asked suspiciously, in a thick German accent. Glottal stops and narrowed eyes.

"I don't know why I came in," I said. "I'm new here. I'm just checking things out. I'm Wendy."

"Ute," said the woman and, without thinking, I held out my hand for the poor, armless woman to shake.

"Jesus God," Ute said. "Pass my cigarettes from the bag and help me light up, would you? And then you can tell me where you have come from."

"HE'S PUNISHING ME, OF COURSE," SAID SERENA THAT NIGHT. SHE HAD made an effort today, dressing in black and looking every inch as sophisticated as the first time I saw her.

"Who?" I asked.

"Joshua. He left me that nice message while I was away, and now I'm back in town he won't reply to a single one of mine. I've told him I'm back with a charming companion in tow and he shows not the slightest interest. We shall have to entertain ourselves." She eyed my sketchpad. "What have you got there?" And she made me show her my drawing. She chuckled. "Oh, dear. Is this how you're feeling? You look so bereft. I never knew you drew. It's very northern, isn't it? You've taken Kilburn and made it look as if Lowry was here." She tossed the book back to me.

"Joshua," she grumbled. "I didn't think I'd ever be running after a man like this again. Well, it's no good. I shan't leave any more messages. I've compromised myself quite enough."

"Is he your lover?" I asked.

"Goodness, no. Though he is attractive. Rather out of bounds to me."

"Gay?"

"No, but he's very curious. He has turned inwards, somewhat, in recent years, which only adds to his allure. He has devoted his life to his work. I call it work, but it would be, for anyone else, a hobby. I think I said before that he collects things. Art objects, installations, pictures and pottery. He has a remarkable eye. He and his daughter subsist on virtually no money. Katy is nine and has become a surly, uncommunicative creature." Serena shook herself out of her doldrums. "Let's get you dressed up, Wendy, and we should go out and look at something. Pictures, a play, other people. Anything to get out of this place. Have a look through Time Out and see if you can find us anything."

Serena went upstairs to change into something more suitable for looking at things.

"My life has become a quagmire," said Serena, in a cocktail bar in Soho, "and a masquerade." She didn't enlarge on that just yet.

They hadn't looked at anything much tonight, apart from the frosted pitcher of margheritas Serena had called for.

"You must make sure that you are cleverer than I am," she told Wendy.

In Covent Garden they dodged past crowds watching street

performers and Serena made clucking noises. "I despise jugglers. When I see them walking on stilts I long to push them over."

"On the Royal Mile in the Festival, there were fire-eaters," said Wendy.

"Now that, I love. I would stop to watch a man eat fire." She stopped. "Will you come to the opera with me? Your aunt never will. She went once and loathed it. She kept riffling the programme and asking how long until the interval. She made me take her to see *Cats* and *Starlight Express*."

"Aunty Anne would like shows with lots of dancing in," I said, thinking of her legs and her vaunted high kicks.

"Oh, her and dancing," said Serena.

THAT MORNING, A POSTCARD FROM TIMON.

> 'Bed and breakfast in the western isles, hon. Filming the sky. I'm filling tape after tape and I haven't written a word in days. Snow on the mountains and Belinda tramps around like Julie Andrews. XX.'

And a very short letter from Mandy.

> 'Happy New Year and I'm still in the Professor's house, where he cooks for me and makes me put up my feet while I write page after page. He says I must have a novel ready—even a very short one—by the time my story comes out in *BritLit Four*, that anthology I'm in. Blackpool has come up very clear in my writing and it worries me that I'll never go back, or if I do, it won't be the same. Of course, it's not the same. Our Linda's married the insurance man, all very sudden and quick—did you know? They're in Luxor. Love to you—Mandy.'

"Your sister Mandy has it all sorted out, doesn't she?" Serena said. "I think she has made some admirable choices."

"I think she should have stayed in Manchester," I said. "Done her studies and not got mixed up in the world of men."

"A woman's lot," said Serena. "You have to get mixed up in the world of men. No mistaking it. Mandy can go off, eventually, if she wants to study women's issues, if that's what she wants. But she has to have truck with the world of men. Men are fixed in space, you see, Wendy. They are the solid objects women have to negotiate and slink between. A woman has no real place in this world and she has to make a strength out of that. We can fix ourselves anywhere."

That seemed true of Mandy, of Aunty Anne, of Serena herself. Then I thought of our mam, who stayed most persistently in the same place, in Blackpool, with her kids. In her case it was the fella who moved out, who made a change in his life. Similarly, Timon was the changeable one, who picked up and moved on and threw in his lot with someone he'd just met.

Serena just said, "Gender can be very fickle. People eventually find their roles. It takes money or bravery, or both." She eyed me. "Maybe you will have both."

THIRTY-ONE

THEY WERE AT THE TATE LOOKING AT AN INSTALLATION CALLED 'ON THE Farm' when Serena first properly broached the subject of her past. The exhibition was of severed animal heads afloat in glass pots of various sizes, ranged in a group on the floor. There were twenty-four of them: the largest a bull's glaring, neckless head and the smallest, a newly-hatched chicken's, which looked like a ball of yellow fluff. All of them were being left to deliquesce gently in their columns of glass.

"It's quite affecting," said Serna, stalking round the wooden floor. "Seeing the flesh dropping off like this. It makes you want to return again and again to see their progress."

Wendy said gloomily, "This show will run and run."

"I'm sorry, my dear," said Serena, realising. "And you in mourning still. This is terrible of me. Let's go and look at the Rothko's instead."

So in a room of canvases that were just slabs of wet-looking paint, Serena began to talk to herself. "I remember being tiny, in a very expensive school and I stuck out like a thumb. A sore thumb, I mean, and I suppose I was too much like you: the under-achiever in my class. I sat at the back and I was staring at the sky while we were talking French. They made us learn French early. Mine is very imperfect. I was staring at the sun, daring myself to stare straight at it, stare it out. I like these Rothkos because they are all one colour, like light. The after-image of looking at a clear, sun-filled sky."

To Wendy her sky seemed a bit murky.

"And I sat one day and I saw the plane before the rest of the class did. Soon the noise was unmistakable. It was enough of an event, or the lesson was boring enough, to make all of the girls jump up from their desks—the desks were the colour of toffee, I remember, sticky with varnish—and rush to the windows. We watched the small plane circle and circle, as if it could write a message for us. Even our teacher, Mme. Merle, came to see.

"We watched the sun glaring off its windows and wings. It came in lower, passing over us and we even worried that we'd be bombed. Still we watched. Then, incredibly, it brought itself down and landed safely on the neat green fields beyond our windows. It slowed, slowed and stopped. Well, we cheered and clapped and begged to be let out to greet the pilot. Before we could move, or Mme Merle could give in, the door on the small plane opened and the pilot stepped into the sunshine. She was in black, with a leather helmet, goggles, everything. "It's a woman!" someone shouted and the excitement was, as they say, palpable. Mme. Merle shooed us out then and we ran out into the field to see this woman." Serena smiled at Wendy.

"Who was she?" Wendy asked.

"When we ran up to her I stared. It was *me*. She looked exactly how I would look when I was older. I was sure. That stunning, stunting aviatrix looked exactly as I look now. I am sure of that."

She led Wendy back through the cool halls of the Tate.

"I suppose you were right," Serena said. "That exhibit of heads was ghastly. What are those people thinking of?"

"I like paintings," said Wendy. "I suppose that's old-fashioned."

"No, I adore paintings too. Joshua does watercolours sometimes, you know. Perhaps he'll show you one day, when we eventually get to see him. Now come on, let's get back home before your aunt arrives. I have dinner to prepare."

Aunty Anne was due that evening. It was the later train from Darlington. She had left her Buddha, her fat man in the council house. Last night she had phoned and declared herself free of his pious encumbrance (as Serena gladly put it). And... Aunty Anne had news—thrilling news—for Wendy.

As ever, Wendy took news from her aunty with care.

"There's something in this, though," Serena said, as they walked along the river towards Pimlico tube station. "I've never heard Anne so agitated. She could barely contain herself."

SHE CAME TO THE DOOR IN A TAXI, WHICH WASN'T IN ITSELF SURPRISING, since she hated the tube. Once she said that when she was underground, her nerves went jangly and made her legs jump up and tremble. The escalators were so much more perilous than those in department stores. Wendy and Serena stood on the doorstep, staring past the leafy garden and what did startle them was the ten pound tip Anne flourished in the air, in the sherbert-coloured street light, before pushing it into the driver's hand.

She had brought a whole load of bags, which they had to help her with. She pulled Wendy into a stiff, cold embrace. That same old yellow coat seemed strange here in London. "Hey, I'm freezing. I thought London was meant to be a few degrees warmer?"

"Are you all right, then?" Wendy asked. "Serena said about... you arguing with your man."

"No argument. I took one look at the old slob and thought: I'm not having my life dictated to me by the likes of him. The big pig."

"That's not how you talked about him before."

"Well, absence makes the heart grow fonder, or something. I'd forgotten the reasons I was so glad to leave and go to Blackpool in the first place. So that's that."

She struggled into Serena's living room and flung herself down on the William Morris sofa. "You've been making a few changes in here, Serena." She kicked off her shoes and examined her feet for signs of travel-damage. Her hair was blonde again.

"Yes," said Serena thoughtfully. "Let's have a drink."

"God, yes. Do you know, he had a whole posse of these devout, fawning, bored women around him. They were tending to his every need, apparently, and now he never leaves the house at all. He doesn't need to.

Hasn't tried for months. Doesn't even think he could manage it. I looked at him and thought, I don't need the likes of you."

"Hear, hear!" said Serena, passing her a Pimm's.

"I never liked all the god business anyway," said Anne. "And he had the nerve to ask me if I'd been faithful all the time I'd been away. Not a word about poor old Pat! Not a dicky bird!" She took a long slurp.

"You're here now, anyway," said Serena, sitting herself carefully opposite. Wendy took her own glass and sat down too.

"And I'm staying," said Anne firmly.

"Here?"

"For now, if you'll have me. But I'm buying my own place. In London. You're always telling me this is the place where it's all happening. That I have to get with it. So here I am. I want in, now."

"Right," said Serena, her mouth going up at one side. Wendy knew enough about her by now to know it wasn't wry amusement, it was nervousness.

"So you've got a full house now," laughed Anne.

"So I have."

"Just wait till she," Anne nodded at Wendy, "starts inviting all her pals. You'll have women with no legs, fat mad women, blacks and allsorts on your doorstep."

Wendy realised that Anne had already been drinking.

"She'll turn this house of yours into the same as Pat's place. A home for freaks and skivers."

"Oh..." said Serena mildly, as if about to say that she wouldn't mind, but then she decided that she rather would.

"No, I won't," said Wendy. "And don't call them freaks. It includes you too, Aunty Anne."

"Of course!" she grinned, raising her glass in a toast. "And I'm the Queen of the Freaks. I'm the Queen of the frigging Freaks." Then she burst into loud, wet sobs.

Serena, who couldn't deal with tears, ducked into the kitchen to check on dinner. She was doing something complicated in parcels of pastry, she said, and had spent an age twisting them into just the right shape. Wendy was left to comfort her aunty, which she did awkwardly.

"I'm rich, now," Aunty Anne said, and blew her nose. "Look! Black snot. I've only been here for half an hour." She looked at Wendy, gauging her reaction. "I've come into what they used to call a fortune."

"Uncle Pat?" asked Wendy, and her aunty nodded.

Serena was back in the room as if called. "So you really are going to move to London?"

"A nice big house," said Anne. "Of my own. At last." She smiled blearily at Serena. "I'll need help."

"And you'll get it. So this was your news! Wonderful!"

"Colin's still abroad with that friend of his."

"David," said Wendy.

"He doesn't know about the will yet. He gets enough, and the flat in the Royal Circus, of course."

"Bless him," said Serena. "I can help you shop for furniture, fabrics, things... you must have a garden, of course, and..."

"It's not the only news," said Aunty Anne. She looked at Wendy. Wendy felt herself blush, guessing what was coming next.

"I don't..." Wendy began.

"Three million pounds," Aunty Anne said, in a curious, toneless voice. "That's how much he left you."

Serena dropped back into her chair. She stared at Wendy. "You clever thing!"

Anne glared at her. "What do you mean by that?"

"Why... just... I mean, nothing."

"You can take it back," Wendy spluttered, as if her Aunty had offered her cash. "It's not mine. Give it to Colin..."

"Won't Colin be furious?" asked Serena. "He was the son and heir. Doesn't this cut down his share?"

"Apparently," said Anne, draining her glass, "he already knew about the whole thing. He didn't want much anyway. Pat said so in the will."

It sounded to Wendy like her uncle had been talking again, from beyond the grave. She wanted to hear him, to argue the toss with him. Just to hear him again. Parachuting, he had said, was like coming all over the sky. But trains made him vibrate too much. She wanted to ask, what did dying feel like, then? She started to cry and the others didn't notice.

"That's why Colin took himself out of the country," said Anne. "To be out of the way when this happened."

"Three million pounds,' Serena repeated softly. Her hands, her long white hands, had flown up to her throat and they were still resting there.

"Can I contest it?" Wendy asked.

They looked at her sharply. "Can you what?"

"I don't need it. I can do without it."

"You Uncle Pat," said Anne, "wanted you to prosper. He said as much. He said he wanted to put wind in your sails. To use your imagination. He wanted to see what came of you."

"But he can't," Wendy mumbled through her tears. "He's dead. The money won't help that."

Serena came to stand beside her. She touched Wendy's hair. "It has its consolations, Wendy. You'll see in the end, that life is all about finding consolations."

Anne helped herself to another drink. "After I get the house underway, guess what's next?"

They looked at her.

"Tummy tuck, bum lift, face lift, liposuction. The whole kit-kaboodle. I want to bring all of me into line with my legs before the new millennium." Then she danced a quick two-step on Serena's hand-woven rugs.

I WAS ALWAYS THINKING ABOUT THE NEXT THING. I KNOW I GAVE that impression of drifting along and latching onto people, or letting people latch onto me, whichever way you want to put it. I gave the impression there was nothing I wanted to do, nothing in particular. I couldn't answer when they asked me what I wanted to do. My junior school teacher said I could sing. Miss Kaye made me sing out notes loud as I could go and she felt for my diaphragm, said it had a silent g. She said that I really could sing and that I should learn. After that I never thought about it again: I thought I already could, just by her laying hands on me. Mandy said, Linda said, Timon said, Aunty Anne said: ambitions are things you have to work at. I suppose they despaired at me that I never got behind one of my ambitions, like they said they did to theirs, and pushed for all I was worth. I got caught up in other things and if I gave the impression I didn't care, well, it was false, because I did care. I was always thinking about the next thing.

The next thing would stun me into inactivity. I knew it was out there, Jaws-like, waiting for its moment. It hypnotised me. I went from friend to friend, home to home, knowing that, eventually, it would come to me.

Money comes as a great relief to anyone, of course, and it comes as a special relief to people who—forgive the cliché, Colin—live on their nerves. I was trapped moment to moment, unable, unwilling, to see the larger sweep of time. My mother was dead and I couldn't get by inside her living experience. I had nothing to project my own experience against. When I got to know the hairdresser, Lisa Turmoil, I was jealous of her because she was doing the job, living the life, that her mother had done before her, and her mother before that. They slotted in like Russian dolls. If my women role models were Russian dolls, they were a mix-matched set, and no one got the right bottoms and tops and some were even left without one half.

I made excuses for myself.

I want you to see how I managed, or didn't manage, to handle my life, my fortune, and my eventual husband.

I was aware of all the other lottery winners in London, in the country over. I was one of them now, by default. Since it had started in 1993 the National Lottery had created a fair number of overnight millionaires whose lives, although they various protested this wouldn't be the case, were changed utterly. I was aware of my fellow millionaires, new to their lots, when Serena and Aunty Anne took me out to the big shops. We were like zombies, acquiring cards and new agendas, replacing everything we already owned, and dreaming up the things we had got by without until then. Funny thing was, I never saw a brazen new millionaire, mouthing off in a department store, demanding the best of everything and more. They were, we were, rather shy, as if the money had come to us through dodgy dealings. I felt a fraud.

When Uncle Pat won his fortune it was a Rollover week. That was what they called it when weeks had gone by without a jackpot winner, and the Saturday totals had rubbed up together and multiplied and the pile of dirty money mounted ever higher. He never went on the telly to receive his cheque and crow at the watching multitudes. No congratulations from a top star. No Astrology Annie, the bizarrely witchy presenter who used arcane lore to foretell the week's lucky viewers. Uncle Pat took the money and hid. He didn't go out buying things in London.

I did. It was like one of those stories, about the father who takes his young son to the whorehouse at the edge of town. He leads the boy to the pro, pays her handsomely, and instructs her to give the boy a birthday rite of passage he'll never forget. Afterwards, the father takes his son back, tips and woman and says: "Thank you for turning my boy into a man." And, in the old, old story, the boy glows with spent pride.

Aunty Anne and Serena led me into Piccadilly, then Knightsbridge, with fatherly care. They took me to the correct glass altars and made me spend. Aunty Anne did her own spending, collecting valuables for her new home. She was like the father who, to pass the time, diddles the brothel-keeper, an old friend of his.

I couldn't get very excited about all of this. You were meant to come out of the revolving doors swinging your heavy shopping bags by their gold braid handles and you were meant to be ecstatic. I couldn't keep up the ardour. My excitement—and I did try hard, for the sake of the others—pretty much flopped.

While Aunty Anne and Serena tried on clothes I slunk off to a gleaming coffee bar and wrote out large cheques to Mandy, Linda and Timon. I told Mandy to leave her Professor, Linda to leave her boring new husband, and Timon to come with Belinda to see me. I posted them off and decided I wasn't going to spend another penny that day.

I would try to think more clearly about the whole thing. About the next thing.

The ladies found me sitting at a table at a Rennie-Mackintosh fountain, following the iron curlicues of a peacock's tail with my gaze, completely absorbed, and to them I looked morose. I was so out of step with them. They were in their glory days, I realised. Aunty Anne's independence had come at last. They were free to live the high life they had always wanted, and had goaded each other into finding. In an old Hollywood film, this period in Aunty Anne's life would be represented by a breathless, luminous montage of her having a whale of a time: riding in taxis, pointing impulsively out of the window, measuring new, vast windows for curtains, instructing removal men and artisans, trying on a range of fabulous hats, going to the races and stepping out of those eternally revolving doors, swinging her shopping bags.

THE FIRST THING THAT CAME BACK FROM TIMON AND BELINDA WAS A spray of pink lilies, delivered one morning to Serena's flat in Kilburn. A tight, frosty morning, newly February. The man carried the flowers to Wendy like they were a baby, swaddled in polythene. The outward furling petals looked so exotic, bobbing on their stalks. The orange stamens goggled as Wendy took the prize."Lilies are for funerals," said Aunty Anne. "Haven't we had enough of those?"

Serena fussed around Wendy. "Oh, they're for any time. These are magnificent. So fleshy and cool. Who sent them?"

Wendy read the card. "Timon and Belinda. They found a florist in the Western Isles."

She read:

> We're coming to see you! And we're bringing back the cheque so you can rip it up—very kind of you and all, but—well, anyway, we'll talk about it when we get there—in the wicked city—we're going to be famous, Wendy!—we've got some footage!—breath-taking world-shocking mother-fucking footage!—This will be as big as the 1967 Big Foot home movie, when the lady Big Foot was filmed running back into the snowy woods through the fallen logs—and as talked about as the alien autopsy at Roswell in 1947—oh, boy—you'll see, Wendy—you'll see what we've seen!—Just wait!
>
> Love to you,
> Timon and Belinda.

Wendy looked up. "They've filmed some UFOs."

Aunty Anne tutted.

"They've got evidence?" asked Serena sharply. At Christmas she had heard all about Belinda's preoccupations.

"Apparently. They're bringing it to show us."

"They're coming here?"

"To London. I don't know where they want to stay."

Aunty Anne looked at Serena as if to say, see? Now you'll see. Here come all of Wendy's funny friends.

Aunty Anne was about to move out to Putney at last.

ANNE HAD RIDDEN ALL OVER LONDON ON THE TOPS OF BUSES AND IN HER taxis, her A to Z flat on her lap, spying out her perfect house. "And it has to be perfect," she said, "because this is me, now. This will be the place where I will eventually drop. I mean, I'll stay there—in bliss—until my dying day. No compromise this time. I'll know exactly what I want when I see it."

It turned out that the best she could imagine for herself was a tall, narrow house in Putney. It was just across from a florist and a chain French restaurant, here she soon enjoyed going for late breakfasts. Serena was gently scornful of Anne's choice of mansion home. But her friend had fallen in love at first sight. "Look," said Anne. "All these beautiful, empty white rooms. I don't need any more than these."

She started to ask Wendy when she would move in with her.

Wendy saw, suddenly, that she was in a tricky position. Serena stepped in. This was over pastries and bowls of coffee in Café Blanc, opposite the new, empty house. "I don't think Wendy knows what her plans are yet."

"What are you, her secretary?"

"Perhaps Wendy is going to buy her own home?"

"She isn't even eighteen. Of course she isn't. I'm the one looking after her."

Wendy sighed. There was no use intervening in skirmishes between her aunty and her friend. Wendy and her homelessness were the ostensible subjects, but this exchange had more to do with a host of historical entanglements the two women had got themselves into. They were cool with each other for the rest of that day, rallying only later, when Anne bought Serena a very smart handbag.

IT WAS AT ABOUT THIS TIME THAT WENDY WENT THROUGH PICCADILLY late one night, bored with waiting for the number twenty-two to Aunty Anne's, and she joined the loud gaggle standing around Eros. He looked so flimsy up there, Wendy thought sadly. The whole of Piccadilly Circus had seemed disappointingly small to her, the first time she saw it. It was just like the Golden Mile in the round. There was a dreadful place, a kind of museum of pop music, and they had duff waxworks standing on balconies, high above the hectic streets. With beseeching arms, Tina Turner, Mick Jagger and Brenda Soobie stood looking very unlifelike in the air above Eros.

Standing there, Wendy watched the people hanging around in groups. Tramps and dossers and the homeless, drug users and pushers, boys and girl she supposed were selling sex. She tried to tell who was who and felt absurdly like a bird watcher, clutching her Observer Book.

I know nothing really, she thought. I've never spent a night on the streets. Not even outdoors in a tent. She thought about sunbathing in Gayfield Square with Colin, and how they realised they were being stared at by the pissheads over the low wall.

I could be mugged, thought Wendy, who had two hundred pounds in her pockets. Anything could happen to me. And this is London. No one would care. No one would stop to see what was happening. She was in an old T shirt and jeans again, her trainers were ripped and flapping apart. Or I could disappear here and turn up anywhere. Just another teenaged girl in London.

She counted out the money in her pockets and took a deep breath. Then, walking back to the bus stop by the cinema, pushed ten pound notes into the hands of everyone she passed. Some blessed her, some told her to fuck off. By the time her bus came, she still couldn't decide whether it was deeply unsatisfying or not.

In the new house Aunty Anne was standing red-faced with arms akimbo. She was among her freshly-delivered cases and boxes. How few old things she had. She'd jettisoned her old things as easily as she had Pat's. Some of these boxes bore the names of smart shops. Nothing was unpacked yet, apart from what looked like a banana tree in the living room.

"What's the matter?" Wendy asked, seeing her face.

"We have a visitor," said her Aunty Anne and, as if on cue, the downstairs toilet flushed thunderously and out came Captain Simon, rubbing his wet hands on his yellow coat.

"Wendy!" he cried. She hugged him and was sure that his white moustache had flourished since they'd been apart. He looked older.

"He isn't staying," said Aunty Anne flatly.

"Ohh,' Wendy waved her away and brought the old man through to the kitchen, which was the only habitable room. The surfaces were strewn with unspotted and fragrant herbs and crumbs of black earth. "Are you going to stay with us?"

"I'm in a hotel," he smiled. "She needn't worry."

"It's lovely to see you," said Wendy, and meant it.

"I've left the flat empty," he said, twinkling at her. "Belinda will have a fit. I'm meant to be looking after plants and making sure burglars don't get in. But, to tell you the truth, I couldn't stick the Royal Circus with everyone gone. I had nowhere to go! No pals to visit!"

"I know," said Wendy.

"So I made some plans of my own."

Anne appeared in the doorway. "Don't let him go begging after any of your money."

"Don't be so foul," said Wendy.

"The old devil."

Captain Simon shook his head at her, whistling. "You're a terrible woman, Anne."

"I know."

"I heard about your good fortune, of course. Pat told me something about his plans."

"Don't go expecting..."

"I certainly don't," he said, with some dignity. "I don't need anything. He left me a little gift, but I was never after money from him. He was the best pal a fella could want."

Anne came down the few steps into the kitchen. "He was, wasn't he?"

"Here," said Simon. "Let me see you."

They hugged hard under the new strip lighting.

When they stepped apart, Wendy had slipped away upstairs.

I THOUGHT MAYBE ROMANCE WAS IN THE AIR FOR THE TWO OF THEM. I've always had that sentimental streak. Next morning, though, Captain Simon had gone. I never saw him until years after that. He flew to Africa on safari, and went to look at things in their natural habitats.

"I was quite harsh on him before," Aunty Anne said.

"You were," I said as I saw to our breakfast.

"He's a simple, loyal man."

"That's right."

"But I don't need a man hanging round me. I've had enough of all that."

"Serena says you have to involve yourself in the world of men, only if you have no other choice."

"That sounds like her. And it's true. Now I'm gladly beyond the pale." She eyed me. "But you're not."

"If it does anything, the money means I never have to be dependent."

Aunty Anne shrugged. She looked at her still unpotted herbs. "There are all sorts of thing to be dependent on somebody for."

This was the morning Timon and Belinda were due to arrive and I was queasy with excitement. Timon had become a distant figure again. All I got were his irregular few lines in the post. Nowadays Belinda had a hand in them, and his letters and cards read differently. It must be love, I thought, if she's effecting his prose style.

Aunty Anne and I listened to the February rain plop down and rattle on her backyard. Her courtyard, she called it, and had installed a statuette of a cupid, tottering on one chubby foot. It was festooned in fairy lights which had already fused.

THIRTY-TWO

DURING THEIR TIME TOGETHER IN THE WESTERN ISLES THEY HAD discovered the gently erotic art of bickering. Now on the Central Line and heading for the BBC, Timon and Belinda were nervous and they indulged themselves in an edgy ribbing that was starting to get on Wendy's nerves. She was going along with them for moral support, while they did their live interview.

"I hope my sneezes stop," said a red, wheezing Belinda. She was in an armless, backless silver dress, clutching a handkerchief. She had been in this state ever since they arrived at Serena's house (Aunty Anne wouldn't have them staying at the Putney house) and she had decided that she was allergic to the goose down in the heavy duvet and the luxury pillows.

"Might be the pollution, hon," said Timon. "You *would* have to have a special reaction, wouldn't you?"

"Hm?"

"Anyone ordinary would get allergic to duck down or nylon, something common like that."

She rallied. "I can't help it! And I suppose you're allergic to even more exotic things?"

"Yeah?" he laughed.

"I bet you're allergic to peacock feathers. You'd have to have a duvet woven from a peacock's fan tail, just so you could suffer exquisitely and get everyone's sympathy."

"Well," he said. "You'd have a duvet knitted out of old hair."

"Hair!" she cried. "You'd have hair pulled out of a baboon's red backside and you'd love that."

"I wish the two of you would calm down," said Wendy. At this rate they would both be hysterical by the time they got them to the stage. They wouldn't be able to talk sensibly at all.

Their tape, their priceless footage, had gone on ahead of them. It was waiting to be unspooled live on television, unleashed upon a late night audience. The viewing figures for *Strange Matter* were growing weekly. It was a fairly jokey show that came out live, with the brief to astonish, perplex and outrage the millions-strong public. From Argyle Timon and Belinda had posted a copy of their magic tape and the invite had come almost by return of post. They already knew what they had was hot. And they wouldn't let Wendy watch it until she came to see the show.

SERENA WAS WATCHING AT HOME WITH AUNTY ANNE. THEY SAT ON HIGH stools with the portable in her kitchen.

"They're going to make fools of themselves," muttered Aunty Anne.

They were watching *Beyond The Poseidon Adventure* which starred Telly Savalas, and which had to end before *Strange Matter* came on. The film showed no sign of ending yet.

"Maybe there's something in it," said Serena. "Let's face it, if there was such a thing as visitors from outer space, Belinda and Timon would be exactly the kind to bump into them." She laughed. "You're just jealous because it's you that wants to be on the telly, Anne."

"I've been on the telly."

"Oh, yes." Serena remembered Anne's autumn of TV appearances, a few years ago. She got herself into the studio audience of all the daytime discussion shows. By phoning in and claiming to be the victim of bad holiday insurance, of a mad dog, of a house fire, of a serial killer, of a polygamous rat and finally 'a woman who can't say no'. She had managed to get herself onto three Kilroys, two Esthers, four Vanessas and only once on *The Time, The Place*. Eventually the producers cottoned on and saw through Anne's disguise of dying her hair for each appearance.

One producer said to her, "You must be the most afflicted woman in the country."

"I am!" she cried, and left the green room in high dudgeon. Yet she had slaked her thirst for getting on the telly. For the last one, about 'women who can't say no', she was among a number of women claiming to be in their sixties and that they were miraculous grandmothers. One woman wore a very short dress and closed the show lip-synching to Tina Turner's 'Simply the Best'. Anne thought it should have been her, flashing her marvellous legs all over the credits. The sight of this other woman sickened her.

"I don't need the publicity anymore," said Anne sniffily.

"Timon does," said Serena. "He's trying to get on the television, by making a fuss about Belinda and the visitors, just so he can cash in with his book."

"His book," tutted Anne. On her way to the loo upstairs at Serena's she had pushed into the guest room and, after minimal poking around, found the bound manuscript. It seemed complete. A neatly-written slim hardcover with the title page spelled out in a childish hand.

Pieces of Belinda
By Timon.

Aunt Anne flicked through. It began:

> 'My name is Belinda. I haven't moved much in my life, but the things I've seen!
>
> It is true, though, that I like a view, but I like to sit with my back turned to it.'

Anne's hands were damp and she found herself blotting and wrinkling pages. She flicked.

'I have met a genius only twice in my life and both times
it was like a bell rang in my head.
I met Marlene Dietrich, and I met Timon, my lover.'

Anne rolled her eyes. Who would read this?

Then she found what she called to herself, in her own mind, the dirty bits.

Pieces of Belinda, indeed.

With shaking fingers she put the book down, where she was sure she had found it.

She returned to the kitchen, the telly and Serena and tried to put the thing out of her mind. Nothing got her adrenalin going like poking around in other people's belongings.

As Telly Savalas came to the end of his struggle to find the survivors of the Poseidon wreck, Anne said: "I could fetch his book from upstairs... and we could have a little read, if you like."

"Anne..." purred Serena. She pursed her lips. "If you must you must. I won't read a word of it." She smiled. "So you will have to read aloud to me."

"THIS IS WHERE THE TV LICENSE MONEY GOES," SAID WENDY WHILE they were waiting in the BBC reception. It was a new glass walled edifice with a vast, clean floor. The ceiling high above was white and scalloped. It looked like the inverted hull of a cruise liner. They were called through the bleeping turnstiles and given passes. Belinda had to find the toilet and didn't listen properly to their directions. Timon studied the map. They were to sit in the studio audience until called down. There were no rehearsals: there wasn't time. They were expected to be spontaneous. *Strange Matter* had the reputation of being spontaneous and that was its special attraction. The show didn't like to flatten its guests' oddities by making them do anything mundane like rehearse. Belinda went to the ladies' to throw up.

"I've just seen Astrology Annie!" she gushed when she emerged. "When I said what I as doing here she wished me luck. And then she put a blessing on me for the lottery."

"Oh, boy," said Wendy.

"And she gave me a go with her lippy." Belinda's lips were bilberry blue.

"I hope she hasn't got herpes," said Wendy.

"As if!" said Belinda. Then they fell quiet as Astrology Annie swept out of the toilets, her cape brushing the walls of the corridor. Instinctively they shrunk back.

"Good luck again, Belinda," she said in her dire Transylvanian accent. "And you must be Timon."

Timon gave a little bow.

"I shall be watching," said Astrology Annie, and glided off down the passageway.

Belinda had a soppy grin on her face. "Captain Simon will be madly jealous," she hissed. "He's crazy about her."

"THIS," SERENA SAID, "IS STRONG STUFF."

"I don't understand the woman. Letting him put filthy words in her mouth like this."

They pored over the pages.

"I thought she looked like a very naïve woman," Serena whispered.

"Look at this!" Anne pointed to the phrase 'moist cleft'.

They both drew in a breath.

Anne said, "Do you think she's read this?"

Serena shrugged.

The book fell open at Chapter Seventeen. 'Love at the Royal Circus'. "I'm in this!" shrilled Anne. "Listen! 'Her legs were like monuments—they were her twin monuments—her podiums on which she displayed herself—they were her pride—she existed only for her podiums—she strutted them—she strode about—she wore boots which made her amble and roll along—she was her monument to herself.' What kind of compliment is that?"

"I'm not sure that it is."

"Chapter Six. 'My Brother is Replaced'. Chapter Ten. 'An Orphan Comes to Stay'. This is outrageous! She, I mean he, has turned our lives into some kind of... sex comedy."

"A farce," said Serena.

"I'm keeping hold of this." Anne looked around. "Shall we burn it?"

"No!" Serena made a grab for the book.

Anne was on her feet. "It's scurrilous. I'm going to destroy it."

"It looks like his single copy."

Anne was standing at the gas stove, clicking the ignition. "Good!"

"I can't let you do this, Anne," said Serena, advancing on her. "Give me the book."

"He'll publish it and I'll be a laughing stock. The woman with huge fat legs."

"He won't publish it. It's low-grade pornography, written in dreadful stream of consciousness. No one will touch this."

"Stream of lies!" She couldn't get the ring to light.

"Give me it and I'll keep it safe."

"Will you?"

"You can't burn a book, Anne."

Serena reached out one of her large, perfect hands and took the volume off her friend. She would keep it till later, and examine it carefully in private.

One of the many things Joshua collected was erotic works of fiction. They had to be hand-written, the pages sweated over. The value for him was lessened the wider the readership had been. He liked no one to come between himself and the author's presence. She would phone him and perhaps insinuate herself back into his life. When she went back to him, it would have to be with a present, since she seemed to be out of favour just now. The book went into the knife drawer.

"The film's finished," said Anne, sitting herself disgruntled on her stool again.

They watched an advert for a hospital series, then a murder series, and one about firemen. Then the credits for *Strange Matter* began.

THEY SAT BELINDA AND TIMON RIGHT ON THE GANGWAY SO THAT, WHEN the time came, they could have easy access to the stage area. There was a whole barrage of cameras, cables, technicians and floor managers for them to get through before they would reach the brightly-lit podium and science fiction backdrop and, as they were instructed in the art of whooping, Belinda began to fret.

"I'll get all out of breath going down there," she hissed. "I'll arrive at the bottom looking like a sweating pig." She was already frayed around the edges. She'd been wise, Wendy thought, not to wear a top that would show perspiration.

Timon was clutching her hand and patting it. "You'll be fine, hon." His eyes were avid, staring at the set, which featured large photographic blow-ups of UFOs and unnameable creatures.

The warm-up man was goading the audience, making the first few rows laugh with his Kenneth Williams impressions. Then they all had to do Mexican waves, back and forth, to get into the party spirit. Still chatting, Wendy and the others absent-mindedly stood when the wave hit them, then they flomped back down again.

"We're going to look like fools, aren't we?" said Belinda.

"No hon, we're not."

"Now we need some more whooping," the warm-up man said. "Whenever I hold up this card during broadcast, I want you all to whoop. Whenever someone new comes on, or there's a joke. I shall signal the jokes, and when you have to laugh. Apart from that—be spontaneous. Now, altogether—Whoop!"

They whooped.

Beside Wendy there was an excitable woman who kept coming in too fast with her whoops. She couldn't quite believe that she was in a TV studio, actually seeing *Strange Matter*. She gabbled to Wendy that she had the last two seasons of the show taped on video and knew them virtually off by heart. She wore a black T shirt with a silver unicorn on the front, its horn appliqued diamante. The woman saw Wendy staring. "I'm a member of the Church of the Silver Unicorn? Have you heard of us?"

"Never," said Wendy.

"Perhaps I can tell you about it afterwards?" said the woman hurriedly, because the floor manager had started to count them down from twenty, to going live into the credits. They had to be ready to give on almighty whoop. Wendy found herself taking a deep breath in preparation. The unicorn woman said quickly, as an afterthought, "We aren't a cult, you know?"

Then the show began in earnest.

From the dawn of time the mind of man has been asking himself the big, big questions. Who am I? Why am I here? Where do I begin? And he has to find his own answers. There are other mysteries, too, that the mind of man has worried at. About magic, religion, extraterrestrial life, and the inner world. Perhaps we can shed some light, some tiny chink of light on our profoundly dark darkness as tonight we consider once more... the world of Strange Matter.

The audience whooped.

FOR ME, AT ANY RATE, THEIR APPEARANCE, THEIR DEBUT, PASSED IN A blur. First we had the carrot-haired, obnoxious host Julian, coming on and cracking wiseguy jokes at the expense of those credulous enough to watch his show. A drummer underlined his punchlines, and he waggled his glasses like Eric Morecambe to make the crowd, who weren't offended by his ribbing, laugh even louder. Justin the host drew the cameras' attention to the section of the audience populated by those who had come dressed as aliens from *Babylon 5* and *Blake's 7*. We looked (and whooped) at the monitor screens showing people seeming embarrassed in their tin foil and painted bubble wrap. Then there was a short film about a Christ who wept coke in Venezuela (it was boring) and then, before we knew it, Timon and Belinda were yanked out of their seats, paraded down the stairs and onto the stage. In all the clapping and yelling (as if they'd won something) the woman from the Church of the Silver Unicorn kept nudging me and saying, "It's your friends! Look, it's your friends!"

Justin introduced them briefly. "Timon what?"

"Just Timon."

Justin pulled a 'get him!' expression at the camera. But the camera was busy loving Timon. He looked absolutely calm and assured as he sat on the overlarge settee. He really had the air of someone who had witnessed the extraordinary.

"Now," said Justin chummily. "Tell us all about your film."

Belinda became earnest. "You mustn't treat it like a silly thing. It isn't a funny home movie clip like someone falling on a cake at a wedding, or being attacked by a cat. What we've filmed is... well, it's..."

"All right," waved Justin crossly. "Roll VT." He sat back heavily as the lights dimmed.

We all stared at the vast back projection.

"That was telling him!" Serena smiled.

"He's an arrogant ginger gobshite," said Aunty Anne. "I'm glad his wife walked out on him."

They stared at the portable's screen.

"Jesus God," said Aunty Anne.

THIRTY-THREE

I'M GOING TO TELL YOU WHAT I SAW. WE WATCHED THE TAPES MANY times after that, both their original footage and the recording of the TV show, complete with cutaway shots of a delighted, aghast, drop-jawed audience. The film—only fifty-two seconds of it—caused a sensation first here in this country, and then abroad. Hundreds of thousands of people have viewed and reviewed it since, dredging over its frames individually and in sequence. They have been through its murk with a fine-toothed comb, looking for extra clues in the corners of its blatant obviousness. But I am going to tell you what I saw that first time.

And you must understand—hard to think back now, this side of the millennium—that up until then, what did we have for evidence of visitor incursions? A few crappy shots of lights-in-the-sky, like fag ends glowing in the fog. Or discs that could have been just about anything, or descriptions of individuals that were downright embarrassing. Grey men with faces like a foetus indeed.

What we saw was this:

The bulked, black headland of a portion of Scottish coastline in

January. A night with a storm pending: the firm, tussocky grass steeping in violet, quagmire juices. Timon and Belinda are lugging the lightweight camera and the picture jerks around. We see Belinda in wellies, looking a fright with her hair hanging down (the audience laughs) then she's jumping up and down and pointing straight up and up and up zooms the camera, swishing messily into focus, out again, until it finds the craft. Then the picture clicks into absolute clarity on a dark brown mass, the size of a council house in the air. There are small panels, glowing a gentle lemony yellow, and bodies clustered, peering out. The soundtrack is filled with Belinda's shrill wails and she dashes towards the mass as its lurches onto the dark beach, sending up fans of damp sand, which crash and patter onto her and Timon and the camera, which goes dead.

The audience moans, thinking this is all. But it isn't.

There is fuzzing and crackling and we see the grass and the swampy ground again, very close-up, as if Timon the cameraman is lying on his stomach. Vaguely we can see the opened vessel, its belly gashed apart, spilling light like a wild house party, but one going on in silence. There are figures scattered on the rough ground. We see Belinda, drenched and lathered with mud, nearly unrecognisable. She howls at the figures. They look at us.

For five whole seconds we see a group shot and they look like an outing of friends. There is a woman in a sheer pink frock which is meant to seem see-through. She sits in a wheelchair, a slash up her dress showing off her legs, a yellow wig that sweeps up from her face. She is pushed by a soldierly-looking gent with a moustache and a yellow jacket. There are others: an old man in a scarlet dressing gown, a fat woman with an anxious look about her. Beside them there is a white horse.

The shot slides away into darkness and the film goes dead.

JUSTIN THE SLICK TV HOST DIDN'T KNOW WHAT TO SAY TO THAT. HIS autocue, his script, his own words failed him. The audience were on their feet and the floor manager tried to calm them down. They wanted to see the film again. And again. They wanted to hear Timon and Belinda talk it through.

The show overran by half an hour. The BBC switchboard was—as they say—jammed.

Astrology Annie came on. She was meant to talk about horoscopes in Ancient Egypt but all she could go on about was the footage and surely that woman in the wheelchair was... but it couldn't be... but it was... *Marlene Dietrich.*

At the end of it all, when we were finally allowed to leave, we were called taxis and ushered out of a side door, as if we had done something wrong.

I took charge. Come hell or high water we were going out to dinner. I shouted my instructions and we ended up with almost twenty people coming with us, to an upstairs room of a restaurant in Greek Street that Astrology Annie suggested. When we walked in we caused a stir. The place had been quiet until we turned up.

After the main course, which had arrived past midnight because there were so many finicky eaters in their number, Wendy went to the loo and decided to phone Kilburn from the payphone on the stairs.

"Wendy! Where are you?" It was Serena.

"We're having dinner. Did you see it?"

"My dear, I saw *something*... What is going on?"

"No fucking idea! Is Aunty Anne there?"

"She's furious."

"Why?"

"She thinks you'll be a laughing stock."

"She always thinks that."

"Was it a fake?"

"How could it be?"

"But it was so... ridiculous."

"Did you see them?" Wendy was laughing. "Did you see the visitors?"

"I saw some people. They looked like pensioners."

"What did Aunty Anne say?"

"That she wants absolutely nothing more to do with the pair of them."

Wendy was down the other end of the table from Timon and Belinda, who were being toasted and feted by a gaggle of production staff, audience members and apparently scientific experts. Belinda looked beatific, carefully answering their questions, and Timon seemed wary, eating very little of the banquet that was paraded before them. Wendy hadn't been able to ask them anything yet. She found herself sitting with the Unicorn woman, Astrology Annie and another woman, with lank brown hair, who she didn't know, and who kept disappearing into the toilet. Wendy tried to make conversation that had nothing to do with UFOs.

"You brought my uncle luck, you know," she told Astrology Annie.

"Did I? Where is he?"

"He's dead now."

"Not that much luck, then."

"I mean, he won the lottery in a Rollover week. He died a millionaire. And you predicted it. You said that week it would be someone just like him."

Astrology Annie sighed. "I wish people would write in and tell me when that happens. I might get a rise. Everyone thinks I'm a joke." Then she went off to refresh her bilberry-blue lipstick. It took a lot of concentration, because she had to invoke her spirit guide to help her get it on straight. "I'm slightly wall-eyed, you see," she said, staring past Wendy. Wendy had already noticed and said something pleasantly about that giving Astrology Annie a special psychic look. "Hmm," sighed Astrology Annie.

"I don't know what my church will make of this?" said the Unicorn woman, from over the dessert menu. "Strictly, I don't think we believe in extraterrestrials of any kind? This might be banned?" She looked gloomy. "I might be guilty of blasphemy even now, just by being here?"

Wendy asked, "So what do you believe in?"

She looked at Wendy. "Horses with horns on their heads?"

"Everyone!" called the produced of *Strange Matter*. "I give you a toast. To our intrepid souls here. Tonight we have seen something that might prove to be a landmark in the history of the unknown. I give you... Timon and Belinda!"

We all applauded and shouted raucously. The Unicorn woman whooped.

Timon was called upon to make a speech. He smiled shyly and, I'm sure, won the hearts of everyone there. He said, "Something new, coming true."

We all applauded again.

Timon coughed and said on more thing. "I've... um... written a little book about..." He was besieged by cries and quickly disappeared behind the backs of those who had risen from their chairs to talk with him. People were getting up from other tables, no doubt earwigging on it all. Some of them had actually seen the show. The next morning I learned Timon had been offered six contracts of varying generosity before he got to his peach melba sorbet.

Astrology Annie came back from the toilet. "Oh, is something happening?" She sat down and nodded at the unknown woman's vacant seat. "I found her in the Ladies'. I thought she was throwing up. All this green business in the sink."

The Unicorn woman shook her head. "That's my friend, Lizzie. And it's not sick? It's ectoplasm?" She looked disgusted with Astrology Annie. "You should know all about that?"

SERENA CHECKED THE HOUSE. NO ONE, SURELY, KNEW THAT TIMON AND Belinda were staying here. Still she peered out into Plympton Road and tried to make out shapes hiding in her garden. She knew the press would be round like a shot. But there was nothing.

Annie had flown to her room some time ago and hadn't returned. Serena was too dazed, thinking too fast about all sorts of things to wonder why her friend seemed so upset.

Switching off lights, turning off the oven, checking doors were locked, slipping into shoes sensible enough for the cold night. She stopped and thought hard for a moment. Then she picked up her mobile and called for a cab.

The book was in a knife drawer. She took it out.

Serena checked to the final page and it seemed complete. The pages were numbered, even. It felt warm in her hands, as if Timon had only just set it down, newly-done.

The taxi honked once discreetly at her kerb, like a cough. Serena slipped out and clicked the lock after her.

"Greenwich, please," she told the cabbie and gave him Joshua's exact address.

By the time they tumbled out into Charing Cross Road it was the early hours. Timon had pockets filled with scraps of phone numbers. The producer slapped his back and said he'd phone tomorrow. Belinda was shivering, pulling Timon's jacket over her backless dress. We decided to head towards Trafalgar Square, looking for a taxi. "We should have phoned from the restaurant," said Belinda dreamily.

"They were glad to see the back of us," I said.

"Who paid for all that?'

"I did."

"Oh, Wendy... you can't."

I shrugged. Raised my arms. I was drunk. "I'm a big heiress now, aren't I? A big fucking humdinger of a rich heiress!" Using Colin's favourite word made me miss him suddenly. I imagined his reaction to tonight.

"Hey, hon," said Timon, becoming himself again. "That reminds me." From his wallet he produced the cheque I'd written them and he started to rip it up.

"Don't do that!" I made a grab and rescued it.

"Don't fight, you two," said Belinda, looking round. "That lot are still behind us, watching."

It was true. Astrology Annie had dashed off ages ago, to write the whole thing up for her spooky column in the *Telegraph*. But behind us the Unicorn woman was helping Lizzie along. The ectoplasm woman had her handbag held up over her chin.

"Oh, let's get out of here, kids," said Timon. "I'm thinking of a nice goose-down bed."

"I want you to have this money," I said.

"We don't want it."

"I didn't want it, either!" I shouted. "Uncle Pat gave me no choice!"

"He loved you, Wendy," said Belinda.

"He loved you fellas as well," I yelled. "Jesus God. Just go and spend it, will you? For me?"

"Well...."

"I don't want the responsibility for all that money."

"I'll make money anyway," said Timon blithely. "I'm going to publish my book. *Pieces of Belinda* will make us a fortune."

Belinda glowed.

"Is that what you've called it?"

He nodded, watching out for a cab. Then he told me, "You can't please everyone, you know. You'll try to, but you can't."

Our taxi came.

"Yeah, well," I said. "I can try, can't I?" A thought struck me as we clambered aboard. "You do have a copy of that tape, don't you? I mean, we haven't left the only one back there?"

"We've got copies," he grinned. "Plympton Road, please. The pictures are out in the world now, anyway, hon. You'll see. By tomorrow they'll be in everyone's eyes."

The cabbie asked us, "Did you see the telly tonight?"

"We saw."

"Fakkin aliens! The fakkers've landed! And they looked just like fakkin ordinary people!"

"We know."

THE PAPERS NEXT MORNING GAVE THEIR COVERS TO TIMON AND BELINDA. Almost all of them used Belinda's chosen word 'visitors' and this word was repeated in bold across all the front pages.

Imagine an old film at this point. That thing they used to do, spinning the front pages, one after another, up to the camera.

The pictures they took from the video stills came out rather badly. Dark fuzz with tiddly figures. It was disappointing, so the papers mostly elected to use shots of Timon and Belinda themselves, stepping out of the BBC's side entrance.

I was first up next morning. The phone was already ringing and it never stopped all that day. I checked the answerphone was on and let it be. Belinda and Timon lay in, under their goose down, and I could hear Belinda sneezing in her sleep. No sign of Aunty Anne, and Serena's bedroom door was open, her bed untouched.

I went out for a walk down Kilburn High Street and bought all the papers.

I went to the launderette to see what Ute thought. I arrived just in time to turn the page for her. Please turn to page two and three for full story.

"Jesus God," said Ute. "The aliens come and they look like this fat woman and black man."

"They're just the people who saw them," I explained. "Those two aren't the visitors."

"That's not what the *Sun* is saying," said Ute.

"It was true. Their banner read: VISITORS GO HOME and underneath it, Belinda and Timon's faces looking startled, almost affronted.

THIRTY-FOUR

ALL THIS TIME MANDY WAS PREGNANT IN THE NORTH. AND SHE WAS getting huge, she wrote. She wrote and told me she was like the swans on the canal by the Professor's house, where he walked each morning to clear her head from writing through the night. She wrote at night to keep the Professor from seducing her.

She felt like the swans, full-breasted, heavy-bodied, on the frozen canal. They had nowhere to swim and Mandy said she laughed when she saw them skidding from bank to bank, trying to crack the ice. If they cracked the ice with their weight they'd still have nowhere to swim, she said.

She wrote and asked what I meant by sending her money. That was the beginning and end of her qualms about accepting it and she cashed the cheque, put it to good use. She stored it up for her escape from the Professor, the learned, bearded Sultan who kept her all that winter and sometimes, she said, he tried to get his end away with her. He knew she never wanted him really and he turned glum and folded in upon himself. He carried his years and learning heavily that winter. When she read—her voice getting stronger and surer—chapter by inevitable chapter, he sometimes played with himself surreptitiously in the firelight and she didn't mind.

She wrote and asked what was all this fuss about Timon and Belinda. No TV in the Professor's house. That was how he kept himself free from the pernicious hold of the everyday. He didn't know anything he didn't want to know: he had no inadvertent knowledge. Only Mandy could surprise him, or he permitted her to. But they both read the papers when they knew Timon and Belinda were in them.

Had the world gone mad? Mandy wanted to know. Listening as it was to Timon and his funny, old girlfriend. They had been on telly again and again those early months of the year. And there was talk of Timon having a book out, the literary companion to his short film. The papers talked about the book being published soon, though Timon held them off. An artist, such an artist, Mandy said. He'll be finicking the details and holding his publication off. Booting up his price. Mandy hoped he'd keep holding them off, since she wanted to be the first in print. Her story was coming out in March, her novel was almost complete. Hers and Timon's was a race to get into print, a wager they'd made way back in Blackpool. I'd never heard of their wager before.

Mandy said that when her story came out in March, she would come to London and see me at last. In April her baby ought to be ready to drop.

The Professor's hold over her was by no means complete. She pitied him now. He was a Sultan only in his own house, masturbating over her nightly tales.

That winter and Mandy's letters seemed so clear to me now. Yet that was a time when none of us yet knew her daughter, Lindsey, who still hadn't been born. Mandy wasn't yet published, she was waiting. Those facts make it seem a very long time ago. What also makes it seem an ago to me, is that I still hadn't met my Joshua, my eventual husband, and his daughter. That was all about to happen.

Mandy hadn't yet had her reviews for her story in March. Those reviews, I remember, drove her crazy. It was very full of meaning, they said, it was laden with a—big breath—superfluity of meanings, resonances, allusions. And so it was a success. Her story was called 'Me in the Monster Museum' and that was to be the name of the novel too: a sprawling, compendious book, written and finished off during that winter.

"Allusions? What fucking allusions?" our Mandy asked when she read the reviews in London. "They'll say I was cheating next." And, like many a successful woman, they wanted to know about the man they felt sure was behind her. Sure enough, they turfed out the Professor, her hirsute beaming Professor, although the Professor didn't need much turfing.

They thought she was Collette and he was her Willy.

'What?!' Mandy shouted.

WHEN SHE ARRIVED AT KING'S CROSS THAT MARCH SHE DIDN'T THINK TO ask for a porter to help with her bags. Down the platform she came, her face in a rictus. I went running through the oncoming crowd to help her. I hadn't seen my sister for most of a year and the changes were alarming. I hadn't reckoned on seeing her big like this, with the baby virtually poking its head out of her. She was still Mandy to me, Mandy who would never get caught, Mandy who knew a thing or two.

Still drinking and smoking though, even with the lump in front of her. We dragged her cases into the pub at King's Cross that was meant to look like a country pub, with flock wallpaper and horse brasses. She looked very pale and her face was luminous with sweat. It was two in the afternoon and she made me fetch two pints of lager for us. "I'll never get on the Tube with this little lot," she said numbly, taking in her lump with her baggage.

"We don't have to, do we?" I said. We hadn't said much to each other yet. We were still testing the waters. She looked at me dubiously, as if I was something that had fallen out of her nest and been returned to her.

"I know what you're thinking, Wendy. I always did."

"And what's that?"

"You're looking at me funny because I've made myself look stupid, taking up with two stupid men, one after another."

"I never said a word."

"But it's just the way it ended up. I loved Daniel, I really did. The way he used to read that woman's books. Maybe I just wanted to be her and get all of his attention."

I looked at her.

"Ok, it's trite, but it's my life, right? Anyway, he lost interest when Lindsey came along."

"It's going to be a girl? You've already named her?"

"Yep. And the Professor... just happened. But you can't cut yourself out from the disastrous relationships, Wendy. The things that aren't quite right. You can't hold yourself up pure and separate."

"And that's what I'm doing, is it?"

"You're looking at me funny. Judgemental."

"No I'm not! And I'm not trying to be separate about anything."

"This money of yours is a problem, you know." She swished the remains of her pint. "If it means you'll never have to compromise or depend on anyone. It'll be trouble if it means people only ever depend on you. You'll get too far out of ordinary life."

"No I won't. I haven't yet."

"Hm."

WHEN MANDY ARRIVED AND SAID ALL THIS, LIKE A LIST OF THINGS SHE'D prepared on the train, she disturbed me. Because just that week I had met Joshua for the first time. He came unexpectedly to Serena's house while I was there. This was the rare, bold Joshua whose appearance she had built up to, fearing him lost to her. He came in laughing (a good sign) and treated Serena like his oldest, best friend. She became twitchy and animated and her house took on a new atmosphere that afternoon. She felt included again.

I heard him moving about downstairs and listened a while before coming down. He was turning off music and replacing it with his own choice—Rimsky-Korsakov, I think—all heady and *Arabian Nights*-ish. He was saying, "Serena, anyone would think you had a teenager living with you. Or that you'd discovered a second, a third, a fourth youth of your own."

"I have," she said, laughing.

"You've become the good mother at last, have you? Taking in this girl?"

"Don't make her sound like a waif and stray, Josh. She's hardly that."

"Well."

When I came into the William Morris room I found him sitting indolently on that settee that sucked you in and made it very difficult to move again. Joshua, though, was out of it in one movement that was meant to be sinuous, but he faltered at the last moment, dropping his cigarette on the African coffee table and swearing. He shook my hand and smiled and sank back down. "I'm Joshua," he said.

He was then about thirty, I suppose. Serena had explained she'd taken him up to join her friends when he was quite young, but he had never really become part of their set. He was forever offending them. "Not that he sets out to," Serena explained. "Josh likes who he likes and he's very loyal, I suppose. But if he takes against you at first sight, you'd never know it. Only, eventually, he'd say something to take your breath away." Even on first meeting Serena, who claimed to be one of the people he was closest to, he had, during dinner, told her she was 'wonderfully greedy and self-centred' and that was why she'd insisted on not having a dessert, but trying spoonfuls filched from everyone else's.

That first day in Kilburn he was in a tangerine linen suit, quite crumpled, with the shoulders rucked up from the way he'd thrown himself down. He had the Saturday papers already spread out across his lap carelessly, and his shirt was so white, his hands so clean, that you couldn't help but worry that he'd cover himself in newsprint. And this was my first reaction to Josh: an involuntary twinge, because he set out so clean and obviously he took care of himself, but he immediately messed it all up. He was smoking impatiently, taking swift gulps and blowing it noisily out of one side of his mouth like Popeye. His head was shaved almost completely, his features large and sensuous, with a jaw that dimpled when he read. He was unshaven and I found that very sexy from the start: his tiny blond hairs everywhere which, he once told me, sometimes grew in pairs in the same place, and simply slid out of his face when pulled gently. Later on he would let me try that. He was looking at me over his trendy half-moon glasses, which were very dirty. When Serena entered the room with a tray laden with her Mexican pottery tea service, he shot his cuffs to show he was wearing scarlet cufflinks.

"They're beautiful," I said. "Like burning coals."

"Would you like them?" He grinned at me, stubbing out his cigarette quickly and fiddling with his cuffs. "I'd gone off them anyway, actually."

He pursed his fleshy, succinct-looking lips, uncrewed the links, and handed them to me. "I'm sure you'll find a use for them."

I didn't know what to say, so I took them.

Serena seemed very nervous, perching herself on her usual chair, looking at us. "The tea's passion fruit."

"Oh, fuck," said Joshua. "Why do you always have to push the boat out? Something strong and sweet and ordinary would have done for me. And this girl's from the north, isn't she?" He inspected the tea service. "But your ceramics are rather nice." He felt over the warmed surface of the mustard and purple glaze as if he was reading Braille. When Serena poured his large cup he let it cool all the way through his visit, only drinking it at the end, in a single, gulping swallow. He only ever stayed long enough to let the tea cool. Josh always gave that impression of having to be off, with other things to do, but when you went with him and found out what those things were, it was most often another cup of tea he had to wait to let cool and another pile of newspapers he could riffle and dirty himself with. I ended up loving the way he read the papers, seemingly cover to cover, every column. I watched his eyes flick back and forth. He spent hours, but it was the only thing he did fast. It turned out he knew everything about what was in the papers. "Oh god," he'd say. "Listen to this." The bits he found to read to me were always to do with somebody's ineptitude.

"Of course I know better than everyone," he would say when challenged. "I just can't *do* anything, can I? It's when you try to go and do things that you fuck it all up. I like intentions. They're fine, and as long as they stay in your head, they stay that way."

"He's very anal," Serena put in.

"If I was anal, I'd be forever on the point of doing something," he said briskly. "As it is, I'm not. I know better than that. Coleridge would have been a finer poet if he'd fallen asleep for all of his poems. If the person from Porlock had come knocking every time he was trying to write up what he'd pieced together. Imagine having a reputation for brilliance and nothing to show for it! There would be nothing for anyone to pick over and tell you you were actually rubbish." I liked the rolling way he said 'rubbish'. He said it with tremendous relish (which is one of his phrases, actually, not mine) in his cultivated accent, his exemplary, buffed-up BBC voice. "Coleridge was the last man to claim he'd read everything that had been published up to that point," Joshua went on. "Imagine being him! He didn't have to write a single word. He could go round being the universal expert, the only one in a position to judge. He could go round telling people—that's rubbish, they're rubbish, and you're rubbish as well." Joshua sighed and lit himself another cigarette, snatching it out of his mouth while he was still inhaling. "Yet he had to go on writing things. He fucked his happiness good and truly. Mind, he wrote some lovely things."

I hadn't read Coleridge then, so I didn't say anything.

Serena began: "'In Xanadu, did Kubla Khan...'"

"Yes, yes," said Joshua, to shut her up. "Now explain to me again why you haven't been in touch with me. Not since I sent you that lovely message at Christmas." He looked at Serena over his glasses and his eyes were blue and hurt.

"I left you lots of messages!'

"Did you?"

"Yes! Then I gave up because you were snubbing me."

"I don't snub people. I just don't listen properly to messages. You know that. When I get in and press the button, there's so many things to do. There's the child to look after."

"You don't do anything! You've got all of those women doing everything for you!'

"There's the child to talk to," he said. "It was you who said I shouldn't ignore her. To talk to her like an adult."

"How is she?" asked Serena eagerly.

"Nine going on forty-nine. I've had to buy her a huge computer so she can... *surf the net*. If that's what they call it, but she's shown me what it can do and really, it's more like paddling. She's writing a horror novel, drawing some horribly lurid pictures. She's going on about something called *Girl Power* and starting to fret about her weight because she's getting teased at school. I pay a fortune to keep her at that school and this is the treatment she gets." He squished his cigarette and took up a fresh one. "Ow. I've got a headache. She isn't fat, by the way," he told Wendy. "But girls at that age, I'm sure you know, can be poisonous. Katy is just tall and rather well-made, even if I do say so myself."

"Your best accomplishment," said Serena.

He pulled a face. "You don't create children in that way. They just happen. I don't believe in biology."

"That's ridiculous!" She seemed to be angry with him.

"Don't give me your pre- or post-feminist rubbish, Serena. I can only speak for myself and, to me, it seemed that Katy just happened. Although I'm glad she did. She'll be a good companion in my old age. I warned her, though, not to grow much more. She looked at me so seriously. I said, women should be like the best books. Not too long, and certainly not padded out."

"You're a horrible father." Serena tried to pour more tea for us, but I'd had enough of the flowery stuff and Joshua's cup was still full.

"I'm more like a brother to her. Free not to tell her all the things a parent should tell her. I can tell her all the wrong things and she loves me for it. She'll be fine and rebellious and thoroughly cynical."

Serena looked dubious.

I realised that she and Joshua knew each other very well and that they had talked this through many times. Perhaps by now it was ritualised, or a performance for my benefit, as I sat listening and not saying much. For the first time it struck me that it might not always be for the best when two friends knew each other that well. It could even be inconvenient.

'Will you come and see us?" Joshua asked me suddenly. "We live in Greenwich. The deep, dark South of the river. Serena will bring you. Katy would love to meet you. Outside of her ridiculous school she hardly sees anyone nearer her own age."

"Wendy's twice the girl's age!"

"I bet she can still get on with her though," said Joshua. "Will you come?"

I nodded. "Of course."

Then he was drinking down his tea, tugging his clothes straight, and preparing to leave.

"And you," he told Serena firmly, "had better act more fondly next time you see me. I think Scotland has made you hard and cold."

"Oh, rubbish," she snapped. Then he pulled her into a sudden warm hug and was gone.

Serena lingered thoughtfully over collecting up the tea things. "I'm sorry if Joshua is a bore. He's in a world of his own. You don't have to go round there if you don't really want to..."

"I meant it," I said. "He's all right."

"I worry about my friends meeting up like this. I've had some awful disasters. And in the disasters, Joshua is usually involved. He met a friend of mine once at a wedding and she was so nervous about a dress she'd bought months earlier for the occasion. He came striding over— he was clad in midnight blue velveteen—and told her she looked like a hooker and had that been the point?" She smiled her lopsided smile at me. "He seemed to take to *you*, though."

"I liked him."

"He seems different. Rather downcast. He was slower, too, in his way of talking. As if he was on Prozac, maybe. He did say last year he was thinking of giving it a whirl."

OUR TRIP TO GREENWICH WAS FIXED FOR THE FOLLOWING FRIDAY. WE saw him sooner though, and with his daughter, when we went swimming at an old-fashioned pool that Serena insisted I had to see. I had to see the mosaic walls and the Art Nouveau ceiling. She wore a black one-piece and sat smoking at the edge, tapping her ash into a sea shell and gazing at the glass ceiling with its swirling peacock design and I swam lengths, loving the warm choppiness of the water, its voluptuous pull. This was exactly how I had imagined the place under Astrid's launderette on Leith Walk, even down to the rows of green changing cubicles along the side of the pool.

We had taxied all the way across London just to be there that afternoon and we had come, without realising it, quite near to Joshua's house. The first I knew that he was there with the child, as he sometimes called her, was a cry that went up from Serena. She was waving and I stopped at the deep end, watching heads turn to see her hurrying across the wet tiles to talk to the new arrivals, who both had rolled orange towels under their arms. Joshua was in white linen today, with a soft pink shirt. His daughter looked sullen in cycling shorts and a *Strange Matter* T shirt. I plunged back into my lengths, trying to follow the madly distorting lines painted at the bottom of the pool.

When I stopped next I caught my breath and drifted over to where Joshua and Serena sat talking. He wasn't even wet yet. His soft fair hair, all over his chest, round his tiny, pale nipples and on his neat stomach, was completely dry. They were talking and watching Katy, who clung to the edge some distance away, thoughtfully playing with handfuls of water, as if she was studying and comparing them.

Joshua caught my glance and laughed. "Did Serena bully you into buying that swimsuit?"

I felt my face burn. She had, of course.

"It won't wash well, you know. Those fashionable ones never do. If you're planning to swim properly and a lot, it will fade like a dishrag."

"Such a fucking expert," muttered Serena. The only time I heard her swear was when she was with Josh. I hauled myself out to sit adjacent to them, so that I could have a good look at his body. I took my goggles off first.

He was beautifully made, of course, with wide, muscled shoulders and a small waist. His thick thighs were squashed down on the tiles and I watched them work as he absently kicked at the water. His chest was small and later I was to hear him bemoan his lack of pectorals. He was an unashamed narcissist, but only, he claimed, because he knew he looked less than perfect. But he carried his body with easy, negligent pride, changing his clothes (as he did, three times a day) in front of anyone who happened to be around. He was covered with cappuccino-coloured moles that he would inspect routinely for cancerous danger signs. I was staring at the rounded nub of his collar bone, evidence that he'd once broken it and had it inexpertly set, when Serena suddenly said: "Look at her, staring at you! You'd think she'd never seen a naked man before!"

"I'm not naked!" he protested, and jammed his legs together self-consciously. "And she can look all she likes. As long as I can stare back." He gave me a good looking-over then and smiled approvingly at my breasts, which had always been big and now the nipples were standing on end. It was the chill after the swimming, but it seemed like he did it just by looking at me. Josh was always very frank about his sexuality: it was part of his indolence. Or maybe vice versa. He wanted you and he wanted to lie curled up with you all the time, and he never got bored, he never wanted you to get up, ring the changes, open the curtains, wash the sheets.

"You should meet Katy," Serena said. "Katy, sweetheart?"

"What?" Katy thundered, still cupping her handfuls of water

Joshua explained, "She's trying to catch the reflections of the stained glass in her hands. We've been coming here since she was tiny. I've told her she should swim, but she can't be bothered. She thinks she can take the reflections home with her."

"A collector just like her father," said Serena.

"Not really," he sighed. "She's always breaking things." He brushed carefully at his chest, at a pale scar he seemed self-conscious about.

I asked, "What happened to your collarbone?"

"Is it that noticeable?"

I shook my head.

"I used to row, at Oxford."

"That's how he got his lovely muscles," Serena said.

"Hilarious, isn't it? That was ten years ago and I haven't done a stroke of exercise since. I should be a blob."

"And he eats like there is no tomorrow."

"Anyway, I broke my collarbone at a boating club do. I fell off a chair. Some complete fucking fool set it like this, half an inch out of place and wouldn't put it right again. Said they'd have to break it again to put it straight. I said, that's ok, if that's what it takes, but they wouldn't. They let it knit back like this, like the hunchback of Notre fucking Dame."

"It's not like that..." I said.

"And do you know what the surgeon said?" He looked incredulous. "He said, it's not as if you're going to be a model, is it?"

Serena tutted and looked away.

"I mean, I'd never considered modelling, but to have it taken away like that, and decided for me... I felt like a freak."

Katy came over to us then. She'd let her reflections go and she came to float beside her father's legs.

"Hullo," he said and she scowled. "This is Serena's friend, Wendy."

The child looked at me. "You've got big tits."

"I know."

"Serena hasn't. Serena's hardly got any."

"Now, Katy. I've told you before about upsetting Serena."

"I'm not upset," said Serena. "It just... for god's sake, Josh, she's nine years old. She's old enough to know what she's saying."

"Of course she is. And she knows what she's saying, don't you?"

"Yeah."

"Then, I wish she'd learn some manners."

"Manners are for people who want to hide something," said the child. It was obviously something she'd been told many times.

"Yeah," said Joshua. "Manners suck. My lovely daughter and I are on a crusade to rid the world of manners, aren't we? And tell people what we think of them?"

"Yeah, Serena, you're..."

"That's enough, Katy."

IT WAS THE DAY BEFORE WE WERE DUE TO VISIT THEM AT GREENWICH that Mandy arrived at King's Cross with her few bags, her unborn baby and her author's copy of the book in which her story was printed. She signed this and gave it to me on the way to Aunty Anne's house. "I can't take your copy!" It was a thick paperback, over five hundred pages of stories, with a union jack on the cover. *BritLit Four: New Stories for a New Britain.*

"Have it," she sad. "I'll pinch another at the launch party."

Which was next week, at SuperBooks in Charing Cross Road.

"Are you nervous about it? About being launched?"

"Am I hell." She glanced outside as we heaved around the corner into Sloane Square. "It's only a story."

HER HOUSE ALMOST COMPLETED, FILLED WITH THE SPOILS OF MANY consultations and shopping trips with Serena, Aunty Anne was spending a lot of time at home in Putney. It seemed to me that the place didn't quite suit her. It was all that minimalism—far too much of it—good for the soul as it apparently was. She had lots of space to move around in, which she liked, but the walls were bare apart from a few examples of chilly abstract corporate art, which she didn't like much anyway. "I'm investing," she explained, "in bloody horrible stripes and dots."

When we turned up she didn't seem very pleased to see Mandy.

"And you're keeping well?" she asked. "No problems?"

"Having babies is easy so far," said Mandy. "I'm a text book case." Mandy had already told me that she was having sleepless nights, not only because of the writing. And she had gory morning sickness. When she talked about the muscles of her stomach stretching apart to make room, I thought of butterfly wings being pulled off and it made me feel cold. As always, Mandy spared me no details. Aunty Anne was quizzing her about her plans, subtly making it clear that she wouldn't be welcome to stay here forever.

"I'm looking for a place of my own to rent. I thought maybe I'd stay her. See what literary London has to offer."

"You wont' be doing much in literary London with a kiddie to see to. Why don't you go back up home?"

Mandy didn't answer that one. "I was sorry to hear about Uncle Pat."

"He had a rough time at the end." For weeks Aunty Anne had been silent on the subject of Pat.

"I remember him telling me how chickens drowned in the rain. He told me that years ago."

"He was always telling you daft things," smiled Anne.

"I wish I'd come up to Edinburgh."

"You were busy," said her aunty, and pursed her lips.

"It was a busy year," said Mandy.

"I'll help you put your things upstairs," I said. Upstairs, the guest rooms were perfect, untouched.

"She's going to live in a completely empty place," said Mandy. "She'll be all alone and go bitter."

"She's a funny woman," I said.

"When she first came to Blackpool last summer, you thought she was marvellous."

"Did I?"

"That's just you. You get swept up into people's atmospheres. Their auras. Who is it now, then?"

"Oh..." I said. "No one."

AUNTY ANNE HADN'T SAID ANYTHING ABOUT UNCLE PAT SINCE SHE SAID to me, just after the *Strange Matter* show: "It was him, wasn't it?"

"Who? When?"

"Tell me you saw him as well. On that stupid bit of film your friends had. I know they're playing games. And I think it's cruel. I feel got at, personally. I don't know what they're doing, but..."

"What are you talking about, Aunty Anne?"

"They've sliced and spliced their film up, haven't they? To make that fake spaceship landing. They've got their publicity and everyone thinks they've very clever, but I'm hurt, Wendy. It was a horrible thing to do."

I think I knew what she meant.

She went on, "Those people coming out of that... that thing they filmed. The spaceship. Your Uncle Pat was there, wasn't he? They put him there, on that fake film."

"I don't know what it was, Aunty Anne. They believe in it. I don't think it was a fake." This was at the time that Timon and Belinda were making their rounds of the late night chat shows, magazine interviews, and we didn't see much of them just then. They were living in a hotel, and planning to go to New York, taking their film with them. I had watched it repeatedly and really couldn't believe it was faked. Aunty Anne said, "I wouldn't put anything past them. That Belinda wants so much to believe in it all, and Timon is helping her out with her delusions. But I think it's wicked and cruel, putting Pat on there. Didn't they realise how it would make me feel?" She tried to drop the subject, and couldn't. "And Captain Simon, for god's sake! Large as life and coming out of a spaceship! Pushing Marlene Dietrich in a wheelchair!" She left the room then, to check on dinner.

What surprised me more that Aunty Anne's grievances was that she had failed to see what I saw, the first time I watched that footage in the TV studio. Standing behind Marlene, with Uncle Pat and Captain Simon and the horse, almost a silhouette in the glare of the weird light, was Mam.

So we didn't come back to the subject of Uncle Pat again until Timon and Belinda were about to return from New York. By then, Mandy had launched her writing career with *BritLit Four* in Charing Cross Road. I had been round Joshua's house in Greenwich, and Colin had arrived, fresh from Paris.

It was only then that we heard that, en route to Heathrow, Belinda had completely vanished while in first class, leaving a half full glass of champagne, and Timon in the toilet.

THIRTY-FIVE

It was Serena's joke that Josh was an aesthete and a dilettante collector of valuable odds and ends. She made him into a monster of unappealing material appetites. And it was true, he was a demon in a junk shop, scattering lesser items and rival browsers, spending his little cash on useless, often bizarre gee-gaws. He had an eye all right, but not one like anyone else. He had taste, but it was quite strange.

He wasn't the snob Serena thought. She made him out to be someone who always had to have the best. What he really liked were things that drew the eye. So although he didn't himself drink, he had a drinks cabinet stocked with every bottle you could think of, just because it was a funny old, red lacquered thing.

Serena came with me those first few times I went to the house in Greenwich. It was a curious, red-bricked house which stood alone, just a slice of air between it and the houses either side. When Serena was there she relaxed into the oddity of Joshua's home, into the purple room, the orange room, the underwater dining room and she always made a point of extolling his taste. I used to think she was living out her own idea of her friend. When he met him, at Oxford, he was quite young and she took him up and started to mould that taste of his with bursts, prolonged or brief, to a whole range of aesthetics. Now that his taste was formed and very nearly complete, she admired her own handiwork, ignoring those parts that didn't accord with the original plan. Funny woman.

The Josh I think of is much more ramshackle. It's the Josh who, yes, dressed himself up three times a day in colourful outfits, but fretted and asked me continually if he was going out into the world looking a fool. Whose exquisite jacket pockets were held together by the tiniest of safety pins. He always liked shopping in the most expensive shops and bought two of everything he liked (one for best, one for everyday), but only in the sales, when he could become quite fierce and managed to get forty, fifty, sixty pounds knocked off his total. His bookshelves were replete with shining hardbacks, many of them first editions, but he was no reader. Serena gasped over his wide and eclectic tastes. Later he confessed to me that hardly a spine on that shelf was sufficiently cracked to prove that he'd opened those books even once. Text worried him and made him feel insecure. Younger, he'd been braver, and read widely, dismissing and commending authors as he still did the columnists of newspapers and the people they wrote about. Text that came loose in newspaper sheets, he had no problem with. When it came bound up in covers (and the only hardcovers he bought were perfect bound: he despised those glued-up fakes), then that text stole his nerve away. Nevertheless, the gleaming, colourful shelves in the underwater dining room, floor to ceiling, looked wonderfully expensive. The room was called the underwater dining room because Katy had covered the windows with blue and green cellophane, casting us in aquamarine shade. Mermaids and octopi appeared everywhere, as cut-outs, standing figures, rubber toys. Other rooms were similarly given over to whatever father and daughter could dream up. The white marble fireplace in the living room was, as Serena said, as finely dressed as the shoulders of a Duchess, with antique clocks flashing their expensive innards, porcelain figures and full-bellied cases, but there was also a plastic Godzilla and a string of fluffy parrots.

Joshua made no explanations of his taste. He wasn't a bore who talked you around his every acquisition. When I asked, though, he did tell me about the four pictures in the hallway. They came from a children's book he had found in a junk shop. They were grey and framed in grey, the only other colour being orange, for the oranges that a girl was shaking out of a tree and her hair, which was styled in a vivid bob. I loved those pictures, ripped from four moments in the book's adventure. I asked Josh, but he could never remember what book it had been. It was ages ago, and he hadn't taken much notice. He just liked the drawings.

He had his reasons for liking everything, according to his own, quiet scheme of things. And so if he liked you, you automatically felt vaguely pleased with yourself.

He drove a petrol blue Skoda, which was the biggest challenge to Serena's blithe assertion that he always bought himself the best. He'd snapped it up for seven hundred pounds and boasted that it had never given him a moment's bother. He had a car tape deck that slid out of its place in the dashboard and when he left the car he brought this with him. He carried that tape deck by its plastic handle and it looked like a compact metal handbag and I told him so.

When he drove me around London, when he drove me anywhere, I used to love sitting beside him. I would look at the night road, until he noticed out of the corner of his eye and look back at me. "What?" He would fumble for a cigarette. I would slide my hand under his thigh while he drove. I don't remember how that started. I just liked the warmth and weight of him. He got used to me doing that. When I forgot, and neglected to absently slide my hand between the seat and his thigh, he would turn and look aggrieved. "Mm! Hand!" When he was pleased he would tilt his head side to side and didn't know he did this until I pointed it out.

I sometimes think the whole pattern of my falling in love with Joshua was in my pointing out things he did naturally. I noticed them, said them, and he'd feel silly until I told him they were lovely things to do unconsciously and so we'd go on.

Yet I'm getting ahead of myself. I've already told you I fell in love with the fella, and Serena and I haven't even visited Greenwich yet.

They were still only getting to grips with building the Millennium Dome at that time. They were nailing thick metal sheets onto the struts. They looked like plates over a skull. When it was up and finished and empty, I thought, Joshua would have a smashing view.

That night early in March we arrived and Joshua was still busy preparing himself. Serena treated the place like her own, hanging our coats on racks dangerously overladen with Joshua's and Katy's array of outdoor things. She went through to poke about in his tiny galley kitchen which, she said, she approved of because everything in it was white and cobalt blue. On the way she pointed things out and I caught my first glimpse of the grey and orange pictures, the clockwork owl, and the Peruvian armoire freighted with Art Deco tableware. Serena was stopped on her way by a woman she obviously knew and hadn't been expecting. She executed an embarrassingly phoney double-take as the woman, an ample, mumsy figure in flattering black, looked up and smiled.

"Wendy, this is Melissa. Joshua's sister."

The woman rose to offer a plump, ringed hand. She had been sitting with Katy and they'd been listening to our approach. Between them they had a Sega Megadrive console upturned and opened like a patient on an operating table. Melissa waved a baby screwdriver at us. "We knocked this contraption over and buggered it up." She sighed. She had a pronounced Welsh accent, which was surprising if she was meant to be Josh's sister. She looked at Katy. "Sorry lovey. I don't think I can fix this."

Katy tutted. "I shouldn't have bothered asking you. Can you mend things?" she asked me.

"Me? Oh god, no."

"He shouldn't leave fragile things out," said Melissa primly.

"Joshua," said Serena, "has a horror of unbreakable things. He thinks people who keep indestructible things around them must be dangerous."

"I've never heard him say that," his sister snapped.

"He obviously has other things to say to you."

Between the two women there was a palpable air of antagonism.

Something has happened to my language.
When I set out on this thing, ducking and
diving through my early life I was
switching points of view and first
person was something I dipped
into and out and I was quite

different
Now I've switched on one mode
I'm coloured by another time in
my life
Back then I would just have said:
"Them two women hated each other's guts."
Now,
something has happened.

"You haven't introduced your friend, lovey," Melissa told Serena.

"This is Wendy. You remember my very good friend, Anne? She's Anne's niece."

Melissa snorted. "That coarse woman from Blackpool? The one who kept talking about her legs and her millionaire husband?"

"That's the one."

"I must say, you don't look anything like your aunty."

I didn't say anything.

"Ah now," said Josh's sister. "Look, I've offended you. You mustn't listen to me. I'm an idiot and a bore. I interfere and I always know better than the other person. I'm sure your Aunty is a tremendous person."

"After your brother," said Serena stiffly, "she is my closest friend."

"That's no recommendation, eh lovey?" Melissa gave a deep laugh. "My brother and Serena here are about the flakiest people I know. It's all greed and taste with them."

Serena looked mortified.

"Yet they're happy in their own way. And Katy here is an absolutely midget gem."

Katy looked at me again. "My dad fancies you."

"Katy!" said Serena.

"He said! After the baths the other day, he said... I could give her one."

"He did, did he?" cackled Melissa. She looked like a bird, sitting on her great haunches, twisting her head to listen to Katy. I found out later that she was slightly deaf, and used this as an excuse to talk that bit louder and cut across what others were saying. Next to me, Serena's irritation was such that her hair was just about standing on end.

One thing I had to get used to was how late Josh always was. In that respect he really did live in a world of his own. He could never quite see that by keeping people waiting he could piss them off. I'd find him, terribly late already, partly dressed and staring at two pairs of neatly-ironed socks, making up his mind which colour. Once we rowed about his returning from a meeting he had out of town, some business connection. He was due back at ten, didn't arrive until half past two, hadn't phoned and didn't see why, when he showed up, I was beside myself.

Eventually that night he appeared, barefoot, reeking of some obnoxious Harrods aftershave, in slim, black Italian trousers and a black ribbed top that clung to him. He had shaved, which was disappointing to me.

He hugged me quickly, impulsively, crushing me to his tight chest. "I love these breasts," he said. "I could push myself up against them all night."

"Josh!" cried Serena, grabbing her own hug. "You've turned all rough."

"I don't care," he said lightly. "Now, have you all been introduced? I can't bear doing that stuff."

"They've already started to fight," said Katy.

"Good. I think we should eat straight away."

In the underwater dining room we ate trout by candlelight and Katy made a big show of pulling out her fish's crisped eyes and snipping at their roots. I laughed. There was a salad of nothing but cherry tomatoes in mustard and oil. Josh was crazy about cherry tomatoes, bursting them between his teeth like grapes when he read the papers.

"I shall have to make a file-card out on you, lovey," said Melissa, from across the table.

"Oh yes?"

Josh said, "My sister is so stupid that she forgets everything about everyone. She pokes her beaky nose in everywhere, but retains nothing. At home she has a boxful of little cards, with all the details written in. All the gossip."

"It's my system," said Melissa, helping herself to more of the runny and tart summer pudding. "It's so I can keep up with what the world is up to."

"I hope you haven't got one on me," said Serena frostily.

"Actually... I haven't."

FROM HIS GALLEY KITCHEN JOSH HAD A FIRE ESCAPE DOWN INTO HIS garden which was invisible in the night. I sat with him there for a while, amongst the potted pansies and the garden gnomes. He picked one of these up. "We call this one The Shagging Gnome because it props the kitchen door open when it's hot. It looks like he's, um... shagging the bottom of the door."

"Shagging is such a ridiculous word," I said.

"I'm sorry my sister was here. She turned up and I couldn't..."

"I think she's funny. She takes the wind right out of Serena's sails."

"That's good for Serena, once in a while, when the likes of your aunt spend their time puffing her up." He looked at me. "You never flatter Serena. You treat her like you treat everyone else."

"And how's that?"

"I'm not sure yet." He blew out his smoke in that way he had, all in one rush. "A nice way, I hope."

"We're daft sitting out in the cold."

"It's good." He was thoughtful. "Sometimes I think our family has spoiled itself. Melissa the way she is, like a character out of Congreve. Married to that husband of hers. Me frittering my time away. Tootling and footling my time."

"Hey, you say that, too!"

"There's only Katy with a level head on her shoulders."

"She's got that all right."

"My family's drifted about and split apart. The parts don't know each other at all."

"So's mine," I said. "When Mam died we all broke up and went off. It's in the blood, though, I think. You grow up together and something tells you to get away. For a while at least."

Josh looked sad. "Whatever that is, it isn't in our blood. Melissa and I were adopted. Our adopted parents were old. They both died. There's only us."

"Oh." I took the cigarette's lost, hot drag. "I wondered about her accent."

"Well," he said. "She lays that on a bit thick, anyway."

"Did you never want to see your biological mother?"

He turned cold. "No. I couldn't. My parents were my real parents. I didn't need others."

"Did Melissa want to meet hers?"

"She did. And she found her mother. A different one to mine. And it didn't work out. The woman didn't want to know." He finished his own cigarette. "Poor Melissa. She laughs at herself, but most of the time she's quite unhappy. Shall we go back in? I'm fucking frozen."

I laughed as we stood up. "Do you know something. It's daft, but... I love the way you say 'fucking'."

"What?"

"So refined and proper."

"Fucking fucking fucking fucking."

Behind us, Melinda coughed. "Lovies, Katy wants to say goodnight to everyone."

WENDY WATCHED HIM KISS HIS DAUGHTER GOODNIGHT. FROM THE doorway she could see walls covered with Spice Girls things and Disney things, but there was some evidence that these had been displaced recently and a whole new space, for a new preoccupation, had opened up. While Josh fussed over Katy, Wendy stared at the wall opposite her and saw a mass of newspaper print, interspersed with glossy magazine clippings. Amongst the text were pictures that Wendy herself knew off by heart. The deep chocolate brown and lemon glow of the video stills grabbed from Timon's video. The slight, pin-prick figures in the light. And, repeated all around Katy's collage, the faces of Timon and Belinda themselves, looking alarmed in the photographers' glare, then more composed and intent, when interviewed. She thought: Katy is a fan of my friends. Then she remembered seeing the child in the baths in a *Strange Matter* T shirt.

"Wendy looks like she's going to throw up," Katy observed.

Joshua frowned. "That'll be the trout."

"I wish you wouldn't cook things with bones in, dad."

"I was just looking at your bits out of the papers," said Wendy.

Katy brightened up at this and, in showing her enthusiasm, seemed for the first time like a nine year old. "Timon and Belinda," she smiled.

Joshua laughed. "Katy has a crush on both of them."

"I know them," said Wendy. "I know them very well."

"No..." whispered Katy. "Are they really from space?"

"Timon's from Blackpool."

"And we thought it would be us introducing Wendy to the great and the good!' said Josh, tucking his daughter in. "Sleep now. We'll talk about it tomorrow."

"Can we meet them?" Katy insisted. "Can I go and meet them?"

"They're in New York just now, but... yeah. I'm sure they'd love to meet you."

Katy lay rigid, her eyes wide. "Something new, coming true! That's what Timon always says."

"I know," said Wendy as Joshua led the way out of the child's room. "And it's true, too, hon."

WHILE THE OTHERS WERE GONE, LEAVING SERENA AND MELISSA IN THE sitting room, the plumper woman stopped fluttering and concentrated on the visitor. Her head went on one side and she considered Serena for some time before saying, "You've been very successful, haven't you, lovey?"

Serena poured herself another Martini and then enjoyed carefully lacing the sweetness with vodka. "What do you mean by that?"

"I'm sure it will all work out fine—Godwilling—but you can't pretend you aren't putting them together for a reason."

"Ah. Do you mean you're objecting to Wendy? What is she, too young? Too stupid? Too northern?"

"None of those things, I'm sure. I'm rather worried about her."

"I don't see why you should be."

"I like the girl, the little of her I've seen. She's a match for Joshua in many ways."

"Then maybe it's all right," smiled Serena. "And you needn't fret."

"Can I be frank, lovey?"

"Be my guest."

"It's you I can't stick. I've told Joshua, too. You took him up and did for him. I think you're a horrid, snobby old bitch."

"Well...!"

"And when you get together with Joshua, it's like a nasty commingling of natures and you encourage him to behave worse than he is. Alone, I'm sure you're safe enough. When you're round Joshua, though, I tend to get protective."

"The protective older sister."

"That's right."

"Not that he's even your natural brother."

"That doesn't matter a jot." Melissa clicked her fingers and Serena laughed.

"You might like Wendy, but she thinks you're a pain. You should have seen the looks she was giving me," said Serena.

"I don't care. I don't need to be liked."

"That's just as well.

"I can still warn her that Joshua will make her miserable."

"Oh, keep out of it. You're like a black albatross hanging in everyone's faces. You depress everyone. And if you call me 'lovey' just once more I shall slap you."

"Giving Wendy to Joshua is like throwing good money after bad."

"Your brother is bad money?"

"He's a risk, I think."

"And you don't approve of Wendy's money?"

"I don't know if she's got any."

"She's stinking."

Melissa craned her heard, mishearing this. "She's what, lovey?"

"I said, she's stinking rich." A thunderous, dead tone.

"Good for her," cackled Melissa. "She should watch herself."

"What's this about?" asked Joshua, frowning, coming in with Wendy.

Serena swore under her breath. "Two old ladies gossiping, what else?"

"What?" asked Melissa, who really was having trouble with her ears. "You know, I've asked to be syringed again, but..."

Joshua was glaring at Serena. "Wendy tells me that those alien people, Timon and Belinda, are friends of hers. You never told me that." His voice was flat and full of warning.

"Didn't I?" She looked flustered. "I mustn't have thought it very interesting. It's a lot of nonsense, isn't it?"

"Not to Timon and Belinda it isn't," said Wendy, going to fetch their coats. "I'll phone a cab." The atmosphere seemed to have gone out of the night. It was time to head home.

"I like those alien people," Melissa chuckled, catching up at last. "Especially the big black one. Anytime he liked he could take me into space."

He didn't want to stay in London for longer than an afternoon. He explained, as they sat with ice creams in Russell Square, that he didn't want to see his mother.

"She'd love to see you, Colin," Wendy told him. "She's always asking if you've been in touch."

"I don't want to give her the satisfaction of seeing me alone. You know how she was when I got it together with David."

The square was teeming with people catching the unseasonal warmth. Pigeons strutted and bickered on the paths, pumping their heads and tidying litter. Colin looked at Wendy and went on. "It's finished. He got up one morning and decided he wasn't queer after all. It took him months to figure it out. He got a good deal on it, though. Weeks in a hotel with a miraculous Paris view, getting his cock sucked while he thought it over."

Colin was white and thinner. He had shaved off his odd little beard and looked even more drawn. His clothes were expensive and hanging off him.

"Where is he now?"

"He went straight off to Scotland, just before the weekend. They've offered him a better job in Glasgow, some record shop. He's doing a management course and moving there."

"Are you going after him?"

"I want to talk to him. I'm catching the four o'clock. There's the flat in the Circus to sort out, to air and clean up. We've left it empty for ages. We could have squatters."

"And you'll talk it through with David?"

"It's because I'm positive, you know. It's not just him getting cold feet. He wasn't faking it. You can't, can you?"

"When did you tell him you were positive?"

"Oh, he guessed at the start. All the signs. The extra care I took."

"He'll deal with it. He'll realise."

"I'm not in love with the fella. But... he's all right. I mean, he wasn't the love of my life. I don't believe in that. But we had a good time."

"You were paying for everything, too. Splashing your money around. Maybe he can't handle that, either."

"We'll see." He looked at Russell Square. "When I'm here, I think of Virginia Woolf when she was writing *Mrs Dalloway*. She came running through here at night, going doo-lally and confused, ripping her clothes off. No one to help her."

"Why is it everyone else I know knows about books and I don't?"

"I wish I was staying, really. Then I could meet your Mandy at last. We were kids last time. Now she's going to be a writer."

"It's the do, the day after tomorrow."

"I can't stay, though. I'll come down again, maybe soon."

Wendy sighed. "I miss your dad, Colin."

"I know."

"He had sense. He could sort things out." Wendy wondered whether to ask Colin about Joshua. She found she couldn't sort out a picture of Josh to describe to him. She couldn't put him into words.

"What have you done with the money?" he asked.

"Given chunks away. Nothing much. There's a friend of Serena's, someone I've been seeing—well, not seeing as in seeing, but seeing around—who said he had a few tips for investing it. I'm going to invest it."

"Who's this friend?"

"Joshua Black."

"Oh, god. Him."

"What's wrong with Josh?"

"I met him ages ago. When Serena was dragging me and mum around her London social whirl. There was something funny about him."

"So I shouldn't invest?"

"Nope. He made all his money in the City in the Eighties and then he gave the working bit up. The money he put into a whole range of ideas. Made a fortune, but it sounded very dodgy to me. And he was such a condescending get, too. You've not been doing filthy things with him, have you...?"

"No..."

"You should get away from that Serena. I don't like her."

They had coffee and cakes and stopped at a small bookshop. There, in a display, they found early copies of the union-jacketed, brick-thick *BritLit Four*. Automatically loyal, Wendy flipped to Mandy's story. She showed Colin.

"'Me in the Monster Museum.' That sounds about right." He bought it. "Something to read on the train. She's five pages long. That's a page an hour."

They walked up the bright, leafy streets to King's Cross.

"There's five hundred pages of other smart young things in there," said Wendy.

"All writing about raves and acid and kicking each others' heads in. Dreary internal monologues about S&M and Welsh football hooligans on joyrides. No thanks."

"I hope that's not what Mandy's story is like," Wendy said. "She claimed she was writing about our family."

"Jesus God," smiled Colin.

SUPERBOOKS WAS WELL-LIT AND USER-FRIENDLY, OPEN UNTIL ELEVEN AT night and priding itself on its readings and launches. It was, it proclaimed, the world's first chain of literary supermarkets. Browsers who'd come in after work to choose something to read on the tube were used to getting startled by faces famous from flyleafs intoning their deathless prose. The do for *BritLit Four* had the shop full to overflowing, mostly with the ninety-eight contributors and their friends and family members. Editors, agents and British Council people milled about the stands with plastic cups of wine, all knowing each other. The new young writers were in a kind of roped-in paddock, wearing flashy name badges and eyeing each other. The editors of the anthology, Alfie Smart and Lucy Webb, both of whom had been (as their respective blurbs had it) active and seminal since the nineteen-sixties, seemed wary of their paddock of ninety-eight authors under thirty.

"I'm not standing with that lot," Mandy told her sister, so they kept to one side, nursing their drinks. Only six of the authors had been chosen to read, three minutes each. Mandy was one of them. She felt sick. "I look like a space hopper," she said. "An orange maternity dress. What was I thinking of? Draw a face on the bump and I'll look like a frigging space hopper."

"Shall I?" asked Wendy.

Mandy marched up to a bookshop boy, who was writing out last minute name cards with a blue marker. She took it off him and told Wendy to draw the face in the middle of her orange belly. "Space Hoppers had shaggy eyebrows and a kind of whiskery, doggy face."

A young woman with waxed, fair hair came up, clutching a drink and a stack of books. "Nuala, from Lucifer and Lucifer. I think your story is by far the best."

"Oh," said Mandy, cheering up as Wendy drew on her.

"It seems to me that you're taking risks at the level of language..."

"You mean, no one understands what I'm going on about. That's nowt new."

"I was with you every word. I was born in Didsbury," said Nuala, as if that explained it. "Have you got a novel?"

"Actually," said Mandy, "It's in my bag."

"My boss would like to see it. He sent me here to see you. He's skiing, but he's the publisher at Lucifer and Lucifer. Have you got an agent?"

Mandy said that she hadn't and took the woman's card and then, with a smile, the woman moved off.

"Taking risks at the level of language," Mandy laughed.

"Don't lose your elasticity," Wendy said.

"What?"

"Don't let it turn your head."

Then they were met by a tall, curly-haired man in a black velvet suit. Last year he had published his first novel, which was based on the Fred and Rosemary West case and it had been a fantastic success. Cher and Bob Hoskins were going to be in the movie. "Mandy," he purred, fag ash all down his velvet lapels. "Fantastic. You are exactly how I imagined you." Then he too started going on about the risks she took at the level of language. Mandy's eyes glazed when he went on to bring in what the French Feminists had to say about the language of the pre-oedipal womb. "Christ," he suddenly muttered, seeing that his agent was trying to attract his attention through the crowd. "There'll be a call coming in. Cher is apparently shitting herself because she's just seen photos of Rosemary West and now she's not too keen on the part. Excuse me." He squeezed through the crush.

"Prick," said Mandy after him.

"Oh, boy," Wendy said.

"Daniel should be here. He used to love talking about things like that. Lulu Iffygay – or someone - was one of his biggies, in the days when he was obsessed with French Feminist criticism. The Speculum of the Other Woman. He said you had to read inside a woman's body to see what she was on about."

"The dirty pig." Wendy got them refills. "You've beaten Timon to this, anyway..."

"Timon wouldn't be interested in all of this."

"Yeah, but he wants his book to come out. It's called *Pieces of Belinda*."

Mandy loved that. "Shit. Which pieces?"

"He's fobbing off the publisher. Actually—that's Lucifer and Lucifer, too. We should have asked that Nuala woman. He's got a massive advance and they're knocking up the cover as we speak. Timon and Belinda falling through the stars. But the thing is... he's gone and lost the only copy of the manuscript he had." Wendy kept her voice down. "He's been going frantic."

"He always was daft."

"He reckons it's been nicked."

Just then the editors started calling everyone to attention.

"Jesus God," said Mandy. "Now I've got to read."

YOU COULD TELL SHE WAS NERVOUS WHEN SHE GOT UP IN FRONT OF Everyone. She was the first one, so it was difficult, but as soon as she opened her mouth her voice took over. Her voice had grown strong and evenly-pitched through her winter of muttering to herself, walking all over frozen Lancaster, and reading to the Professor in the night. She wedged her unborn baby above the table, displaying the Space Hopper face, and read her few pages.

"In Blackpool, at drear day. The seabirds shout yes-nay yes-nay, yes-nay. Big sky. Small lights. Jackpot garlands of golden coins. All along the Prom, the girls come. All along the Prom, the boys come. Yes-nay. Yes-nay."

Mandy's story went on like this for some time.

"My mother had a monster love. Not monstrous, of the morbid, the decadent, confined to the box. That which rose unbidden. Strong Freudian stuff. Whiff of sulphur, of menses, of that which dare not speak. Yes-nay. Steady, sure as the waves on the shingle. We could hear up in the gods at night. We lived in the cheap seats of our flats at night on the Terrace. My mother fed her youngest child. We stared at her tits as she fed our sister sat on the fat, orange settee."

When she finished, overrunning her three minutes, we all clapped.

I couldn't get to Mandy for a while after the readers were done with. People were bending her ear. I was stopped by a woman I recognized. She was still in her black sweatshirt with the unicorn on the front. "Hey?" she said. "Remember me?"

"What are you doing here?"

"I wrote something for the anthology? I wrote 'Manifesto for the Church of the Silver Unicorn?' Page four hundred and twelve? They seemed to think it was a fantastic story?"

"Is your ectoplasm friend here?"

"She's at Church, of course? I got permission to come here? Was that your sister up there reading? She looks like you?"

I nodded.

"I see your alien friends are being very successful? When's his book coming out?"

"Sweetheart!" It was Serena at my elbow. "I knew it was tonight. We missed the reading. Is your sister here?"

Behind her, I saw Joshua and he was wearing scarlet and green tartan. He'd left his face unshaven again and I grinned. Maybe I felt funny after Colin's warning about him, but he was so reassuring in the flesh. "Serena got us in," he said. "She knows everyone."

I was about to introduce the unicorn woman to them, but Serena had burst out squealing and she was dragging on the arm of the man who had written about Fred and Rosemary West.

"Cher's pulled out," he glowered. "Now they're talking about Julia Roberts. And I have to write some fucking songs."

"I think that was a wicked book you wrote?" said the unicorn woman.

"Oh yes?"

"I think modern fiction has lost all its moral value?"

The man in black velvet curled his lip. "And what do you believe in?"

As the woman opened her mouth to reply, I said to Joshua, "Let's find Mandy. You haven't met her yet."

MANDY SAID THAT IF SHE WENT OUT TO DINNER SHE WOULD BE EXTREMELY ill. She was very—as they say—near her time, and what she really fancied was chewing on a kebab.

"Your time of confinement," Josh was saying as we left the party in the shop.

"That what they used to call it," said Mandy, warming to him. "But I reckon I've already had that bit."

We stood outside a takeaway a few doors down from the bookshop and got our fingers sticky, pulling out ribbons of unidentifiable meat and warm lettuce. We watched the bookshop people leaving and fights breaking out amongst the ninety-seven under thirty. It started to rain and the police came.

We found Josh's Skoda and Mandy had to sit up front with her bump, of course, so I couldn't slide my hand under his thigh.

The plan was to drop her in Putney with Aunty Anne. I was meant to be at Serena's that night, but she had vanished with the man in crushed velvet. I supposed we would discuss where I was going on the way. Things were moving.

In Putney, Aunty Anne was waiting up in her dressing gown.

"Have you seen the news?" she asked us urgently in the hallway. "I suppose you've been too busy swanning about." She saw Joshua, stepping into her house. "So this is your fancy man," she said to me, raising her eyebrows and wrinkling her cold cream.

"We've met before," said Josh. "Through Serena."

"I know," she said.

"What's the news?" asked Mandy.

"You've ruined that maternity dress. What's that supposed to be? A face?"

"Space Hopper chic," said Mandy.

"The late news is coming on."

She led us into the spartan front room.

That was when we learned that, as she was flying back into London, Belinda had managed to make herself vanish into thin air.

THIRTY-SEVEN

If I skip a few years now, it's like, oh yes, then we had the end of the century.

But we did.

The big humdinger, Colin would call it.

For a long time Timon was inconsolable. No one could tell him where Belinda had gone. There was the usual investigative flurry, interviews and reports. They never even found a hair, not a single wispy silver hair, clinging to the plush of her first class seat. We had to take that well-worn phrase 'without a trace' and apply it to the not-inconsiderable substance of someone we knew very well.

When Katy eventually met Timon in the flesh he was almost speechless with grief. He was like a king in exile. On the telly he made pleas to whoever had taken his beloved. There came nothing in reply. The papers blamed her vanishing on everything she knew. Their video footage was shown all over again.

Timon sunk into himself for those next couple of years. He lived in London. Then he drifted back to Blackpool, and then to the Royal Circus in Edinburgh. He was casting about. We even lost touch with each other for a while.

He had lost his manuscript, too. He didn't kick up a fuss. He secretly imagined that *Pieces of Belinda* had gone the same way as the whole woman herself. He returned to the north to write his book again. Heart-aching work without Belinda's help.

Mandy published her novel with Lucifer and Lucifer, who were glad to have something to console and tide themselves over through Timon's hiatus. They were particularly glad because *Me in the Monster Museum* partly concerned itself with the early life of someone very much like him. There were connections here, the reviewers muttered. They started to talk about a Blackpool movement. Mandy's book was fairly well-received. There was some bleating about how magical realism or surrealism didn't quite wash in books about ordinary, working class people. It was something more appropriate for exotic places. Others praised her for her risks at the level of language. The Professor began appearing in London, begged her to be his lover again, and made it known far and wide that he had ghostwritten her book.

"My book is full of ghosts," Mandy snapped. "That old lecher is only one of many."

Then we heard that the Professor had started hanging round with a weird, cultish set. He was distracted by the possibility of actually becoming someone.

Mandy sold about five hundred copies in hardback and went off to write a second. That was harder going. Not least because she had the baby to see to. Lindsey was born early in May 1998. Everyone adored her, of course. She had small, marmalade fluffy curls. Even Katy took to her, Katy who seemed suspicious around the new arrival at first. She was writing a horror novel for children about incubi and succubi. I could never tell the difference. Katy had seen, from her Aunty Mandy's progress, how simple a process it was, bringing a novel out.

Her Aunty Mandy. Because by then, of course, I had married Joshua. And what a fuss they made about it. Serena, in the end, seemed to have misgivings. Aunty Anne couldn't see why I didn't marry someone richer and better connected. I had my pick, she said. Colin buried his qualms, as he always did, and came south for the ceremony and the little party we held in the Greenwich house, where we had decided to live. Colin even conceded that Joshua could make himself quite good company. He went so far as to say that he thought Joshua was probably gay, underneath everything. He couldn't persuade me of that. Colin hadn't managed to persuade his erstwhile lover David of anything. His lover had moved to Glasgow to be successful, and that was an end to it.

For the wedding, Joshua filled the house with orchids.

His sister took an attack of the vapours, fell against the mantelpiece reeling in black satin and swept it clean of most of its objets. She smashed a valuable clock, so that it was stuck forever after at midnight.

Midnight.

We spent the rest of the century, with Katy, on a cruise liner travelling to the most exotic ports in the world and returned just before the New Year.

As fin-de-siecle's go, it was all right.

They had the Queen Mother installed in her emerald casket in the Greenwich Dome, and this was the spectacle we queued, along with everyone else, to see at the end.

And for a few years after that, life went on pretty quietly.

I was happy.

THIRTY-EIGHT

"NO, I DON'T WANT TO BUY ANYTHING. I WANT TO SEE THE MANAGER."

The woman was holding up the queue. Behind her, teenagers were rapping their empty CD cases on the cash desk. The assistant told her straight. "The manager is incredibly busy. Can I help?"

The woman's face tightened at this. The assistant winced. You could tell there had been some severe plastic surgery there, the way her skin went tight under her hair. "It is David Moore, isn't it? Your manager?"

"Yes, but..."

"I want to see him."

SMILING, THE MANAGER LET HER IN. HE WAS IN THE STAFF POLO SHIRT, looking slightly older and more careworn since the last she'd seen him. His desk was covered in printout and the fax machine was chattering to itself. "Anne..." he said warmly. "You've changed."

"For the better, I hope," she said gruffly as she sat down, and poked her legs out before his desk.

"Yes, you look years younger."

"Good. Now, I heard you were in London these days. Colin told me."

"Ah yes. Three months nearly." They had given him the smaller of the Oxford Street shops to manage, and he still couldn't hide his glee. After Glasgow there had only been one place to move up to. "How is Colin?"

"He's not too well. Still in Edinburgh." She gave David a dark look. "But that's not to be helped. I want you to come by my house for some supper tonight. I need a favour."

"I can't, Anne. I'm seeing someone."

"A man?" she asked bluntly.

"A woman." He flushed.

"Colin told me about your recapitulation."

"So I can't come, anyway."

"It's just a small favour," she said, softening. "I thought, since you were so... successful now, you'd have no trouble fixing it."

"What is it?"

"My niece's step-daughter."

"Wendy's step-daughter?"

"She needs a job. She's going wild."

"I'm sorry, but..."

"Two thousand quid."

"Anne, I can't take bribes to..."

"Three."

"I won't take your money."

"Please come, David. Have supper. It'll be like old times."

"I'm not sure about that."

"Please. For the sake of an old—but still shapely—woman."

He grinned. "All right."

Anne jumped up and gave him directions. "Nine o'clock. On the dot. I knew you were a good boy, really, even if you did dash my poor son's hopes."

"Anne..."

"I know, I know. I shan't interfere. Now, be prompt."

He opened the office door for her and she tugged his ear.

"I knew you were a good'un. Remember, when me and Wendy first went up to Edinburgh together? You were on the same train. Off to find your fortune. Such a roughie-toughie skinhead you looked. I thought you'd go tootling and footling your time away."

"How is Wendy?"

She sniffed. "As well as can be expected."

HER ROOMS WERE STILL MINIMALIST, AS SHE STILL CALLED IT, BUT THAT was all right because minimalism had recently come back in. In her tucked, trimmed and tautened new body, Aunty Anne was finding herself the height of fashion.

She was an Aunty again, to Lindsey, nearly seven, and Katy, who was sixteen by now and who had left school gladly, against the judgment of her betters. She spent the weekends in Putney with her Aunty Anne, but Anne suspected that because she had friends in the area. Katy was at an age when she soon tired of spending much time with her father and Wendy. They were too intense together, either bickering or clambering all over each other and it turned the girl's stomach.

"I blame that funny school they had you at," said Anne that night. "That's what put you off education. It was all cutting shapes out of paper and dancing around, wasn't it?"

Katy was bored, tapping at her aunt's new computer. "Hm."

"Not that there's anything wrong with dancing. Did you ever see me dance?"

"Yep."

"But you need to learn more than that at school. That's your three R's. Wendy would never learn. That's how she went the way she did. She left school at sixteen, too."

"Wendy's all right."

"She could have done better for herself."

Katy went red and didn't say anything.

Anne thought she might have offended her, and was about to say something else, but was interrupted by the doorbell going and it was Serena. They kissed each other briskly. "Did you get him?" asked Serena.

"Ah-hah," nodded Anne.

"Get who?" asked Katy, who had come to listen.

Aunty Anne sighed. Katy was in a nylon patterned blouse of red and purple, a miniskirt of green diamonds, and white leather boots. Retro-chic was back in again. Aunty Anne remembered dressing like that to go out dancing at the Troccadero. So she was almost a grandmother after all.

DAVID ARRIVED SWEATING FROM WORK, WITH A SUIT JACKET PULLED OVER his T shirt. He seemed ready to interview a prospective staff member, but Anne put a gin and tonic in his hand, made him sit, and started working—to Serena's mortification—on an immense fry-up. David got up to look at the framed photos along one wall.

"Wendy's wedding?" he called through.

"Yes," said Serena with a sigh. "It seems so long ago now. You weren't there, were you?"

"Busy in Scotland," he said tiredly. "I didn't even know it was happening."

He found Colin's face in a rowdy black and white group picture. He recognised a few other faces. In one picture Anne was hosting up her matron's dress to show her legs and, beside her, Wendy stood in her vast satin gown and rolled her eyes to heaven, hands on hips.

"He looks like a good-looking fella, her husband," said David.

"Joshua," said Serena. "My best friend."

David stared at one odd photograph. It was of Astrid from the Leith Walk launderette. Her wheelchair was pulled up next to a woman with no arms. They both stared straight out. In biro someone had written on the glossy print, "Jesus God."

"I heard about Belinda," said David, sipping his drink. "Wasn't she here for the wedding?"

"She'd already gone by then," sighed Serena. "I never knew her. If you ask me, she did a runner. The whole thing was a lousy fake. Her nerve went."

Anne appeared, along with the aroma of bacon and sausages. "Ready soon. Oh, you've seen my little gallery."

"I should go and see Wendy," he said. "She's happy, isn't she? When I saw you before you sounded ambivalent."

"I don't know the meaning of that word," Anne sniffed. "You know what I'm like. I wanted the best for her."

"Josh is the best," put in Serena.

"I suppose you're happy enough," Anne conceded.

Serena looked round. "Katy," she said, startled. The girl had a way of just appearing. "This is an old friend of Anne's. David Moore."

He held out his hand and smiled.

Katy looked at him and gave a rare, unexpected grin. She took his hand. "Something new, coming true," she said.

SO THIS IS A MARRIAGE, AND WHAT HAVE I LEARNED? THAT EVEN WHEN he was a long distance away there was stuff still to be learned. That the substance left behind when he went was stuff for me to take on and learn. I learned him. He went away and further on and this was our marriage and I learned.

I learned our marriage like the rule of thumb and the ins and outs of our ups and down started to come easy to me. Even when he was away and I went sniffing round and alone I was suspicious, even then we had ups and down. I never thought we could have ups and downs like that, when we were apart and only one, but we did, we managed it because that was our marriage and we were learning. My aunty said marriage is a thing you work at, look at mine and learn. Oh boy.

THIS WAS HOW MANDY STARTED HER SECOND, SLIM NOVEL. IT WAS about the joys of marriage and togetherness, then apartness and togetherness again. She called it *Mardy Cow* and it went on in this vein for some time. It lost her many of the readers her first had gained. She wasn't writing much about funny people or places anymore. *Mardy Cow* was about relationships. Or rather, 'the destructive mutuality of the relationship from hell' as her editor at Lucifer and Lucifer wrote on her inner flap.

I said to Joshua, "What does our Mandy know about marriage anyway?'

"He said, "She's probably picked up a thing or two here or there."

Timon sent us a card from Scotland. Older, wiser, widowed Timon had just read Mandy's second novel.

'It isn't funny stories and accidents, hon. She used to put them in to make us laugh or hold our breath. She's lost it all. She's just taking risks at the level of language, I think.'

Although there were accidents in our Mandy's second book, which arrived at the house in Greenwich in a plain white cover, they weren't happy or funny ones. By then Mandy was living in a flat of her own in Kilburn, around the corner from Serena. She was sharing with a woman she got on well with, a woman who was a production assistant at Pinewood. This friend was working on the new James Bond movie, because they had cast a new Bond, a midget lady called Sheila. Brenda Soobie was singing the theme tune, just as she had back in the Sixties. Brenda Soobie was seventy now and still giving it some. Mandy's friend had even met her at Pinewood when she shot the title sequence and said she was a cow.

I met Mandy's flatmate when Serena held a Seven Deadly Sins party, uncharacteristically throwing open her house. It was our Katy's sixteenth birthday and Serena had taken control. Serena was Madame Whiplash, the wicked hostess, in her little-light-bondage outfit. Mandy came as a Space Hopper again, because she couldn't decide and her friend came as the kid out of the *Exorcist*, in a baby doll nightie which she covered in green spew and hung a tinfoil crucifix around her neck. Late that night we ended up in Mandy's flat, in her friend's attic room, watching her cook up carrot and coriander soup on a tiny stove. It made me feel terrifically sick. I thought, surely the handmaiden to the new James Bond could afford a nicer flat than this.

That party was the last time I saw Mandy before *Mardy Cow* arrived in the post. Funny, but living in London made us keep in touch less frequently than ever. She had her own life, I suppose. At the Seven Deadly Sins party I saw her telling Katy that now she would give her copies of her books. "You're old enough to read the dirty bits now."

Katy, who had painted herself head to toe in bright green paint and come as envy, tutted. "Well, it's nice of you anyway. But I wasn't a kid before."

"Yes, you were," Mandy smiled.

"I'll read them."

"You might find out all about this family of ours."

"Whoopee."

Serena brought the cake in then, which she'd had a friend design, construct and deliver. It was a monstrous pink cock, with a flaming bristle of pubic hair, which poor Katy had to blow out in front of everyone. She pulled back her own long hair in case the pubes set it alight. It was a lurid, nasty cake, really, and I didn't fancy my bit—a frosted slice of helmet—at all.

Katy had with her a new beau. This was a recent thing and very hush-hush. We weren't to say a word until we met him. That she'd discovered this man through work, her new work at the Megastore on Oxford Street, should have rang alarm bells for me. I should known they were all—Aunty Anne, Serena, Katy—cooking up something else beside this phallic confection.

Lo and behold and dressed as, for some reason, a McDonalds employee, David came tripping into the party. Just before I caught sight of him Katy tried to prepare me. "He's very nervous about meeting you, Wendy."

"Why? I'm not..."

"Because you already know him."

I stared at her, at her glaring white eyes in all that green paint.

"It's David Moore. Aunt Anne said that..."

"What's he doing here? What are you doing with him?"

"Nothing yet. He's managing the store I'm working at, and..."

Then, coming through the crush of people, was David.

"This is kind of embarrassing for me, Wendy," he said.

Even in a stripy apron and a baseball hat he looked wonderful.

"Fuck you!" Suddenly everyone was listening. "What are you planning to do, David? Sleep with everyone in my family?"

"Wendy," hissed Katy.

"I don't care. He's outrageous."

"It's not like that," he mumbled.

"Like shite it's not. You've been manoeuvred into this, you dope. Who's put you up to this?"

David shook his head. "No one, Wendy. I just met Katy recently. Coincidentally."

"She's a child!"

Katy was furious now. "You can be such a bloody old puritan, Wendy."

"No, I can't!"

"Who was it wouldn't let me read Aunty Mandy's book when it came out?"

I turned on my heel and went looking for Aunty Anne and Serena.

I hunted through every floor of Serena's house, and every room was brimming with her arty friends, most of whom I didn't know. The bathroom had been turned into Cleopatra's, a sign on the door said so, and I stormed into find all these men standing around another man, who lay in an enamel bath filled with milk.

"I'm looking for Serena," I said, trying not to notice they all had their knobs hanging out.

"She's not here," said the man in the bath. I'm teling you, Michael—you piss on me and you'll curdle the milk. I'll never speak to you again."

I left them to it.

I wished Joshua was there. When we first got the invitation he'd bolted upright and said he couldn't make it.

"It's your daughter's sixteenth birthday party!" I couldn't believe him, but this was the way he was going. Forgetting things and sloping off. Danger signs.

"It's not her actual birthday," he said crossly.

"No—but it's the day Serena—your brilliant mate Serena—has organised her bash. You've got to be there."

"I can't."

"Why can't you?"

"Business."

Usually I would leave it at that. His funny business had caused ructions before. There was meant to be a truce now, because last time we argued, he said his business connections, all his investments and the money they brought, were all that gave him a sense of self-respect. I shut up and listened to him. For the sake of his own bruised self respect in these days of being kept by his heiress wife, I listened and maybe I shouldn't have. It was all too easy for him to make me feel guilty for supporting us. I had to let him go away from time to time, to fix his shady connections.

"Katy's going to be disappointed."

"I'll take her out to dinner for her actual day. Just me and her."

"What about me?"

"Do you want to come?" he asked, looking blank.

Oh, I've made it sound as though we were in one of those rough patches just then. Bits of it were, in fact, rough as a bear's arse, but it wasn't all like that. We were lasting, we were. But he was forgetting things and sloping off.

And then Mandy's new book appeared, with a perfunctory note and a 'For Wendy' in a plain white wrapper and, it turned out, it was all about a marriage and a woman whose husband starts forgetting things and sloping off.

Aunty Anne and Serena were sitting on the top stairs at the very top of the house. Serena was dangling the woollen strands she had taped on her homemade cat o' nine tails and was listening to Aunty Anne going on.

"Hey, Wendy. I was telling Serena about the fortune I made out of all those horse ornaments that belonged to your mother. We dined out on that, remember? Horses everywhere, she had."

I said, "Tell me you didn't set it up."

"Here it comes," said Serena.

"Katy with David. Tell me you didn't set that up."

"I don't know what you're talking about."

"Don't you fucking smirk," I shouted at Serena. "I'm sick of you poking your beak in."

"No, you look here," said Aunty Anne.

"Yes?"

"I got Katy that job. I set it up. And yes, I did call on David because I knew he was here." She looked at me levelly out of eyes which were now quite slanted and narrow. "There's nothing wrong with calling in old favours."

"What favours did you ever do him?"

"Leave them alone, Wendy," said Aunty Anne. "If you interfere with Katy's life, she'll hate you forever."

I glared at them.

Aunty Anne went on. "Anyway, what does it matter to you? Why are you so bothered about David?"

Serena shoved her oar in then. "Everything's all right between you and Josh, isn't it?"

"Oh, you'd love that, wouldn't you? To get your teeth into Josh after all this time."

"Go home, Wendy," said Serena. "If you can't get into the party mood, you should never have come out tonight."

"Right," I said. "I'm fucking going." Then I said, "And you do know, don't you, that you've got four hairy blokes in leather harnesses getting into your bath and pissing on each other?"

Serena barked with laughter. "Good!"

So I ended up over the road at Mandy's flat, with her and her mate, the production assistant to the new, midget James Bond. While she cooked up her carrot soup, Mandy and me sat on her bare mattress on the floor.

"I'm up at five tomorrow to go to Pinewood!" said the friend dismally. Then she found us a photo of the new James Bond.

"She looks like a proper bull dyke,' said Mandy. "Fantastic." Then she started on about her new book again and how I'd be getting my copy very soon. She said she was nervous about it.

"I had a good time tonight," Mandy said, lying back. "I don't get out much, what with the kid and everything."

"Ah, Lindsey," said the friend, stirring her soup.

"Do you know what this reminds me of, Wendy?" said Mandy. "It's like when we used to sit up all night in the kitchen in Blackpool, entertaining Timon, and Timon entertaining us."

"Does it?" I thought back. "That seems hundreds of years ago now."

"What's new and coming true for Timon now?"

"I think he's given up on Belinda at last."

"Has he written the book again?"

"A little bit. He says it isn't the same."

"Poor Timon."

"He's the only one," said the strange friend, "who isn't tied down."

I walked home. I don't know how I found the way. It was dawn by the time I came back to Greenwich. I walked miles that night and I could have been anywhere. Walking in any of the places where I'd walked through the night.

The Millennium Dome was gone by then. There was nothing to look at but wasteground out of his windows.

In the tender light I traipsed around our house. I looked for the first time, properly, at all the things Josh had been buying. He'd been branching out, spending more, making his collecting a more expensive hobby. Whole rooms were turned over to odd contraptions in silver, bronze and tin. Assorted TVs played video installations around the clock. I looked at his study and he had more things in there, with more books he had never read.

He had the horse's head on his desk. One of the farmyard pieces in a tube of glass from the Tate, which I'd seen, years before with Serena. That artist had hit hard times, his installations were broken up and sold off, and Josh had snapped up this little beauty, and that had caused a row again. I looked into the horse's eyes.

I dozed on the bed settee for a while, gazing at the horse's eyes. And, down amongst the cushions, I found a hardbacked book wedged right in there. It had a cracked red cover and, handwritten inside, I discovered:

Pieces of Belinda. By Timon.

And she was in there, piece by piece, lovingly detailed.

THIRTY-NINE

HE'S CLINGY, ISN'T HE? I NEVER THOUGHT YOU WOULD TIE YOURSELF down with a clingy man. This was Aunty Anne. It doesn't do to let them get too clingy, you know.

Girl, I've got something to tell you.
So listen up and pay attention
to a woman
who knows her way around a man or two.
It doesn't pay to
let them hang on
to let them hang about your neck
like a trophy a garland of
idle male flesh
medallion
man
because he'll depend on you
he'll ride out your wishes
your

I cut Aunty Anne short. I wasn't buying this. Josh wasn't clingy.
He wants to be with me
wants my every iota
Oh yes, she said, kicking up her legs
oh yes, I remember that
and dancing
with the men who promised
their all and pledged
their all and worshipped
every scrap of me

and Anne still had this fixation about not living her life to the utmost. In later life utmost was Aunty Anne's word and she reckoned she was just about getting it now, on her own. Well, good luck to her, I thought, but she shouldn't criticise Josh.

She had this thing about the Marianne Faithfull song about the woman who never got her utmost. About Lucy Jordan, who at the age of thirty-seven realises that she'll never drive in a sports car through Paris with 'the warm wind in her hair'. Aunty Anne would say: listen and weep, and I said, Aunty Anne you've been to Paris again and again and you've been in sports cars galore. You've had that warm wind.

Don't be funny, she said. And the Paris I'm thinking of is a place I'll never ever go now.

I said, anyway, riding through Paris in sports cars will never be the same thing again, it's not the same thing after Diana died. Riding through Paris in sports cars at the age of thirty-seven is no longer just a dream of the utmost, it means closure now, it means—

She said, don't give me your analysis
girl, don't give me your Open
University view on the world
because by then I'd started studying
and I was reading things
in a hundred different ways
maybe more like Timon and Mandy read
Aunty Anne would never listen to me

but I was trying to warn her
and tell her I was happy
and I couldn't live inside her experience
of the things that would make only her
happier and I could never be in that sports car
underpass-bound.

"Hey," said Mandy recently. "There are these funny bits in your text."

We were talking again. This was quite recently: our rift was sealed. I even let her read my work-in-progress.

"Don't you like them?"

Mandy was doing her Womens' Studies degree at last, she was reading the French feminists at last, she was graduating next July.

"It's like Kristevan Woman's Time. It's like Babble. It's like a Wild Zone."

"Oh boy. Is that good?"

"Because woman is eternal and part of nature..."

"Yeah?"

"She exists, at times, in her own time and space. You're opening up your text to allow her that space. These are like songs in an old MGM musical. When the woman gets to bear her soul."

I thought about that. "I just set I out how I fancied it." Then I thought some more. "But it isn't just a woman's space. Look at Captain Simon as Uncle Pat's deathbed. He sings, too."

"Oh," said Mandy. "Then maybe you're confounding blithe assumptions about gender. Men have Women's Time, too."

"Don't men have Men's Time?"

"Yes, that's what they have."

"And is it different to Women's Time?"

"Oh, yes," nodded Mandy.

I used to wonder if dogs, cats, insects had a different experience of time to us. Did their minds and eyes move slower to compensate for a shorter, faster life? I hated it that there was no way we could ever know this. And those things, like butterflies and wasps, that only lasted a day or so. They'd have to have a different experience of time altogether, otherwise tragedy, what we understand of tragedy, ending too soon, would to them be as much of a condition of living as flight.

JOSHUA WOULD DO HIS DOG THING. HE WOULD COME PADDING AND panting up to me, usually when I was busy and pin me to the chair, the bed, the floor, and lick at me. He would lick my ears to be sexy, but he made them wet. He would fall in my lap. And for some reason he would sniff the back of my neck, which smelled of me, he said, he didn't know why, but it did and he liked it. He sometimes forgot himself and sniffed my neck when we were in company, coming up behind me and taking in great lungfuls in short little sniffs. Maybe it was to do with heat. Aunty Anne used to say you had to wear a woolly hat in winter, because your body heat escaped out of your head and if that got cold you were done for. For someone who wanted to keep glamorous, Aunty Anne was full of old lady wisdom. She thought that was the best combination of qualities. I thought maybe my heat escaped out of the nape of my neck and for Josh it was perfumed, and coded with my essence.

He did his dog things. He even made dog noises. Not barking like barking mad. Odd whines when he was wanting something, queer dipthongs from low in his throat. Woofs of pleasure, sometimes. This was what drove Katy away, seeing her only natural parent revert like this. We embarrassed her. I embarrassed her by giving in to her father's tender, dogged ministrations.

Serena thought she had housetrained my husband years before.

You have to leave spread newspaper at each door for a puppy. Josh would come in, pick it up, read it. You have to listen for them scratching at the door and telling you when they want to be out. A puppy doesn't really want to foul his own basket, so you have to be alert to scratches. Joshua took to going out at strange hours. You have to tap a puppy on the nose sometimes to tell them no. Joshua perfected hurt, puppy eyes. And they get frisky, puppies, and try to hump your leg. They'd hump anyone's leg, their little cocks easing out like lipstick. They'd do the conga with you if they could. Sometimes you have to brush them off, or they'll keep you all the time. And they can't see past the next five minutes.

Was Joshua living in doggy time?

Odd thing was, he never preferred taking me in what is embarrassingly called doggy fashion. Sometimes I like it, to feel him inside me in a different way, swivelled all the way round like that—versatile as a Kenwood chef. He liked to fuck me with my legs over his shoulders and him looking right into my face and he'd lick my ears when he knew I couldn't do much more than twist underneath him and sometimes that would make me laugh and sometimes it wouldn't. He had a flair for fucking, did Joshua, and came over all abashed when I told him so. But he did and it isn't everyone. He was just right. He could be snug and pounding and gentle and slow and frantic in all the right combinations. I think he listened to my body. A retriever in the long grass with his head cocked. Let the dog see the rabbit.

I'm saying it all past tense. Tense is so cruel. I can't believe I'll never fuck him again. Dogs are fickle, you know.

JOSHUA CAME BACK THE NEXT AFTERNOON AS IF NOTHING WAS STRANGE and I said nothing about the book I had found. I slipped it back between the bed settee cushions as if I had never seen it. I would decide what to do about it after my little trip. Katy and I were going away together for a few days.

"What do you mean you forgot?"

"You told me you were going to Scotland. I forgot it was this week." He looked affronted that we were packing when he finally showed up at home. Katy gave her father a quick peck, as she wandered from room to room with armfuls of ironed clothes. She still had a faint green tinge. Neither of us had mentioned David Moore. Katy had enough sense not to bring him up.

I didn't know what to think about finding Timon's book. I went on packing. Joshua sat himself in his study, beside his pickled horse's head and read the paper, eating cherry tomatoes. He'd be there for hours.

"Look," I said at last. "We can stay here a couple of extra days. We don't have to meet Timon till then. We'll stay a little longer."

He cheered up. "I wanted to take you both out to dinner, for Katy's birthday." He was out of his chair and clutching me. "I thought you were leaving me alone out of revenge!"

"This has been planned for weeks, Josh."

"I know. You know what I'm like."

"Yeah."

"I'll do anything. I won't stay out anymore. I'll even chuck away that bloody horrible horse's head."

"Whatever, Joshua."

"Why are you calling me by my full name?" He stared at me. "You only do that when there's something wrong."

"Do I?"

"I listen to you."

"But there is something wrong, isn't there?"

SO WE WENT OUT TO DINNER, TWO NIGHTS RUNNING. JOSHUA PUSHING the boat out, delighted with our company, showing off.

"Shame your young man couldn't be here," Josh said to Katy, who scowled. David hadn't been invited. Josh must have been talking to Serena, I thought.

"Tell me again," he said brightly. "Tell me what this trip is all about. Should I be coming with you?"

We were in an old, converted, high-domed bank. Our table seemed a hundred miles from all the others. We had potted palms secluding us, dangling their lush fingers over our plates. On a platform a woman was singing breathily into a microphone, Burt Bacharach songs.

"We're going to Edinburgh to meet up with Timon," said Katy eagerly. This was a pilgrimage for her, because she was still a fan. I'd seen her pressing and packing her old *Strange Matter* T shirt, even though it was faded and tight. "Then we head out into the Highlands. Across to Argyle."

"And then," Josh knocked back his brandy. "You watch the sky."

Katy pulled a face.

Hang on. Josh knocked back the golden brandy remains in one practised gulp. And Josh who didn't drink ordered another. For the first time in ages it came back to me, Belinda's sombre convictions, that when you least expected it, your friends and family got replaced.

This wasn't my Josh. I sat back from the table.

In the Nineties the telephone company ran this scheme where you got discounts on your phone calls if you listed your most frequent callees.

You listed your ten family and friends who you called the most. What if, I wondered, those lists got into the wrong hands? Someone could have a hit-list. Maybe someone had mine.

Then I remembered Mandy's short story, 'Friends and Family', which was published in her collection 'Women in Gloves'. In that, a woman whose flatmate moves out wins the phone company competition that sends her on holiday with her ten most-phoned pals and relations. This South American carnival jamboree is filmed for the phone company advertisements. Most people would be pleased to go, to become an advert, but in Mandy's story it turned out that the absent flatmate made all the most frequent calls. Mandy's heroine is sent abroad, to be joyous in public with a bunch of strangers. I laughed, thinking about it, and Josh and Katy both looked at me.

"What's funny?"

"Nothing." I gave him a look. If he really was a replacement, would I ever know? Besides drinking like a fish, was he really doing anything that went against continuity? That hidden book, perhaps. Bluebearded away down the settee cushions. But I'd found before, years before, Joshua's dirty books. Salty, crinkled, eighteenth century tomes of turgid and unsettling prose, describing acts that the woodcuts painstakingly filled out. He was a fan, it turned out, of other people's sex. And that wasn't such a strange preoccupation. He'd collected up Timon's book for the sexy bits. Yet he knew, he must have known, what he had in that book: all of Timon's past and future bound up in one. Timon's life was thwarted and cracked in two, as much by the loss of his manuscript as by Belinda's.

"You don't seriously expect her to come back, do you?" he asked me.

I was startled. "Who?"

"Belinda. That's who all this is for, isn't it?"

OF COURSE IT WAS. ON THE NEWS THAT NIGHT THERE WAS A TINY segment, the weirdy-obsessive, it's-a-funny-old-world, slice-of-life story at the end of the nine o'clock news. "Followers of the infamous Church of the Silver Unicorn are gathering in Glencoe in the west of Scotland to mark the seventh anniversary of the disappearance of Belinda Simon. Ms Simon was the UFO enthusiast who, in 1997, produced footage of what appeared to be evidence of visitor incursion and caused a brief scandal and flurry of fin-de-siecle excitement. Just as soon however, it was all over and Belinda Simon vanished for her seat on Concorde, en route to Heathrow from New York."

All through this item they showed the footage again, like an old friend, a favourite B movie clip. We saw the Silver Unicorn people assembling, we saw Timon's talking head. It was saying: "We aren't spotting lights in the sky this time. That's not what it's about. We're marking the passing and celebrating the life of a remarkable woman."

Then we saw the unicorn people pitching tents on the glen. They looked like hippy protestors, and they had a number of exhausted-looking horses with them, with fake horns glued to their foreheads. And, worst of all, they were represented by a new leader, or High Priest, as the caption said.

"It's Mandy's Professor!" I shouted over his first few words. "That horrible man she lived with in Lancaster!" And it was. Her professor had left the academy for unicorns in the Highlands. He looked zealous and bright.

"She will come again!" he was ranting. "Belinda's story isn't over yet! She has been sending her scrambled interstitial messages to my herd!"

My herd, I tutted. But he looked very impressive, the Professor, with his sultan's beard oiled and curled. This was a head-and-shoulders shot too, and you could almost imagine that he would rear up at any moment with a great big whinny, revealing the torso, flanks and shining hooves of a centaur. But the news team cut back to the studio.

"Jesus God," said Josh. "Are you really going to hang out with the likes of him?"

"Oh," I said. "It's a trip out, isn't it?"

Katy looked distant. "I really think something will happen. If not now, soon anyway. Belinda couldn't just have vanished."

"People disappear, sweetheart," said Josh. "They leave important things behind. They start a new life for themselves."

This was Josh the orphan speaking and my heart went out to him then.

"They don't just vanish on Concorde," she said angrily. "Belinda wouldn't leave us in the lurch like that."

I had to admit, it was very strange, even by Belinda's terms of seeing the world. To leave and not even send a hologram or a replacement to keep her place.

In the morning's post came Mandy's new book and it was time to go. King's Cross to Edinburgh Waverley and I read all the way there. It was the first time I'd been back to Scotland since Uncle Pat had died. I'd been to Athens, to Rome, New York, San Francisco, Hawaii, Tibet, but not there. This felt like my first journey all over again. I read the first line of *Mardy Cow* and kept reading it until we were clear of North London and the South started to fall back behind me.

Her first line took me ages to get beyond. It fell in, as these things do when you're tired and perplexed, with the train's dependable rhythm:

Where do I begin
to tell the story of
how great a love
can be
the same love story
that is older than the sea
the same love story
of the love he brings to me
Where do I start?

THE BORDER OF SCOTLAND WAS MARKED NOW, WITH AN ENORMOUS archway painted tartan green and red. Katy asked, was it meant to look like a giant in a kilt straddling the mainline?

Bands of bagpipers played at the smaller stations past Berwick-upon-Tweed. They didn't want you forgetting that you were in a different country now. That was something else Timon was in trouble for, besides his seven years late manuscript: his work visa for Scotland was out of date and he was, to all intents and purposes, a fugitive in Edinburgh, making a dangerous show of himself by getting his face on the news.

"What's Mandy's new book like?"

Katy startled me out of it. She was reading *Me in the Monster Museum* and we must have looked like proper Mandy fans. "Is this really you in this one? The younger sister?"

"No, I said. "And this one is confusing. It's like eating ten bags of crisps all at once."

"Is she still taking risks?"

Yes she was. Not necessarily at the level of language. Her book seemed to be about an errant husband who lives in Greenwich, who knows he is orphaned, and in his mid-thirties decides to seek out his birth mother. All the while he is falling out of love with his young wife, who he previously thought he adored. He takes up with all kinds of women, secretly, and tries out the different types. Luckily, Mandy's characterisation was off, the characters were none of them very distinct and there was no one I could recognise in there. Relief.

The orphaning and birth-mothering business bothered me. Now Mandy knew about Joshua's disinterest in researching his birth-mother. I had told her once that we had talked it through, and he had even made the preliminary moves towards tracking her down. He got in touch with the adoption agency, all the while unsure, feeling—I think—bullied by me. He was ready to pull out when he decided that he'd gone far enough. I'd talked to him about this, thinking that his disinterest was maybe something do with the despondent moods Josh sometimes fell into. He needed a mother, I thought. I wasn't going to be it. It disturbed me that neither he nor Katy had a natural mother, but he wouldn't be drawn on the subject of Katy's mother.

So he had the interview and I went with him. He shook and gave mumbled responses to the woman who handed him a thick, ancient file of papers. They were his, she said, his birthright and it was up to him, whatever he chose to do now.

We took the file home, sealed up in an envelope and didn't say a word about it. Josh put it away in his desk. Opening the file would put things in train. He would know where she was then, her name, her last known address. Even letters from her, addressed to him in a name he didn't know. The woman from the agency said his birth-mother had been writing to him year after year.

Joshua cried and wouldn't open the file. It would lie on his desk for years. So long as she was there, under the paperclips, the rubber bands and the dried out pens, he knew where she was. Maybe, he thought, he would let her wait for him, for a change. Maybe he just didn't want to know. The night after we'd picked up the file he wept himself dry and came to bed and wanted to fuck me his favourite way, peering right into my face and licking my ears. He reared all the way up, towering over me, his fine scarred chest and knobbly collarbone all blue in the early light. He rammed into me in tight little squeezes and when we woke our thighs hurt from gripping each other and staying open to each other so long.

In Mandy's book the man had the file unopened in his desk and, when he hit problems with his young wife, he decided to open it and find out at last. And he couldn't talk to his young wife about it, she had become so distant. Instead he talked to her sister, somewhat older and much more beautiful. He opened the file with the sister there, and they learned together. There was a name and an address that was fifteen years old. Then he fucked the sister because that was the kind of intimacy they had drawn up between them. Only they two knew what was in the file and, reading it together, there was nothing for them to do but seek consolation in each other. Consolation with her thighs around his waist, his tongue in her ears.

"Wendy," said Katy. "You look white."

I closed Mandy's new book.

"It's all right," I said. I put it back in my bag with the other papers and things for Timon.

It couldn't all be true. It couldn't be really, because I knew for a fact that Josh had never opened his file. It had stayed in his desk all this time and he had never taken it round anyone's house, let alone Mandy's, to crack apart the yellowed tape. It was all in Mandy's head.

I knew because I had checked the envelope that morning. I had the sealed envelope in my bad now, on the way to Edinburgh. It had never been touched. Joshua had learned nothing yet. I was going to do his learning for him.

In Scotland we skirted the blue coasts and cliffs, the straggling resorts. We skimmed under the busy arms and walkways of a colossal nuclear power station. Then, estates and corporations, football grounds and multiplexes. Finally, Edinburgh again.

FORTY

THEY HAD DONE ALL THESE THINGS IN EDINBURGH IN MY YEARS AWAY, like landscaping over the dirty grey glass ceilings of the railway station and building a new shopping mall under Princes Street gardens. Timon said you could sit in John Lewis' coffee rooms now and look up out of the window to see the castle a terrifying and sheer two hundred metres above. It seemed that they had built under and above everything they could find. Levels everywhere.

I knew things would have changed, of course. In the time I'd been living in London, we'd seen a fin-de-millennium built and dismantled. This was all a new start now.

The change to the Royal Circus was the biggest shock. We were only staying one night before going out to Glencoe, but it was long enough to take in what had become of the place. It had turned rough. The Georgian splendour, the gracious living, the monument to Appollonian culture as Serena put it, all of it had become tawdry and over-used. Gone, in short, to the bad. The old building where I had lived those months in the late Nineties, seemed to be swarming with ragged children. They sat on the stars with unwashed hair and catcalled us as we went up. The doors to the dark flats were open and you could glimpse the rot and the horror within. The entire place had let itself go. Cobwebs mapped the vertical spaces between banisters.

Timon didn't prepare us for any of this. He was pleased to see us, and talkative, but everything he talked about was Belinda this and Belinda that. He was obsessed with the vigil tomorrow night, with making it a right-and-proper memorial to his lost beloved. "And if that bastard Professor mucks and fucks it up," he said, with unusual vehemence, "I'll rip his heart out."

Timon, who took books very seriously of course, thought he had extra info on the Professor, because he had read Mandy's first novel, which ends with her Scheherezading the Professor to sleep. To Timon's mind, the Professor had always been a villain. Muscling in on Mandy and now on the memory of Belinda.

"I wish we could have all had quiet lives," said Timon, as he led the way to Colin's flat above.

Katy said very little. She was still awe-struck by Timon in the flesh, even though she had seen him before. He was too preoccupied to notice her silence or my dismay at how the custardy walls of the stairwell had turned to streaky brown.

"I haven't aired the rooms yet," said Colin, sitting heavily down at the table. "I forgot. And it's so hot in here."

The flat felt as if no one had opened the windows or doors in months. Colin looked terrible. He was in a dressing gown, a purple one much too large for him, and he wore nothing on his feet. When he'd let us in and walked down the hall, you could see his soles were black from soot, fag ash and dirt.

"Are you alone here?" I asked, knowing the answer.

He laughed. "Me and Timon are alone together in our two flats. We both go drifting around and sometimes we have a drink together." He opened a couple of bottles of wine. "Drink. I won't, though." He rubbed his face. "Wendy, remember when I said that you see ghosts only if you've suffered?"

I didn't want him to go into this now. I must really have felt like a parent to Katy, because I wanted all the talk around her to be pleasant and distracting. Nothing like this.

"It must have been you who suffered in the end, Wendy. Because me and Timon are the ghosts, aren't we? We became the ghosts in the end."

"Don't talk like that."

Colin turned on Katy then. "You've got a new young man, haven't you?"

Oh god, I thought. He's heard.

But all Colin said was, "Look after him. He's a good fella."

Katy nodded, her eyes wide. Nervously she fiddled with her overfull glass of wine.

Colin asked, "I've not thought properly about entertaining you all on your brief stay. Is there anything you'd like to do tonight in Edinburgh? Anything special?

But there wasn't. We wanted an early night, so we could be up in time to drive to Glencoe. Timon had a car, an unreliable old thing. We had to pick up Astrid from the launderette's back door at half past five in the morning. Timon made easy work of strapping her wheelchair to the roof rack.

"Wendy," said Astrid as we watched him work. "I have been praying for your happiness, but I have got the feeling that you are not, and am I right?"

I made sure Katy was out of earshot. "I think Josh is doing something he shouldn't."

"Jesus God."

Then we drove out of early morning Edinburgh, leaving the ruined Royal Circus and Colin behind. The country unfurled before us into ranges of hills mottled with the startling colours of marble sponge cake. We were quiet with each other at first, till Timon relaxed into his driving, put on a tape and started singing to it. The atmosphere became lighter the further we drove. The roads wound about the hills, the day crept on and we sang along. Rather gradually, it became a holiday.

THEY STOPPED HALFWAY FOR TEA IN THE GARDEN OF A PUB. THE TEA things were brought to them on a tray by a woman who couldn't stop laughing. "Don't mind me!" she went, and left them to it.

"I told you," said Timon, "that we'd see the biggest hedge in the world." For the past hour in the car he'd been telling them about this café, on the roadside beside the world's biggest hedge. The hedge was in the record books. Thirsty, they had kept an eye out for it.

"That can't be it," Wendy had moaned. "That hedge is only about four foot tall."

Until, eventually, they drove alongside a green wall one hundred and fifty feet high. They crawled along in its shadow, peering up out of their windows. Wendy couldn't help but imagine this was the perimeter to the most terrible maze in the world. There would be no light whatsoever inside.

And here they were at a picnic bench, with Katy fetching Astrid's cigarettes, which she'd left in the car. Katy and the German woman had taken a shine to each other.

"Is Joshua still filling the house with bric-bracs and nick-a-nacks?"

"Oh, yes," said Katy. "More than ever. His taste is even weirder than before. I said, Dad, you'll never get old. And he won't. He's always finding out new stuff."

"And Wendy," said Astrid. "What have you been permitted to do to the house? Have you filled it with your obsessions too?"

Wendy smiled. "I haven't contributed much. Joshua has taste enough for both of us."

"But that is no good!" burst Astrid. "We are like the animals, you know, and we must mark our habitats. Otherwise it means we are not staying. You remember, of course, how I have my launderette full of my pictures?" Pictures mostly of Marlene Dietrich, Wendy recalled, including the picture of Marlene leaving the private jet in Edinburgh, smiling on the arm of her fancy man. The very day she was abducted. How often the younger Wendy had started at that picture, imagining Belinda just off the edge of it, breathless at all the glamour.

After ten and before setting off again, Katy wheeled Astrid off to the loos inside the pub.

Timon looked at Wendy. "Hon, something's chewing you up."

She nodded.

He said, "Sorry I've not been much use. I've been sleepwalking for ages. Years."

"You're my oldest friend, Timon."

"Besides your sisters."

She exhaled loudly. "Haven't heard from our Linda in ages. And Mandy... I don't know, Timon. I don't trust her. That sounds awful, right?"

He looked at her levelly. "You've been reading the book, haven't you?"

"Yes. On the train."

"I read an earlier version, but I think it's the same. Like I said in my card, I don't think it's up to much. But it's got you worried, hasn't it?"

"How can it not? How can she do this to me?"

"You think it's about her and Joshua." Timon shook his head, smiling. "But if that was true, how could she be so up front about it? Could Mandy be two-faced like that?"

"I think she could. Really, she's only ever been out for herself."

"Oh, hon," he said.

"But she hasn't opened his file from the adoption agency. I know that much."

"All that was true?"

"Even down to the drawer he kept it in. That's what I mean, Timon. It's like she's trodden right through my life. But I know she hasn't seen inside his file."

"How?"

"Because I've got it. It's untouched. I've..." I looked at Timon. "I've nicked it."

He was shocked. "You can't go stealing Josh's stuff like that! It's his! It's important... his past."

"I bit my tongue, in case I said too much here. "Josh has some funny priorities of his own about things like that."

"You shouldn't have told me this, Wendy. It's his birth-mother inside of there. Her name... everything he doesn't know about her."

Katy and Astrid were emerging from the pub, into the sun. Astrid waved. "We are getting back into the car!"

Timon stood up. "I think you're acting daft, Wendy. Joshua loves you. You've got all het up about something you've read in a piece of fiction. Allow Mandy to have an imagination, hon. And stop yours going mad on this."

I wanted to tell him all sorts of things, but I couldn't.

"Let's get on," he said, and led the way through the garden to the car.

"Don't look in that file, Wendy. If you did and used the information, Josh will never forgive you. I wouldn't if I was him."

Of course: Timon was an orphan as well.

THERE WERE MORE OF THE UNICORN PEOPLE THAN WE HAD BARGAINED for. Luckily we had booked the hotel rooms in advance, and moved easily into our own twin rooms above the bar. Last time he was here, with Belinda, Timon had had his eye on this hotel, in the shadow of the almost completely pyramidical mountain. The hotel had looked luxurious to them and at that time they couldn't afford it. We were shown directly to our rooms. The kind of place that puts bowls of pot pourri by your bed and you end up putting your hand into it in the middle of the night. The management knew who we were and we were escorted neatly away from the others in the foyer, all of them wearing black appliqued sweatshirts.

"They must be the richer unicorn people," said Astrid disgustedly as we sat on the beds. "The others are sleeping out in old tents."

Timon was peering out of the chintz curtains. "The day's turned gloomy. Just like it was the last time we were here."

I hope he wasn't banking on a repeat performance. I'd noticed his video camera in the car boot.

"I hate those unicorn church people," Astrid went on. "They have opened a church down Leith Walk."

"I didn't know that," said Katy, who liked to keep up with this business.

"Jesus God, yes. And they come into my launderette—not to wash and talk nicely, oh no. They want me to talk about Belinda, to pick my brains, as if she was a goddamn goddess or a saint. And she was just my friend." Astrid was getting herself upset. "They do not really love Belinda. Not like we did. I think they are using her."

Timon said, "Come and see this."

In a field just close enough to see, their ragged encampment was staked out. And, as the light lowered, you could still make out individual figures on the glen. Someone was exercising the horses. They were a startling white against the murky land, and running in a wide and endless ring.

FORTY-ONE

JESUS JESUS GOD.

This is my part of the story now, my account of it all that night of the vigil. This is the testament von Astrid.

And the first thing, the worst thing I must recount as I launch off into this piece is to complain about the rutted fucking ground, the terrible Jesus-love-it place with its bogs and creeping damp and long grass that stuck in my wheels and spokes and tried to snag me down as we headed off into the night to see the vigil. To be the vigil, I mean, we would have been the vigil anyway, we were there for our beloved sister Belinda. And the others, the rabble of hangers-on were making a spectacle of themselves, but we couldn't help that, we couldn't help looking at them.

They cavorted and danced whirling dervishes, that's what they were doing, the selfish things, making a sport of poor Belinda. Their camp fires were up and roasting, some of them shooting flames straight up twenty feet into the sky and so the sky was darkened anyway by the smoke and glare, so how could we see anything at all, should it start to happen? Did these people have any sense and Jesus God, apparently not. Katy the youngest, strongest in our team was pushing me, her heroic effort getting me through the quagmire and Timon was finding it hard too but he wasn't swearing and cursing like I was at the hazardous trekking we did. He was wordless and filming all of this going on and you couldn't help feel sorry for him. I always feel sorry for people capturing their former glory, for it is always a mistake, a big embarrassment. Yet there is a fascinating thing about seeing them in decline, these people, at the big ending when all is gone and you see them lying in the same muck as we all of us live in. Like seeing Marlene at last behind the green door in Paris, up the crawling cranking life shaft. She called out Belinda old girl, she was the same as us. But now Belinda is a long-vanished goddess as well.

They had an effigy in bracken and twigs stuffed with fruit and god knows what. They raved and danced around it in all the smoke. They drummed and the noise came rolling out without stops and added to that the wailing of the people, who had thrown off their horrible unicorn sweaters and many now were barechested, with black horses daubed on their breasts. Their skins were painted, plastered white, white clay powder. Their faces sweated, their limbs were wet, they whirled and danced. We came to watch and Wendy was disgusted.

"They've got a wicka-Belinda," said Timon.

The effigy stood tall and goggled its horrible May Queen white queen eyes. Its face was ghastly in rotted and stinking vegetables no good even for soup and nasty fruit. Acrimboldo. Its arms flailed and it shed feathers and crumbs of dead wood each time the dancers shook it and turned. No mistaking it for anyone other than Belinda, though, her wild white hair, indeed, her fatness, even yards of pink cloth for one of her funny dresses. Oh, poor Belinda up there and would they set fire to her? Is that what they were meaning to do? The horses shrieked and brayed, running circles about this encampment all the while, it was terrifying in the noise and murk. The horses were corralling us, these shiny splinters of bone, ivory tipped, nailed into their foreheads. Cross-eyed horses: they circled the dancers' den.

"They're all on something,' Wendy said.

Timon said, "The Silver Unicorns are well known for it. They're always off their tits."

"But when I met them before, six, seven years ago, they seemed harmless. Pitiful cranks."

Katy snorted. "It's taken off since then. Since they got the Professor in, and let him take over. This is their New Age. Things have changed since they adopted Belinda as their masthead and personal saviour."

Wendy shook her head. "Belinda couldn't even get her shopping in for herself. Some saviour."

"It's true." Timon smiled. "I had to go with her every time. She was always distracted down some other aisle."

No sign of the Professor as he still called himself though by now, of course, he was the High Priest, the Big Cheesy. Self-styled priest and scaremonger, he like to tell all, to tell all the world and sundry that Belinda's visitors were imminent and that he and his herd were the ones going, galloping off with that bandwagon. And Belinda had shown them the way. Seven years since Belinda had gone and seven was their—they reckoned—sacred number.

"Where are we going to go?" asked Wendy. They've filled the place. I don't want to be here at midnight, with all them going daft."

Katy was fascinated and pulled in. "I like watching them."

Timon looked defeated, the way I'd seen him looking a lot lately when he comes down to the launderette and he has not much to say for himself. "Jesus God, Timon," I try to goad and egg him. "You life has to go on. You have people to meet! Books to write!" The trouble of course was his book is Belinda, all about Belinda, all Belinda's pieces and he can't as a consequence and result shake off her hold. You have to try and distract Timon away from his sombreness. I try to make people like that look forward to something and often it works. But I told Timon to look forward to coming to this vigil, to make his final fond farewells to Belinda, farewells in peace and be ready to move on again. But this circus has come up now and Timon looks despondent. They are drumming false hope into him and shattering his peace of mind. When he says, "We should never have come," I believe in him and I think he is right.

Belinda looking down from on high will think we are turncoats and fools, tootling and footling with these—Jesus God—these maniacs. Playing with fire, with a burning brand each, brandishing and tossing them into the dark and dropping them so that sparks rush out of all quarters and it's a bloody old dangerous place to be. I'm thinking especially if you are confined to a wheelchair and stuck in the goddamn mud.

We decide to look for a quiet spot. We push off and try to move us away from these mad people and loonies. The horses are rushing out of the night, and they are terrified, you can hear their squeals and we could be killed and dashed beneath their hooves when they come pushing and pelting out.

We make a special effort, hard pushing through the dire terrain. Until we rest on a small hummocky tussock and can see more of the sky, lemon scudding clouds and the moon licked clean underneath, creamy like taking a milk foil bottle top off when the fat rises to the top. From here the party mad people, dancing and drugged stand out alone in a ring around their fires and the wicka-Belinda, goggling her fruity eyes, watching her horses, the fake unicorns trampling around, held in the unity of that ring by someone's power of will, I don't know, maybe the Professor's power of will. They are rowdy and shocking, making themselves heard and now they are nude but at least up here we can listen to ourselves thinking.

"What time is it?" asks Katy, the child.

It was almost half past eleven and midnight was our marker again.

The dancers sing:

I beg you to hold me
while I am slippery

between her and the Indescribable Witch
then such a grand grown up lady
in this valley between her thighs

out of the fire come essences
weather and the money
out of the fire comes
everything
forced to go against the Indescribable Witch
and get bruised in her service

We'll leave you here, to practise
your progress of stories
while I get my thoughts together, pack a bag
a tempest's coming up
with long afternoon walks and expensive boxes
of chocolates
the beckoning waves
let the devil
let the devil
take the rest.

I had this goddamn throwback or is it they call it a flashback, yes. I had this flashing back anyway in all the brilliance and plumy fury of our vigil and the singing and we were alone with our thoughts of god bless Belinda. I saw me and Belinda at Leith Walk Juniors, which is still there, looking a lot smaller these days, grey beside the extra red of the post sorting office. Me in school with no legs and even smaller, Belinda already fat and spending break times cramming her face with sweeties I swear she would give you anything though, even her last bit of chocolate. And he would fling herself over the railings if she heard the ice cream van coming. The kids would laugh and call there she goes and she would vault with extra cunning prowess over those railings and come back with a wafer ice cream sandwich, cream all around her mouth.

I was living at the foot of the Walk and Belinda would come to eat with us. I think she had it rough at home, especially while her brother was away and gone a-soldiering. We bonded as girls at school when one of her fathers says to his daughter, "You're hanging aboot with a lassie with nae legs. A kraut and a paki with no legs tae boot!" And the other's father says to his daughter, "Jesus God, Astrid, that girl is a monstrous blemish. A size she is, my eyes, what a size!" Yet she came to ours, to our flat above the launderette where my mother kept everything going, churning and churning, everything clean.

Belinda saw her first UFO with me. We walked and toiled up Arthur's Seat up all the crags and it was tough work for us with a chair and much extra ballast to heave and push. We looked out over the city and the docks and the castle and we let it get darker and later than we ought and we got scared. And it was—is it a comet? Is it a bird or is it a plane? But it was none of those and it was Belinda's first sign and glimpse of her visitors.

Ah, my eyes were always duff and no good. I squinted and squirmed, but Belinda said that the lights had passed. Jesus God.

AFTER MIDNIGHT THE MOON WAS CLOUDED OVER AND THE REVELS HADN'T ended. The group on the small, separate hill waited a half hour.

At last Astrid said, "Look at those cocksuckers. Still dancing and blazing. Have they no respect for the dead?"

Wendy actually flinched at the word 'dead'. That's what it took, though. Someone had to say the word, and brutally break the spell.

"That's that then," Timon turned on them with a smile. "We've seen her off in style. I reckon she's with Marlene and Pat and Wendy's mum and they're having a whale of a time somewhere. Somewhere much more fun than this."

"More than that lot could ever have," said Katy, nodding at the unicorn people.

Down there they were torching the wicker effigy. There was a puff of luminous flame, small exploding fruits and gourds and a nimbus of burning leaves, pulling Belinda into horrible life. "I want to go back," Astrid said. "I want to go back to the hotel."

Katy started to push her through the grass and down the hill. Wendy and Timon were lingering. "We'll see you there," Wendy said quietly. Astrid nodded and waved Katy on.

"I know we were a joke," said Timon. "When we were set up, when everyone waited to see us meet. I would see she was fat and she would see me and maybe it would be a shock I was black. But we'd told all about ourselves really. We already knew that we loved each other. And all the visitor business, we knew that made us jokes, too. But we didn't care." They watched the fires. Then they watched Astrid and Katy vanish into the dark fields, hotel-bound. Faintly, Astrid's voice: "Jesus God!" in frustration. They watched the revels again. Belinda's vast dummy caved in, her rib cage cracking in numerous golden splinters and gouts of flame spurting up.

"I only wish I had my book," he said.

Wendy bit her lip.

"Belinda and me were jokes before we even met," he said. "Only separately. I was a joke when I first met you, hon. Asking to come back to your mother's flat, asking to be part of your family. What was I like?"

"Lovely, Timon," she said. "Always lovely."

He relaxed in her arms then and grinned. He kissed her, quietly and unexpectedly and how soft and full his lips were. His teeth gave her lips a playful nip and stayed there, just for a breath, then he pushed at her again, pulling her into his warmth, where she rested.

"If we make love," Wendy said, "it won't be..."

He hushed her and started to undress her, pushing the warmed clothes down onto the sodden ground. She felt her skin tighten in the cool air and tasted the soot that lined her throat. And tasted Timon's mouth on her again. She smoothed his chest as his shirt dropped away, fumbled with his belt. Felt her knees crack as she bent to lie beneath him, heard his belt and keys and money jingle as he came to straddle her, his feet tangled and tied together. She laughed. "I'm fucking soaked now."

He brushed her hair back, pulled leaves and twigs away and eased some feeling back into her. He tugged his cock free of his tangle of clothes and she thought, in a rush: old pal, hiya, you're the first proper cock I ever saw and at last, after all this, he was sliding it into her and he lay on her breasts and sobbed as he held it there inside her. Wendy gripped his sides and felt his feverish sweat slick her thighs, her hands and she thought, not for the first time, that she and Timon had been each other's consolation prizes all along, right from the start.

KATY PUSHED ASTRID STRAIGHT INTO THE WAITING PARTY. MORE TENTS had been struck right at the edge of the glen. A less raucous gaggle of unicorn followers awaited them. Even the horses were quiet and watching. Astrid's wheels squeaked and protested. "Shit," Katy said.

Astrid never said a word.

The followers of the church lit torches and came out to meet them. With them came the Professor. He wore a neat black suit, but he was huge and lording it over everyone present.

He laughed, loud and deep inside his gullet to see them struggling, stuck in the rutted mud like this.

"Bring them to the camp," he chuckled.

The followers helped Katy with the chair.

Katy clung on. "Take me to your leader," she muttered.

"More for our happy gang, our wondrous breed," the Professor laughed. "Our ever-expanding troop."

Astrid's face contorted in anger. She could have spat in his eye. "We don't have anything to do with you. You are spoiling the memory of Belinda."

"A rival faction," he purred thoughtfully.

"Faction my arse," said Astrid.

"My dear," he said. "What are you like, riding that fine, steel steed of yours? You are like a little centaur. A plucky centaurina. Perhaps we could adopt you as our new figurehead. You can be an emblem of the challenges we face as we ride onwards, ever onwards."

"Do you really believe all your own shite?" asked Katy bluntly.

"Oh, yes," said the Professor. "And come morning, all the world will see how much we believe."

"Yeah, yeah," said Katy.

"Take them," said the Professor quickly, and Astrid was plucked wriggling out of her chair by willing, dead-eyed stagehands. Her chair—with its lacquer of nail varnish and twists of old tinsel—was booted into the fire.

"Cocksuckers!" screamed Astrid, held struggling and suspended. Katy was pinned to the ground.

"These two reek of the corrupted world," glowered the Professor, raising his voice to carry to the others. "They are sullying the air and the chaste minds of the true followers. These two have renounced nothing. They are in our midst and they bring with them poisonous thoughts." He clicked his fingers. "Bring them to my tent."

His harem tent was larger than all the others. It was dark and smelled of fish and chips, which one of his lackeys had brought out for him from the hotel. Astrid and Katy were pushed down on the lumpy cushions and bound with coarse cloths.

"Jesus God," said Astrid. "I think this is it."

They were left for some moment while the Professor addressed his closest followers. They heard him through the canvas.

"I will teach these two myself and convert them to the purer way. Even though our journey is almost over and morning will see us reunited with the visitors and long-gone from here, we still have time for two more conversions. I shall take that burden upon myself."

The rabble were clapping and jeering him on and he was ranting, spittle flecking his perfect, neat beard. He talked once more about the perfect, sexless visitors, all reason and perfection, who would pass by soon and take the purest home.

"They all want to be horses," said Astrid.

Katy was thrashing about in her bonds to free herself and fell into a jumble of the Professor's personal effects. His stinking clothes. She cursed. Tins of Heinz soup, a little stove, a portable Byron, a tin opener and a white sliced load, half gone. She twisted and swore and scratched the flesh off her wrists getting the tin opener into one hand.

Then up went the tent flap and the Professor was crouching over them while the followers guarded his read.

"Which of you lovely converts is going to be the first?" he grunted.

"Mandy was right about you," Astrid shouted.

"Mandy?" he asked, mildly surprised.

"Everything she wrote in her book. Everything she said."

"Do you know the beautiful and treacherous Mandy?" he smiled. "My Scheherazade?" He unloosened his suit trousers, closed the tent flaps behind him with a cough. Then he yanked down his boxer shorts and pumped furiously at his fat purple cock. "And will you two tell me stories to delay my coming? What elegant circumlocutions can you describe?" He advanced on Astrid. Hmm. No legs."

"Leave her the fuck alone!" Katy yelled. "She's got no fucking legs."

"I know," he said gleefully. "Isn't it convenient? I'd prefer her with no arms as well. But what can you do?"

Katy lashed out with her whole bound body and tripped him so he fell, heavily between them. He bolted up, surprisingly fast for his state and size. He lunged at Katy.

"I don't know what or who to do first!" he cried.

"You've promised these people impossible and horrible things," said Astrid.

"They've done it to themselves," he bellowed, drawing up onto his knees, making a playful grab at Katy. "They had the fucked up space-agey ideas in the first place. They want to think space is all unicorns and happiness and purity—so who am I to stop them? I want to believe that too! That's what I long for. Purity!"

His hands shot out to grab Katy then, and with enormous strength he pulled her down to him. He dragged on her hair and set about pushing his wet cock in her face. She rolled all too compliantly, the tin-opener's stubby blade glinting once, brightly on the air, held up close to her face as she made one untidy gash at the base of his cock, squishing it neatly into his balls.

He stared down and his look at first seemed to be one of puzzlement at the way he was losing his erection, and then at the blood rushing out and the wormy silver threads of the tubes from his balls spilling apart in dirty festoons. Then he howled and pitched over onto his side.

There was a pause before the unicorn people came running.

"I know," breathed Katy. "Jesus God. Jesus fucking God."

"Katy," said Astrid. "That is blasphemy."

The tent flap shot open. "He's had a heart attack!" Katy shouted, to buy them time.

"He was trying to be fucking us both," Astrid added, "and he took a massive fatal attack of the heart!"

By then Katy was attacking her own bindings with the tin-opener. Free, she pushed past the stricken followers and dragged Astrid bodily out of the tent.

By the time his followers managed to pull the wailing bulk of the Professor onto his back and discovered his wounds, the women were gone. Katy staggered headlong into the grass, half a German sikh grasped in both arms.

"Murder, Katy," Astrid was whimpering. "This is murder we have created."

Nothing more was said until they were back in the hotel room they were sharing.

They looked out the window and saw the fires still raging. There was no sound from Timon and Wendy's room. There were no policemen at the door, axing their way in, no management calling, no ambulance bawling. They were out in the wilds and the fuss was dying down.

Bloodied and sooty, Katy and Astrid slept.

TIMON AND WENDY SLEPT HALF-NAKED IN THE GRASS AND THEY HADN'T fucked at all. He'd fallen asleep inside of her at his first thrust and shrivelled and crept back out and she'd slept too, holding him tightly.

When dawn came they were the first on the whole glen to wake up.

The fires were smouldering gently and sending out purplish, dirty-looking smoke as they died. The horses were all gone. Fled at last. And the dancers, the revellers, the followers of the Professor's church, lay still on the ground.

"Everyone slept out of doors last night," said Wendy, dressing hurriedly.

She and Timon stumbled down the hillock towards the fires' remains. Each member of the church lay oddly straight, at regular intervals on the ground, describing a ragged circle. Each had a square of blue silk over their faces, their chest and arms.

Elsewhere, in the smaller camp, it was the same.

All had neat blue silk covering their faces, except the tortured remains of the Professor, and the last surviving member, the woman in the black sweatshirt whom Wendy had met years before. She was the Church's very first member and author of their manifesto. She had been laying them out till dawn, until now, when she was sure she was almost too late to catch the Starship as it passed. Quickly she took the pill and lay down beside the fire where the black charred wheelchair sat in a heap of hot rubble. She swallowed the pill down, thinking the Professor was doing some very strange things last night and maybe his ending wasn't what he had planned. She was thinking that maybe they were wrong to let him get so extreme. Maybe last night he was showing a true underneath self. The unicorn woman couldn't think straight about it. Yet it was too late now, with everyone following the plan to its end at last. All of them gone home like this. All she could think of was her glimpse of the dying Professor's ruptured scrotum and those pale ribbons hanging out. She'd thought: That's all his power spilling away, spilling into the mud? That's his words, that's his long sentences coming out of his punctured balls?

She swallowed her pill down and lay straight in the filthy earth and tugged the silk that she'd kept for herself into a neat diamond over her face. She closed her eyes to wait.

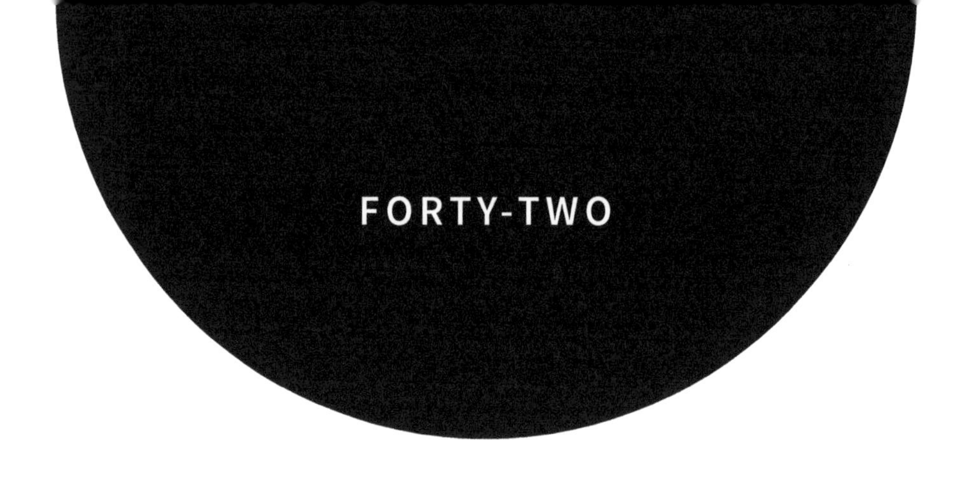

FORTY-TWO

IN THE END ALL YOU WANT TO DO IS PROTECT THEM. I'D SPENT SO LONG in the years of being married to Josh wondering if Katy could feel like my daughter. It didn't matter in the end. She was mine because I wanted to protect her, an urge that came out of nowhere and pushed me to go after her, to check who she was with, what she was doing, that she was safe. When she took up with David—and she did, she took up with him again as soon as we returned to London—I was meant to be jealous and cross, maybe eventually concede and realise that I'd grown older, and let him go by. I never felt like that. Maybe at first I did. What I felt in the end about Katy with David was relieved, that I knew him, and that he was all right really and he'd be good with her. After Argyle she was in a peculiar state. We all were, but it hit Katy worst. We found both her and Astrid the morning after and they looked like a bomb had dropped. They were past being surprised by the deaths of the church people and how the followers had turned on the Professor and killed him in his tent and pulled his balls off him. Katy looked stricken, and Astrid just looked at Katy, as if waiting to take her cue. 'Jesus God! What a surprise!'

Timon looked guilty. He thought he and Belinda had caused the deaths. You couldn't get it through to him that there'll always be people to hang their suffering and needs on something you've done. They used you, Timon, I tried to say. He wouldn't have it. He drove us back to Edinburgh a couple of days later, once all the circus around the cult had died down. We had to answer questions. Timon was conspicuous, was known to the media and the police, but they also knew the reason he was in Argyle. His relative fame protected him. He was treated carefully, as the surviving partner of a woman worshipped by a suicide cult. We were given counselling, emergency support talks in the lounge at the back of the hotel. I couldn't say much about it really, and I don't suppose Katy or Astrid did either. They had seen less than we had.

All the sombre way back to Edinburgh, I wondered about the Professor. He thought he was protecting his church, his herd. In the videotapes they had made in their London headquarters—and sent, in advance, to the BBC and ITN—you could see his love for his people, how they believed they were going on to something better. While we stayed on in Argyle the tapes were broadcast, full of dire warnings of what they intended to do to themselves. The members looked certain and delirious with anticipation. Of one last rabble-rousing festival and then... off with the visitors. They were getting what they wanted. They knew the non-church world would never approve or understand. They sent messages explaining to their individual families, and those people had to watch their children changed, visionary, thinner, posthumous on the nine o'clock news, days after the event, saying that they were happy and sure.

The Professor loved his herd. You could see that much. And he was protecting them in the only way he could think of.

Since all my friends were split up by then and living in different cities, many of the fantasies we spun out when we talked on the phone was that we could all get together and stay that way, just for a while. Deadlines would come up, events for us to gather round. My wedding had been one and we seemed nearly complete then. The century's end was another: one of those turning points you wouldn't want to go through without seeing everyone, like it's your last day on earth. But that New Year, and all the ones since, have seen everyone in separate places they wanted to be.

The Professor got all of his people together.

He managed it, for one final bash.

AT SCHOOL—I MUST HAVE BEEN THIRTEEN—WE HAD A KINDLY biology teacher who was coming up for retirement, but he hadn't lost the knack of talking to people our age. Nothing creepy or too pally in the way he went on with us. He was a smiling, sandy-coloured man and he pulled no punches, spared us no silly jokes when he told us, as he had to that year, all the facts of life. When he said about crabs 'in your hair down below' and about your monthly periods and the way you might feel, there was always this very proper sympathy coming from him. He died and there was a special assembly and lots of us cried. We didn't know him well, but it seemed like we had.

Once he'd done some elementary physics with us. He made one girl hold my upper arm in front of the whole class. "Now, what do you think," he asked us, "if she kept hold of Wendy's arm like that for a thousand years, would her arm wear away eventually? Or..." and he instructed the girl to rub my arm gently in one spot, like she was swabbing me for an injection. "Would it wear away in less than a thousand years like this?"

I always thought of that lesson in friction when Josh held me in one of his doggy hugs and when he decided it was time to break apart he would rub my upper arms briskly as a signal. Usually it was me pulling away first, wriggling and impatient. But the time he rubbed my arms I thought: in less than a thousand years he'll wear me down to nothing, and then I won't have to look after everyone.

So it was true that if you held on tight to someone and didn't move at all, they lasted longer.

Now I knew that wasn't true, but my implacable thirteen year old self would still occasionally remind me.

We said goodbye to Timon and Astrid at Waverley station and we were bound for London again. I waved at Timon, who'd held still inside of me, as if friction was the last thing he'd wanted to cause.

WITHIN A YEAR TIMON PUBLISHED HIS BOOK AT LAST, A SLIM, NARROW, rewritten hardback with photographs, which sold shitloads. It sold on the back of the cultists' suicides and there were rumours that Timon had sorted the whole thing. The whole kit-kaboodle, said Aunty Anne, who turned out to be one of the murmurers . She read the book and thought it was disgusting. In this version of the book Timon made heavier use of the letters that had flown between Belinda and himself before their first meeting. He admitted to me later that they were there to fill up space.

"And now everyone thinks they know Belinda," he said. "They can't see the difference between knowing someone in the flesh, and having read about them."

I thought this was startling coming from him. He'd thought he'd known everything about Belinda just from having read those same letters. He'd changed his mind, now there was no physical presence to back them up. Yet he published the letters virtually intact, and let everyone think they were getting to know someone in all their glory.

Because there were photos, I appeared in the book. The atrocious Polaroids of our Christmas together, right before Serena appeared. They made a double page spread in the book. I had a raft of footnotes to myself. I am footnote girl.

Dear Timon,

One day I would like to come to Blackpool and see you at work. I wouldn't tell you I was coming. I'd let it be a surprise. Wendy always tells me that surprises are the devil's work and that we should avoid them—did she say that when you knew her? I think she wants an easy life and one shock-free.

I would walk in your fish restaurant and emporium and order something special. Scampi or, as some of the fish shops here do, lobster and chips. Something to make me stand out. I've got what they used to call a quiet face and, actually, haven't done much out of the ordinary in my life, but I would order something special, and you would look up in surprise and, in an instant, you would realise it was me.

Dear Timon,

My brother is a soldier and I don't think he'll ever stop. He's vigorous and vigilant and in his seventies and walks the streets cursing ne'er-do-wells and slackers, or anyone who looks like they're heading that way. One day he'll get himself into trouble. Somehow he thinks he must always do the right thing. I think someone—the army, I suppose—took great care to drill this attitude into him. He looks upon me, his only sister, as someone who has gone to seed. He's given up on my ever doing the right thing. I'm a hopeless case according to him, selfish and really, I suppose I am. I'm not public-spirited. I don't believe in it. We make our own way. Don't we?

Dear Timon,

I told you last time about going on holiday with Astrid's family. We were twelve and her family let me come along, but her father wasn't keen on me. Her mother thought Astrid should be mixing more at school and I was the mixer. Did I tell you about the pony-trekking? They rigged Astrid into a special harness thing so she could hold on safe. She was delighted because we'd assumed she wouldn't get a go (my friend has no legs at all but she's a lovely girl and spirited). She made me laugh going up the narrow hill paths because I was going in front and she was shouting to me about how my horse was doing a shit as it trundled along. She gave a running talk about it and the pony people were cross and horrified, because—for some reason—because Astrid was disabled and they'd laid on special provision for her, she shouldn't be rude and act up. She shouldn't be laughing like a drain and going: 'Jesus God! It's a hole not a crack that the shit is coming out of! It is shitting out bricks!'

When we finished back at the stables Astrid's pony, freed of its harness, skipped about happily and lay on the grass, rubbing its back. 'It is glad to be free of me!' Astrid laughed. 'I can't be such a weight!'

All of this came back to me when we were held captive by the visitors. We saw them rarely in those days we were prisoners. But we could hear them approach, the measured canter in the corridor beyond our door. Their steady trip-trapping sounded all wrong indoors. They walked on all fours, of course, but you could never think of mounting one. When we were in the ice fields, allowed to walk and exercise ourselves under careful, baleful supervision, Marlene and I saw the visitors run and they ran like creatures that had never been ridden in their lives. They drummed up a sheeny mist of ice chips as they pelted into the distance and I worried that they would crack the ice clean across and lose themselves. They ran in formation, but we couldn't tell one from another. They never spoke of course, and when we were in their care and sharing their shapeless, cavernous rooms, they simply looked at us with mild curiosity. Whenever they had a finickity task to carry out, one that required manual dexterity, they would lower their noble heads and use the single, silver digit they had attached to their brows.

Dear Timon,

Wendy and I rode out on the bus to the coast, to sit on a scrubby beach looking up at the Forth Bridge. I took all your letters to read. I can't tell you how happy I am to have a real correspondent. Yet I'm this plump, white-haired fiftyish spinster. You must have guessed that by now. I felt safe writing anything I wanted to you, because I knew you were listening.

Dear Timon,

Because I felt safe I wrote things about myself no one knows properly, not even Astrid who still lives close by. Because I knew you were listening I also felt free to invent, freely, wildly, because I never had to meet you, not really. We could stop this exchange any time and it could be like neither of us ever existed to the other.

Dear Timon,

I felt free, at first, to invent a different me, one you could fall for, one you would want. I laid her foundations and got you on the scent. Of course now I want to make a clean breast of it.

Dear Timon,

No clean breasts, no fresh slates. Whatever you've got written from me is the whole truth. It has to be, because it comes from me, and there is nothing more.

Dear Timon,

So I'm doing the dance of the Seven Veils, am I? Sorry, lovey, but I'm not sure I follow the allusion. But come to Edinburgh, and bring your head on a silver platter. Ha!

Dear Timon,

Are you really coming up?

FORTY-THREE

I COULDN'T SETTLE. I CAME BACK TO LONDON AND AUNTY ANNE SAID that's always been my problem, that I couldn't sit still. She said she's lucky, but she's been able to pick up her pieces wherever she is and make it her home. She's had to, she's had to up sticks and settle elsewhere again and again.

I sat at dinner with them and I wondered: how did I end up with you lot? They were like somebody else's friends and family. In the underwater dining room, welcoming David into the fold again in his different guise as Katy's new fella. Joshua had cooked dish after dish, all of them brightly coloured and quite bizarre. He made us laugh at them all, the things he's been trying out and inventing in our honour. He would never tire of trying things out. The only disaster was a side dish of shredded courgette deep fried in olive oil. It was me who had to tell him how horrible it was, acrid and cindery. Josh shrugged and handed me a dish of cherry tomatoes and yellow star fruit slivers.

His sister Melissa, that black old crow, picked a fight with Serena, annoyed that Joshua's flash friend, as she saw her, seemed prepared to fly herself to Paris to visit an optician's. Make two trips for tests and fittings, just to get the glasses she wanted: tiny octagonal frames that would change the way she saw the world. Serena said frames were everything. "But they could send them through the post to you, lovey! I'm sure they would!" Melissa exclaimed.

"You don't see the point," Serena snapped. "It's the getting of the thing myself. It's a trip."

"A trip." Melissa tutted.

"Look. Those are my new eyes we're talking about. I have to see everything through them."

Aunty Anne was pursing her lips. I could tell she was torn between Serena's extravagance and Melissa's prudence, so she kept out of it.

Katy and David seemed pleased with themselves.

Katy was wearing a wry, lopsided smile.

I had seen before somewhere.

And I'm not working up to ending this with a wedding

It's what everyone wants

but they like a wedding before everything stops

Well, not here.

Serena, become an accomplice to Katy and David, was making plans. I listened, astonished, as Josh hung on her every word. She thought the young couple should strike while their iron was hot, and get themselves hitched. Don't let your golden chances pass you by, all that. Even more amazing, Katy was talking it all in, too. I thought maybe she was different since Argyle.

I didn't like the way Joshua let Serena make plans. She leaned across the table, keeping her chin low, her eyes big. I remembered the times Josh was away and Serena was my link and how glad I was of her company. How glad she made me of her company.

It was late. Our guests were staying over. Camping out all over the house.

It was a cold night. Our guests were drifting about the upper landings, hunting out blankets, spare pillows, filling hot water bottles.

Josh stopped me in the hall. "You don't look right," he said.

It was like being caught not looking convincing. "I don't?"

"Like everyone's getting under your feet."

I shrugged. "I wish Mandy had come round."

He looked pale at this. "She's playing it cool."

"Because I didn't like her new book."

Josh hadn't read it, of course. I wondered what he'd think. I hadn't told him what it had made me think.

In the confusion of everyone going off to bed, I slipped out of the house, taking only one bag.

The last thing I saw of Joshua: him going off to bed with his hot water bottle.

I WALKED OUT OF GREENWICH AND, STUPIDLY, STOOD IN THE MIDDLE of the mostly-empty road to check my bag for necessities. It would be too embarrassing to go back now. Tampons, ciggies, cheque book, cards, Joshua's adoption folder. I was almost in New Cross before I could flag down a cab with its yellow light on.

He asked me where to.

"A fair distance," I said. "Out of London, I think. Not sure yet. Hang on." I slammed the door shut and slid back into the dark, cool seat. "Just drive."

He shrugged, and drove.

In the meagre, fleeting light, I opened my bag, lit a ciggie quickly, took a deep breath and ripped open the brown envelope.

A sheaf of crumbling papers and I scanned them quickly for a place name, anything. It seemed indecent, being too hasty, when the information had lain hidden so long. Yet maybe haste would make it current again. The driver was impatient.

"Any ideas yet, hon?" he growled.

Then I found it. Her name was Lisa Turmoil. She was a hairstylist, or at least, that's what she used to be. And she was in the North of England. We would be driving all through the night.

"Well?" he asked again.

"Blackpool," I said. "We're going to Blackpool."

WHAT I WAS DOING WAS BRAVE. I TOLD MYSELF THIS AGAIN AND AGAIN AS we gunned up the various motorways.

Now we were in the twisted guts and intestinal chambers of the country.

Now we were in the clogged and sooty bronchial tubes.

I lay on the back seat and listened to the easy motor, my driver swearing and muttering, the regular thunk of the meter. It was counting down and ravelling up my fortune, portion by tiny portion.

I WOKE IN THE NORTH OF ENGLAND, IN BLACKPOOL, AT DREAR DAY.

There were sea gulls making rich pickings of the crap left on pavements the night before on the Golden Mile. Nothing had changed. We pulled up in an empty side street and the cabby and I stretched our legs.

"I have to get some breakfast," he grunted, and wanted paying there and then. I wrote a quick cheque, one so fast I barely had time to register the amount as I wrote it out, or to make sure that I had done it right, but it didn't matter. The cheque vanished into the driver's wallet. "You're bloody mad, love," he sighed. "What made it so important that you couldn't wait and get the train up instead?"

I laughed. "All of this. I wouldn't have got to see the morning like this and in Blackpool. Taste the air."

"Fish." He sniffed. "And birds crapping everywhere. Same as anywhere you go."

"Not to me."

Don't get all sentimental, Wendy. It's only the place you started out.

AND NO ONE KNEW SHE WAS HERE. NOT YET. NO ONE COULD FIND her, unless they tracked her whereabouts all the way back to her childhood. That might take ages. It had certainly taken her ages. She smiled at the cabby. "Well, thanks, then." Poor bloke. She'd dragged him out, through the night, all the way from South London.

He sighed and tutted and started to move off. "Are you sure you're all right?"

Of course. She was.

She went off down the Prom.

I STILL KNOW MY WAY AROUND HERE. I USED TO RUN AROUND ALL these streets. I check the address on the old certificate again and I'm sure I even know the hairdressers' shop it mentions there: the street not far from our one-time home.

FORTY-FOUR

SHE REMEMBERED READING A REALLY BAD NOVEL ABOUT THREE WOMEN in New York. It must have been in the Fifties or something because it had seemed old fashioned to Wendy. The three women worked in jobs like advertising and showbusiness and modelling and they all fell in love with men who gave them—as Aunty Anne would say—the runaround.

Wendy never finished the book because it was too long and she got sick of all the characters and then her Mandy said it was crap anyway and that she was wasting her time. All the women in the book were so traumatised by their goings-on that they started taking pills. That was the upshot.

Then thing that Wendy remembered most, and especially the morning after her night of passion with the old comic Billy Franks, was the moment when the main character in the book eventually copped off with her boyfriend. She went to bed with him and Wendy waited for all the gory details but they never came. The women in the book had been worried that she 'couldn't give her all' to a man and when she found that—shazam!—she could, then she'd come out with something that had stuck in Wendy's head.

'I function. I am a woman.'

Whatever that meant.

When she got up early for breakfast, ravenous and clutching her sheets for the washer, Wendy repeated the words to herself. I am a woman. I function.

She felt curiously clear-headed.

She was bundling messy sheets into the washing machine when she realised that she wasn't alone in the kitchen. Aunty Anne was sitting at the table on the swivel chair. She was in her fleecy nightdress, clutching a pillow to her chest. The bottle of Glemorangie was open in front of her.

"You look like you haven't slept a wink," said Wendy.

"Pat had another bad night."

"Oh."

"You kept him out late enough."

"He met up with his old pal..."

"Yes, I heard a whole lot of noise in the night. All sorts. That's what woke me up. I got up and found Pat calling out for help, half fallen out of bed. You could hardly hear him for the racket."

"Oh god," Wendy said.

"Hm," said Anne. She was quite drunk, Wendy realised. There was only a finger or two of whiskey left in the bottle. Her aunt was looking at her.

"What were you doing telling him to take you out of his will?"

"Not this again," said Wendy.

"If the old man wants you to have his money, then you should take it."

Wendy turned to leave. "I'm going to check on him."

"No," said Anne, standing woozily. "He's sleeping."

"Right." Wendy turned to the washer and fiddled with the programme.

"I've got some whites that could have gone in with that load."

"It's started now." Wendy sat down with her Aunt, who dropped back into her swivel chair.

"You just go charging in, doing what you want, getting your own way."

"Me?" Wendy couldn't believe this.

"Yes, you. And you get away with it because you're young and attractive. You don't even know that everyone is giving you your own way.

You just expect it."

"Uh-huh," said Wendy.

"Ever since your poor mum died, you've turned ever so hard."

"Maybe I have."

"First you want to get your hands on your uncle's money, then you don't. You get me to get you in with him, get you set up for life. And then you decide you've got principles and you're too good for that. And so you make him take you out of the will. A poor dying old man's will and you make him faff on with it. You've got everyone doing the hokey bloody cokey."

"All you care about," said Wendy levelly, "is what you want, Aunty Anne. Let's face it."

"I want you to be happy." Her aunt looked tearful.

Wendy tossed her head.

"What, you think I'm lying?"

"I don't know anymore."

"Of course I want you to be happy, you stupid little bitch."

Wendy had a burst of inspiration. "I reckon what pisses you off and gets right up your nose is that Uncle Pat hasn't asked you what you want. No one's asked you want you want. They haven't done for years. You're completely terrified that you're past it and out of the game for good."

Aunty Anne picked up her tumbler and flung it at the wall behind Wendy's head. The crash of the glass startled both of them.

They were silent for a moment.

"You'll see how it feels," Aunty Anne promised.

"What would happen if I took the money, Aunty Anne? It would still be the same me."

"You wouldn't have to deal with the ordinary shit. The shit that's held back me and everyone else we know."

"If I got that much money," said Wendy, "I'd only blow it. I'd be surrounded by people telling me what to do. I'd listen to all of them and get properly fucked up. Look at me now! I haven't got a penny to my name and it still happens to me! People are always telling me what I should do with my life."

"Because," her Aunt sighed, "because you're already rich, Wendy.

You're surrounded by people who want to have your youth, your time, your looks..."

"Oh, crap."

"It's true. I would call that being rich."

The washing machine was going into its next cycle. Wendy said, over the noise, "If I got the money I'd get right away from all of you. What would you think of me then?"

Aunty Anne shrugged.

"I'd leave you all. And then I'd find some bloke. I'd spend it all on some bloke who would probably be wrong for me. The first bloke who said he loved me for who I am."

Aunty Anne was shaking her head.

"And I'd blow that million pounds. I'd chuck it away on the first fancy man that came along."

"How did you get to be so bitter, Wendy?"

"It's not bitterness."

"Sounds it to me."

"I've just listened a lot."

"You should learn from what other people say, but you shouldn't let it put you off."

Wendy got up to go.

"We'll get you that money, Wendy."

ANNE WATCHED HER NIECE GO BACK TO HER ROOM.

Then she looked up at the suds sliding down the window of the washer and the wet folds of sheets as they pressed themselves on the glass and pulled away.

Anne hugged the pillow from Pat's bed to her chest. What she had told Wendy was true. Pat was sleeping restfully now, of his own accord.

Last night she had sat with him after his funny turn. The room still smelled of vomit, even after she had scrubbed at the carpet and stripped down the bed as he slumped on one corner of the mattress. To her, the room seemed tainted by his sickness: the smell was in the air, touching every available object and surface. This whole flat was full of sickness, she thought, watching Pat start at last to fall asleep in his clean bed.

When Anne went out to work in the fleamarket and car boot sales, even though she was immaculate and fit as a fiddle, Anne was sure that others, strangers, could smell and detect that lingering hint of sickness, as if it had rubbed off on her.

She listened to his flutey snores. She watched the tiny tremors in his white eyelids.

He hadn't needed money or prestige or any of the rest of it to make him dignified. He always had that about him. It was natural. She'd recognized that much, the first time she'd seen him, doing a rubbishy magician's turn on talent night in a Manchester pub. She would say—though not to his face, in case it made him big-headed—that it was a natural aristocracy that Patrick had. He would behave like a gentleman if he lived in a slum.

Tonight she had seen him shivering, calling out in a weak, high voice. She had seen him sitting on the edge of the bed, caked in his own sick and shit and the whole mess smelling of alcohol. She had seen him crying and cursing himself. When she sponged his naked body down she had been crying too. His seemed like a body she had never seen before. She had become just a nurse.

Now he slept.

And she watched him, as she held the pillow to her bosom. She cradled it like she had once cradled Colin, when he was so tiny Pat had hardly dared touch him in case he broke. At the time Anne thought Pat wouldn't hold the child because he wasn't his. He was above such things. He'd taken them in, married her, adopted the baby, but he wouldn't claim him as his own. But Anne had been wrong. Colin was far more Pat's child than hers.

Pat was never indifferent. He was scared and puzzled. He was bewildered, perhaps, but he was never aloof. He had loved them.

Anne held the pillow out and held it a little way above his face. Silently, silently. She didn't want to wake him. She wondered what it would feel like. It might be rather nice. All that clean warm white pressing down. Taking you in. She would have to press down hard enough. She would die if there had to be a struggle to the end.

And from down the uncarpeted corridor she could hear the sounds from Wendy's room. Squeals and panting and muffled thuds.

Did you press it down hard like a surprise or did you lower it gently so the feeling was imperceptible? So the dense weight touched his face and it would be like a slow, everlasting kiss?

She didn't know.

It was almost dawn.

She had let the dawn creep in.

She didn't know now, how this had to be done.

For a second though, Anne felt more powerful than she had in years. But she couldn't do it.

She pulled the pillow back to her breast and cuddled it there, as if to keep it away from Pat's face.

Then she got up and went heavily to the kitchen to drink, to get drunk, and wait for Wendy.

Aunty Anne watched the skylight turn a bright and fresher shade of blue and the stars go out over the Royal Circus.

She thought: if I'd been a different sort of woman, tonight I could have committed the biggest act of my life.

But if she'd killed Pat, shouldn't she have killed her sister, too? Wouldn't she then be guilty of letting Lindsey suffer needlessly?

Anne hadn't acted in either case and she was glad. Not glad for them, but glad for herself.

None of these things, she told herself, are for me to sort out.

AFTERWORD

Fancy Man was written under the influence of Henry James and Shirley Bassey and Jeremy Hoad, to whom it is dedicated, with love.

With *Fancy Man* I moved away from Newton Aycliffe,
from the town of my growing up, from
the Phoenix Court trilogy.
I went elsewhere, like I did in life, ages ago.
I still want to write about the North.
I've lived in and written about the North East,
the North West, and Edinburgh.
And it isn't really all about the bleak working class north,
and travelling south.
Wendy goes south and my quandary as much as hers, as well as Isabel
Archer's before us, was where to stay put.
Your fancy man always tries to take you elsewhere.
Newton Aycliffe and Phoenix Court still drew me back, of course.
It's where Aunty Anne's own fancy man wedged his glorious bulk and
from where he refused to budge.
Perhaps I'm as drawn to origins as I am to the way we reinvent ourselves.
I'm always interested in survivors.
My characters, my family, my friends are survivors.

This book also comes with thanks and love to another long list of people who have influenced me and go on doing so.

GLITTERING
FAG

"All the lighting in here is from candles," said Katy, staring across the oyster bar. "It's like sitting in a cave." It was atmospheric here, they all decided. It was coming up to midnight and it was even snowing outside.

They were in a bar under the dripping stone arches in the east end of the city. After the shops shut town was almost empty. Katy, Simon, Douggie and Shelley had come out to celebrate and do tequila stammers. Lick-slam-suck. Chins gleaming with salt and lemon juice. Puddles of Montezuma on the table, soaking the Rizla papers. They'd had nachos, of course, and the orange mess of their leftovers sat with them all night. 'Wonderwall' came uninterruptedly on the juke box: someone's favourite.

In her spare time Katy was a painter, but she worked in an office. "The way the fight here is moving...it's like that cartoon. Remember *Roobarb and Custard*? It was done with scribbly felt tip so the colours jogged about and hurt your eyes. It's like that here."

It was Katy's birthday. She'd already had a bottle of wine at work. Her friends' presents were laid out on the table. Housey things because she'd moved in with Simon.

"But he'll get the benefit of these too!"

Simon ran a self-conscious hand over his new-shaved head. "Smart."

Matisse-blue salt and pepper shakers. A fun orange plastic cafetiere, more show than use. A silly collage pasted into a green frame, from Douggie, a painter friend of Katy's. "This means," she said gloomily to Simon, "we're really fucking married now!" Quite suddenly she felt like crying. She went to the loo and sat there for a while. There was no paper. She found a few shredded bits in her pocket.

What had Simon bought her? A food mixer. So she could make her home-made hummous even better. Four cloves of garlic, just how he loved it. He'd waited till tonight, to give her card and present with the others. Blithely he'd let her leave the fiat this morning, her birthday unacknowledged. This made her cry as soon as she reached work and the doorman told her many-happy-returns. Simon looked gorgeous with his hair new and fluffed up. The goldy studs of his piercings glinted and his clever hands picked scabs of wax off the bottle.

Shelley had brought After Eights. She didn't have much money because she was doing voluntary work down the homeless centre. She came all dreaded up like a crusty, and got everyone to use the black envelopes the mints came in to send each other silly messages. Simon wrote one for Katy that said he wanted to go down on her when he got her home and Douggie got it by mistake. Simon coloured.

He and Katy lived four flights up a red fire escape in Thistle Street, the centre of town. The fire escape was the only way in and out of their new flat. To them it seemed quite hazardous, quite glamorous.

After midnight they found the empty city frozen and sheeted with ice. Their party stuck together for half an hour, sliding about on the ice. In St. David's square, taking long running jumps and skating easily. Then they broke up, leaving Katy and Simon to go back to their canyon of warehouses. A streetlamp was level with their front window and shone in yellow on them as she laid him down on the sofa, their hard, green, 1950s sofa. She undressed him slowly, like a present.

"I'm the same old thing inside," he said. She couldn't disagree. The same old salty taste of him.

He gave her something in a home-made box. Something arty farty. It was a packet of Marlboro Lights with only one in. He had dipped a single ciggie in pink glitter. She held it up and laughed.

"A camp fag!" she said. "A glittering fag," he said.

Before he could stop her she'd lit it and taken a drag. She coughed and coughed and he thumped her back and the cigarette, dropped in the ashtray, put itself out.

Shelley and Douggie couldn't call it a night. They shared a flat further out of town and wanted to make the best of being here. As usual Douggie was pulling them towards the Queer Triangle, towards CC's and dancing. "I'm tired," Shelley wailed, standing in the abandoned main street. He was skipping ahead, oblivious to the cold now he felt he was getting his own way. Shelley wore six layers, jumper on jumper and two denim jackets. She had worn these in the advice centre office, where the clients came off the freezing street in even more layers. Layer-chic, Douggie called it. Like all the gay boys here he wore his clothes as small and tight and thin as they would go.

Tonight he suddenly disappeared over the black iron fence into the private gardens along Queen Street. His jeans were a vivid orange in the murky, untouched snow beyond. It was a different world. "It's not fair that it's private in here!"

"We're free to break in," Shelley pointed out reasonably, throwing her leg over the fence.

They lay in the snow and made angel shapes, flapping their arms to brush and make wings. Then they rolled balls of creaking snow larger and larger, to build a snowman.

"I was thinking about mum,' Shelley said. Douggie adored her mother, not least when she cooked a meal round her daughter's flat. Funny greasy little Chinese parcels of wontons, seaweed and tofu. Her mum drank half pints of gin and brayed with laughter. She wore a burgundy rabbit fur jacket from Oxfam and talked at length about tampons and how the last one she used tended to dry up some of her juices as well as the blood and it took some getting out. Katy blanched and made it clear she didn't approve of Shelley's mum at all.

"What's the matter with you? Hey, leave your boyfriend behind. He's got an old lady he could be cheering up, here."

Simon shrugged helplessly. Wearing his trendy footballer's top. Katy could have punched him, grinning like that. Shelley's mum looked her square in the eye. "Hey, I'm not a wicked person. You'ye got to believe that." She sounded so desperate, but spoiled that by very deliberately fetching one of Katy's ciggies and taking a long drag. "I'm really not a wicked person."

Their snowman is finished. Douggie did a sculpture unit on his art foundation course, so this isn't your usual three blobs with eyes and buttons. "He's a bit of a hunk!" says Shelley, stepping back to survey.

"I hate that phrase," says Douggie, who can be prissy. He's taken off his jacket, showing off his muscles and his green checky shirt. "Hunky. Like men were edible."

Yet he has made a sexy snowman who, if he were ice cream or sparkling icing sugar, Shelley would have no qualms over eating.

"Race you," says Douggie as he turns and runs out of the park. He leaves his sexy snowman, his flatmate, his jacket behind and he vaults the iron fence, back onto Queen Street. He's pelting towards CC's.

She's used to him running off. Usually on their ad hoc nights out he's never to be seen again and she knows he's gone off with some feller.

Tonight, breathless, she catches up with him at the crowded bar. Karaoke night at CC's. Two dykes are up doing Meatloaf. 'Real Dead Ringer For Love.' "Same old lot in here," says Shelley, jabbing him in the ribs.

With a pint each they struggle through the upper floor, the black and white lino, the pressed bodies in denim, plaid, leather and Lycra, through the scents of two dozen aftershaves. Downstairs it's Step-Back-In-Time night. They dance desultorily — loving it — to the Nolans, Tight Fit, Boney M. Someone shoves poppers under their nose and says she's "Tanya, from Texas!" Douggie see Tanya in the gents later, handing her little bottle along the blokes at the urinal.

Past three there's a new arrival in the sweaty basement.

He swaggers in wearing Douggie's abandoned jacket and nothing else. The crush of bodies pulls back when he appears. Startled by his presence, his nakedness. His cool.

Shelley tries to tell Douggie. The newcomer dances at his shoulder. Breaking into his space.

I know he's there, Douggie's eyes tell her. Hers tell him: You've cracked it.

She draws back to let Douggie flirt.

Abba is on. Douggie dances with his new man. Soon it is time to go. Shelley tugs his elbow. "You can't take him home!"

"Why not?"

"He isn't real!"

"He's real as anyone else here!"

"But...he'll melt!"

Douggie laughs at her. His new man waits to be propositioned and taken home on the nightbus.

Shelley gets on the same bus at the top of Leith Walk. She feels like she's walking three paces behind, so she won't cramp his style. From the back seat she watches Douggie laugh and joke with his snow man. She stares at their twinned, white, shaved necks. The snowman's is, of course, the whiter. As the bus slides through the glossy dark Douggie's arm goes round his new feller's shoulders. His hand kneads gently at the sexy back of that neck. The pressure and warmth of that gesture, she knows, is melting the snowman already. His flesh is glittering. Shelley stares at the streets going by and knows that next morning she'll be there to talk it through with Douggie, when there's nothing left.

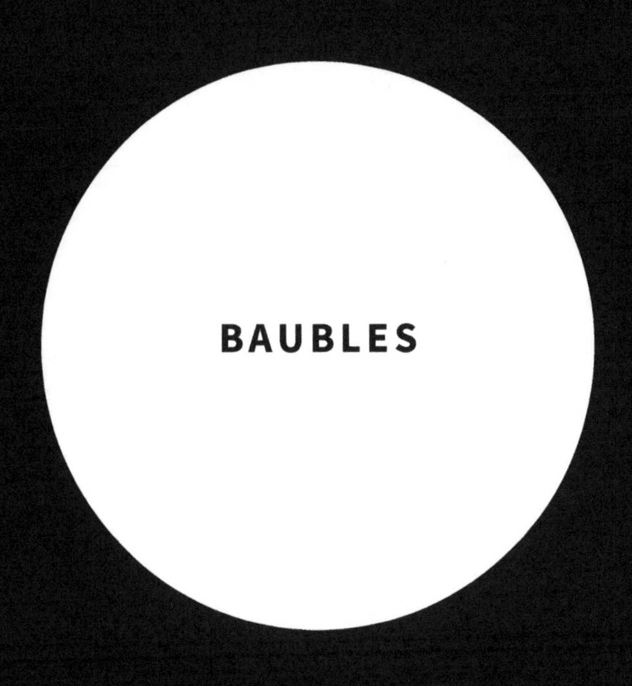

BAUBLES

Out Of Season

"Don't knock it Robert," she told him.

Aunty Jane was getting cross as she clip-clopped across the piazza di San Marco clutching her useless sun hat, swinging her bag and scattering the evil pigeons as she went. "We can't help the time of year," she went on. "It's cheap, all right? That's all that matters." Robert took a last look at the towers, domes and scaffolding, and followed her across to the arcade of shops. They were glowing with coloured crystal and glass, beckoning to her through the fog.

That's all she wanted to come for, he found himself thinking. The shopping. The shopping and the Italian men. Outside an expensive café a mini orchestra had started to play. 'We Are the Champions'.

He hurried after his aunty knowing that, by the time he caught up with her, her mood with him would have changed. It always did. They were best mates really. Otherwise, how could they work together? How could they come on holiday together.

SANTA'S LITTLE HELPERS

Back at home in Whitby, they even had rooms next door to each other in the Christmas Hotel. They were high in the attic, far from the paying guests.

When Robert had been down on his luck and, after a new direction for his pitiful career, it had been Aunty Jane's suggestion that he join her in the fishing town and become an elf, one of Santa's happy little helpers in the Christmas Hotel.

The Edwardian hotel looked out blearily across the wet black rocks of the shore and the crumbling priory. It was filled mainly with pensioners and run by an evil-looking woman with grotesquely swollen legs, whose idea of fun was to celebrate Christmas every day of the year. The ancient visitors lapped her sales gimmicks up.

All summer Robert had waited on, ran around and been a general kind of servant, all dressed as an elf in a skin-tight green costume and a red hat. The outfit had shown off his packet something chronic: his festive little holly spring, Aunty Jane had laughed, something else to cheer up the old dears.

Hard work in the Christmas Hotel, pandering and present-wrapping, all summer long. Then came autumn and meagre, rather begrudged bonuses and the determination in both nephew and aunt alike that they had to get away on holiday. Away from the churning froth of the North Sea and the keening, kamikaze gulls. Time to fly on some cheap airline to Italy and hopefully catch the last of the sun.

They took the kind of flight where you have to pay up for even a glass of water and the stewardesses sell things like aftershave and bikinis up and down the gangway.

PEACHY

They'd been in Venice for a day. It was misty and the drizzle was warm. Like dishwater, as Robert put it: dropping on them slowly as they sat in pavement cafes, traipsed foggy, perplexing alleys, and minded their steps on slippery humpbacked bridges. "Well, I think it's downright romantic, seeing it off-season and autumnal," Aunty Jane announced just this morning as they embarked on their exploration of the Left Bank. "When it's foggy like this, you never know who you might end up bumping into, coming around the next corner."

Aunty Jane was coming up to fifty. Robert had to admit she'd kept herself nice. She was slim and still, as she put it, with-it. She'd bought a caseful of patterned summer frocks. She was here, she said, to take in the culture: the music, buildings and paintings. All Robert had seen her looking at was the men.

Having bruschetta and a glass of the local pink Pinot Grigio in an off-licence last night, she'd told him: "I've finished with those chat-and-date phone lines. Never again. All those fellas want to know is what dress size you are, and are you still pretty, have you got your hair done nice. And when it comes to them, they don't want to tell you anything. Well, then you go to meet them in some godawful wine bar — a place too young for both of you — and he's sat there waiting and he looks like Wurzel Gummidge. Oh, no. Not for me. No more shooting in the dark."

Once she'd thought that she was bound to find someone, working in a big hotel. Some millionaire with a rakish glint in his eye as she brought his fried breakfast. Someone with cash to spend on a smart, mature person like her; who couldn't believe his luck, meeting her in Whitby, where he'd come to spend an unseasonable Christmas. She wouldn't mind if he was eccentric.

But no one at the hotel had caught her eye. More to the point, she hadn't caught theirs.

Robert and his Aunty Jane sat at the high stools of the off-licence bar for a couple of hours, drinking the pale, murky wine served to them by a bloke who looked like Harvey Keitel. They talked about love like they never really had before. The conversation was an eye-opener for both of them.

They drifted out, bought peaches off a fruit stall gondola and sat on the steps of a white stone bridge. The evening mist and dark came down and they talked about their ideal men, and how sick they had become of turkey, tinsel, and the blazing blue Christmas puddings.

"Look at him," Robert suddenly said, laughing and pointing at an old man strolling by the closed up front of a church.

"He's ancient," his aunt said, wiping peach juice off her chin.

He had a huge white beard and a scarlet face. He was a skinny old thing in a checked sleeveless shirt and Bermuda shorts.

"It's Santa Claus!" Robert laughed, choking. "On holiday!"

They both laughed until the old bloke was out of sight. "He must wear padding at Christmas time," Aunty Jane said, and then shuddered. "Oh, don't talk about Christmas to me."

WATCH THE BIRDIE

"But who could afford all this? And how would you carry it back in your luggage?"

They were looking at the coloured glass objects in the shop windows.

Twisted, sculpted glass with crimson and aquamarine seeping clouded and frozen in spirals and whorls like ink dropped rough water. The two of them gazed for an hour or more at jewellery and vases and bottles and, finally, a whole tree of blown glass that teemed with life-sized and haughty-looking parrots.

It was as they were studying the glass birds that Robert glimpsed a familiar figure inside the shop.

"Don't look now," Robert hissed. "But there's Santa again."

Santa was having something carefully wrapped in green tissue paper. His Bermuda shorts showed off his pale, hairless legs and sandals. He looked affluent and pleased with himself, scratching at his magnificent beard.

"Oh, no," said Jane. "Let's ignore him. God, I hope he didn't hear us laughing at him last night..."

She was blushing as the old man came out of the glass shop, struggling with his precious parcel and the awkward door. Aunty Jane looked away, but Robert was watching.

Santa fixed them with a genial frown, his feathery eyebrows pulled together. He waited until Aunty Jane met his glance.

Then he said, "Ho, ho, ho!" and she gasped.

The old man moved off into the narrow, bustling arcade and soon he was lost to them amongst the brolleys, damp fleeces and shopping bags.

REGRET TASTES OF COFFEE

They had tiny cups of bitter, gritty coffee at a table by their hotel.

"The canals smell of damp wool," Robert said, staring at the milky green water. He looked at his despondent Aunty Jane and sighed. A litre of wine at lunchtime in the Peggy Guggenheim museum hadn't been such a good idea. The sour wine had tasted like rainwater, like tears, and as they'd trooped around, dutifully taking in the surrealist pieces (nightmare interiors by Ernst and Magritte, driftwood assemblages knocked up by Picasso), Robert had watched his slender, nervy Aunty Jane sink into a deep depression.

She bolted back the rest of her espresso like medicine, pursed her lips and told him: "Don't you ever turn out like me, Robert."

"How do you mean?" He'd found he was watching the gondoliers again, as they rested on the opposite side of the canal. Larking about in a foreign language, shoving each other, lazing in the afternoon sun as the cobbles gave off wreaths of warm mist.

"I was your age in the Seventies and I thought I had it all in front of me. I was like one of Pan's People off *Top of the Pops*. That's what I looked like. And I called it sexist at the time, the way all the blokes looked at me and tried to chat me up. I just breezed through and then it was a decade later and I was a housewife for a bit. Poodle perm, batwing mohair sweaters, negative equity, the lot. And by the time I'd got myself out of all that, I found I'd turned into a little old lady, like this..."

"You're not a little old lady..." he murmured. One of the gondoliers was climbing back aboard his boat and Robert was watching him: the curious, wiry strength of him, the overdeveloped calf muscles.

"I may as well be," she said. "And who has looked at me during this holiday, eh? Who has looked my way?"

Robert's heart went out to her, because his Aunty took such a pride in her appearance, and it was a shame if no one paid her any attention. But he had seen men looking, in the Departures lounge at Standsted, in that shop in Pisa.

"Them?" she gasped. "They were perverts. I don't want perverts looking at me."

SLIPPING AWAY

It was a strange city, and not for the reasons they expected.

Not because of the weird, overlapping sounds of the canals at night, or the fog that slipped down and swapped all the streets around so that nothing was in the same place as before. And not because of the thought of ancient ballrooms, casinos and bordellos sunk underwater, preserved somewhere beneath their feet, with monstrous fish drifting about through gilded rooms, under chandeliers bearded with lichen and weed.

It was strange because it seemed empty to Robert and Jane. They were here together, but they were both looking for other people. There was a sense of something here for both of them, but neither knew how to find it.

"We may as well be invisible," Aunty Jane said. "We're like ghosts in a city that's sinking..."

Robert didn't like it much when her thoughts went morbid and lurid like this and she told him all about it. Each night, when he knew she was sleeping, he slipped out of their shared hotel room and went hunting around the Academia bridge. There were men hanging around, sure enough, smoking fags and following him when he attempted to lead them a merry dance.

But they didn't play the rest of the game like they were meant to. They had some other cryptic purpose, knocking about the woolly-smelling canals in the dark. Robert couldn't figure it out.

Their holiday was taking a bleak, sour turn and reluctantly Robert had to put it all down to sex. We're on what could be a romantic trip, he thought: that's why. All this romance is just like rubbing our faces in it.

Waiting On

They ate in a trattoria with a courtyard out back. Their waitress kept pinching Robert's cheek and his ciggies and came over to gabble at them in Italian, as if they understood every word.

"She's very insinuating," Aunty Jane said, flicking her menu. She had come up in terrible bumps from insect bites and was itchy, dizzy and cross. "She's much too familiar. I don't like her."

Aunty Jane considered herself to be a very fine waitress and took great interest in how others behaved on the job.

"I think they're all ex-prostitutes, who run this place." Robert was studying the plastic lobsters on the walls and the mirrors with disturbing clowns painted on. Everything was garlanded with fairy lights. "They're all retired and they've set up a co-op and now they're raking it in."

"Their bread buns aren't very fresh," Jane sighed.

The waitress was back. She wasn't that helpful with explaining the menu. "Oh, lasagna, tagliatelle, spaghetti...is all the same." Then she was nudging Robert with her bony elbow. She was wrinkled from the sun, but very pale and her dyed black hair had gone thin on top. "She your mama, yes? Your lover, no?"

"Oh no," said Aunty Jane.

"No, no," said Robert. "My aunt. Just my aunt. My friend."

The waitress didn't understand and passed him a rose. "Che bello," she told him, and ruffled his hair.

Aunty Jane was looking aghast, but not at him.

"What's the matter?" At a table in the ramshackle courtyard of the trattoria, Santa Claus was wearing a pink linen suit and sitting hunched over by guttering candlelight. He was polishing off a dressed crab and beaming to himself.

"He's following us about," Aunty Jane said, transfixed by that formidable beard.

"Never," Robert laughed. "It's a small town, really. Like Whitby. You're bound to bump into people again and again...it's like maze with everyone going round..."

She shook her head, looking grim. She fiddled fearfully with her long dark hair. "No. He's a pervert. He's a Santa Claus pervert and he's coming after me."

Robert had to laugh.

Christmas Stalking

The old man finished his dinner and paid up just as they were going. He didn't make it obvious and neither of them noticed him casting sidelong glances their way, but somehow he timed it so he was leaving the noisy, shabby trattoria just as they were.

Their waitress was hugging Robert goodbye and Aunty Jane was hissing, "told you!" as Santa squashed by, grinning.

They took the dark back alleys to their hotel. Aunty Jane had them scooting along, shooting backwards glances all the way, until Robert lost patience with her.

It was true, though. The bearded man in the pink linen suit was ambling after them, all the way to their hotel.

They'd been lucky with their hotel, managing to get a room with an arched window at water level, right on the Grand Canal. They had a pedestal table and wickerwork chairs, where they could sit to watch vaporetti chugging past.

"He must be staying in the same hotel," Robert told her.

His aunt was getting far too jumpy. She had two high spots of pink on her cheeks.

"It's the way he went 'Ho, ho, ho,'" she said, coming out of the en suite, brushing her teeth. "It sent a chill right through me..."

SEASON'S GREETING

The next morning they were sitting at their window and waving at the vaporetti, trying to get the passengers to wave back.

"Well! The cheeky devil!" Aunt Jane burst out suddenly. Robert looked and saw why. It was Santa, up on the top deck of the passing bus. He was waving both arms at her energetically, grinning his head off through his beard.

It was Jane's idea that the two of them split up for that morning and do some exploring alone. She felt Robert may be tiring of her nerviness and want to get away. lie shrugged, nonplussed.

Jane found herself drifting about not too far from the hotel, since she'd come without her map. It was a cautious exploration, with her clothes sticking to her.

She sat right out on the front of the bay, where the choppy Adriatic came up to the front of the newsagents and bistros. She sat a table and ordered a coffee and then she saw the two waitresses from last night's trattoria ambling along the prom, carrying between them what looked like a big bag of leftovers, a huge doggy bag, one handle each. It was as if they had been working in that tatty restaurant all night and were only now setting off home on aching feet, looking even more ancient in the lemony-grey morning light.

Jane had a kind of future-shock then. One of her sudden, horrible glimpses of what might be in store for her. She often tortured herself like this. In these queer flash-forwards, she never saw things going well for herself. She saw herself as a real old lady (really, she knew she wasn't one yet) and she was still grafting away at the Christmas Hotel. And Robert was still with her, twenty years and they were still finishing their backbreakingly festive shifts and struggling home together at the end of them, just like these two gamey old birds — who had noticed her by now, and were waving at her as she sat under her awning, blowing On her coffee.

They were jeering at her really; two wizened old death's head crones, knowing that her life might as well be over already and it was always going to be the same.

She gulped her coffee and refused to wave back. They moved on, out of sight. And then Santa was pulling up one of the aluminium chairs, scraping it on the cobbles and seating himself heavily at her table.

Jane narrowed her eyes, deciding to treat him, if not with contempt, then at least as an hallucination. Sunspots. Fever. Malaria from her insect bites.

"Ho, ho!" he said.

WINTER BREAKS

"Go away," she hissed, mustering the nerve to swear at him.

He looked hurt in an exaggerated way, an operatic way. "You treat me like exactly the kind of man who you don't want to meet. But look at me! I'm perfect! I'm doing everything to catch your eye." He laid a bunch of bedraggled, wilting anemones on the table. Their petals were like wet rags. "Is it my age?"

"No, no," she sighed. "I'm just not used to being pursued across a strange city by..."

He chuckled. "Pursued..."I

"It's very disconcerting."

"You act as if I appal you. Am I so grotesque?"

She relented for a second. "I don't even know you."

He twinkled at her. "Are you sure?"

She pulled a face savagely. "You're so bloody jolly and good. Every time we've seen you on this horrible holiday, you've looked so, well, happy..."

"Is it really a horrible holiday you're having?"

She realised her mistake. "No, not really. It's fine, actually."

He leaned forward conspiratorially. "You know, Jane...you've got me all wrong."

"I have?"

"I'm not the man you think I am."

"You're not."

"I do have my darker side."

"You do?"

He nodded happily. "If I really was the man you think I am, don't you think I could have solved all the world's problems? Conquered famine, and hunger and disease? Oh, but I'm too selfish for that."

Her eyes were swimming in the dappled light from the sea. She tried to snap out of it: "I don't know what you're talking about."

"If I was the man you thought I was I'd be a very powerful, magical old man, very remiss in my duties, leaving the world so mixed up and sad. I'm too selfish to use my powers to put everything right." He stroked his luxurious side-whiskers and beamed at her. "You were quite right about who I am. But I'm a very limited, selfish, sexy kind of Santa Claus. Nothing to do with your preconceptions. Nothing to do with Christmas."

She snorted. "I've had Christmas coming out of my ears."

She was staring at him. Could she think of Santa as an erotic object? It seemed perverted, almost.

He whispered, "I promise, you'll only have Christmas when you want it. Only the bits you like. If you come with me."

She flushed. "Come with you where?"

"I know you think your life is over. That it holds no more surprises for you. All I can say is, if you carry on in your regulated life, sticking with your nephew and living in a hotel where every day is necessarily the same...of course that will be true. Your life will be smooth and predictable till the end of your days."

He produced another present for her then. It was wrapped in tissue paper. She took it like an unexploded bomb and unwrapped it in front of him. It was the glittering blue bauble he had bought in the glass shop yesterday.

"You can walk across the surface of your own life forever," he said softly. "Round and round the same old world. Or..."

She looked up sharply, despite herself, wanting to know now what was the alternative.

"Or you can come inside. Into your own life."

He really was a cheeky old thing. Now he was getting up to leave. And she found herself disappointed.

"Meet me tonight," he said. "On the bridge by the hotel. One o'clock. Bring the glass."

"Why?" she asked, bracing it in her fingers like a crystal ball.

He was gone.

I've never been given a magic object before, she thought. No one's ever promised to take me out of my life.

I wouldn't have to stay for long. And If I didn't like it, I could come back.

She got up and started putting her things into her bag; purse, and then the glass bauble, which she dropped and smashed on the wet cobbles. She gave a short, anguished cry.

She picked up the pieces, careful not to cut herself. She put them all into the tissue paper, wanting to cry with shame. Th glass was so thing. It was like blue spun sugar. Well, now she'd just have to go and meet him.

To explain. To apologise. For being so clumsy and hopeless. So dangerous and out of control of her life.

Final Fling

After a long day spent alone Robert was full of pasta and wine. He was nodding off as he watched black water pushing against the steps up to their windowsill. He was mesmerized by the reflections of lights on the waves.

Aunty Jane's complaints from across their room had quietened to murmurs. He managed to block out her twittering and drift off.

Then he awoke with a jerk in the dark. The hotel room lights had been dimmed right down and it was much quieter.

He looked over at Aunty Jane and made out the rigid bump of her, lying under a single white sheet. She even slept tidily.

He stood stiffly and woozily, grimacing as the wickerwork creaked beneath him.

Just once more round the block, he thought. Just a little scout around in the dark before dawn. Get some of that muggy air into his lungs on their last night in town. Might get lucky this time.

There wasn't a peep out of Aunty Jane. He took his key and slipped out into the corridor.

DREAMING OF A WHITE CHRISTMAS

He was drawn to the steps of the Academia bridge.

For a while, no one came past. Then, one or two late stragglers came and went and left Robert to his business. He smoked and watched the sudsy clouds passing over the moon.

He stared at the bridge.

There was his Aunty Jane. Standing there like a sleepwalker, in full view of anyone who cared to look.

She tricked me, he thought. She slipped out of the hotel before even I did.

There wasn't much space between her and Santa Claus.

They were in hushed, urgent conference.

Aunty Jane looked flustered and hot, even in her loose nightie. Santa was chuckling at her, lifting up his great beard, rippling his fingers in the humid air. Uncertainly, Jane was joining in with his echoing laughter.

When Santa snapped his fingers, Robert could hear the click.

A solid transparent sphere shimmered around both figures on the bridge. It looked brittle and faintly blue, like Murano glass.

Aunty Jane stared at the old man in wonder and he was laughing again. The glass started to mist over and it was harder for Robert to see them. He realised that it was snowing inside the bauble. A perfect, miniature snowstorm was raging just inside the sphere. Santa had taken Robert's aunt and trapped her with him in a bubble of winter.

All around them in that hermetic space, silent clots and specks of snow were whirling, and colliding with his Aunty Jane's overheated flesh.

He's doing it, Robert thought suddenly, to prove that he is real.

Santa's doing it to prove it all true.

Aunty Jane was frozen in that moment; aghast, awhirl. Her breath was crystallizing. Robert could see his aunt's gasp of amazement hanging in front of her and it was like a large white question mark.

Santa bent forward to kiss her. He'd be melting the flakes on her face, her eyelashes.

Then he reached up and pricked the bubble from within. It burst like soap and the glass and the hectic blizzard melted in an instant. The hot wet air of the Venetian night came flooding back.

"I'll catch my death," Robert heard his aunty say.

Santa was peering over the side of the bridge, down to the canal, where a great dark shape had drifted up and was waiting for him.

"Time for home, Jane," he said, in an unexpected accent.

Jane let Santa lead her down to the gondola. He nodded to the boy in the boatnecked jumper, who was bracing his slight weight on the slant of the gondola's stern. Robert stared as the boy doffed his yellow straw hat at Jane, revealing his nascent horns, their rounded nubs poking out of close-cropped hair. Reindeer, Robert realised. The boy had cloven hooves.

He watched his aunt rubbing her arms, though she must be warmed through again by now. She was stepping aboard. She looked dainty as she sat down in the cushions, hugging her knees as Santa joined her.

The gondolier shoved their small boat away from the crumbling shore. As they went sailing off into the dark, Robert heard his aunt come out of her trance with a gasp.

It wasn't really like her, taking off like that.

PAUL MAGRS

1997

ABOUT THE AUTHOR

Paul Magrs lives and writes in Manchester. In a twenty-odd year writing career he has published novels in every genre from Literary to Gothic Mystery to Science Fiction. His most recent books are *The Heart of Mars* (Firefly Press) and *Fellowship of Ink* (Snowbooks). He has taught Creative Writing at both the University of East Anglia and Manchester Metropolitan University, and now writes full time.

MARKED FOR LIFE

Meet: Mark Kelly – a man tattooed with glorious designs over every inch of his body. He's married to the slightly unhinged Sam and has a young daughter who's about to be kidnapped at Christmas by an escaped convict and old flame of our hero's. Over one snowy festive season the whole family sets off in perilous pursuit... accompanied by Sam's mother, who's become a nudist lesbian and her girlfriend, who claims to be a time-transcending novelist known as Iris Wildthyme...

DOES IT SHOW?

Meet: Penny Robinson, who's a sixteen year old with witchy powers and an impossibly glamorous and overbearing mother called Liz. They've just moved into the neighbourhood and the friendships they make will start off a bizarre chain of events involving love affairs with hunky bus drivers, people dressing up as dogs, raucous nights out with the ladies and a very surprising revelation on the dance floor during Goth Night in Darlington...

COULD IT BE MAGIC?

Meet: Andy, a young gay man who finds himself quite unexpectedly pregnant. Andy runs away to Edinburgh to sample the delights of the wicked city and to give birth to a child of his own: one covered in golden leopard fur...

Lightning Source UK Ltd.
Milton Keynes UK
UKHW04f2347010918
328189UK00001B/43/P